BEFORE EUREKA!

The Adventures of Young Archimedes

A Novel by
Bryan Bunch

Bryan Bunch

ACKNOWLEDGMENTS

As this is my first work of fiction, I was helped immeasurably by the
FRIDAY FICTION FOLKS: Marie-Therese Miller, Susanna Hill, Angela Batchelor, and Kathy Morris, who read and improved every stage of each scroll;
as well as close reading of several drafts and many helpful suggestions from my frequent coauthor Jenny Tesar;
and an important final reading and corrections from my beloved wife Mary,

Copyright © 2014 Bryan H. Bunch

All rights reserved.

ISBN-10: 978-1503381575
ISBN-13: 1503381579

For Julia, Jesse, Zoe, Jude, Toby, and Lydia

[A] charge was made that gold had been abstracted and an equivalent weight of silver had been added in the manufacture of the crown. Hiero, thinking it an outrage that he had been tricked, and yet not knowing how to detect the theft, requested Archimedes to consider the matter. The latter, while the case was still on his mind, happened to go to the bath, and on getting into a tub observed that the more his body sank into it the more water ran out over the tub. As this pointed out the way to explain the case in question, he jumped out of the tub and rushed home naked, crying with a loud voice that he had found what he was seeking; for as he ran he shouted repeatedly in Greek, "Εὕρηκα, εὕρηκα" [= "Eureka, eureka" = "I have found (it), I have found (it)"].

From THE TEN BOOKS ON ARCHITECTURE by

Marcus Vitruvious Pollio

Although my book is intended mainly for the entertainment of boys and girls, I hope that it will not be shunned by men and women on that account, for part of my plan has been to pleasantly remind adults of what they once were themselves, and how they felt and thought and talked, and what queer enterprises they sometimes engaged in.
From THE ADVENTURES OF TOM SAWYER by

Mark Twain

SCROLL 1

◆ *The boy Figures dreamed of cakes, cakes shaped like animals or fruit, cakes that covered the table. A pear lay between a sheep's legs, an ox's head tucked under the sheep's chin. In his dream he moved the cakes, seeking a repeating pattern, one with each group fitting neatly into another with the same arrangement. But there were gaps. Annoyed, he pushed the edges of the cakes, making the animals and fruits into triangles, all the same size and shape. The triangles covered the surface completely. Happy now, he combined the triangles into squares that also fit together. Cutting the squares back into triangles again, he arranged six triangles at a time into hexagons, stretching the triangles to fit. He covered the surface with the hexagons, leaving no space between them. Then he pushed five triangles together to make a pentagon. His father had once said that a pentagon was a special shape, but Figures could not remember what was special about it. He could not fit pentagons together on the flat surface. But he could stick their edges together to build something like a ball. He kicked the ball off the cloth that covered his sleeping body.*

The festival of Diasia, which would start at sunset, had inspired his food dream. Today his family and their household slaves would make cakes shaped as animals or fruits. But instead of eating the cakes, they would burn them as a sacrifice to the god Zeus. The part of the festival that excited him was that he would receive the gift of a Diasia present. He did not know what it would be, but he liked to get presents.

Diasia was one of very few occasions when his family sacrificed anything to a god or goddess. His parents said that many traditional Greek festivals were disgusting. They seldom even mentioned the gods, not even Artemis, the goddess beloved in Syracuse for creating the Arethusa fountain, the beginning of the city.

Ten days earlier, he had asked his mother why he could not join his friends in celebrating the full-moon festival.

That day his mother, Andromeda, replied, "Was there something that you wanted from the festival, Archimedes? Something your friends got?" Andromeda always called Figures by his real name, Archimedes, instead of his nickname.

He said, "Phyllis, Herc, and Jason all got toy wine casks as presents."

"Those were not toys. The little casks were filled with wine, and your friends were expected to spill some on the ground for the gods and then drink the rest. You know that we don't let you drink wine."

His father, Phidias, added, "We don't allow children to drink wine, and none of us eat meat. Your mother and I disapprove of animal sacrifice, so we cannot be a part of most offerings to the gods. No one knows who an animal was before it was born. You might be sacrificing your grandfather. The gods, such as they are, do not seem to mind us ignoring them. They have never come down from Mount Olympus to punish us for failure to participate in their worship."

Andromeda said, "Someday you will understand why we live the way we do. For now, however, just remember that this is they way we live. I don't want to hear that your friend Phyllis has taken you hunting, for example. We live our way, and she goes the way that her family does. And we sometimes sacrifice to a god when no animal is killed. For Diasia we make and burn cakes, so when Diasia comes in a few days, although you will not get a little wine cask, you will get a Diasia present."

He had liked this idea. "What will I get?"

Andromeda replied, "I can't tell you. It will be a surprise. If you knew, it would not be a surprise."

He still wanted to know, but knew better than to ask, so

he said, "It seems like a waste to make cakes and then burn them."

Phidias said, "The gods are supposed to benefit from the smoke. It is not clear to me why, if they are gods, they need cake smoke."

Andromeda added, "And it would be good if you could eat cakes or something to put some weight on, Archimedes. You are very thin, even for a young boy. I would not want you to be fat like your friend Herc, but I worry sometimes that you don't pay attention to food, except sometimes to use it as a drawing board for geometric shapes."

He thought that there might be some connection between not participating in Greek festivals that involved animal sacrifice and his not attending a school like the other boys who lived in the Epipolae neighborhood of Syracuse. He asked, "Is it because they sometimes have animal sacrifices that I don't go to school?"

Phidias replied, "School costs a fair amount of money. We have a nice place to live, with room to grow our fruits and vegetables and to keep some animals for milk, eggs, and wool, but we do not have much money. My parents made a good living creating objects from gold and silver, but after they were gone I used all their savings to buy this land and build this house. Teaching brings me a small amount of spending money. And, since I am a teacher of men, I think I can teach my child better than most schoolmasters. I don't really trust the men who have started schools for boys. I think they treat their boys as playthings rather than as students."

Andromeda said, "Phidias! I don't think you should talk that way to Archimedes. He is only nine."

"He is very bright for his age, which is I am sure more your influence than mine. He should understand how the world works. When you read Homer with him, there are passages that deal with men and boys."

"He will read those himself, I am sure. You stick to the music, mathematics, and astronomy. I will teach him how the world works at the proper time."

Unlike most Greek women, Andromeda could read and write well, having been taught by Phidias. He claimed that he taught her so that she could help him by taking notes as he observed stars, but Figures suspected that his father just believed that women should be educated. Besides, since she ran the household, she needed an elementary grasp of arithmetic and numbers.

He decided that nothing more would be said about the Diasia gift, so he took a charred stick from the fire and started sketching geometric shapes on his leg. His parents went on talking to each other, mostly about the siege of Syracuse by Carthage. They soon forgot that he was listening, but he was interested in everything and remembered everything they said.

⬟ On the morning of the Diasia festival, he was the first one in the family to awake and rise, although the slaves had been up since before dawn. His father generally slept late, claiming that astronomy, with its long nights, gave him an excuse to stay in bed. Figures found his blanket at the foot of the couch he slept on, and awkwardly wrapped his body in it. After he had made his morning trip to the latrine and had a drink of water, he folded the blanket and put on a chiton, a long shirt appropriate for a young boy. His father, Phidias wore the same woolen toga he slept in. When Andromeda pointed out that the current toga was soiled, Phidias simply switched to his other while the household slaves, Dromio and Luce, washed the dirty one.

Phidias affected the look of a philosopher, leaving his beard unshaved but trimmed. Like Figures he was lanky, but lack of physical exercise had given him a small pot that he hid beneath the folds of his toga. Although his hair, trimmed to a moderate length, was still black, his beard was already flecked with gray. Phidias' brown eyes were attractive but had become inefficient, for he found that he was beginning to need to hold a scroll farther away to read it. Sometime he used a curved piece of glass that he placed on the letters of a scroll. This enlarged them, although it also made the letters misshapen. But he could still see the stars and planets without help.

Neither Figures nor Phidias nor Andromeda ate breakfast. As soon as they woke and dressed, they went about their business. Once in a while he was allowed to accompany his father on his daily stroll to the agora where Phidias might talk with other citizens of Syracuse about the events of the day, currently the ongoing siege of Syracuse by a Carthaginian army from the other side of Sicily. Or they might meet a philosopher and converse with him about the stars. Phidias also had some paying pupils to whom he taught astronomy and mathematics. Figures was usually pleased when he got a chance to hear a lesson being taught, although he did not enjoy it if the student argued with his father. He tried to avoid being present for lessons with the Carthaginian Malchus, who abused Greek ways, although he lived in Syracuse, and asked rude questions of his father. Most days, however, Phidias went to Ortygia alone and Figures stayed in Epipolae.

On the morning of the Diasia festival, he remained at home with his mother. Andromeda usually stayed in the house, directing the slaves on food preparation, cleaning, and other household tasks. She also supervised the garden and the care of the animals. Although there were two household slaves and three that took care of the garden and animals, Andromeda often did small chores herself, and like most Greek wives she spent some of her day making yarn or weaving.

She was trim and both shorter and younger than Phidias by a considerable amount. Figures thought that her curly hair was her most dramatic feature, usually worn piled high on her head and pinned to keep it out of the way. Although her face in repose was grave, a result of having a prominent straight nose above a generous mouth and widely spaced eyes, it usually was actively expressing emotions, always reflected in rapid gestures. When she was working on the household finances, she would push her lips together tightly and hold that expression until she finished. Like most female citizens, she wore a long pleated dress when she was directing the household but added a small toga on top of the dress when she went out or when there was company.

⬟ Although it was winter, the weather was comfortable in Epipolae, on the outskirts of Syracuse. Syracuse lies on the coast of Sicily, where summers are very hot, but the rest of the year is mild. The top of nearby Mount Etna, however, is covered in snow. As the days had been growing shorter, it had rained nearly one day in three. So Diasia fell on a lucky day, bright with clear skies.

Diasia was not one of the really big festivals, so school was still going on. He would not see any of the boys he knew until school was out, but he could probably find Phyllis. He told Andromeda he was going out to play.

He took the path toward the nearby house where Phyllis lived with her parents and her younger brother, Herc. Herc would be in town during the morning, since he attended the school of Pelekos. Herc's family could afford to send their son to school, since they owned a large tract of land and had many slaves. While the mother managed the slaves and other business, the father devoted himself to writing a history of Syracuse. His history had not yet reached the age of Gelo, more than 200 years earlier, however, perhaps because he preferred research to actual writing.

Figures did not have the muscular build of an athlete or even that of a powerful young boy, but constant activity had given his thin legs and arms more strength than an observer might think at first. But he stumbled going out of the door. Although strong and bright, he was incurably clumsy.

As he stumbled along the path to his neighbor's house, he thought about their nicknames. Greeks were very fond of nicknames. His father had told him that most people only knew the most famous philosopher by his nickname, Plato, which means "wide." He received that name when he was a young wrestler, and it stuck for all his life. Phidias had told Figures about Plato when he learned that boys were calling his son Archimedes "Figures" because he was known for drawing squares or triangles in the sand or even in spilled food. Archimedes had resented the nickname at first, but his father convinced him that if he accepted it, he could change it from a derisive comment to a compliment. Figures did not think that "Figures" had become a compliment, but he had become so used to it that it was now just his name.

He seldom thought of Herc and Phyllis by their real names either, which were Heracleides and Cleoboule. Herc's father had called Heracleides "baby Hercules" when he was a plump toddler with a strong grip. The hero Hercules, according to a popular story, had been strong enough when still a child to strangle snakes. Figure's friend, however, had not grown to be a demigod with superhuman strength, but instead had become a chubby and rather lazy boy of eight. The family found "Hercules" inappropriate, but it was close to the real name of Heracleides, so both were combined and shortened to "Herc."

His sister, a year older, was as thin as Herc was chubby. The family had begun calling her by a variety of names that suggested her skinny frame. Willow was one of the first, since she was long and thin like a willow leaf. Then they just called her Leaf. Finally, the name Phyllis, which is a way of saying "leaf," seemed to work best. The original Phyllis was a princess who died from grief and turned into an almond tree. Even though it was the name of a princess, it seemed to Phyllis less like a girl's name than Willow or Leaf, and she hated her real name of Cleoboule. In Greek, which everyone in Syracuse spoke, names ending in "-s" most often indicated boys.

⬟ As he walked along the path, he looked for something new to count. He had long since counted the steps, the palm trees, and the stones, so he turned his gaze toward the sky, hoping at least for clouds with interesting shapes. He failed to notice Phyllis in the path and bumped into her as he stumbled over a tree root. She was dressed in a chiton also, but carried a small woven bag over her shoulder. She looked very much like Figures, although taller. Her wavy black hair was cropped short to nearly the same length as his straight hair. A person seeing them for the first time might think they were two brothers, or, after a closer look, brother and sister.

"Figures! Stop thinking about whatever you are thinking about so hard and listen to me."

He straightened and waited.

"I was visited in a dream last night by the Goddess Artemis. She came to me dressed for hunting, carrying her bow and a spear. I was afraid at first because of the weapons, but her face was smiling, even radiant, and I was immediately at ease when she looked on me. 'Why are you here?' I asked. She said she had a message, and it was for you. The Goddess referred to you as Archimedes, the way your mother does, and she called me Cleoboule, which no one else does. She said you must go to the harbor where you will learn something of great importance. Isn't it exciting? You have the special protection of the Goddess. And I am her messenger."

He groaned inwardly. He liked Phyllis as a friend. Often she was the only one who would go exploring. Herc was lazy and other boys seemed to have nothing but sport on their minds. Anyway most boys were more likely to tease than befriend him. When he lost his temper, which often happened, he would start fights, fights he always lost.

So Phyllis was his best friend. But he could not understand why she treated the goddess Artemis as real. When his father or mother spoke of the gods, it was just a way of talking. Everyone said "the gods this" and "the gods that," but it did not mean much. It was easy to say "the gods brought rain for the garden" or "thank the gods that I have a new student, for we need the money." But neither Andromeda nor Phidias seemed to think there were real gods at work; rain came and went unpredictably and students did as well. Who could believe that the stories of the gods were real? Of course Phyllis was a girl, even though she dressed or acted like a boy. But Phyllis not only thought the gods were responsible for everything, she also seemed to consider Artemis, the twin sister of Apollo, her personal friend.

His mother had taught him some of the poetry of Homer. In Homer's stories the gods behaved like Phyllis' Artemis and changed events in favor of their favorite mortals. But those stories from Homer were made up long ago about events even before Homer's time, so he thought that the parts about the gods were just put in because people no longer knew what really happened, just like his father thought that the figures in the sky, the constellations, were made up to help remember which stars were which.

Despite all this, he was glad to accept Artemis' command to visit the great harbor. He had already planned to suggest this to Phyllis, but for a more rational reason. He always enjoyed the great harbor. He liked to watch the men of Syracuse and their slaves move goods on and off the ships. He loved the interplay of the blue sea and blue sky, always alike and always different. Although Sicily is such a large island that it seems like a small continent, nearly all the life there is lived near the sea and few love the sea more than Greeks, no matter where they live. The smaller harbor was much closer to their homes in Epipolae but seldom had anything more exciting than fisherman bringing their catch ashore. But his mother and father had said to each other that big ships were coming to the great harbor, and he wanted to be there to see them.

⬟ No one would miss Figures and Phyllis for a few hours. The streets of Epipolae were a safe playground for any children not in school. But they soon left Epipolae, going down the hill along a path to the small harbor and then turning toward the narrow strait that separated the island of Ortygia from the rest of Syracuse. Past that strait lay the docks where sailing freighters landed cargoes from Alexandria or left with goods for such Greek city-states as

Corinth and Athens.

Phyllis chattered on as they walked the path. "You know that Artemis comes here often because she was actually born on Ortygia, where her mother had been chased by Hera. And of course Artemis is the one who changed the nymph Arethusa into the famous fresh-water spring on Ortygia where the wild papyrus grows."

He decided he wanted no more talk of gods and goddesses, so he interrupted Phyllis. "My father told my mother that the great Greek general and 'sometime king' (whatever that means) Pyrrhus would be arriving today with his army. He also said 'As you know there are secret members of the Society, and the one in Pyrrhus' camp has kept me informed'. I like to learn secrets. What do think the 'Society' might be?"

Phyllis said, "It's a secret society, so we are not supposed to know. The Egyptians and Romans have secret societies. I didn't know there were Greek secret societies."

"Maybe that's because they are secret. Anyway, father said that Pyrrhus had won two great battles against Rome, but after the second battle Pyrrhus claimed, 'Another victory like that one and I will be completely undone' because he had lost so many troops. After that Pyrrhus was ready to quit fighting Rome and come here to fight for us."

Phyllis said, "Perhaps that's what my dream means: Artemis knows that you will become involved with Pyrrhus, and so she wanted us to be there when he arrives. If we go to the temple of Artemis on Ortygia, it is on the highest point, so we can see if the ships are actually coming."

This seemed like a good idea, so they crossed the short causeway into Ortygia and traveled up to the temple. The air was so clear that from the temple steps they could see the entire great harbor and beyond.

⬟ The harbor is among the best in all the seas of the Mediterranean, a main reason why Greeks from Corinth had chosen the island when they started their colony almost five hundred years earlier. A fleet of ships began to enter the harbor. The great sails of many colors gleamed in the sun.

He said, "Let's go closer and see the ships land." They ran back toward the causeway.

Syracuse is not a tiny village, but a great city with perhaps a hundred thousand people living in four of its five neighborhoods, if you count women, children, and slaves as well as citizens. After running across the causeway, they were in Achradina, the commercial center of Syracuse, heading toward the docks. There were very few women other than female slaves to be seen down near the harbor wall, although Phyllis was not much noticed, for most thought she was another young boy.

When they arrived at the harbor, running as only children run from place to place, they climbed the steps and stood on the wall, looking at the ships. For a short while, they were content to lean over the harbor wall and watch the ships approaching. He admired the different shapes of the sails and wondered how to know which shape was best. A triangle had only half the area of a rectangle, but there must be some advantages or shipbuilders would not use them.

Soon Phyllis tired of waiting for the ships to dock. She suggested a game of hide-and-seek. Both young Greeks were thin and agile and could find hiding places that most persons would not be able to enter. He crawled into a large empty amphora, the common jar used for transporting goods

⬟ From his hiding place in the amphora, he heard a familiar voice, which belonged to someone he definitely did not want to see, so he stayed quiet. The voice, with its slight Punic accent, belonged to the Carthaginian Malchus, one of his father's paying students until a few weeks earlier. When Malchus visited their home for lessons in mathematics and astronomy, he acted as if the whole place, slaves and all, belonged to him. He would pick fruit off a tree or off the kitchen table and eat it without even asking. Figures' father argued with Malchus about Malchus's god, Baal, and

Malchus quit the lessons, leaving without paying the money owed. Phidias was furious about not being paid and planned to hire a lawyer to sue Malchus in the Assembly.

He heard Malchus say, " I believe that Carthage will fail to capture Syracuse this time. Pyrrhus will make a difference."

A different and much gruffer voice asked, "Can we speak Punic so fewer will understand us?"

"No, Atban," Malchus said. "We will be recognized sooner if passerby hears Punic—and many in Syracuse would understand anyway. We can speak Greek softly." He lowered his voice, so Figures had to strain to hear him. "The siege of Syracuse by Carthage is not going to succeed."

Atban whispered in Greek with a strong Punic accent, "It is far too easy to run that blockade at night. My ship does it regularly. But now even that porous blockade is being abandoned since our Carthaginian admirals prefer not to engage Pyrrhus. When Pyrrhus and his armies settle in Syracuse, the Carthaginian army will no doubt lift the siege. Everyone fears Pyrrhus."

Malchus said, "This fine harbor rightly belongs to the world's greatest sea power, not to a bunch of displaced Greeks. Carthage will eventually prevail. I plan to stay on the winning side. The great god Baal will displace that weak female Artemis, and the people of Syracuse will sacrifice to the true ruler of the universe. I consulted the priests of Baal on what we need to insure a Carthaginian victory. We need to sacrifice a virgin boy to him. Baal wants the boy taken to the molten lava pit on Mount Etna and thrown him into it."

Atban said, "If you can lead me to a virgin boy, I can take him to Etna and see that he is properly sacrificed by priests."

"I can arrange that. I know just the boy. His father was my teacher, but we quarreled. There is some mystery about this teacher; I know he is hiding something, but what? The boy, his son, is I am sure a virgin, for he has never been to school away from home. He would be the perfect sacrifice." Not so loud, Malchus. Come back to my ship with me. I can help kidnap the boy provided you lead me to him."

SCROLL 2

● Neither speaker said more for what seemed a long while. Figures peeked out of the amphora. Malchus, a short, olive-skinned, beardless man with frighteningly blue eyes, despite pitch-black hair, was nowhere to be seen.

Figures' legs trembled with terror, but he was one of those lucky people whose mind focuses more in an emergency than when facing day-to-day challenges of ordinary living. He organized his thoughts. He must inform Phidias of the plot. Once his father learned Malchus's plan, he would protect his son. Figures did not know where his father was now, and he would not be home until suppertime. Nothing could be done at that moment to stop the plot to sacrifice him to Baal. Malchus clearly meant to take him from his father's house and offer him to Baal. For now he felt safer away from home, since Malchus and Atban would seek him there. Since he was not sure how he could find his father in town, he should spend the day with Phyllis away from Epipolae.

He climbed out of his jar and looked for Phyllis. A large crowd watched elephants being unloaded. Phyllis would be there, and he soon found her in the crowd. She explained, "I never saw an elephant before. I started watching and forgot to look for you."

Like Phyllis, Figures had never seen a live elephant, although he heard of the giant gray animal with what appeared to be a tail at both ends. He was astonished at the size of the beasts. Before this he had never seen an animal larger than an ox. He kept count as the elephants descended a special gangplank. Soon the last of eighteen elephants had been led from its ship and herded toward the edge of the city for pasture. He tried to compute an elephant's weight by comparing an elephant to the weight of a sheep. This helped keep his mind off thoughts of what swimming in boiling lava might be like.

Phyllis said, "Look at those beasts. But I don't think that they are your fate. Artemis would not have sent us to the harbor only to see elephants. I am sure that your destiny is entwined with that of Pyrrhus in some way."

Figures said, "I think that an elephant must weigh more than forty full-grown sheep."

But try as he might, the elephants occupied only a small corner of his mind. So he lingered in the crowd, indulging in his habitual eavesdropping, hoping to learn more about Pyrrhus and about elephants. Phyllis asked direct questions of strangers, forgetting that she was just a young girl and not supposed to address adult men. Together they learned the basics. These were Asian elephants that Pyrrhus had obtained from India, more easily handled than the African elephants used by Carthaginian armies. Armies used elephants to scatter the opposing forces.

Pyrrhus was called King Pyrrhus because he was the king of Epirus, a small, mountainous city-state in Greece tucked next to Macedon. Pyrrhus was said to believe that if his late neighbor and cousin Alexander had been able to conquer half the known world, he ought to be able to do even better. At one point Pyrrhus had added the throne of Macedon to that of Epirus, but the Macedonian reign only lasted seven years--although Pyrrhus still considered himself the rightful king of Macedon anyway. While he was away from Epirus in Macedon, the Epirotes removed him as king, but he soon took power again. Despite remaining king of Epirus, it had been three years since he had lived in that land, for he had been busy leading his armies against the Romans.

What Figures had heard from the inside the amphora was true, also. Hiketas had turned Syracuse over to Pyrrhus. Furthermore, nearly everyone expected that the siege of Syracuse would be lifted and the Carthaginians return to Africa rather than fight Pyrrhus. He was happy because this was what his father and mother wanted, although his family had not been much affected by the siege since their own tiny farm produced much of what they needed.

The bag Phyllis carried held bread and cheese for lunch. He still felt safer in Ortygia than at home, so he accepted lunch from Phyllis but suggested that they walk back to the agora, where he hoped his father might be found, to eat it, instead of trying to find a quiet place in the crowded harbor. He told Phyllis that he was looking for his father, but he did not want to frighten her by explaining why he needed Phidias. But he did not see his father at the agora, so after lunch they wandered back to watch the ships still unloading.

Figures studied the crowd, looking for Malchus. He did not appear to be among the men at the harbor now, which reassured him somewhat. He would have searched for Atban, too, but did not know what Atban looked like.

⬟ The elephants had all been led away to graze temporarily in the grassy portions of Neapolis. The crowd at the harbor had returned to its normal size and composition, with many dockworkers and few local residents. Phyllis glanced at the Sun as it lowered over the sails of the ships.

"Figures, it is almost time for Herc to get out of school. Why don't we go meet him and tell him about the elephants? Then we can walk home with him and perhaps mother will have some dried figs and honey for us. You can help us make and burn the Diasia cakes in honor of Hera." The school was in Epipolae, in the direction of home.

Figures said, "Diasia cakes are sacrifices to Zeus, not to his wife Hera. And I should go home for our own Diasia celebration."

"Some people think the cakes are for Zeus, but some think they are for Hera. I prefer to sacrifice to Hera myself. Actually I am more excited about the next festival, when we make stag-shaped cakes from dough, honey, and sesame seeds for Artemis. Herc loves both occasions, mostly because he enjoys making cakes. Although I know he would like it even more if he made cakes that he could eat."

"In our house, I don't think mother and father care whether the cakes are for Zeus or Hera, although I think that the slaves dedicate their cakes to Zeus."

They arrived at the school and settled down to wait for Herc. He made sure that they were situated where he could watch anyone approaching. His plan, if he saw Malchus nearby, was to run into the house where school was kept, thinking he might hide among the other young boys. If they went to Phyllis' house, he would have company until being very near home. By waiting he could be surer that his father would be home before he arrived himself.

⬟ The school that Herc attended met in the home of the schoolmaster, Pelekos. In good weather, teaching took place in the courtyard, just inside the wall of the house. If it rained, the small class moved to the corner room that in most houses was reserved for men to meet and entertain each other or to hold discussions or conduct business. In Syracuse, of course, the weather was good most of the year, although often very hot and dry in summer. Today was an average winter day--cool but with no rain. Class was in the courtyard, where there was no way to see students from outside.

While they waited for Herc and the other pupils to emerge, Figures began to sketch geometric diagrams in the sand. Phyllis observed him break up a right triangle into smaller triangles, which led her to reach into her bag and pull out a smaller cloth bag. "Look, Figures. We can do geometry together. I brought the Bellyache in case we had some time to play with it." And she emptied the bag onto the ground.

The bag produced fourteen pieces of wood, a dozen triangles of various sizes along with a large piece with four straight sides and another with five sides. The Bellyache is a special kind of puzzle or toy with pieces that can be arranged in many shapes. It got its name because trying to make a square from the pieces is enough to give anyone--except Figures--a bellyache. He quickly picked up the pieces and arranged them into a square.

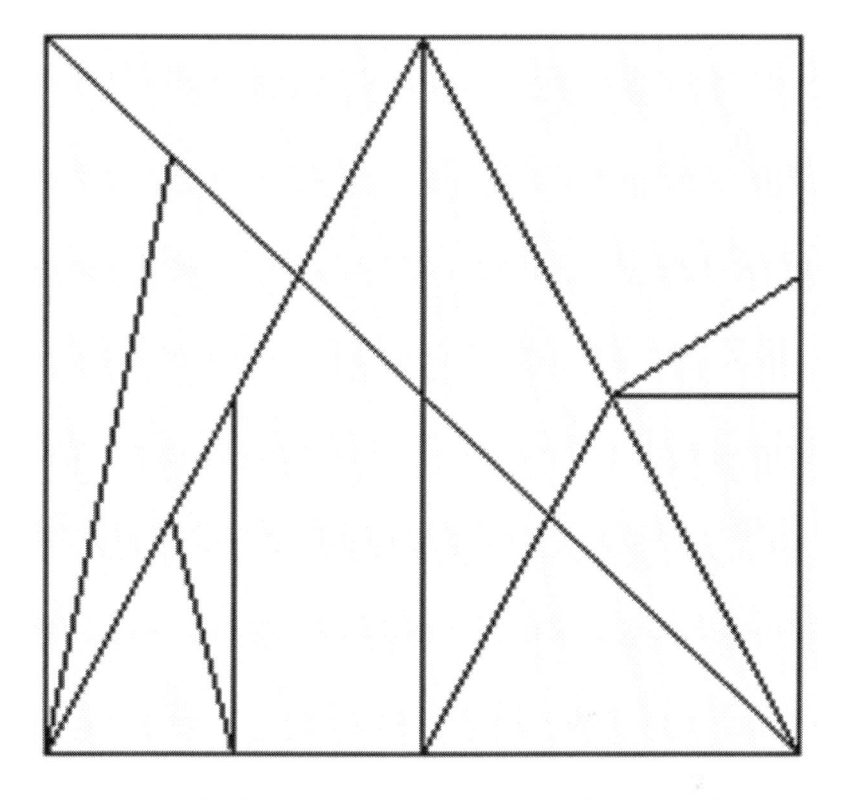

Phyllis said, "I want to make something more interesting. I think we can take these pieces and make them into the shape of an elephant like the ones we saw down at the harbor. Let me try."

She started playing with the pieces and soon produced her elephant.

He admired her elephant, but took the pieces and created a square again, but this time with the pieces in different places. He said, "I can make a square with these pieces in many different ways, Phyllis. I could count all the ways if I had my own Bellyache." But Phyllis was not interested in squares and picked up the puzzle pieces and made a swan swimming in the water. Figures showed her another square, although it took longer than before, as he had to work it out. Working on the puzzles, he found, kept his mind off his fears. Then Phyllis made a lopsided star and challenged Figures to make a flying goose. While he was trying to get his pieces in order, school let out. So they scooped up the Bellyache pieces and put them back in the bag and put that little bag back in Phyllis' bigger one.

⬟ Pelekos' school was small. When it let out for the day Narcissus, Jason, and Faunus, who were the same age as Figures, and a few older boys ran out of the door. Herc, not only the youngest pupil but also the fattest, was last to emerge. Figures and Phyllis knew the younger boys. Narcissus and Faunus were fast friends with each other; they had given Figures his nickname, but otherwise did not interact with him—nor with Phyllis, who after all was a girl. Jason, however, lived near Herc and Phyllis and often joined them and Figures in climbing trees or other important activities.

Pelekos gave Narcissus a friendly pat of farewell and closed the door. It was apparent that Narcissus was the favorite pupil.

"Guess what we saw, Herc," Phyllis exclaimed. "We went down to the harbor and there were a lot of ships. They brought elephants and many soldiers along with a man called King Pyrrhus, who is going to chase away the Carthaginians. I knew something important was going to happen today because Artemis told me in a dream."

Even Narcissus and Faunus were interested in elephants and soldiers. They stayed with Herc and Figures and listened to Phyllis describe the ships, the elephants, and the soldiers. She finished, "And I think some of the soldiers were Greeks, but most of them appeared to be barbarians."

Figures wanted to be a part of the excitement as well, so he interjected, "They all came from over Italy, where Pyrrhus has been winning great battles against the Romans." He did not want to tell these boys about Malchus. They would accuse him of inventing stories.

Narcissus asked haughtily, "How would you know where they came from, Figures? You never know anything.

You don't run or say anything interesting or wrestle or play war games. You just draw shapes or numbers in the sand. I see you have been doing it here in the dust that belongs to Pelekos."

He did not really have anything to say to that, so he just kept quiet and hung his head. He wondered whether if he went to school with them, they would respect him more. Then he thought that perhaps it was better to be schooled at home. Whenever he quoted a poem he had memorized or corrected something another boy had wrong, the boys seemed to like him less rather than respect him more. He did better keeping his mouth shut.

He thought, but was afraid to say, that Narcissus possessed the self-love of his namesake. Everyone knew the story of the beautiful young man named Narcissus who fell in love with his own image. A flower grew where the earlier Narcissus drowned himself in a pool while staring at his own reflection, and that flower is now called Narcissus in his honor. The boy Narcissus that he knew was more like a weed than a flower, however.

⬟ After everyone except Figures had given their views on what the coming of Pyrrhus and his armies might mean to Syracuse, Narcissus suggested that they should pretend that they were athletes at the Games, noting that Pelekos' lessons that day mentioned several of the heroes of the Syracuse Games who had later won events in the main Games at Olympus.

Narcissus said, "Someday the name 'Narcissus' will be among those of the athlete heroes. But I do need to practice. Let's have our own little Game. We can race to that olive tree at the end of the street and back here. Each of us has to circle the olive and then come back. Herc can stay here and be the judge. What do you say?"

Jason and Faunus agreed that this would be fun. Jason was always for any sport. Phyllis also said she would race, but Narcissus said that girls were not allowed. Figures, who knew that he was no runner, stayed quiet.

Narcissus said, "What's the matter, Figures? Afraid you'll lose? There isn't any prize--just the glory of winning and the shame of losing. You can chance that, can't you?"

He replied, "I am not likely to win. I am not a fast runner. I might do better in some other contest." After he said that, he worried that perhaps Narcissus would propose boxing or another challenge that might result in a worse defeat than losing a race.

Phyllis said, "Come on, Figures, give it a try. If I can't race, I'll pull some olive branches down from the tree and make a wreath for a prize."

Narcissus said, "Maybe you would rather wrestle, Figures." Narcissus was heavier than Figures, but the extra weight appeared to be all muscle. Figures suddenly had a more immediate problem than Malchus, although less serious. He said, "I'll race." But he worried that the idea of wrestling might take hold in Narcissus' mind.

Herc said, "I'm the judge. Let's get started." He looked around for a way to mark the start and finish of the race. Runners in the Games start by placing their toes in grooves on a flat piece of rock, called a balbis. Herc did not have a rock, but drew two lines in the dust to represent the grooves. Each of the four runners lined up with the toes of the right foot placed on one line and the toes of the left on the other. Figures had not been taught about the Games, so he simply did what the others did. All four boys then extended both arms in front, the starting position for racers.

Phyllis had in the meantime walked up to the olive tree that would be their turning point and picked some twigs from a low-growing branch. She started back, while weaving the twigs into a wreath about the size to fit on a boy's head.

Narcissus called, "Hey, Leaf. Get out of the way. The race is about to begin."

Phyllis glared at him, but moved aside.

Herc called "Foot by foot" and the racers made sure their toes were aligned with the marks, then "Go!"

Before *Eureka!*

⬟ It was not much of a race. Although Faunus made the best start, Narcissus was well ahead by the time he reached the olive tree. Just as Narcissus started back, however, a tall woman seemed to come from between two houses and crossed directly in front of Narcissus. At this point, Figures was just rounding the olive, so he started to catch up a bit as Narcissus slowed because of the woman. Figures immediately thought that it was unfair to take advantage of the incident, so he also slowed down. In fact, he slowed down more than Narcissus had, although the woman was not in his way at all. Neither Jason nor Faunus was similarly thoughtful, so both maintained their highest speed. As a result, Faunus came in first, then Narcissus, next Jason, and Figures was last. Phyllis was there at the finish line with Herc and put the wreath on Faunus' head.

Narcissus said, "No fair. I would have won if that woman had not got in the way. Where'd she come from, anyway?" He looked around for someone to punish for his loss. He heard Phyllis whispering to Figures, "Why did you slow down. Artemis wanted you to win. That tall woman may have been Artemis in disguise, just the way Athena disguised herself to advise Odysseus."

Narcissus did not have any idea what she was talking about, but the whisper called his attention to Figures. "Let's have another game. I think it is time for wrestling. I challenge Figures to a match." He did not wait for him to answer, but stepped over to him and threw him to the ground.

"That's one," said Narcissus, meaning that it was one fall. It took three falls to win, and any time the opponent was on the ground was considered a fall.

Figures rose to his feet and complained, "That was not fair. You did not give me a chance to get into position." Narcissus answered him by grabbing him by the shoulders and throwing him to the ground somewhat harder than the first time.

"Second fall," crowed Narcissus. "But you are no fun to

wrestle with. You don't fight back. Maybe I should wrestle Faunus instead, since he won the olive crown unfairly."

Figures by now, however, had lost his temper, which he did rarely but always completely. He rushed at Narcissus and the force of his head hitting Narcissus in the chest knocked the surprised bigger boy off his feet.

Narcissus hollered, "That was a slip. It doesn't count." He got up and this time he approached Figures with his arms extended and curved inward, more like a real wrestler than like a playground bully. Figures caught Narcissus wrists and tried to push Narcissus over sideways. But Narcissus was clearly stronger and heavier; so without even taking hold of Figures, he was able to push him far enough down to bring him to his knees.

"Third fall. The match is over. I win," Narcissus cried. He snatched the olive wreath from Faunus' brow and placed it on his own." Faunus made a grab for the wreath, but Narcissus began running away with it. Faunus followed and soon the two of them had run down the road and away from the others.

It was time to go home, anyway, for Pelekos had come out from his door to see what the commotion was. He would not tolerate fighting between the pupils in his school, unless he arranged it himself. Of course, he did not care what Figures and Phyllis did, so long as they didn't bother his pupils, but he glared menacingly at them anyway.

Figures, Phyllis, and Herc said goodbye to Jason. Figures looked at the Sun and decided it was now late enough that his father would be home. He told Phyllis "I don't think I should go home with you today. My mother will expect me to help make and bake Diasia cakes with her and our household. And I want to see what my present will be. But I will walk with you to your house."

So the three walked together, with Figures in the middle, until they reached Phyllis and Herc's house. He said goodbye and set off on the path, breaking into a run when he saw that he was alone. As he ran the short distance between the homes, decided he would say nothing about the fight with Narcissus or the race. He rehearsed the way he would tell his father about Malchus.

SCROLL 3

⬟ As Figures ran toward home, he kept looking around for Malchus. When a lizard ran off the path into a pile of leaves, Figures' heart jumped in his chest. Maybe telling his father about Malchus and Atban would not be enough, for he had become terrified to be alone. He must make sure that he was never alone until the threat from Malchus and Atban was completely eliminated.

As he often did, He tried to think of a number he could compute to take his mind away from something unpleasant. He considered that he was in his second race of the day. How fast was he running? To find speed, he needed to know distance and time. Distance was easy, because he could count his steps, but there was no good way to measure time. Still, he thought he was running faster than in the race with the boys earlier. Fear gave him the motivation. If he was going to be in athletic contests in the future, he needed to improve his motives for winning.

Although Epipolae is part of the city of Syracuse, it is more like country than town. Each house has its own patch of land that supports household animals and small plots of lentils or wheat. He shortened his run by cutting through the fields. He felt safer away from roads, and even safer as he reached the door of his home.

⬟ When he passed through the door, however, he was surprised to find his mother and a large stranger in the courtyard garden. This man was dressed as a soldier—maybe a sailor. Could he be Atban? Why was he with Andromeda? His mother never met strange men in the house.

"Archimedes," said his mother. "Do you know who this is? You have not seen him since you were very small. It is my cousin Hiero. He is a mercenary in the army, which means that he is paid to be a soldier for whomever hires him. For several years he has been fighting in wars far distant from

Syracuse. Now that the famous general Pyrrhus is going to come to aid Syracuse, we sent Hiero a message to return home and help Pyrrhus defend the city against the Carthaginians."

"Pyrrhus is already here. Phyllis and I saw him arrive down by the harbor. He brought elephants."

Hiero said, "Archimedes, I am glad to see you again. But if Pyrrhus is here I should not linger too long with your family.

Figures remembered his manners. "I am glad to greet my mother's cousin. It is good to see you again." He had often heard his mother speak of 'cousin Hiero,' but had no recollection of seeing him before.

Hiero said, "I am going to apply for an officer's rank in Pyrrhus' army. I have been fighting all over Europe and Africa, so I can offer Pyrrhus that experience. Now I want to fight for Syracuse. Did you learn where Pyrrhus' headquarters will be located?"

Andromeda said, "There is no need to be in a hurry. Phidias will know where it is. After all the years away, you surely can stay with us for a while. It has been too long since we were together. You can make Diasia cakes with us." Then, to Figures, "You know that Hiero is more like a brother than cousin to me, for we lived together as children. My father's sister died long before you were born, and Hiero, who had no father, grew up in our household."

After more discussion, Hiero agreed to stay the night. Phidias soon returned and welcomed Hiero warmly. Phidias was full of questions about what Hiero had seen on his travels: where were the stars different? What were the barbarians like? Is the land surrounded everywhere by a great ocean? Are other volcanoes like Etna, the great volcano a few dozen stadiums from Syracuse.

Figures had been interested in all the answers, but the topic of volcanoes reminded him once again of the danger he was in. He was especially terrified by the description Phidias gave of the pools of boiling rock on Etna. He quieted his nerves by making a more careful study of his cousin.

Hiero, like Andromeda, was quite handsome. About 30 years old and at the height of a man's physical powers, he seemed to fill the room with his presence. He was dressed for battle, wearing a thick leather jacket and a short skirt as well as strong boots. His nose and chin both were sharp, and jutted from his face, although not so far as to interfere with his overall good looks, which he did not deign to cover with a beard. Soldiers seldom wore beards, which were more appropriate to philosophers like Phidias. Hiero's hair was not especially curly, but he wore it slightly longer than most people and got the most curl out of it that he could. Like many soldiers, his model for hair and dress was Alexander the Great, the standard by which all generals and would-be generals were judged. A band tied around Hiero's head kept the hair out of his eyes. Figures also observed a small pile of weapons deposited against the wall. There was a short sword, a longer spear, and a shield. All appeared to have received a lot of use, especially the shield.

The plan to study his cousin backfired. Hiero's large size, weapons, and soldier's garb also frightened Figures. He wanted to tell Phidias that Malchus planned to take to Etna and sacrifice him to Baal. He decided to wait until he could get Phidias alone.

The household slaves bringing in the dough for the Diasia cakes interrupted his thoughts. Soon the entire group, including Hiero and the slaves, were making cakes. The family laughingly complained to each other about how little most of the cakes looked like the animals or fruits they were supposed to be. Phidias took the easy way out and made a pear. Figures tried to use geometric shapes to make a sheep. Hiero produced a credible horse, while Dromio and Luce each contented themselves with bunches of grapes. Andromeda won the informal competition with an ox that everyone said was too beautiful to burn. But then they built a small fire in the courtyard and burned them all.

"There," said Phidias. "Our duties to the gods are done."

Before *Eureka!*

Figures said, "Isn't there supposed to be one more part of Diasia?"

Andromeda said, "Of course. You are to get a present." She went to another room and brought it out. It was a Bellyache game like the one that Phyllis had. Figures was delighted and showed Hiero some of the shapes he already knew, included several different ways to make a square. Hiero appeared to be quite impressed by the ease with which Figures assembled the pieces into the shapes he wanted to show. Phidias bragged, "I have been schooling Archimedes myself, and he is a better student than most of the adults who pay me."

Hiero began to question Figures about what he had learned. He asked questions based on the lives of the Greek heroes Hercules and Achilles, which he answered correctly. Hiero also made him demonstrate his ability with numbers by multiplying and dividing.

He was embarrassed to parade his knowledge in front of this older man but also proud that he knew the correct answers. He continued to be slightly afraid, as if Hiero might at any second pick up the sword that leaned against the wall and attack him and his family. But since Hiero was his mother's relative, he might be counted on to help protect him against Malchus. He tried to balance his fears against his faith. He was not used to having two contradictory emotions at once, so he felt quite confused; he had little understanding of his own motives or emotional life. Often he knew the conventional feelings people expected of him, but he was not sure that he experienced those feelings himself.

⬟ After the Sun went down, his mother insisted that he go to bed. Although the disappointed Figures went into his room, he was too excited and also frightened to go to sleep right away. So he listened as best he could to the adults talking in the other room, which largely consisted of his mother quizzing her cousin on what women he had met on his travels and teasing him for not being married yet, and his father explaining the political situation in Syracuse and in Italy to Hiero.

Phidias repeated the story of Pyrrhus winning two battles against the Romans, but losing so many men in the process that he had said that another win like those would leave him completely undone. "After these battles that Pyrrhus won so disastrously, we asked Pyrrhus to abandon his fight against Rome and leave Italy. Syracuse would welcome him as our new leader. We thought that Pyrrhus would defeat Carthage and lift the siege. As it turned out, Carthage chose to withdraw rather than face the famous general."

Hiero said, "Pyrrhus may have had another motive in coming. Because of so many wars on the island and because many men fled from Italy in the face of Roman domination, Sicily is home to large numbers of soldiers that Pyrrhus can enlist to refill the ranks. Once he gets his army rebuilt, Pyrrhus can return to his plan to conquer Rome.

"Pyrrhus claims that he can overcome all Sicily. From Sicily it is a short distance across the sea to Carthage. Sicily is even closer to Roman lands in Italy. Pyrrhus could use Syracuse as his base to become the new Alexander."

The conversations with Hiero about war and politics went on and on after this, slowly putting Figures to sleep, despite his continuing fears. Now he was less certain of what the threat he had overheard from within the amphora meant. Would Malchus try to kidnap him from his home? He really needed his father's help.

⬟ Gradually his thoughts merged into a dream. *He was playing with the Bellyache. He began to calculate all the ways that he could make human beings out of the 14 shapes in the Bellyache. When he arranged the pieces, they sometimes became Hiero and sometimes became Malchus. Phyllis was there with her Bellyache, so he made Hiero from one and Malchus from the other. The two shapes began to move and soon were fighting. It looked as if Malchus might win, but*

Figures took him apart and made him into a square. Then he took Hiero apart and made him into a square also. He looked at the 28 pieces that made up the two squares and then tried to combine all the pieces to make one big square. If the length of the side of one of the two small squares was used as the unit, so that each small square had an area of one square unit, then the large square he was trying to make must have an area of two square units. But he could not succeed making the large square with the 28 pieces he had. At this point in the dream Phyllis gave him a third Bellyache, so now the large square would have an area of three square units. But he tried and tried and could not make a square with an area of three units. Phyllis gave him a fourth Bellyache and he had no trouble making the square with an area of four units, since he could just make four of the small squares and join them. He could make squares with numbers of Bellyaches that were also squares, so 1, 4, 9, 16, and so forth would be no problem. But the number of Bellyaches could not be some other number. He was so excited by this discovery that he made a large human being using all the pieces. The large Hiero then turned into Malchus and chased Figures back into a deeper sleep.

⬟ When he woke up the next morning he was surprised and very unhappy to discover Phidias was gone. His mother explained that Hiero was used to a soldier's habit of early rising, and Phidias had risen early to join him. They had gone to see Pyrrhus.

Andromeda could not predict when Phidias and Hiero would return, so he decided to tell his mother about Malchus and Atban. Although she might not be able to help the way Phidias could, he had to tell someone, but the conversation did not go the way he expected or wanted.

He began, "Mother. I must tell you about what I heard down by the harbor yesterday."

"It must have been very exciting to see the elephants, Archimedes. Did you actually see King Pyrrhus or just his army?"

"Not Pyrrhus himself, although we heard a lot about him. But I encountered father's former student, Malchus. He frightened me"

"Oh, don't be scared of Malchus, although I never did like him. He still owes Phidias money for the lessons they didn't finish. He should be taken before the Assembly and made to pay us. And apologize, too. He said dreadful things to Phidias. But he is just a Carthaginian who does not have Greek beliefs about honesty and fairness."

"Mother, you don't understand. Malchus was threatening me. I heard him say something that sounded like he was going to kill me."

"No! Did he try to hurt you? Did he touch you?"

"No—I just heard him say that he was going to sacrifice a boy to Baal. And he clearly meant that I was the boy."

"He is just another bloodthirsty Carthaginian with their crazy ideas about Baal. I will have to get Phidias to make charges against him. There is no reason he should threaten a child because he has a quarrel with his father. What did he say to you?"

"He did not speak to me directly. I just overheard the threat. He was talking to a sailor. In fact, Malchus did not even know that I was there."

"Then we can get the sailor to testify against him. In the meantime, Archimedes, stay away from Malchus. I cannot believe that he really might do you harm, but the threat is enough. I will talk to Phidias about bringing charges. We can have Malchus exiled. But don't you worry about it. Now get to your studies—you could not do anything last night with Hiero here." She turned and left for the women's rooms.

He was about to follow her to make clear the danger he faced. But first, he described it to himself aloud. "While I was hiding in an amphora, Malchus and someone with a Punic accent decided to take me to Etna and kill me by throwing me into a pool of melted rock." As he uttered these words, he began to doubt what he heard. The only sacrifices he knew about were animal sacrifices at the temples. He could not imagine a human sacrifice. Why would a god want such a thing? Maybe he was just imagining that Malchus might kidnap him. He needed to get his father's opinion on this. His father knew Malchus and could better tell how serious the threat might be.

Despite these doubts, he did not want to play outside, for Malchus certainly knew where he lived. He wandered around aimlessly in the inner courtyard for a while, wondering what to do until Phidias came home. When he talked to his father, either his father would convince him not to worry or his father would find a way to protect him.

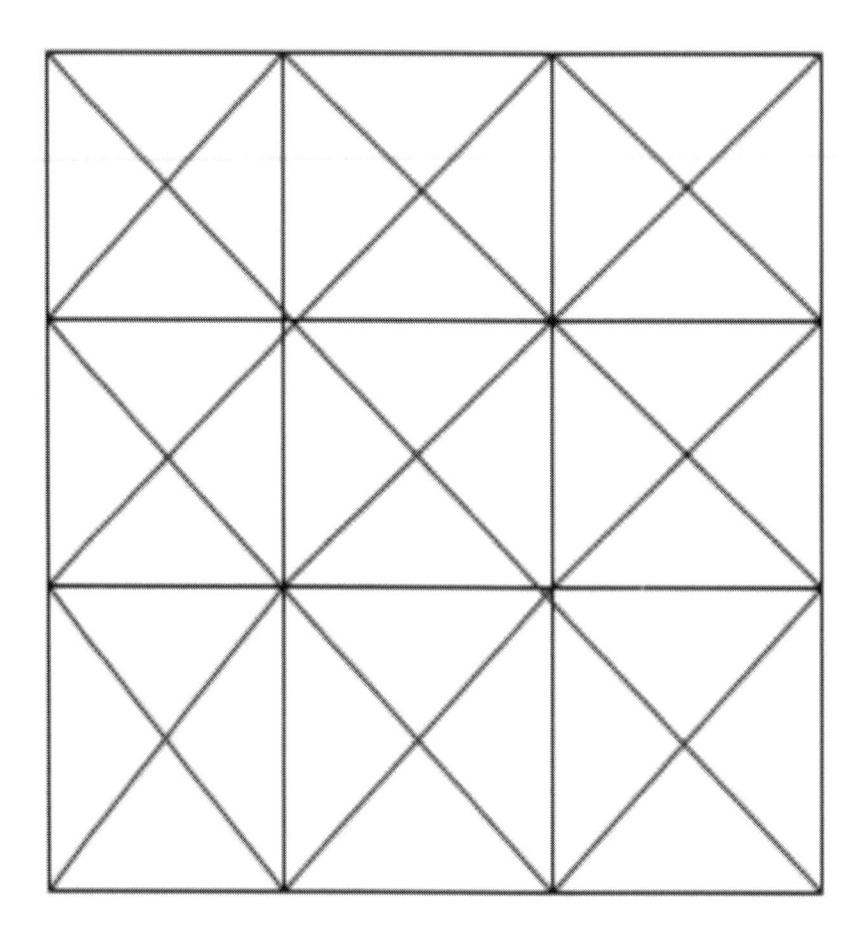

SCROLL 4

⬟ Figures spent the rest of the morning in his room, drawing diagrams to take his mind off Malchus and Atban. He studied the famous theorem of Pythagoras--squares on the two shorter sides of the right triangle added together have the same area as the square on the long side. Figures smeared oil on the floor and drew a right triangle and the three squares with his finger. His right triangle had nearly equal short sides. He thought it might be easier if the short sides were fully equal and drew a second diagram. Gazing at the new

Before *Eureka!*

diagram he had an idea. He broke the squares into triangles and covered part of the floor with triangles drawn in the oil.

Choosing one of the small triangles as the right triangle, the squares on its short two short sides are each two triangles, so the squares on the two small sides together are equal to four triangles. The big square on the long side is also formed from four triangles, so Pythagoras was correct for triangles with equal-length short sides. Now he began to draw diagrams showing patterns of right triangles with different sized short sides. The squares on the side had three different sizes, so he needed a different kind of proof.

His mother entered the room and found him drawing lines in oil on the floor. She said, "Little children make messes and play in them, not boys old enough to be in school. Now look what you have done, Archimedes! The slaves must clean that mess up. Suppose someone slips and falls. You should be ashamed."

"I was just working on my mathematics."

"Nonsense; your father would never tell you to pour oil on the floor as part of a math lesson. You are old enough to help around the house, not mess it up. With Hiero visiting, I don't have time to spend teaching you, either. What could you do today to help? I know. You can help Tono stack wood."

A Greek boy had little need to work unless his family was quite poor. Slaves handled cleaning and tending plants and animals. Figures had few possessions to organize or keep in working order. Still, Figures was given chores.

He knew that Andromeda assigned tasks to keep him moving. He had heard his mother explain to Phidias, "Archimedes is not fat like Herc, but he will grow up weak if he does not move around more. Other boys his age are already thinking about the Games and what events they will enter. He has shown no interest in wrestling or running or throwing objects, although he does wander about the woods. So I am going to ask him to gather wood, to help keep the animal's yard and shed clean, and any other light task I can think of to build up his strength." And Phidias agreed.

⬟ The last thing he wanted was to go outside, where he might be kidnapped. But he could not disobey his mother. At least stacking wood would take place near the house, and he would have someone with him. Perhaps that would be safe. But it was still vital to talk to his father and have him deal with Malchus and Atban. At nine, he thought his father was all-powerful. Although Phidias had no official role in Syracuse, those who did run the city admired the astronomer's broad knowledge and apparent good judgment. If anyone could protect Figures from the boiling lava, Phidias could.

Figures went to work with the new farm slave Tono, trying to keep between Tono and the house at all times. The less exposed the better. Furthermore, surely Tono would alert him if anyone approached from behind.

Tono had been captured in a raid on the Sikels, the original inhabitants of Sicily. Few of the Sikels in the remote mountains had ever met the Greek and Punic speakers of the coasts, and these were considered fair game for slave traders. Phidias got Tono for a bargain price because Tono didn't speak Greek, but Phidias knew enough words in Tono's native Sikeliot that they could communicate, and he was happy to save money on the purchase.

He had made a good bargain, for the Sikeliot slave was strong, healthy, and an excellent carpenter, his profession before capture. Tono was beginning to learn Greek, although his progress was slow.

As they stacked firewood, Figures passed the time trying to teach Tono more words in Greek. He thought: Tono cleans up after the animals; I can tell him about how Hercules cleaned the Augean stables. Hercules was not exactly a god, but was a great hero and half god, famous not only in Syracuse but in every place where people spoke Greek. He said, "Tono. Story about cleaning manure. I tell you."

Tono knew the Greek words for *story, cleaning,* and

manure already, especially since his work included plenty of cleaning and also gathering manure to use on the fields. He was not sure what Figures had in mind, however, since they were now stacking wood, not cleaning up manure.

Figures continued, "Hercules. You know Hercules?" He held up two pieces of wood like weights and tried to make his muscles bulge."

Tono said, "Herculeesa."

"Yes, Hercules. He cleaned manure for King. Big pile manure. Had to clean in one day."

Tono repeated, "One day?" Figures raised his index figure and pointed at the Sun.

"In one day. Very big pile manure. How?"

Tono asked, "How?"

"Took river." Figures stopped because he did not expect Tono to know the Greek word for *river*. "River." He used a piece of wood to draw a winding river with a couple of tributaries in the dirt. "River." Tono still looked as if he did not know what was meant. Figures pointed to his sketch of a river and said, "Water. Water in river."

Tono repeated, "Water. River. River water."

"Good, Tono. Hercules moved river." Figures drew a line for a dam across the river and then showed the river turning aside and following a different course. "River moved. Water cleaned manure. In one day. Hercules great hero." Maybe Tono had the idea of the story, which was that Hercules had re-routed the river through King Augeas' stables to clean up the manure, but the only new word Tono might have learned was *river*. He tried to think of another one of Hercules' labors and give Tono another word. He became involved with his own task of teaching Tono that he forgot for a moment to be frightened.

⬟ Suddenly, Tono said something in Sikeliot (or perhaps really bad Greek) and rapidly walked into a nearby shed. Probably he intended fetch some object they needed, maybe a covering for the woodpile. Figures never found out what it was, however, for as he pressed himself against the house to wait for Tono to return, Malchus and a much taller man with a very dark complexion rushed from behind the shed and tossed a net over him. As the dark man pulled a rope the net bound his arms to his sides. Another jerk took his feet from under him. He was completely wrapped in what he recognized as the kind of draw-net he had seen fishermen use. The rope circled its edges through loops so that it could be quickly pulled tight. He was swept up like a squid pulled out of the water. He screamed and called "help!" as loud as he could.

The net was strong enough that the kidnappers were able to lift the thin, young boy off the ground. They slung the netted boy between them and started running.

He guessed that the tall, dark man must be Atban. He did not look like any human he had seen before. Malchus and Atban must have been watching all morning for him to be outside alone.

Figures shouted, "help!" again. The kidnappers stopped running, and Atban hit him hard in the head. "If you continue shouting, I will kill you," Atban said with a heavy Punic accent.

He stopped shouting. They were going to kill him eventually, but at least if they did not kill him immediately, he might have a chance to escape. He concentrated finding a way out. Fear was put aside; he needed to solve the immediate problem — if he could.

The two carried him onto a path into the woods, now moving at a brisk walk.

He recognized the path, which led through olive groves to a small harbor used by fishermen. Clearly they planned to take him north to Etna by boat, faster than traveling overland. Then, after appropriate prayers by a priest of Baal, he would be thrown into the fiery lava. He was annoyed that he would be killed to no purpose, since neither Baal, nor any mythical god, influenced human affairs. Part of the plan must be to harm his father by killing his only son.

He was bounced around as the two carried him along. Although the net was strong, some openings enlarged slightly from the jostling. He could make them bigger by pushing the twine apart. With enough time, he could enlarge one opening enough to escape. If they left him alone and out of sight, he was sure he could free himself. But he might not get that chance. He began to widen one opening of the net where neither Malchus nor Atban could see.

⬟ The distance to the harbor was not great. When they reached the sea, Malchus and Atban dumped their heavy burden on the ground and begin to launch a rowboat. As Figures landed on his back, the opening he had made was in plain sight. He rolled over to hide the escape route, but it was too late.

Malchus exclaimed, "Look! He can get out of that net if we turn our backs on him for a second."

Atban said, "I expected that. Knots can slip. I have better way to hold him. I brought one of the goat pens from the ship."

"Goat pen?"

"We stay out at sea for weeks. We need fresh food, not just salted meat and hard bread. So we carry a few goats and chickens in cages. A goat cage from the ship is just about the right size for a young boy."

Atban lifted a piece of sailcloth that had covered the cage. Figures could see that when he was put inside it, there would be no way to stand up and not much room even to crouch. Malchus stepped into the boat and went over to the cage to open it so they could put Figures inside.

"How does this thing open, Atban? It seems stuck"

"The latch is very heavy. Goats reach through the bars and lift ordinary latches with their teeth. But they are not strong enough to lift this kind of lock. Try it again."

Malchus lifted the latch with some difficulty, then dropped it closed. "This is as heavy as gold."

"Lead, not gold. Hurry and open the gate. Let's get this

boy in the cage and to the ship before someone from the house follows us."

Malchus lifted the heavy latch again and pulled the door open. Atban shoved Figures roughly into the cage, and Malchus dropped the latch back into place. Malchus said, "I don't think the boy can move that latch. I hurt my arm lifting it myself."

Atban said, "Hurt or not, help me put the cage in the boat." The two lifted the cage and dropped it heavily into the back of the rowboat.

His two captors pulled up their robes above their waists and with some difficulty pushed the heavy boat into the sea. Atban held the boat with one hand and his toga with the other while Malchus climbed aboard. Atban then easily pulled himself in.

"Move to one side, Malchus. This boat is too heavy to row alone. You take one oar with both hands and I will sit beside you and pull the other." As soon as they could arrange themselves, both of the men began rowing together, Malchus not nearly as expertly as Atban.

Figures was still in the net, but soon with a lot of wriggling, much of it involving very uncomfortable positions, he freed himself and reached through to try the latch. At the angle he could grasp, the latch was unmovable. It was just too heavy. He was not going to be able to get out of that cage.

● Malchus shouted, "Look! On the shore! Phidias and two other men! They must have followed us. But we have a head start and they don't have a boat, so there is not much they can do." Figures could not see the shore, but whatever was happening had to be helpful, for without help no escape was possible.

"Row harder! A woman is showing the men a boat."

The rowers increased the tempo but Malchus's inexpert rowing became even more inept when he tried to speed up. He moved the oars rapidly, but they did not catch much water. Atban pushed powerfully in deep strokes. The boat began to turn toward Malchus's side.

Malchus exclaimed, " The woman is pushing them off. All three men have oars. " The boat Figures was in continued to turn in a wide arc.

"That boat is a narrow racer so all three can row at once. And it is much lighter than our boat. They will catch us, sooner if you don't row more forcefully."

Malchus asked, "What can we use to fight against them?"

"We have no weapons of any kind. We didn't need swords or spears against a small boy. And, we are outnumbered."

Figures realized he had been holding his breath and started breathing again. In short order, he would be saved.

Malchus said, " We can beat them back with the oars."

"They are closing in fast. The large man in the back has a sword. We are doomed."

"Phidias is not dangerous, but the other two appear to be seasoned fighters. I think they have us."

Atban said, "We can still escape. The boy is the prize. Let's sacrifice him now. Then they won't have any reason to chase us."

"They will kill us for revenge. "

Figures could not see the other boat, but the man with the sword must be Hiero, so probably his father and Hiero had come back to the house in time to hear from Tono that he had been kidnapped. "Not if we throw the cage overboard. The sea is deep and he will go right to the bottom. It will sink like a rock and the boy will drown. But they will stop and try in vain to save him. I am sure Baal will be just as happy with a drowned sacrifice as if we burned him alive. Say your prayers to Baal while we tip this cage overboard."

As his cage was lifted to the side of the boat, Figures could hear his father shouting "No!" in the distance. The other boat was too far away to stop the cage from being pushed into the water.

Figures took a big gulp of air. A second later he was in the sea and sinking rapidly toward the bottom.

SCROLL 5

⬟ The cage with Figures trapped inside fell through the salty water. It swirled and turned until the latched door faced downward, and the rushing water pushed Figures to the top. The fall was oddly silent, although he could feel the water flowing past. He could not reach the latch on the cage's door, but his only chance was to open the gate and swim out. He hoped his air would last long enough.

He grabbed the mesh on the side of the cage and pushed his body down against the strong upward flow. Holding tight with one hand, he pushed the latch with the other. This time it opened easily, but the ascending water kept the door closed. He twisted inside the cage, still hanging onto the mesh. The cage rotated slightly, but not enough for the door to open. From his new position he got his feet on the door. As he pushed against the door it opened partway, and his feet were out of the cage.

There was a tremendous thump as the edge of the cage hit a large rock. The door slammed Figures' feet back into the cage. The cage spun around again and the current of water stopped. Now the cage rested on the sand with its floor at the bottom once again. The latch swung down, locking the door.

He was where he started, locked a cage with a latch he could not lift--except now the cage was at the bottom of the sea. And the air that he had sucked in before going under was nearly gone.

⬟ Once again Figures tried to lift the latch. To his surprise it moved. The latch underwater was lighter than on the boat. With his last bit of energy, he lifted the latch, pushed open the door, and propelled himself into the open sea.

The Greeks say of a stupid person, "He is so dull that he does not know how to swim." Figures was not at all stupid and had been swimming since before he could walk. But he was out of air and exhausted by struggling with the net, the latch, and the sea. He thought: If I stay motionless, I will float to the surface. When I can breathe air, I can swim. But I must not breathe in water on the way.

But it was too far to the surface. He lost consciousness from lack of air before reaching it. His mouth, freed from his willing not to breath, opened, and he began to gasp seawater into his lungs. The cold water in his mouth and throat woke him just for a second, and he knew that he was doomed.

At that point something pasted itself over his face. He no longer could breathe water or anything else. He passed out again.

⬟ Figures was in a strange boat, and his father was blowing air into his lungs. After several breaths from his father, and a push on his stomach from Hiero, he began breathing on his own.

Phidias cried out, "He lives!" The two men pulled him into a sitting position. He gazed at the anxious face of his father and a damp Hiero and Tono.

"Did you get them?" was the first thing he said when he felt able to talk.

"No," Phidias replied, "We got you instead. We saw them throw the cage overboard. We were close enough to see you inside. We thought you were lost."

"How did you find me?"

Phidias said, "When we reached home, Tono shouted that two men stole you and started running down the path to the small harbor. We ran after him."

Hiero interrupted. "But we thought we were too late. When we reached the beach, all we saw were two men rowing out to sea."

Phidias picked up the story. "Then a woman came out of the woods and told us that the men had put a boy in a net into a cage and the cage into the boat. We were in despair. Their rowboat was already a half stadium from shore. Even if we could swim to it, we couldn't to board it--they would use the oars to push us away."

"The woman said, 'I have a fast boat. Take it and fetch the

boy.' She pointed. There was a boat we had not noticed. It was a light vessel with three sets of oars--perfect for us. We jumped in without even a word of thanks. The woman pushed the boat into the sea. I could not believe how strong she was. She launched a boat with three oarsmen all by herself."

Phidias said, "We started gaining on them immediately. They saw us and rowed faster, although not very straight. We could catch them. We got closer, and I recognized Malchus. The other man was a huge African I had never seen before. Suddenly they stopped rowing and lifted the cage to the side of the boat and tipped it over. My heart stopped. I thought you were lost to me forever."

Figures said, "They knew you would try to rescue me instead of chasing them."

"They were right. We rowed to where you had been thrown overboard, and Hiero and Tono dived into the water to swim to the bottom. But you popped out of the sea, more dead than alive. I pulled you into the boat. You're lucky that you did not swallow or breathe in a lot of water or we might have lost you."

"Something covered my face," Figures said. "I don't know what it was."

"Whatever saved you, we thank the gods that you made it," Hiero said. "What were those two doing? Why did they try to kill you?"

"Malchus wants to sacrifice me to Baal. He thinks a sacrifice will help Carthage defeat Syracuse."

Phidias said, "Utter nonsense! He may have had more than that in mind. He started out as my student, but quickly became my enemy. He never was an honest student. He may have been sent by my enemies."

"You have enemies, Phidias? That is hard to imagine." Hiero's view of Phidias was based on what Andromeda had told him, and Andromeda seldom offered more than praise.

"Everyone has enemies of some kind, Hiero. Mine don't single me out because of anything I did, but hate me for what

I believe, which makes it worse."

Figures was astonished to hear his father say he had enemies, for Phidias harmed no one. But he would not tolerate anyone treating animals or slaves badly and spoke harshly to those who were cruel.

Hiero said, "Malchus has escaped for now. We have to see that Malchus and his friends are kept out of Syracuse. I was already against Carthage, but this is beyond any civilized act. It may be necessary to sacrifice a bull now and then to propitiate the gods, but to sacrifice a human is barbarism at its worst."

Phidias said, "When Greeks sacrifice a bull to Zeus, they make sure that some good comes of it. After the priest dismembers the dead animal, and wraps the bones and internal organs in the fat, the bundle is burned so that the smoke can nourish the god, but the edible meat is divided among the priests and those who have come to worship. So the meat-eaters have a good meal and the sacrifice is not wasted. I disapprove of animal sacrifice, but Carthaginians have even worst practices. At least they don't eat the flesh of the victims they sacrifice to Baal. They are not cannibals."

Hiero added, "Only the god benefits."

At that point they stopped rowing as the boat began to scrape its bottom on the sand.

Hiero jumped out and pulled the boat on shore. "Now where is the owner of this boat? She is the one to thank for your rescue." They looked up and down the beach, but she was nowhere to be seen. They turned the boat over on shore and left it there. Hiero picked up Figures and they followed the path toward their house. This time he did not mind being carried. He realized that he was no longer afraid of Hiero.

♠ The next day Figures wanted to talk about his capture and escape. He told his mother that he was going to visit Phyllis and Herc, but she was reluctant to let him go. She was still ashamed that she had not seen how serious Malchus' threats had been, and now she wanted to keep her son in sight every moment. He argued that Malchus must have sailed away with Atban, and anyway he could not stay in the house forever. Finally she agreed and he started out. He did not completely believe his own arguments, so he kept looking around for danger. Instead he saw Andromeda standing in the doorway as long as he was in sight.

When he arrived at his friends' house and entered the courtyard, he found Herc helping the kitchen slave, chopping almonds and walnuts while the kitchen slave stirred a mixture of eggs, flour, and honey.

"Where is Phyllis?"

"My sister is not here. I'm helping Labda make sweets."

"You don't need sweets. You are too fat already."

"I don't want them to eat—well, not all of them. I plan to trade the sweets at school for other things. Everyone will love them, and I can make some really good trades."

"But what would you trade them for? I bet you plan to trade them for other kinds of food."

"I don't eat that much. I just want to trade them for things that others care less for than they do for a sweet. What is wrong with owning more things?"

"You already have everything you could possibly need. Have you never heard of King Midas?"

Herc said, "Everyone knows that story. He wanted more gold, so the god Bacchus made everything he touched turn to gold. He could not eat any more, for the food turned to gold when it touched his lips. Bacchus punished Midas when he thought he was getting a reward."

At that point, Phyllis walked through the door. "The gods always punish those who want too much. Yesterday, when I was visiting the temple of Artemis, the priestess told me that when someone comes to the temple with a wreath or ribbon to give to the Goddess, so that She may protect a child from harm, Artemis favors those who bring gifts appropriate to the wish. Women who try to buy Her favor with gold threads or a silver wreath often are punished, not helped."

Figures asked, "Why were you at the temple?"

"I had a sudden desire to make an offering. Somewhere a child was in serious trouble, and I pinned my ribbon on Artemis' statue as I prayed that the child might be saved. Afterward I felt a great sense of relief, as if I had saved a child somewhere myself."

Figures said, "I have to tell you about my adventure. Do you remember my telling you about my father's pupil, Malchus? He was quarreling with my father about something, and as part of his quarrel he had me kidnapped."

Herc exclaimed, "Kidnapped! You are here now. How did you escape?"

Figures told his friends the whole story, from first hearing Malchus and Atban plotting to sacrifice a child to Baal, his capture and his time in the cage with the unliftable latch, escaping at the bottom of the sea, and finally his rescue. He left out the woman who supplied the rescue boat; Phyllis always found a way to turn a woman in any event into a goddess' intervention. But he did tell of the feeling that just as he was beginning to breathe water into his lungs, something seemed to cover his mouth and face, which may have saved his life.

"Don't you think it was odd that just as I was praying to have a child saved, the heavy lock on your cage suddenly became so light that you could lift it? Clearly, Artemis helped lift the lock herself. Gods can become invisible, so you did not see her. I must go back to the temple tomorrow to thank her."

"You are certainly wrong. Something about being underwater made the lock weigh less. I am going to experiment when I get home to see if I am right. Water makes us float, and we feel lighter when we are swimming."

"But a heavy lock does not float. I don't think that you can find a natural explanation for it becoming lighter. There are many ways that the gods enter our lives. Everyone knows that. And we also know that we cannot explain why the gods sometimes favor one person over another or one act over another. Why did Athena favor Odysseus so? That is the way gods behave. Artemis favors you "

Figures did not want to get into another argument with Phyllis about the gods, so he changed the subject to talk about how much help Tono had been. Soon they had exhausted the subject of Figures' adventure. By that time Labda had baked the honey-almond sweets, and each child got one as a treat. Herc also took his half of the rest and put it in a jar to trade later.

⬟ After supper, while he was studying, he overheard his mother telling Phidias that Malchus needed to be punished for the kidnapping.

"Too late. Malchus is gone and will not be able to return to Syracuse. Pyrrhus today had his soldiers imprison all Carthaginians, which would certainly include Malchus if he were here."

Andromeda asked, "Did you meet Pyrrhus?"

"Pyrrhus came to the Assembly while Hiero and I were there. While your cousin Hiero is big and strong, Pyrrhus is much more powerful. Hiero compared to Pyrrhus is like what I am compared to Hiero. And Pyrrhus is fierce. He fights battles alongside his men and sometimes fights opposing generals in single combat."

"Hiero is never so foolish as that. They don't usually offer the general for single combat, but their most ferocious fighter in his place. Hiero says he is a more effective soldier than a ferocious one."

Hiero said. "I am ferocious when necessary. Pyrrhus' men recognized me as a fellow warrior. My much-used shield and sword were my introduction. Soon we were listing battles we had fought. They introduced me to Cineas, Pyrrhus' main deputy. He questioned me closely concerning my experience, then told me to report tomorrow. He said 'Say farewell to kinsmen and girlfriends today. Pyrrhus will move against the Carthaginian towns in Sicily tomorrow.' Then he grumbled that Pyrrhus could not stop fighting. He said, 'He should have been content with Epirus. He should have secured Macedon. If he wins Rome and Carthage, which he appears to want, then what difference will it mean? He could be just as happy in Epirus.' But Cineas for all his grumbling seems ready to follow Pyrrhus wherever he fights. That kind of loyalty makes for a strong army."

Phidias said, "We will be sorry to see you leave. Archimedes is much safer with you here. Malchus is gone for now, but I fear that he will be back."

"Malchus can find a young boy to sacrifice to Baal at almost any farmhouse in Sicily. He was already fighting with you. He knew Archimedes and where he lives. So Archimedes was his first choice. But now that he has failed with Archimedes, he is more likely to look for another sacrifice. He can't return to a city warring against his whole tribe."

Phidias replied, "I am not so sure. There may be other reasons that he is attacking my family. But let us enjoy this night when you are still with us."

⬟ That night Hiero and Figures' parents stayed up late drinking wine and telling stories. Figures was allowed up later than usual and listened to the grown-ups talk. Most tales concerned relatives he had never met, people who had lived and died before Figures was born.

Hiero told one story that he found disturbing. Phidias asked about a friend or distant relative, Leon, who lived in Croton in Italy. Hiero knew this man. He had heard that Leon was one of the few remaining dedicated followers of Pythagoras, the Pythagoreans. For this reason he was dragged from his home by a mob led by local priests, and then burned to death—or something like that. Hiero was not certain of the details.

Phidias said, "I knew that Leon was a Pythagorean—many in Croton once were. But I believed followers of Pythagoras were no longer persecuted. This is truly bad news if true."

Figures knew that Pythagoras had been a mathematician and philosopher, but he did not know until this moment that people who followed Pythagoras were endangered.

Phidias continued, " Pythagoras did not believe in conventional gods or animal sacrifices, so members of the Pythagorean society have been attacked by mobs led by priests. When Pythagoras was still alive, a hundred or so years ago, he and his followers controlled Croton. But they drove him out of the city, and later many Pythagoreans in Croton were burned to death in a suspicious fire. Some escaped and started communities elsewhere, even in the lands of barbarians. The Pythagoreans in Greek cities were attacked and their buildings burned. Some lasted longer in Italy, but I doubt that Leon wanted it known that he was a Pythagorean."

Figures said, "But you told me that ideas that come from Pythagoras are true."

"His ideas about harmony and right triangles and the shape of Earth are beyond dispute," Phidias said. "He believed that numbers were the basis of the universe. They can be proved by experiment, by mathematical reasoning, or by careful observation. No one would attack people for believing in those proofs or theories. But priests fear his ideas about religion. They also claim that Pythagoreans practice evil magic."

Hiero said, "Some say they perform secret rituals. I have heard that they communicate among each other all over Italy and Sicily using codes. What else do I know? Let's see. They have a magical symbol, which is the five-pointed star in a pentagram. I don't know what it means. If someone suspects that a neighbor is a secret Pythagorean, the symbol is scratched on the doorway, signaling priests to move against him. That's all I know about Pythagoreans. Leon was identified, then they killed him."

Andromeda asked, "And what of Leon's family? Surely he was married. What happened to his wife? Were there children?"

Hiero answered, "I met his wife and there was also one child. His Italian wife Claudia was justly famed for her beauty. I did not meet their daughter Hypate. No doubt they both were either killed or driven out of town."

At this point Andromeda announced. "It is time for Archimedes to go to bed. All this talk of people being killed is not suitable for a young man to hear, and I know he always is listening."

⬟ As he lay in bed, Figures thought about Pythagoras idea that everything came from numbers; but where did numbers come from? He knew that he could count five figs by matching each fig with a finger, but if matching was all there was to number, he did not think it could account for much. Even for figs, if he cut each one in two, there would still be the same amount of fig to eat, but now he counted ten pieces. He could cut those pieces in half and have twenty, a much bigger number but still the same amount of food.

When he counted, it did not matter what the objects being counted were. He could lay down a fig, a rock, a pot, a frog, and a stick—there were still five things, even though all of them were completely different. And he could count things that did not exist at all, such as Zeus, Hera, Artemis, Aphrodite, and something like a dream. The number five still worked, even when nothing was really there to be counted.

Suppose that nothing at all existed...then what would there be to count?

He then had an exciting idea. If nothing existed, he could count the nothing, which would give him the number one. So if nothing existed, he would have the nothing and also the number one. He had two things he could count. That would mean that the number two also existed. In that case there were three things: nothing, one, and two. He could see that this same line of thought would produce all the numbers, so Pythagoras probably meant that numbers exist independently of everything else.

Happy with this idea, he finally fell asleep.

SCROLL 6

● Early the next morning, Hiero left to report to Pyrrhus. He soon returned, however, saying, "Pyrrhus has changed his mind. His conquest of Sicily is put off until tomorrow. *Today* he studies maps and decides how to deploy armies and elephants. My new commander told us all to take a day to rest up for the campaign. I need to return to camp later, but I have part of this day to spend with you. What shall we do?"

Phidias and Andromeda proposed that they take food and wine to a small grove of palm trees where they could eat outdoors. Andromeda suggested that Figures ask his friends to join them so he would have someone to play with.

He ran along the path to get Phyllis. Herc was in school. Phyllis was home and bored, so quite happy to join the outing.

She asked, "Can I bring my aulos? I am just learning to play, but I am already quite good. " The aulos is a musical instrument played by blowing through a reed clenched between the lips, using fingertips to open and close holes to change pitch. It is difficult to play. Phyllis was rather bold to offer to perform in public, but then she was seldom shy about anything.

"Bring it. Luce will also entertain us with her lute, but perhaps you can play duets."

When they reached the grove and Phyllis met Hiero, she suddenly abandoned her normal bold attitude. She seemed in awe of the soldier, far from her usual manner. She watched Hiero's every move as if he might suddenly stop chatting and attack her with his sword.

Even when they ate or when she blew into the aulos, cheeks puffed out and lips compressed, she kept one eye on Hiero. Hiero did not seem to notice this attention, but Figures thought it was very odd. She did not fear his father or any other man.

Phidias asked her if she were worried that playing the

aulos would affect her beauty.

"Not likely," said Phyllis. "For I have none. Why do you ask?"

"I have been told that the aulos was invented by the goddess Athena. But when she played it, her cheeks puffed out from the effort. The goddess worried that this might ruin her beauty. So she threw the aulos away and never played again."

"What happened to the aulos?"

"I am not expert in all those old stories. You should ask your father who pays more attention to them. These stories make for good poetry, but are not real history. How would we know whether Athena really invented the aulos? Who saw her do it?" He shrugged and went back to eating.

Phyllis did not argue with Phidias, but Figures was sure that she believed that Athena invented the instrument.

Hiero said, "Archimedes, your mother tells me that you are an expert in all your studies. You also spend a lot of time wandering in the woods. Do you hunt?"

"I make maps. I follow a stream down a hillside and sometimes all the way to the sea, then draw its path. I made a machine to figure out how far it is between bends in the stream. Also I include hills and anything of interest, such as a cliff or cave. I've mapped most of Epipolae and I am planning to map Mount Iblei when I am older and father will let me travel that far. And when I am older yet, the volcano Mount Etna."

"How do you measure distances?"

"I use a rope to measure the circumference of a wheel. I make a mark on the wheel that is easy to see. Then I roll the wheel along the place I wish to measure. Each time the mark reaches the top, the wheel has covered the same distance. To count how often the wheel turns I use gravel. As the mark reaches the top, I drop a rock into a bag. When I cover the distance, I count the rocks and multiply by the circumference."

Hiero said "Ingenious! The next time I visit, you must

demonstrate your invention. But now I must return to camp. I promised one of the soldiers that I would meet him this afternoon."

⬟ After Hiero left, Figures asked Phyllis why she had kept staring at Hiero.

"Figures, your cousin was sent by Artemis. He has a special light shining around him that comes from the Goddess. He must be on an important mission in Syracuse. Although I know that the Goddess favors you, she has not shared that shining light with you. But she has with Hiero."

Figures, the skeptic, asked, "What do you think it could mean? Is Hiero going to save Syracuse from Carthage and Rome? I think Pyrrhus is supposed to handle that mission. As far as I know, Hiero is just another soldier, hoping to get an officer's commission in Pyrrhus' army. I suppose that there is one way he could win a great battle. When the opposing army saw a glowing general, they would just turn and run away."

"It's not like that at all. Maybe he is here to save Syracuse or maybe just to save you. Anyway, I don't think that most people can see the light that shines from him. You can't, for example."

⬟ With Malchus out of the country and Hiero in the army, Figures went back to the life he had always known, lessons from his father and mother and playing with his friends.

For an astronomy lesson one night, Phidias led Figures to a high point on the nearby fort of Euryalus, an ancient fortification from the time of Dionysus. From there they could see the sky in all directions.

Phidias reminded Figures how to identify the constellations. He covered his lamp and pointed west.

"You already know the three stars of Orion's belt. Can you see Orion rising over the cliffs along the horizon? Now turn and look directly over the sea. The three bright stars that look a bit like the three stars of Orion's belt are part of the Scorpion, although the middle star is much brighter. Here, I will draw in the dust of this platform the main stars in each. The Scorpion is one of the twelve zodiac constellations." Phidias uncovered his lamp and produced his drawing of the stars.

Figures saw both constellations in the sky, although he did not really see the creatures that were supposed to be in the stars, so he asked, "Why is it that I can't see the shapes better? And who decided that these stars in the east look like Orion the Hunter and those stars in the southeast look like a scorpion in the sky?"

"The shapes are hard to see except for a few, like the Plow, which you also know as the Great Bear, although it looks more like a plow. No one knows who first named these constellations. There are many stories that tell how they were put in the sky by gods or goddesses. "

"Tell me one."

"Artemis, the goddess who some say was born in Syracuse, is supposed to have caused both Orion and the Scorpion to become part of the sky. Orion, according to one story, is said to have done something that made Artemis angry. She commanded a scorpion to bite him on the heel, which resulted in Orion's death. But Orion was a favorite of the god Poseidon--perhaps his son--so Poseidon put Orion in the sky as a constellation. This act made Artemis even angrier. So she put the scorpion in the sky also. But to keep the scorpion safe from Orion stamping on him, she put the scorpion in a distant part of the sky, where he remains today."

Figures said, "Maybe Orion is still afraid of the Scorpion, so he does not arise until he sees that the Scorpion is beginning to set."

"Certainly they keep far apart; whoever first named these constellation understood that although the sky moves, most stars keep their places. We can see both constellations tonight, although each is low on the horizon, but soon Orion will be gone and the Scorpion will rise. Then winter will have turned into spring."

Phidias then began to teach Figures the names of individual stars. He pointed first to one then another and murmured each name almost as an incantation--Sirius, Hesperus, Canopus, Polaris, and on and on, even naming some stars that could not be seen because they were below the horizon.

Figures asked. "How many stars are in the sky, father? A myriad?"

"Not that many. How big is a myriad?" Phidias asked.

"A myriad is the biggest number you have taught me. But it is only ten times ten times ten times ten, or ten times a thousand. It seems to me that there should be a bigger number. For example, ten times ten times ten times ten times ten, or ten myriads. But I said 'a myriad' because you said that it is the biggest number that has a name."

"I have studied the stars all my life. You may be surprised to know that there are not a myriad stars. I know I was. In fact, there are only three thousand stars that you can see from Syracuse on a very clear night, clearer even than tonight."

Figures was surprised at this indeed and not sure that he believed his father. "How can you be sure of the number of stars?"

Phidias pointed to the sky and said, "I have counted them."

"I know that the myriad is not the biggest number. I think those bigger numbers should have names--not just ten myriad but something else. The number of grains of sand on the beach here should have a name."

"Pythagoras would approve of that, I am sure, but that is enough lessons for tonight. I see by the stars that we both should get to our beds and sleep, or one of us at least will be cranky tomorrow, and you would not want it to be me."

As they walked back home, Figures asked Phidias about

something he had worried over since hearing Hiero's story of Leon in Croton. "Why do people harm Pythagoreans like Leon or Claudia and Hypate? Pythagoras was a wise man, not someone who encouraged evil."

"Pythagoras did not believe what everyone else believed. And perhaps some of those who followed his rule were too insistent on making others do as they did. It did not help that the Pythagoreans were a secret society, so people suspected them of much that could not be known."

"You talk as if the Pythagorean Society was in the past. But Leon was killed not long ago for being a Pythagorean."

"Figures, the days when members of the Pythagorean society could live and meet openly are long gone, even though Pythagoras died over 200 years ago."

Figures said, "What will happen to Claudia and Hypate, the wife and daughter of the Pythagorean who was killed?"

Phidias replied, "Among the beliefs of Pythagoras was that women are equal to men and should be educated and encouraged to be leaders. I have no doubt that if Claudia and Hypate escaped, they know how to survive without Leon. Now we are home and must go to bed. "

As Figures slept that night, he dreamed of constellations, but unlike the real sky, the constellations were all easily recognizable figures, the way that the seven stars of the Plow formed a shape that clearly resembled the kind of plow Tono used to turn over soil in their field. Orion was there, but instead of just the three stars of his belt, there were stars showing his head, shoulders, a sword hanging from his belt, and legs stretching across the sky. Far away was the shape of a real scorpion, complete with claws and legs.

At that point he noticed that Artemis was watching him from the nearby wood, carrying her shield and bow, with a quiver of arrows slung over her shoulder. She looked something like Phyllis in his dream. Artemis approached him and said, "You, too, can be a constellation. I can make you one." With that, she grabbed his arm and effortlessly threw him high into the sky. He was still floating upward among the stars when he awoke.

⬟ Figures often overheard his father and mother discussing Pyrrhus. After scaring the Carthaginians from the gates of Syracuse, Pyrrhus had decided that he should clear all Sicily of Carthaginian influence. Phidias said that Pyrrhus likely planned to move on to Africa next and overcome Carthage itself.

Pyrrhus was forcing all young men to join the army and spending much of the Assembly's money on arms. The people of Syracuse were not sure whether to be grateful to Pyrrhus for rescuing them from the Carthaginians and the tyrant Hiketas, or to be alarmed by his expenses and disruption of city life. Soon Pyrrhus was opposed by some of the same members of the Assembly who had invited him to Syracuse. Pyrrhus did not take dissent lightly and had his opponents in the Assembly killed.

Although Figures learned nearly all the political news by eavesdropping, he was told directly about one news event; Andromeda proudly said to Figures, "Our cousin Hiero has become an important officer in Pyrrhus' army."

Phidias added. "With so many new people being pushed into the army, the experienced soldiers like Hiero keep being promoted. He already has a large number of soldiers at his command. He is very popular with the soldiers, so his career is blossoming."

Figures was glad to hear that his cousin Hiero was doing well. Hiero came to visit his mother every few weeks and always spent a lot of time playing with him. Hiero liked to question him about what he had been learning. He recognized during these exchange, that Hiero did not have a great deal of learning himself, especially when it came to geometry and arithmetic. Sometimes he started teaching Hiero, being careful that Hiero never had to reveal his ignorance. In turn, Figures learned from Hiero many of the ways that soldiers used to win battles.

He was especially interested in Hiero's description of the catapult. The catapult was a Syracusan invention that had changed the face of warfare. It was a giant bow that launched heavy bronze arrows or small boulders. The arrow or boulder struck so powerfully that it could take down a wall or other fortification.

Figures built his own catapult, based on the description given by Hiero, but much smaller. In the first trial of the device, the heavy arrow, made from oak instead of bronze, went somewhat farther than Figures had expected. It nearly hit one of the slaves working in the vegetable garden.

Figures' mother cried our, "Archimedes! What are you doing? You could have killed Noto with that thing! You must take it apart at once."

"It is a catapult. I will be careful where I aim it."

"No. You will not aim it anywhere. I will turn it over to Tono to take apart. You cannot play with such a dangerous toy."

Soon after the catapult incident, Andromeda told Figures, "You spend too much time building things and making maps in the woods by yourself," she said. "When you do something with another person, it is nearly always that girl Phyllis. Now I like Phyllis well enough, but you will grow up not knowing how to be with other men. I want you to meet other boys more often and play with them."

⬟ The next day, Figures and Phyllis walked into town and waited at Pelekos' school. But when school let out, Narcissus and Faunus ran right past them, heading toward the harbor on some pursuit of their own. But Jason and Herc seemed happy to see Phyllis and Figures.

Phyllis said, "We thought you two might want to do something this afternoon, and we could join you."

Jason said, "We could go to the field where the contestants for next year's Games are training. We can watch them practice through the fence around the field. We can learn ways to train that we can use for ourselves. The Games are only three years away and I certainly plan to enter the boys' competition. You will, too," ignoring that Phyllis, as a girl, could not have any part of the Games.

Jason's enthusiasm could not be ignored. He led the way to where the athletes were at work.

The young men were training in a smaller amphitheater than the one used every four years for the actual Games. It was similar in design, but instead of being built into a small valley from stone, it stood on a level place and was surrounded by a latticework fence, so that it was possible for someone outside the fence to see the action inside through the gaps between strips of wood.

Figures did not understand what the young men on the field were doing. Some stood with arms outstretched and knees slightly bent, then ran rapidly for a few feet, walked back to their starting place, and did it again. Some had heavy weights that they lifted repeatedly over their heads. Others circled the outskirts of the field over and over. A man played the aulos near men holding weights in each hand. These men swayed to the music then jumped, tossing the weights behind. Nearer to where the friends sat, athletes paired up and carefully placed their hands and arms in position, then pushed or pulled until one of them started to fall.

He was ashamed for not knowing more about sport but did not want to sound stupid before his friends. He thought that if he watched long enough he could determine what the athletes were doing.

Herc was seldom embarrassed, however, and asked, "Jason, what sports are these men practicing? "

"The athletes are training for races, jumping, and wrestling. Some are just building their strength. Tomorrow a different group will be here, throwing the discus and javelin. Because there are athletes practicing all over the field today, no one can throw anything because they might hit one of the others."

Herc said, "Does everyone do every sport?"

"Some just race or box or wrestle, but the best all-round

athletes take part in a kind of combined event called the pentathlon."

Phyllis added, "That's a short race, a long jump, a discus toss, a javelin throw, and wrestling. You have to be really good in all five to win."

"Not really, although it helps to be good in all of them. Winners of the other events wrestle each other to determine which man gets the laurel crown."

Figures asked, "What does the person who comes in second get? If the same athlete is second in all four of the first events, he should have a chance wrestling, too."

Jason seemed astonished. "No one cares who is second. The idea is to be best. If you are not first, then no one really cares. But if you win, you will be famous.

Phyllis added, "At least until the next Games."

Figures asked, "How long is the race? I see that some runners are going around and around the field, which seems to mean that the race covers a long distance.

"There are several different kinds of race. The shortest race is the main measure for distance, the stadium. One part of the pentathlon is a one-stadium race. Then there is a two-stadium race and a long 24-stadium race."

Phyllis said, "And the winner of every event is crowned with bay leaves by the priestess of Artemis."

Jason added, "The Olympic Games in Greece are dedicated to the god Zeus. Boys under 18 cannot compete in the pentathlon because Zeus has declared it unhealthy for them. Here in Syracuse, however, the Games are dedicated to Artemis, who permits boys to race and do the pentathlon."

Phyllis suggested, "Since Artemis is in charge of the Syracuse Games, she should decree that the pentathlon is also suitable for girls."

The boys just laughed. They were used to hearing Phyllis proclaim that girls can do anything that boys are able to accomplish. No one believed her, but they found it not useful to argue. Once she lost her temper and pummeled Jason until other boys rescued him.

● Figures began to calculate the distance the athletes ran during a single trip around the outside of the training field. The field appeared too small for the circumference to be a full stadium.

Although at first look the field seemed circular, each section of fence between posts was straight. He counted the fence sections: 25. Although his foot was shorter than the official length used in Syracuse, he knew that by placing all four fingers close together in front of his toes, the distance from his heel to his little finger was exactly a Syracuse foot, the length of the foot of Apollo at his temple. He had matched his foot-plus-fingers with the statue's foot.

He found a stick and broke it to be one foot long, then used the stick to measure a section of the fence. It was 24 feet, so the whole fence was 24 times 25 feet, or 600 feet, the length of a stadium. That was the length of the fence, but not the length that runners on the circular path inside the field traveled.

Figures interrupted Jason's discourse on the Games to announce, "The field is too small. I just measured the length of the fence. The fence is exactly one stadium in length. But the fence must be longer than any circle inside it, so the length of a run is less than a stadium. The athletes may think that they are running a one-stadium or two-stadium race, but they are short by a few feet. The builders could have got much closer by using a fence with shorter sections, maybe 50 sections instead of 25. The more short sections, the closer the fence is to the circle."

● One winter day Figures picked through his father's scrolls, kept in a chest in his father's room. The name of each set of books was on a wrapper tied around the scrolls. He studied the labels, starting with poetry and philosophy. He had already finished reading both books of Homer and tried (and abandoned) his father's Aristotle. Plato was a lot more interesting, but reading too much philosophy at a time was tiresome. What he liked best were the books about astronomy or mathematics, such as works by Eudoxus. But he had read and re-read all of these already.

After some thought, he lifted from the very back of the chest the *Elements of Geometry* by Hippocrates of Chios. The ribbon around the scroll caught on a narrow chain that lifted out of the chest along with the scroll. The chain vanished into a small hole in the back of the chest. Pulling back the scrolls, Figures could see the hole was inside a rectangle of cracks--a door set flush into the back of the chest. He put his finger in the hole and tried to pull the door open, but it was shut tight. He felt a small bar inside the hole, which moved slightly back and forth when pushed. Figures recognized that a hole in a door with a narrow chain emerging from it must be a lock.

His mother was in charge of the lock on their storeroom. That lock had a larger hole with a strong cord emerging. The cord was attached to a bolt inside the door that prevented the door from opening after the string had been pulled tight.

His mother wore the key on a cord. The key was a notched wooden cylinder with a hole through the end of the cylinder that reached the notch. To open the storeroom door, she threaded the string from the bolt through the hole in the key and out the notch. She pushed the entire key through the hole in the door, keeping both the cords outside. When she pulled on the cord attached to the key the bolt pushed back, and the door could be opened. To re-lock the door, she removed the key and pulled on the cord attached to the bolt.

Figures felt metal bolt with the tip of his finger again. The opening was rimmed with bronze and the chain was bronze. Only the person with the correct key could open the door. This meant that the door was a problem, and Figures loved solving problems.

The easiest solution would be to find the key.

Figures looked around the room for anything that might be the key, but he quickly realized that no one would go to the trouble of making a bronze lock and then leave the key in plain sight. It was his father's chest of books, so he supposed that his father had the key. If he was going to find out what was behind that door--and he was very curious about what might be there--he would have to solve where his father might hide a small brass key on a chain.

Immediately he knew the answer. His father wore a small brass cylindrical whistle on a chain around his neck. Figures had asked him long ago what it was. Phidias had lifted the whistle to his lips and blown a high piercing note. Phidias said that he had used it for years to summon a dog that he had as a boy. After the dog died, he had kept the whistle mostly to remind him of his boyhood companion, but now he sometimes used it to stop arguments when they became too loud and long. This explanation had seemed reasonable to Figures, but now he also realized that the whistle was just the right size to be the key to the bronze lock. What's more, the chain the whistle hung upon was the same type as the chain portion of the lock. And, since there was a passage for air through the whistle, the chain from the lock could be threaded onto the whistle just the way that the string from a wooden lock could be threaded through the hole in his mother's wooden key.

But he could not think of a way that he could test the theory that Phidias' "dog whistle" was actually the key to the lock. He would need to take the whistle from Phidias, but Phidias wore it all the time, even while sleeping or bathing. Although Figures felt close to his father, he did not think he should ask. After all, when he had asked about the whistle earlier, his father had not told him the whole truth. Furthermore, in the past year he had become less close to his parents, as they seemed to worry more about Hiero than about their son. He did not want to admit that he was jealous of his parent's love of Hiero, but deep in his heart he knew that he did feel that way.

What might Phidias have hidden in a secret compartment? Maybe Figures did not want to know. His mother had taught him a story from the ancient poet Hesiod, who lived about Homer's time. In Hesiod's story Zeus did not want men to be as happy as gods, so he created a woman to cause men sorrow. All the gods gave the first woman precious gifts, such as good looks and wit, so she was named *Pandora*, which means "all gifts." One gift was a large jar, but she was told that she must never open it.

Pandora was very curious by nature, so she had to know what was in the jar. She unscrewed the great lid and removed it. But all the world's troubles had been kept in the jar. The troubles suddenly flew out—pride, murder, lust, war, disease, hunger, all the evils of the world. Pandora saw the troubles flying out of the jar and as quickly as she could, she put the lid back and screwed it tight. According to Hesiod, however, all troubles but one had already exited the jar before Pandora closed the lid.

Figures' mother had said, "Hesiod could not know what was trapped in the jar since it was never opened again, although he claims it was *hope*. Other writers say that Pandora shakes the jar and hears something in it. She is so curious that once again she unscrewed the great lid. This time what fluttered out was hope. Hope is the antidote to all the other troubles, so it was good that she opened the jar the second time."

Phidias had come into the courtyard while Figures and Andromeda were finishing the lesson. He said, "Hesiod knew what was trapped in the jar—after all, he wrote the poem. It was not hope. Trapped in the jar was the ability to see the future. Seeing the future lets men know which of the other evils will befall them, so it is another curse like the other curses that Pandora released. Pandora's jar was never opened again, so mankind cannot see the future."

Andromeda said, "Phidias! That is not the kind of thing to tell a young boy. Bad things do not necessarily happen to everyone."

Figures wondered if he might be like Pandora. He might loose all kinds of evil on his family if he opened the door to the secret compartment. Maybe it would be safer if he never found a way to steal the key.

SCROLL 7

⬟ For distraction he opened *Elements of Geometry* by Hippocrates of Chios and began to work through proofs. Soon he became totally involved and forgot the secret compartment for that day. Instead of unlocking the compartment, he unlocked each proof, following how Hippocrates reasoned. He was delighted by an elegant chain of thought in which Hippocrates constructed a curved figure with the same area as a square. The curve outlined a shape like the crescent moon, which Hippocrates called a lune.

Later he told his father how to make a square into a lune. Phidias said, "That is a beautiful proof. We might never have had it if Hippocrates had been a better businessman. When he was defrauded of his money and property, he was reduced to making a living as a mathematics and astronomy teacher. Talents are not all equal. A great mathematician often knows little about practical problems."

Figures thought at first that his father said this because Phidias thought Figures was not very practical. On reflection, however, he concluded that Phidias was admitting that he was not very practical himself.

As he slept that night, he dreamed of the whistle his father carried. The dream Figures blew the whistle, and it made a low sound. He blew harder and the sound rose to a higher pitch. His father said, "Do you remember what I taught you about pitch?" He plucked a string on a lute. Half its length raised the note to the same pitch, but higher. A third or a fourth the length made harmonious notes. His father said, "1, 2, 3, 4 controls the music. The whistle is the same. How did you get my key? No one can have the key." Then Figures no longer had the whistle. His father had it and was using it to open the lock in the scroll chest. But just as the door was about to open, Figures lost the dream and fell sound asleep.

Before *Eureka!*

⬟ The next day Hiero came to stay during a short furlough, filled with stories from battles throughout Sicily. He had started as the commander of a small group of untrained townspeople, whom he quickly forced into shape. Hiero's troops then distinguished themselves in the fighting to take towns that Carthage controlled. Pyrrhus noticed, and Hiero was promoted several times in only a few months. When Hiero returned to the army after his furlough, he would be co-commander of the troops from Syracuse.

Figures' favorite story was about Pyrrhus in Eryx. Hiero said, " Eryx was the toughest city we faced, probably the strongest fortress in Sicily outside of Syracuse. It is almost to the sea at the far western end of the island--about as far from Syracuse as you can get and still be on the island. By the time we had fought our way there, our supply lines were stretched to the limit. We survived by plundering the villages around it. In addition to excellent fortifications surrounding the city on all sides, Eryx also had a large army. We knew we might not be able to defeat them in a fair fight.

"We still had several elephants that had survived the earlier battles. Pyrrhus took the one that best obeyed its trainer and had a ladder built that rode on the elephant's back along with Pyrrhus himself."

Figures shivered at the thought of riding one of the giant elephants he and Phyllis had seen land at the harbor.

"As the Sun rose a small group of our mercenary archers began firing at the openings in the wall around Eryx. The mercenaries' attack provided a distraction while the elephant with Pyrrhus aboard moved swiftly to the wall. Pyrrhus, wearing heavy armor and carrying a sword, a shield, and a spear, put the ladder against the wall and scrambled to the top, killing all defenders who dared approach him. The sight of Pyrrhus slaying their soldiers with abandon seemed to the Carthaginians as if a god had come to fight alongside Pyrrhus, as Homer tells happened often during the Trojan War. While the Carthaginians stared, unable to take their eyes from Pyrrhus--terrified that he might be heading their way--

the rest of our army moved rapidly and got a hundred ladders in place. There was fierce fighting for a while, but Pyrrhus won the battle by himself."

There was a pause as Hiero finished his story. Andromeda said, "I don't know for sure what Pyrrhus has planned, but it seems that with all of Sicily captured, Pyrrhus might be satisfied for a while."

Phidias said, "Pyrrhus will not be satisfied for long. Soon Hiero will be leading the Syracusan troops to Africa or Rome or Macedonia to help Pyrrhus conquer the world."

After a moment Phidias asked Hiero, "What do *you* think Pyrrhus will do next? He may have an army of 30,000, which was enough to take all of Sicily from the Carthaginians, but that will not be enough to defeat Carthage or Rome or Macedonia." Phidias gazed at the ceiling as if he thought the answer might be written there, then continued, "I'll tell you what he will do. He has already put the able-bodied men of Syracuse into his army, whether they wanted to be or not. Now he will command all men to come with him on whatever his next adventure turns out to be. He won't hesitate to induct me and the other old men. And I know of soldiers only slightly older than Archimedes is now, boys only thirteen years old."

Hiero said, "The main problem will not be finding the soldiers. The harder part will be finding a way to get an army across the sea to attack. That makes me think he will attack Rome rather than Carthage or Macedonia. There is only a narrow strait to cross between Sicily and Italy. He could ferry the army across to Italy. A few boats going back and forth each day would do it. Then the army could march on Rome. Also, he has allies in Italy, such as Tarentum. Their armies would love to have help in fighting Rome. So, I think he will gather an army and head for Rome."

⬟ But Hiero had not been able to read Pyrrhus' mind. Pyrrhus soon announced that he would gather a large army and also build ships for a navy to take Carthage. For this he needed sailors and ships even more than fighting men.

Figures asked, "Is Pyrrhus going to make *everyone* go to Carthage and fight? Would that include you? Or me?"

Phidias reassured Figures, "I don't think he will take you or me. I am too old for fighting and you are far too young. We might lose Dromio and some of the other slaves for a few months."

But a few days later, Phidias reported disturbing rumors that were circulating through Syracuse. "They say Pyrrhus is not happy with the number of recruits. Young and old are no longer exempt."

Andromeda asked, "Who will farm and take care of the animals if able men, slaves, and young and old men are taken for the army?"

"Women will have to do it. Pyrrhus says that every man and boy should be part of the war effort. Women without farms should weave extra sails for the new fleet."

Figures asked, "What can an army do with boys and old men?"

"The young will be trained to be soldiers or rowers, front-line warriors that are killed first. The old will assist ship's carpenters or do other work that does not require great strength."

Figures now thought only of the plans for war. He no longer wondered what he might find if he could unlock the secret compartment in the trunk with the scrolls. Everyone he knew also became obsessed with the coming war. For once Jason spoke of something other than sports. Phyllis reported that her father had gold ready to bribe any who came to impress him or Herc into the army or navy.

⬟ Early one morning townsfolk dressed as soldiers arrived at Phidias' house. The dozen men did not wait by the door to be met. They stormed into the courtyard and shouted, "Come out." Figures and his father left their sleeping quarters. Figures recognized some of the "soldiers" from the Assembly.

Phidias cried out, "Arion! Have you come for my slaves?"

Arion appeared to be the leader of the team. The leather soldier outfit did not suit his grossly overweight body and graying hair. "Not just the slaves, Phidias. We must take you. Your knowledge of astronomy will be essential for navigation as Pyrrhus' navy crosses the sea. You can read maps and interpret notes captured from Carthaginian sailors. Pyrrhus needs you."

"And what has he promised in return?" Phidias asked.

"When this war is over, we each will be given regions once ruled by Carthage. We shall be like kings."

"He made no promises to me, and I do not intend to help him fight."

"You have not choice. Take him, men."

As the recruiters grabbed Phidias and began to bind his arms, Figures made a dash for the women's quarters. He had to tell his mother what was happening.

One of the men, a former student of Phidias, ran after him, shouting, "Stay, Archimedes--you are to fight for Pyrrhus also."

Andromeda was startled to see an adult following her son into the women's part of the house. "Orymas! What are you doing here? You know you cannot come into this part of the house. "

"I am truly sorry, Andromeda. But my orders are clear. I am to take Archimedes to fight against Carthage."

" Archimedes is too young for war."

"There is no escape. We are recruiting all able-bodied boys."

"Well, Pyrrhus can't have him. Phidias will stop this nonsense."

At that moment, Arion appeared in the doorway. "Do you have the boy, Orymas?" he asked. "We have Phidias and the slaves. Let's get everyone to Pyrrhus."

Andromeda screamed as the men hustled away her husband, arms tied to his sides. Her son was gripped tightly by two men and forced to stumble along after Phidias. She started to run after them, but Luce grabbed her shoulders and held her back.

"There is nothing you can do, mistress." Luce said. "They have Dromio and Tono, too. All we can do is pray that the war will be short and that our men return safely." Andromeda began to weep uncontrollably.

Every household in Syracuse was similarly torn apart. Narcissus, Faunus, Jason, and Figures were taken to a dormitory for preliminary training. Even Herc, younger and overweight, was taken—his Father's bribe had failed his son. But the recruiters ignored Phyllis and all other girls.

Later Figures learned how Andromeda finally stopped weeping and traveled outside the city walls to ask Hiero for help, begging him to return her husband and son.

He said, "I can do nothing. In a few days the army and navy will sail to Carthage. Pyrrhus believes he can overcome that great city the same way he conquered small towns of Sicily. There is no way to predict how Phidias and Archimedes will fare. I can't promise that either will return. For that matter, I am not sure I will survive."

SCROLL 8

⬟ The makeshift dormitory that housed the boys training to be soldiers had been the former tyrant Hiketas' cattle barn. It still smelled of manure. There were no separate rooms—each boy was assigned a space for sleeping. Hiketas' cattle had been given to Pyrrhus' Epirote soldiers, who had butchered and eaten them.

Cylon, who was in charge of the dormitory was an experienced soldier. He said, "My mission is to teach you military discipline." He organized various strenuous exercises to improve the boys' strength and agility. As they ran, jumped, crawled, fought with sticks, and lifted weights, Cylon studied their skills or lack of them, keeping notes on every one of the dozens of boys.

Figures had never lived with boys his age, not to mention those two to five years older. He soon learned that boys in a group are rough on any boy who seems different. Several times an older boy took food meant for Figures and ate it. Since recruits were served only one meal of bread and a cereal, losing a day's supply meant that he woke up in the night, hungry after dreaming of food. Someone stole his clothes while he slept and hid them. He spent the morning naked and barefoot until Jason learned where the chiton and sandals were hidden.

He did not always understand the conversations of the boys, especially the older ones. He had grown up on a small farm, seeing animals behaving like animals, so he knew about reproduction, but not the slang the other boys used to talk about it, which they did incessantly. The older boys also teased him about sex, accusing him of practices that he did not know what were. He longed to talk about mathematics or politics or books.

One day Figures complained to Aristedes, his sleeping neighbor, that the older boys took too much space for themselves. "I have measured the barn against my own foot.

The main floor is about 5,850 square feet. There are 117 boys here—I counted them myself. Each boy deserves exactly 50 square feet. That should be plenty, but you and your friends have reduced my corner to only 18 square feet."

Aristedes thought for a second and then smiled broadly. He said in a loud voice, "Figures wants more space. Let's give it to him. There is plenty of space on the roof. Figures can have some of that."

He grabbed Figures, who at first fought back. But other boys took his arms and legs and lifted him off the ground, and he surrendered. They carried him to a small ladder that led to a trapdoor on the roof. Aristides climbed the ladder, dragged him onto the roof, and closed the door. When Figures tried the door, the ladder was gone. He was stranded on the roof.

At first he cried. Then he saw the view from the roof. He could see everything below. He sat down and soon watched the recruits being trained. From time to time he opened the trapdoor, but the ladder was still gone. When the stars and planets began to glow, he lay on his back and studied the sky, which from the roof could be seen as a complete dome. The moon was dark, and the stars and planets blazed forth.

He was cataloging the visible constellations and watching for shooting stars, when the sound of the trapdoor opening startled him. The head of their instructor Cylon appeared in the opening. Cylon said, "I thought you had run home to your mother. But when I asked where you were, your neighbor Heracleides, said you were on the roof all day. What do you think you're doing?"

"Watching the stars."

"Not all day. I'll see that you do two days training in one tomorrow."

But Figures was glad to be rescued despite the threat of double training.

⬟ After his stranding on the roof Figures spoke only to the boys he had known before the dormitory life. Narcissus and Faunus might tease him, but they stopped short of taking his food or locking him on the roof—although he had enjoyed the adventure on the barn roof once he recovered from being locked out.

Despite the perilous and uncertain future of the coming war with Carthage, Jason continued to focus on the Syracusan Games. He said, "If I am chosen for the army, long marches will be good for building leg strength, a help in winning races, but being a rower in the navy would strengthen arm and chest muscles, and improve performance in the discus and javelin tosses, not to mention wrestling."

"Whether or not they hold the Games, you have to be alive to compete," said Faunus. "Our chance of living is not good. It is even more dangerous for rowers in a battle than for infantry. Rowers have no weapons and no place to hide. If the other ship grapples yours, their marines will casually kill you on their way to attack the sailors."

Figures wanted to compute their chance of surviving, but knew little to use, for war was not part of his home schooling, unlike the curriculum in most Greek schools. He asked, "What do you mean by 'grapple'? I thought ships sank enemies by ramming."

Faunus said, "Ramming is not often successful. Remember that the other boat is maneuvering to ram *your* ship. But if you can row close enough, you can throw a hook, called a 'grapple', over the side of the other ship and connect the two. After the two ships are pulled together, marines do the fighting."

"Marines?"

"Armed soldiers on fighting ships who try to fight their way onto the other ship so they can kill all its sailors and officers as well as any rowers in the way."

Narcissus said, "When one side gains an advantage, those marines leap across to the other ship. Once on board the other ship, they usually win. The marines are the toughest and best-trained troops, better than soldiers in the regular army. The winning marines kill most of the sailors and the younger or weaker rowers. If we win, some of our own sailors take charge and keep the ship in action, which is another reason grappling is better than ramming."

Faunus said, "The captain who brings a Carthaginian ship into our Navy gets a reward from the City. About half of his reward goes to the marines and sailors who were involved in the fight while the captain keeps the rest."

"Not the rowers?" Jason questioned.

"Not the rowers."

Jason returned to his original idea, "All the same, life as a rower could give you the arm strength to be a better discus tosser or javelin thrower or wrestler."

"Not a better wrestler," Narcissus said. "The secret of wrestling is strong legs. That's why good runners, like me, are the best wrestlers."

Then Cylon caught them talking and sent them racing around the track seven times. To prove his point, Narcissus completed all seven laps while Jason and Faunus were doing six. Figures was a few steps behind.

⬟ After the boys had been training for a few weeks, a ship's captain arrived, needing rowers for the new ships Pyrrhus was having built. Cylon lined up a number of boys for the captain's inspection, but did not include Narcissus, Faunus, or Jason or any of the stronger and more agile older boys. Judging solely by their looks, the captain quickly rejected Herc as too young and fat and Figures as too thin and frail looking, taking mostly the oldest boys available. Jason somehow slipped into the group being shown to the captain. So he was picked for the navy, where he would become a rower. The new rowers were marched off to live on their ships. Figures counted them as they left the dormitory.

A few days later an army officer came to collect boys for the infantry. All remaining boys were displayed except Narcissus, who had become Cylon's favorite, despite frequently drilling in his own way instead strictly following instructions. Cylon had sent Narcissus on an errand that kept him out of the camp for the day.

Cylon had the candidates run, lift weights, and perform exercises with sticks to show how well he had trained them. The officer soon stopped the demonstration, saying, "I'll take them all except that young fat one." But when Figures lined up with the others to leave for camp, the officer grabbed his shoulder. "Archimedes? Are you the boy whose mother is related to Captain Hiero?"

"Yes," replied Figures.

"Then return to your dormitory. Hiero will come for you tomorrow."

Figures was overjoyed, for he was certain Hiero had found a way to obtain his release. He would be able to return home and see his mother. Perhaps his father would be excused also. He told Herc that they would both be able to go home together when Hiero came.

When Narcissus returned to camp, he was furious that he had missed induction into the army, but Cylon assured him that he had a happy surprise coming the next day. After Cylon left, Narcissus said, "I think Cylon plans to keep me as a companion."

Herc was not sure what a companion might be, but it did not sound military. He said, "That would be great. You could escape the war. "

"I prefer to have the glory of fighting. I would fight like one of Homer's heroes, like Hector or Achilles."

Figures said, "Those heroes were both killed. I would prefer to be Odysseus, who survived the war."

⬟ The next day, two visitors arrived. One was a messenger from Hiero, who announced "I have come to take Archimedes to Pyrrhus."

"I am supposed to go home. Do I need to see Pyrrhus first?"

"You are to report to Pyrrhus. Hiero has praised your intelligence and knowledge so much that Pyrrhus that concluded that you will become his personal messenger boy.

Cineas has often urged Pyrrhus to use a messenger."

Cylon introduced Narcissus to the second visitor. "This is a captain of the marines. I want you to display your strength, speed, and agility to him."

After watching Narcissus work out, the marine captain said, "Cylon, you are right. With more training this boy can become a marine."

Cylon said, "That takes care of Archimedes and Narcissus, but what do we do with Heracleides? The Navy and Army have rejected him. I want to close this dormitory and report to my own Marine Company. Can I send Heracleides home without getting into trouble with Pyrrhus? My orders were to place all the boys in the armed services."

The Marine recruiter said, "My uncle commands a troop carrier that will transport soldiers to Africa. He has complained that his ship's cook needs an assistant, but possible candidates are already assigned to the fighting forces. The fat boy could be the answer to his problem." Turning to Herc, "Can you cook, fat boy? "

Herc said, "I have helped our family's cook sometimes."

"Good," said Cylon. "That settles it."

Cylon and the marine captain left with Narcissus and Herc, not even waiting for them to say goodbye to Figures, who was left alone with the messenger from Hiero.

Figures said, "Can I live at home while I work for Pyrrhus?"

"No. You must return each night to this dormitory. Soldiers will occupy it later today and stay there until the navy sails. You will spend all day with Pyrrhus, but sleep here with the soldiers."

⬟ The messenger led Figures to Pyrrhus. He felt much the same as he had the first time he met Hiero. Pyrrhus looked even fiercer than Hiero.

Pyrrhus spoke with the same intensity and volume that Cylon used to order trainees. "Boy! You are to stay near at all times while I am awake, but always out of my way. When I call you, be prepared to do whatever I ask. When I go to bed, return to your dormitory but be at hand when I arise at dawn. You start now."

Figures said, "Start what?"

"Do not speak unless I ask you a question. Start now waiting for orders."

Figures tried to shrink into nothingness. He flattened against the far wall so he was not in Pyrrhus' line of sight. That day he spent gazing at Pyrrhus' many scars, acquired during battles over half the Mediterranean. Various soldiers and Assembly members visited to make petitions to Pyrrhus and then left. Cineas, Pyrrhus' principal advisor, kept track of all of Pyrrhus' activities and commands. No one said anything to Figures until night had fallen. Cineas noticed him and said, "Archimedes, Pyrrhus is ready to rest. I will have a soldier accompany you to your dormitory. Be sure to be back here by dawn."

That night Figures dreamed that he was cupbearer for King Pyrrhus, the person who fills the king's cup with wine taken from its jar, which sat in a storage room.

Pyrrhus had strict rules: His own cup always remains at table, so the cupbearer uses a separate vessel to carry wine from the jar. Pyrrhus' cup when empty must be filled to the brim, but not spill over it. The cupbearer must bring the wine in the fewest number of trips, but no wine can be left in the cupbearer's vessel that the cupbearer might drink.

Pyrrhus' cup was a cylinder and the vessel given to Figures was a cone the same diameter and height as the cylinder. It took three trips back and forth to the wine jar to fill Pyrrhus' cup completely. Pyrrhus complained that it was taking too long, so Figures began to search for a larger cup. There was a cube that was the same height at the cylinder, but he knew it would bring too much wine and he would be in trouble for having wine left in his vessel. Then he found a vessel that was a sphere the same diameter as Pyrrhus' cylinder. Maybe he could fill Pyrrhus' cup in two trips with none left over, but he was not sure. He took the first cup of wine to Pyrrhus in the hemisphere, and it filled more of Pyrrhus' cub than the conical vessel had. But Pyrrhus' cup was more than half full, so he could not use the sphere again. Maybe the conical vessel would fill the remaining space. But Figures became lost on his way back to the wine jar and woke up frightened of Pyrrhus' anger and without knowing if he could exactly fill the cylinder in two trips, using one sphere and one cone. Figures thought about the dream for a moment or two, then fell into a dreamless sleep. It was still dark when a soldier shook him awake next morning. The dream faded from his memory as he hurried to Pyrrhus' headquarters.

⬟ After that first day, Figures was often sent carrying messages or fetching people or things for Pyrrhus, although there continued to be many hours when his only duty was to stand by awaiting commands. He was following Pyrrhus across a short bridge between Achradina and Ortygia when Cineas approached.

Cineas said, "Pyrrhus, I am glad to find you where we can talk for a moment without others listening." Figures, however, was always listening. "I have unpleasant news."

"I always heed your words because you are the one person who tells me the truth, pleasant or unpleasant."

"I have been visiting the Assembly and walking the streets with my ears open. You are rapidly losing your popularity in Syracuse. In the Assembly, old Leptines has been going from person to person saying that you are far worse than the tyrant Hiketas. Your war on Carthage is unpopular and the cause of the people's distress."

"They will love me again when we take Carthage. Victory makes all sacrifices seem worth while."

"Defeat on the other hand encourages citizens to rebel. We must be careful. If the people here in Syracuse are chafing under the burden of getting ready for war, what do you think is happening in the Sicilian towns we conquered such a short time ago? In many of those, the population is more likely to ally with Carthage than fight for you. Some towns were Carthaginian colonies from their first settlement."

"I hear the same story from my spies. In several towns across Sicily, citizens have taken their government back from my soldiers. But we have to let the towns revolt. It would not help our invasion plans at all for me to march back across Sicily and teach the unruly citizens that I am still their tyrant. I need all the troops I can gather. Forget about Sicily for now and think only of Carthage." He paused. "Boy!"

Figures jumped out of the shadows. "Boy!" was always the first word for his next assignment.

"Boy, find Hiero and tell him to recall all garrisons from every encampment across Sicily. Local commanders must make it clear to the Sicilians that if they fail to support me against Carthage, I will return and level their dwellings and temples to the ground. Have you got that?"

"Yes, General. I am to inform Hiero that you wish to bring all the troops to Syracuse that were left behind after you conquered Sicily so everyone can help attack Carthage. Local towns and cities may return to their former rulers but continue to be part of the Sicilian alliance against Carthage. Your revenge will be swift and complete if they fail to support you against the enemy."

"Good. Hiero was right in sending me his clever cousin. Now hurry and find him; and report back to me as soon as possible."

SCROLL 9

● Figures hurried away from Pyrrhus. His cousin now commanded a large body of Sicilian troops and mercenary units, traveling from legion to legion to inspect troops' readiness and discipline, and was constantly on the move. Pyrrhus understood that finding Hiero could take considerable time, so he would not expect Figures back immediately.

As he always did when he thought he could steal enough time from Pyrrhus, Figures started for the newly built navy flagship. It was not a likely location for Hiero, but Figures' father was there.

The shipyards are south of Achradina, so to reach them Figures passed though Achradina, where he was delighted to encounter Phyllis. He had not seen her since the boys and men had been impressed into Pyrrhus' army and navy.

"Phyllis! How are you? Have you seen my mother?"

"Figures! Are you all right? Your mother is fine — weaving and plotting ways to get you home. But do you know anything about Herc?"

Figures grabbed Phyllis and hugged her, something he had never done before. He had missed her more than he knew. He was surprised that her body seemed softer than he expected. He said, "Herc is all right. He is in the navy, but they passed over him for rowing. Instead he is the cook's helper on one of the troopships."

"That is great news. Rowers are killed first, but no one kills cooks if they want to eat. Our mother was worried, but I told her that Artemis promised that neither you nor Herc would go to war. So what are *you* doing that lets you wander all over town?"

"My cousin Hiero arranged for me to be a messenger for Pyrrhus. It is a scary job, but I get to know everything that happens before it happens."

"The best kind of gossip! Working for Pyrrhus does

sound scary. What is he like?"

"As fierce and powerful as everyone says, but only mean when someone disobeys him. What is most amazing is how fast he makes up his mind to do something, and how fast that something gets done. He is very clever as well as being strong. But he cannot hide his ambition, which is to rule the entire world. And you — what are you doing?"

"Trying to avoid weaving sails and the other duties women are supposed to be doing to help prepare for the war. I commune with Artemis in her temple when I can or seek her in the woods. I practice my bow-and-arrow hunting skills to be more like her. I am really bad at weaving and sewing, so mother does not mind so much if I am missing."

"All us boys had to be trained to be soldiers or rowers. They made us all live in an old smelly barn, and our instructor kept us running and doing exercises all day. But some of the other boys played tricks on me when our instructor was not looking. Once they set my hair on fire, and another time they drew diagrams on my forehead while I was asleep."

"If anyone tries to harm you, tell them that you are protected by the gods and they will only create problems for themselves if they tease you. Remind them that Artemis turned Actaeon into a stag when he offended her."

"Yes," said Figures. "And then she shot and killed the stag. She certainly seems mean for a goddess."

"But she can be kind to those she loves. The spring of Arethusa right here in Syracuse is the result of Artemis' changing a beautiful nymph into a different form to protect her from a pursuer."

"Your idea of a goddess who personally interferes with the lives of humans is mathematically impossible. There must be hundreds of thousands of people on Earth. The goddess cannot be everywhere at once, affecting all those lives."

"The gods are *not* everywhere at once; each one exists at one place at a given time, just as humans do. The Gods appear and disappear or take on different aspects, but they are no more able to be two places at once than you are. We are lucky that because she was born here Artemis often visits her temple on Ortygia."

"The greatest temple to Artemis is in Ephesus in Ionia, far from Syracuse. If she spends much time in her temple at Ephesus, then she cannot be here whenever you think you need her."

"A Goddess travels faster than the wind. The priestesses of Artemis know that on certain days she appears in the door into the front gable of a specific temple. Although, she spends time on Mount Olympus with other gods, Artemis is a hunter, so most of the time she is in the forest."

"I still cannot believe that some unseen god changes events in our human world."

"You just don't notice. Several times Artemis changed events in your life, but you thought it was just chance. You need to learn to pay attention more."

"You think it was Artemis. I believe that it was luck. Perhaps I am luckier than most people. If good luck is distributed in uneven portions to everyone on Earth, then by the rules of logic a few people will be lucky all their lives. Maybe I am one of them.

"Athena sometimes helped Odysseus by inspiring him to think clever ideas, but She also sometimes fought alongside him or gave him weapons. You don't know where your best ideas originate, and you fail to notice when you receive extra help. So you think it's luck."

"I am running out of free time. Tell your mother and mine that I miss them a lot. I hope to see you again soon."

They gave each other another quick hug and headed off in separate directions. Figures practically ran to the docks.

● Arriving at the flagship, he announced that he was seeking Hiero with a message from Pyrrhus. He pretended to be dismayed to learn Hiero was not aboard. "I will go then to the astronomer Phidias, who is related to Hiero. He may know Hiero's location." The ship's watchman, who had seen

Figures arrive with "a message for Hiero" before, let him board, and he headed directly for his father.

Phidias looked away from a map and greeted his son warmly. As always, he first asked if there was any news about Andromeda.

"I met Phyllis in Achradina. She reports that mother is weaving cloth for sails like nearly every other woman in Syracuse. But I hear from the soldiers I live with that she is also quietly organizing the women to oppose Pyrrhus any way they can. Her main ally seems to be Leptines' daughter, Philistis. Leptines himself is too old for the army, so he has become by far the most important leader in the Assembly. I heard last night that Leptines is trying stirring up Syracuse against Pyrrhus."

"He'd better be careful! If Pyrrhus learns that Leptines is an enemy, he will have him killed. He has already had one member of the Assembly put to death. But have you heard from Andromeda directly. I miss her more than anything."

"Nothing directly, but Hiero told me that she said 'If you see Phidias and get a chance, ask where a safe place would be for a papyrus from Samos.'"

Phidias became silent and looked very concerned. "I fear that such a papyrus could cause a lot of trouble if she does not have somewhere to keep others from seeing it." He fingered the bronze whistle around his neck and looked intently at Figures. "Tell Hiero that Andromeda should not keep documents in the house, where someone might steal them. In these troubled times it would be safer to put the papyrus in a stout box and bury it in the field. She could make a map and tuck it into my scroll library. If the map is not labeled, no one but Andromeda or I would know what it means."

Figures thought, no one but mother, father, *or I* would know. But he simply told Phidias that he would pass that message along to Hiero.

Phidias said, "I think the navy is nearly ready to sail. They have begun to fill the big tank on the ship they call the cistern, which they use to store fresh water."

Figures stayed with his father for a few more moments. Phidias showed him the maps he was making of the coast of Africa and reported on his successes and failures in trying to teach newly made ship's captains the art of navigating by the stars.

⬟ He gave his father a hug and headed for the army camp to begin a real search for Hiero. It proved to be surprisingly easy. Coming from opposite directions, Figures and Hiero reached the city gate at the same time.

"Cousin Hiero, I have a message for you from Pyrrhus."

"And I have a message for him, Archimedes. I was just on my way to find him."

"My message is that you are to recall the army from posts in Sicily. Tell the soldiers to leave towns where they are stationed now and to return to Syracuse. Pyrrhus wants his whole army together to fight against Carthage. Sicily will have to fend for itself."

"I suppose he thinks that he conquered Sicily easily once, so he can do it again. He is going to have problems with the Sicilian towns; some have already thrown the troops out."

"If it were up to me, I would give up Carthage and be content to rule Sicily, even if it meant taking back the same towns I conquered just a few weeks ago. But Pyrrhus does not seem ready to quit."

"He thinks he is the heir to Alexander and destined to rule the world."

As they talked, Figures steadily led Hiero toward the shipyard, where he had last seen Pyrrhus. "My father and I have a high probability of being killed in Pyrrhus' fruitless attempt to conquer Carthage, and then mother would be caught in an attack on Syracuse without father or me there to help defend her. The Carthaginian Malchus--the one who tried to have me sacrificed to Baal—will be able to find and kill us even if we escape other disasters."

With this gloomy prospect in mind, they reached a short

bridge between Achradina and Ortygia, where they saw Pyrrhus and Cineas were having what appeared to be a tense discussion. Perhaps, thought Figures, Pyrrhus wasn't happy with advice being given by Cineas. Pyrrhus often failed to take advice from Cineas or from anyone.

Pyrrhus turned and said, "Come with us. They headed along the Ortygia shore. Figures tagged along, eavesdropping while trying to stay out of Pyrrhus' field of vision.

"For one thing, the Mamertines in Messana are gathering their forces," Cineas was saying. "Although the Mamertines are not allied with Carthage, neither are they enemies of Carthage. They are your enemies, General. Their leaders hope to rid this part of the world of your leadership, and then, with only Carthage as a foe, take Syracuse and the rest of Sicily for themselves."

Figures had heard of the Mamertines, but knew nothing about them, so he whispered to Hiero, "Who are they?"

"The Mamertines? They worship the god of war. They have occupied Messana, a Sicilian city north of here, for a dozen years or more. They were Italian mercenaries who stayed in Sicily after one of the wars against Carthage ended. Even after Pyrrhus conquered them, he did not try to dislodge them from Messana, where they rule."

Pyrrhus and Cineas overheard the whispered conversation and turned toward the pair. Pyrrhus said, "I am glad you are here, Hiero. Did the boy tell you my orders? I must talk to my generals, gather my troops, renew the commitment of the Assembly, and move out of here."

Hiero said, "Archimedes indicated as much. But it may be too late. Many towns have revolted, and most of the men you left behind have been expelled. The troops left to guard Sicilian towns will have to fight across Sicily to rejoin your forces."

Pyrrhus sighed heavily. "I will have to leave those men scattered across Sicily and take what I have here to Carthage as soon as the new ships are completed."

Cineas said, "We cannot leave soon enough. Carthaginian

warships already head toward Syracuse. Our navy will be attacked before it reaches Carthage." Cineas looked back at the ships in the harbor, which receded swiftly behind the moving foursome. "Carthage's navy is superior to our makeshift group in every way. Pyrrhus, you should retire to Epirus, where they still accept you as king. You could regain rule of Macedonia without much effort. Between the Mamertines in the north sworn to destroy you, and Carthage attacking from the south and probably from the west as well, we are not going to survive."

Figures concluded that Cineas was correct. Attacked on all sides, Pyrrhus and his forces would certainly be destroyed. Although Figures did not believe in Baal, the situation they were in suggested that Malchus and Atban had what they hoped to get from a child sacrifice. If they were lucky, Figures and his mother would be taken as slaves. The ship his father was on would be sunk or boarded and all aboard killed. He was so convinced this would be their fate that he began to cry.

A small crowd began to follow Pyrrhus and his companions as they traveled the shore path toward the agora. Only women and very old men followed, however, for everyone else had been impressed into the armed services. Despite his tears, Figures listened to the comments of the citizens behind them. The women were terrified that their husbands, children, and sometimes fathers were going to be killed in what they saw as a pointless war. The old men predicted defeat and recalled wars of the past, telling how vicious the Carthaginians were as they raped and plundered the conquered population.

Hiero said to Figures, "Stop crying. We must be brave although there is nothing we can do to stop the Carthaginian and Mamertine armies and navies from attack. With so many of our soldiers scattered across the island, and with much of the present army composed of raw recruits and young boys and with our new navy still being built, I fear that we all are doomed to death or slavery."

Figures was as afraid now as he had been when Malchus tried to drown him, maybe more. There seemed to be nothing he could do that would save anyone. But he obeyed Hiero's command and stopped crying.

SCROLL 10

● Soldiers and citizens followed Pyrrhus as he traveled onto Ortygia's shore road, hoping, Figures thought, to hear news of their relatives in the army or navy or of the coming attack on Carthage. In front of the growing parade, Pyrrhus and Cineas continued a quiet conversation that Hiero and Figures, walking behind them, could not hear well enough to follow.

As they neared the fountain of Arethusa, where the wild papyrus grows, the most beautiful girl Figures had ever seen came from the direction of the fountain. Thirteen-year-old Figures was not entirely sure why this girl was so lovely, but he knew she was. Her curly hair, bound by a simple ring of pearls, framed a perfect pair of wide, dark eyes, and her casually draped shift revealed a form similar to the statues of Aphrodite.

Pyrrhus stopped before this unusual beauty as she approached him directly.

"O great general," the girl spoke in a loud, clear voice. "Most people of Sicily, including the fierce Mamertines, are against you. The mighty navy of Carthage approaches. Much of your army and navy is untrained and weak. If you attack Carthage, your mercenaries will desert to the enemy for its superior force and higher pay. You can count only on the Epirotes you brought with you. This war is futile. Instead of gaining Carthage, you are making certain that the good men and boys of Syracuse are slaughtered or taken into slavery by the Carthaginians."

Pyrrhus asked, "How do you know what our situation is? Clearly you are no soldier. Are you a messenger from the gods?"

The girl raised her head further and stared into Pyrrhus' eyes. "I tell you what all Syracuse knows, and what you know yourself. Your cause is doomed. The greatest generals find retreat better than losing. Heed my message and live to fight another day. Ignore my warning at your own peril" With that, she strode past Pyrrhus and disappeared into the crowd.

Pyrrhus stood rigid as a statue. Then he caught his breath and tried to follow, asking, "Where did she go? Who is she?"

Figures pushed through the people, hoping to see her again, but failed. The people were all talking at once. No one claimed to know who she was.

Pyrrhus strode to the edge of the fountain and stood quietly for a few moments. The crowd quieted down. How would Pyrrhus respond? Finally Pyrrhus turned to his companion and said, "Although you have many spies, Cineas, you do not know everything that occurs. Only the gods know everything. But even I sometimes know something."

Pyrrhus raised his voice, so that the entire crowd could hear him. "Remember the Tarentines, who with my aid defeated the Roman legions trying to claim Tarentine lands. When I left Italy to aid Syracuse, I promised the Tarentines I would continue to protect them. Last night I received an urgent message. Roman Legions are entering Tarentine territory, and the Tarentines cannot stop them. The Tarentines' messenger reminded me of my promise and begged me to quit Syracuse and come to Italy to save his people. I cannot go back on my word, so I must go."

Figures—and apparently everyone who heard—was astonished. Could Pyrrhus abandon his attack on Carthage that easily? Figures felt as if a dark cloud had been lifted from his life, a cloud of fear that had surrounded for weeks.

But then new questions occurred that lowered the cloud again. Would Pyrrhus take his new army, including Figures himself, with him to fight Rome. What about the navy and his father? Was Syracuse doomed without Pyrrhus?

Pyrrhus continued to speak in a loud voice, although now he addressed his aide. "My friend Cineas, tell the navy we depart for Italy tomorrow, whether or not the new ships are ready. I will take my Epirotes and the elephants. When combined with the Tarentine troops they will provide enough force to defeat the Romans. Command the men of Epirus to be ready to sail on the morning tide. Not enough ships are finished for the mercenaries or troops from Syracuse to join us—and I would not trust them in any case. Hiero, you and Artemidorus take command of the troops that stay behind. When we have defeated Rome, I will return to Syracuse and use those troops to take Carthage. Do not let the regular troops or mercenaries disband. The men and boys of Syracuse that I have impressed into my army and navy, however, can, if they like, return to their homes. Cineas, start now."

A spontaneous roar of approval arose from the crowd, quickly followed by silence. More news might be heard.

Cineas said, "I am ready. Let us leave Syracuse as a battlefield for the Romans and Carthaginians to covet."

Pyrrhus rapidly walked into his headquarters.

Cineas said, "Hiero, thank you very much for your past services. You know what your mission is now. I will arrange for money to pay you and Artemidorus before we leave, but after that you will have to support your armies in the usual fashion." Even Figures knew that "the usual fashion" was by robbing the population of food and other supplies.

Hiero said, "This adventure is over, Archimedes. Before a new one starts, you need to return to your studies. Find your father on his ship, and both of you go home to Andromeda. Give your mother my love and tell her I will visit as soon as the armies settle down." He left along the direct path to the bridge to the mainland.

Figures remembered the message he carried for his mother. Now he did not have to pass that along. His father could deal with the papyrus from Samos himself.

As much as he wanted to go home, Figures decided to linger near the fountain for a while, hoping to see the amazing girl again.

As the crowd dispersed, a man coming from the other side of the fountain arrived and spoke to the remaining people: "Did you see the amazing event that I saw as I came along the harbor path? The fountain of Arethusa, which has flowed since before the Corinthians founded Syracuse, stopped for a few moments. But then it started again. It was as if the nymph Arethusa left us for a short time."

Figures and the remaining crowd rushed to the side of the fountain, but there was nothing odd to see. It was running just as it had since the day that Artemis saved the beautiful nymph Arethusa from a pursuer by changing her into a fountain.

Figures wondered if an earthquake had briefly stopped the flow. Earthquakes are common in Sicily. But he had not felt the Earth move.

With nothing more to see Figures hurried to tell his father the good news.

⬟ The next morning Figures returned to the docks to learn news of the expected attack by the Carthaginian navy.

But there was no battle. Small groups of Carthaginian ships sailed into the ports along the southern and western coasts of Sicily and reoccupied that part of the island. A larger group attacked ships carrying Pyrrhus and his army to Italy, sinking some and capturing others.

Hiero came to visit Andromeda and Phidias. He reported. "The warlike Mamertines who ruled Messana and the northeast corner of Sicily, learned that Pyrrhus, weakened by the naval battle, was heading for Italy. Messana is just across a narrow strait from Italy, so the Mamertines could reach Italy before Pyrrhus and ambush his army from behind shortly after they landed.

They tried to destroy the remainder of Pyrrhus' army on the Italian shore. The battle was fierce. The two sides fought to a standstill and then retreated to regroup. Pyrrhus himself received a severe head injury in the fighting."

Figures asked, "Was he killed? What happened next?"

"The most powerful Mamertine soldier, having heard of Pyrrhus' bravery atop the walls of Eryx, decided that a way to gain fame and respect would be to challenge

Pyrrhus to single combat. On receiving the challenge, Pyrrhus returned to the battlefield with his head only partially bandaged. He walked straight at the challenger, a giant Mamertine who expected an easy victory over the wounded general. But when Pyrrhus approached, the Mamertine paused for a moment while he looked for the best place to strike. Pyrrhus, on the other hand, did not waste a second. He struck such a strong blow with his sword that he cut the Mamertine into two pieces.

"When the Mamertines saw what Pyrrhus had done to their most powerful soldier, they became terrified. Some say Pyrrhus has magic protection like Achilles. After a brief consultation among their leaders, the Mamertines decided that an invincible warrior is no person to fight, and they sailed back across the strait to Messana."

Figures later learned that Pyrrhus went on to lose barely a great battle with the Romans, and then returned to Epirus and Macedonia. After this, Figures did not hear of Pyrrhus for many years.

⬟ .Syracuse returned to normal life, ruled once again by its own Assembly instead of a tyrant. Figures often overheard his father and mother discussing politics. He heard Phidias tell Andromeda, "Hiero can no longer visit us here. The assembly fears that either Hiero or Artemidorus, because they command the armies, might become a new tyrant. To protect against this, the Assembly has decreed that all troops and commanders of the army must stay outside the city walls at all times. Guards will keep continual watch on the gates so that none of the troops or their commanders—especially the commanders—can sneak into Syracuse. They will check everyone going in or out during the day, and the gates are to be closed and guarded at night ."

Andromeda said, "But we can still see Hiero, can't we?"

"If we visit him outside the walls," which they did when a chance arose. Phidias did not think they had enough money or land to maintain a horse, so Figures and his family walked the long way to the army camp. Hiero took Figures on a tour of the camp, showing him the horses for the cavalry, the camps where the mercenaries decorated their tents with objects from their many and varied homelands, and the giant kitchen that fed everyone.

One day when Figures was visiting Ortygia, he thought he saw Malchus in the crowd at the agora. He did not wait to be certain it was really Malchus; instead, he ran over the bridge and halfway home before he ran out of breath and stopped.

To avoid thinking of Malchus, he began to tackle very difficult mathematical problems. Often he needed to refer to the mathematical scrolls kept in the library box. He always checked the hidden compartment to see if it was still locked. It always was. He thought that the compartment must have been unlocked at least once since his father came home from the navy, for he was sure that the mysterious document from Samos had been stored there.

⬟ Figures and Phyllis still spent parts of a day together when they could, exploring both the city and surrrounding countryside. They visited the great cave in Neapolis, where they made echoes and whispered to each other from a distance, using the cave's unusual acoustic properties. Phyllis told him stories from the history of Syracuse or about the gods, stories she had learned mostly from her father but also from the priestesses at Artemis' temple. He told her about what he was learning--about the constellations, which interested her a lot, and about mathematics, which she found boring but pretended to like because she knew that he was excited by it.

While he had been running errands for Pyrrhus, she had spent much time at the temple for Artemis. During the buildup for the attack on Carthage, she prayed to Artemis that Pyrrhus would go away and let her father and everyone else return to normal.

"And my prayers were answered, weren't they? Artemis

turned Arethusa from being a fountain back into to nymph so that she could stop the war." No one had ever identified the girl who advised Pyrrhus to abandon his plan to attack Carthage. The idea that she was Arethusa was commonly held throughout Syracuse. Many swore that they had been there at the time and seen the girl rise from the fountain as the water stopped flowing, although often these accounts were from young men who could not have been present at that moment.

Figures said, "It was politics more than prayer that took Pyrrhus away," although he also wondered who the beautiful girl had been. "I was glad that we did not have to fight, where I might be wounded or killed, but I really enjoyed being Pyrrhus' messenger boy. I had a lot of freedom and I learned something of how the world works. Time spent learning something you did not know is time not wasted. Next to solving an interesting mathematical problem, learning something new is the best thing there is." By this time he had forgotten his fear of Pyrrhus.

"I learned new things, too. I did not spend all my time at the temple. Since no one was watching over me--except of course Artemis--I borrowed my father's bow and taught myself to hunt. I was out practically every day. I learned first with small animals--rabbits and hares. Eventually I thought I was a good enough shot to kill a deer. I shot a small stag. I got one of the slaves to show me how to skin and dress him, and we invited all the women in the neighborhood to the feast. So I am following in the steps of Artemis, the Goddess of hunting as well as the patron of Syracuse. Sometimes I think I am literally following in her footsteps. She seems to be making a trail for me through the woods, and I sometimes catch glimpses of her in the distance."

Figures was impressed, more by Phyllis' killing a deer than by her stories of the goddess. "What are you going to do next?"

"As a hunter, I am hoping to kill a wild boar, although they are dangerous animals and I must wait until Artemis tells me I am ready. But in the meantime, she has led me to discoveries of many interesting places in the forest--beautiful streams, waterfalls, canyons, and even a cave. These are in the deep forest that is inland from here. One river, the Ánopa, has a deep canyon where it flows down from Mt. Iblei. And the river Ciane, which is just beyond where the Ánopa flows into the sea, starts in a pool that was formed by the tears of the nymph Cyane in sorrow for Persephone, when Persephone was abducted by Pluto and taken to Hades."

"I know about Cyane's pool. That's the best place to gather papyrus, which my father uses for his scrolls. He sometimes lets me have some, too, which I have used to write down some of my own ideas about mathematics. But I have never heard of a cave."

"The cave is in the side of a small cliff on the way to Mt. Iblei, deep in the woods. It takes nearly a half-day to reach it. I did not have materials to start a fire with me the day I found it, so I only explored as far as I could see by the light from the opening. But it appears to be very large."

"I would love to see a big cave. Do you think you can still find it?"

"Yes. I have a very good sense of where things are in the woods now."

"Should we take Herc?"

"I have tried to get him to enter the woods, but he has not been interested. He is constantly scheming to make money by selling goods he can obtain for free. If we told him that we had found gems or anything else he could sell, then he might come. But of course we have not found anything. He might also be interested if we could report that there was some unusual treat to eat--good mushrooms, maybe. I should not criticize him so much, I guess. He does still study, especially history. He takes after our father in that way."

"What about Jason? He would surely want to come with us."

"Jason, Narcissus, Faunus, and all the other boys are only interested in preparing for next year's Games. They all have been training day in and day out at the small stadium. I am surprised that you have not joined them."

"When I am not with you or my father and mother, I am usually working on mathematics. But let's go to the cave. I can add it to my maps. I have not had a chance to map the forest over toward Mt. Iblei. I won't bring any measuring tools, though. This would just be an exploration and a simple sketch with natural features, such as cliffs or streams; approximate distances would do."

⬟ The two decided to go.

Phyllis said, "We should not tell our parents. They may not be pleased to have a thirteen-year-old boy and a thirteen-year-old girl into the woods together." At first Figures was not sure what she meant. He had been spending much of his time with Phyllis for all his life and had long ago ceased to think of her as a girl.

He knew that Greek society tried to separate young boys and young girls, although not always with complete success. His friend Jason had met a girl at a festival, and Jason had told him that the two secretly met alone. Jason bragged about kissing his new girlfriend and hinted at even closer relations. Figures was impressed, but did not feel up to kissing a girl himself. His only experience with kisses was of those his mother occasionally bestowed on him, now as he grew older becoming difficult to endure. Jason hoped that her parents would not give his girlfriend in marriage away for a few years. He himself had no hope of marrying her, he told Figures, because she was so beautiful and sweet tempered that her parents would easily find an older, rich man to marry her.

Figures told Phyllis, "Your parents should not worry. You will be safe with me."

"I think it is the other way around." She paused. "You will be safe with me, for I know how to hunt and I have been learning the paths through the forest." She paused again. "My parents worry over my future a lot. They complain that I am not preparing to become a suitable wife. I have no interest in how mother manages the household. My father says that no one would want a skinny girl like me for a wife anyway. I do not think I am headed for marriage. I don't think I can become one of those women who entertain men, either, those women known as companions. My ability to play the aulos is my only skill. Hunting does not count."

"You would be a wonderful companion. They are paid to be charming and intelligent, which you certainly are. I am not sure how a girl gets to become a companion, however."

"You have to start young. My father employs a companion who went to school. She reads and writes and can recite many short poems. Occasionally she is hired when men visit my father —she is the entertainment. Sometimes I hear her singing one of the poems and accompanying herself on the lyre. One thing about playing the aulos is that you can't sing while playing. But I think I should learn some poetry just in case the gods take me into that profession, however unlikely it seems now."

The two developed a plan for their trip to the cave. Since their parents might forbid the adventure, they would give separate excuses for a day away and meet at the edge of the forest. Phyllis would say t she was spending the day at the temple of Artemis, something she occasionally did. Figures would say he was going to map a nearby stream, close to the truth--although "nearby" was definitely a lie.

SCROLL 11

⬟ Despite Phyllis' prediction that Jason would refuse, Figures asked him to join their cave adventure, but he would not take a day away from training for the Games. The great competition normally occurred every four years, and this had been a Games year, but Pyrrhus had cancelled them. He wanted all able-bodied men and boys available to attack Carthage. Now Pyrrhus was gone, so the Games were back on schedule, and all of the boys and most young men after a late start were in training.

Well, almost all of the boys. Figures was old enough to be eligible for the youth Games but had done nothing to prepare. Jason urged him to practice along with the other boys, but Figures preferred to do mathematics and explore the countryside.

Jason said, "Figures, people make fun of you behind your back. You don't run in races or wrestle. You spend most of your time alone or, even worse, with Phyllis, who no one knows whether she is a girl or a boy. Often when people speak to you, you don't listen--your mind is elsewhere. I like you, but I pay a price for it, since everyone else thinks that you are worthless. You need to be in the Games. You need to make friends with other boys. You would be surprised to find out that what they do is fun."

"What I do is fun for me. The boys I know have no interest in mathematics or reading or anything else important. I don't think the games are important."

But when Figures and his family visited Hiero, camped outside the city with the army, Hiero asked, "What, Archimedes, are you doing back in Epipolae to keep busy?"

"Mostly studying. When I get tired of my reading and writing, I go on expeditions to improve my maps. Now I am mapping the country outside of Syracuse." Then he remembered not to tell Hiero about the plan to visit the cave with Phyllis, since it was a secret from his parents.

"What about getting ready for the Games? Which events

are you going to enter? I hope this silly rule about the army not entering the city is over by the time the Games start. I will have a small rebellion among the soldiers if they can't attend or participate, and also I want to see them myself. I might even enter the race where soldiers wear full armor."

"I don't think I am ready for the games this year. Maybe it would be better for me to wait for four years."

"Nonsense. Every young man in Syracuse who can walk on two legs enters the Games. Furthermore, if you are going to do well in the Games four years from now, you need to start this year. No one does well the first time they compete. While it is true that you are too young to win, simply taking part honors all the competitors. And it is an insult to the Gods if you don't run, jump, wrestle, or toss in their honor."

Figures did not care about offending the gods, but he did care abut offending Hiero. He said, "You are right. I will enter and try to do my best. I hope that you are allowed to come into town to watch.'

On the way home from the camp, Figures told his father and mother that he planned to compete. His father was surprised because he had always assumed that Figures would compete like the other boys his age, although Phidias had never given his son the slightest encouragement in any of the physical activities expected of Greek boys and had not considered training him in any of the sports. But in Figures' family years were identified by famous winners in the Games—for example, Figures' birth year was 'the year after Cimon won all the races in the Syracuse Games' or sometimes 'one year before Herodorus of Megara won his second wreath in the Olympics for playing the trumpet.'

Phidias said, "Of course. You know Pythagoras was a boxer. He was rejected when he applied for the boys' Games, so he entered the adult Games and was champion. This was before he became a philosopher."

His mother said, "Pythagoras should not have taken such a chance. Think what we would have missed if he had been killed. Archimedes, I worry that you are too young, but I supposed you must enter if all the other boys do."

She spent the rest of the walk home telling Figures all the reasons why he should avoid boxing. She recounted a gory tale of how in a famous boxing competition one of the boxers had struck his opponent with an open hand so hard that it entered the victim's body and pulled out the victim's entrails. Figures thought that the story must be a great exaggeration, but nevertheless was convinced to skip boxing. Later Figures learned that boys did not compete in boxing in the Syracuse Games since the sport was considered too dangerous.

⬟ Jason seemed to know everything about the Games. Figures visited him where he was training with the other boys outside the stadium. Figures said, "Perhaps you are right about the Games. It would look really odd if I did not compete. But it would not be good to lose badly. What should I do? I'm not as weak as I look, but also I'm not especially skilled at anything."

Jason picked up a bronze disk and a long spear, then motioned Figures to follow him away from the other boys so that they could talk. He began, "For boys there are both a one-stadium and a two-stadium race and the pentathlon."

"What is a pentathlon?"

"That is the event created by the person for whom I am named—Jason of the Argonauts. He combined five different sports to compete with his friend Peleus and prove himself the better all-around athlete. It includes running, jumping, throwing something heavy and something light, and wrestling, but unless you win a race, jump the longest, or throw the discus or javelin the farthest, you don't get to wrestle. My father won the pentathlon twice, so I think I have a chance. Many boys skip the pentathlon because they want to concentrate on racing. The adult Games have many more events, but the boys' games in Syracuse have just those three—the pentathlon and the two races."

"I am not speedy like Narcissus, so I don't think I should race, and I do not throw well, but I am a pretty good jumper.

Maybe I should try the pentathlon and work on the jumping."

"You need to start training now; one of the rules is that the competitors must swear before the judges that they have prepared for the Games for at least ten months. And you need to train for all parts of the pentathlon."

Figures said, "But I only think I could do well in the long jump."

"You cannot count on winning the pentathlon by winning only one event. You have to win wrestling as well. In the original pentathlon, Peleus was declared the winner because he won the wrestling, even though Jason won the other events. But today you don't even get to wrestle unless you win at least one event."

"I will take the long jump to try to look good. I doubt I'll need to worry about wrestling. What do I need to know about jumping?"

Jason explained the long jump while performing a slow motion demonstration as he talked. "First the jumper picks up a weight in each hand and stands a few feet behind a launching place, which is a board placed flat in the ground. Picture me holding a couple of brass weights." He clutched his hands into fists and put his arms akimbo. "The jumper leans back and squats on his right leg, while he sticks his left leg out in front of him. He holds the two weights in front of him. A musician plays the aulos to help the jumper get the rhythm. The jumper rocks back and forth to the music for a few moments. When he feels in time with the music, he springs forward at a fast run, swinging his weights back and forth in the correct rhythm so that the weights will pull him forward as he reaches the launching place and jumps into space. " Jason took a few steps and jumped a couple of feet. "

"That does not make sense. Why is he carrying weights? That ought to slow him down. Can he really move forward by pulling on the weights? They are not connected to anything."

"Ah, but that is not all he does with the weights. First, the jumper tucks his legs under his body and the weights help pull him into the air. As he nears the pit where he is to land, which has been made softer by tearing up the soil, he pulls himself toward the weights again and then pushes them behind him. Then, just as he is about to land, he lets the weights go and drops into the pit on his feet, which he extends as far as he can. The position of the feet when landing, marked in the softened earth of the pit, shows how long the jump is. The winner, of course, is the one who jumps the farthest. You get three jumps and they use the best."

Jason found a couple of stones to use as weights and tried to demonstrate better how an actual jump would go. Figures pretended to be the aulos player, humming a tune that he hoped had the right rhythm. Jason's jump was not very good; he did not drop the weights until after he had landed. This was not an event that he had practiced much. But Figures observed the general idea, so they exchanged places, and Jason hummed while Figures jumped. Figures did better by about a foot, mainly because he succeeded in using the weights, swinging them forward as he took off and throwing them behind him just before he landed. That was success enough for Figures.

Jason said, "Even if you don't expect to win, you need to know how to compete in all five events. You know how to run whether you do it well or not, but you need to know the techniques for the two tosses." He pointed to the bronze disk and spear. "These are my discus and javelin. My father used them to win in the adult pentathlon twice. In the youth Games he even won the pentathlon without wrestling. That was because he won the race, the jump, and both of the tosses, so there was no one for him to wrestle."

The javelin was long—Figures, the taller boy, could just touch its bronze tip when the base of the pole, or shaft, was on the ground.

Jason pulled something from a fold in his chiton. "This strip of leather is wrapped around the shaft of the javelin before you throw. It gives you extra distance." Jason wound the strip around the shaft, then gripped the shaft with his thumb and two smallest fingers while pulling the leather tight with his other fingers.

Jason said, "I hold the thong and the javelin this way so that when I throw it, I let go of the shaft but keep the thong in my fingers. The thong unwinds and gives the javelin an extra push."

"That is very clever. The arc of the throw will be longer, so you have a lever effect. As it unwinds, the thong will start the javelin spinning, which will help keep it lined up with the direction it is going."

"I don't know how it works. I just know that this is the way my father taught me to do it, and he won both as a youth and as an adult, so it must be right."

Jason then ran a few steps and tossed the javelin a long distance, keeping the strip of leather in his hand. The boys counted the steps as they walked to retrieve it---81 steps.

"Not one of my better tosses," said Jason. "I think I need to reach half a stadium to win."

Figures took the javelin and thong and tried to wrap the thong around the shaft, but he was very clumsy about it and the finished result did not look neat. When he tried to toss it, he let go of the shaft at the wrong part of the throw and released the leather strap as well. The javelin only traveled a few feet and plunged into the ground.

"Be careful! You are going to break it, throwing it like that." Jason exclaimed. "Maybe we should try the discus instead."

They walked back to where Jason had left the bronze disk. It was so big that when Jason held one rim in his hand, the other rim reached past his elbow. Jason said, "This discus is a bit bigger than I really should use, but it was made for my father when he was competing in the adult games. In any case, the boys who win nearly all use an adult discus. Here, hold it yourself." And he handed the discus to Figures.

Figures was surprised by the weight, about the same as a melon—lighter than it looked. It was inscribed with the name of Jason's father and three measurements—79 feet, 92 feet, and 90 feet.

Jason pointed to the inscriptions. "Those were added after father retired. The measurements are the longest tosses of those years. You get five chances, but only the longest one counts. Let me show you how to throw it." He took the discus back and, holding it with both hands, raised it to the same level as his head. "Notice that I am holding it up with my left hand while my right is keeping it steady from above. Now I lift it even higher, transfer the weight completely to my right hand as I bring it back behind me." As Jason made these moves, he bent forward, lowering his left hand and raising his left foot. Then he swung the discus forward, throwing it almost sidearm as he shifted his weight to his left foot. The disk stayed vertical as it spun through the air. When it touched the ground about 60 feet away, it dug into the earth.

They walked over to where the discus lay. Jason handed it to Figures, who began to try to imitate Jason's movements during the earlier toss as best he could remember.

Jason said, "Be careful where you plant your feet. You need to spin on your right leg and then use the left to push off. If you start off with the wrong foot forward, the judge will tap you with his stick and disqualify the throw."

Figures swung around and let the discus fly. Although it did not travel nearly as far as Jason's toss had been, and it seemed to go off at an angle to where Figures thought he had aimed, at least it was not the disaster that his javelin toss had been.

Jason said, "Your form is awful but that is not what counts so long as you basic movements are performed correctly. What counts is how far the discus travels through the air."

"I will concentrate on the long jump and work on the discus for a second Pentathlon event. If I am passable in a couple of events, I may not be teased by the other boys about the Games for the next four years."

Figures once again asked Jason to come with him and Phyllis to explore the cave, but Jason said he thought he was making progress on getting his discus throw perfect for the

Games, so he would rather keep working on that than go off in the woods for a day. He said that if Figures found that the cave was really interesting and exciting, he would come after the Games were over.

● On the day before the planned excursion Figures and Phyllis had the slaves prepare lunches and told their lies to their families. Luce put a jar of yogurt sweetened with honey, some cheese made from goat's milk, a small loaf of bread, a handful of preserved ripe olives, another jar of wine mixed with water, and some dried figs into a basket that had a handle so it could be carried in one hand. Figures thought it was enough food for both of them, but he knew that Phyllis would have a similar lunch to bring along.

Figures was not sure how long the expedition would last, so they might need a torch to find their way home at night. He 'borrowed' the rocks and some wood shavings Dromio used to restart the household fires. These hard rocks when struck properly produced a spark to ignite wood shavings. That small flame was used to light kindling. He practiced setting shavings on fire a few times, then tucked the rocks and some shavings into the basket with the food.

● Figures and Phyllis met at the trail into the forest early the next morning, and Phyllis began to lead the way toward Mount Iblei. The day was warm, but in the forest they were shaded from the strong heat of the Sicilian sun. Although Phyllis claimed that Artemis had laid out a path for her to follow, only she could see it. Figures thought they were just heading through the wilderness. But he knew from the occasional moments when the sun was visible through the trees that they were traveling in the right direction.

As they walked, Phyllis told Figures about a dream. "Sometimes Artemis comes to me during the night and tells me important information. These visions are different from ordinary dreams, which vanish soon after I open my eyes, but Artemis' visits are impossible to forget. Last night, however, I had a dream that was different from the Artemis visions and yet not ordinary at all. I was in the cave. I think you were there, too, but in some other part of the cave. I was completely naked and very frightened. It was as vivid as one of the visits from Artemis. What do you think that could mean?"

"I don't think it means anything. I often have dreams that frighten me. I may be menaced by Malchus. Sometimes I am in the cage at the bottom of the sea again. These dreams are so dreadful that I remember them and think about them the next day. But they are just dreams. You seem to think that what happens in dreams is real."

"Some dreams are messages. This one seemed real to me."

"Most of my dreams are not frightening. Often I dream of shapes or numbers that shift and rearrange themselves. These are my most interesting dreams, but I have trouble remembering exact details."

"Such dreams would not interest me at all, but I never have dreams that don't include gods or people."

Then they stopped talking for a while because, after a long walk under palms and leafy trees, the journey became more difficult. The trees gave way to brush. The sun beat down and the slopes grew steeper.

Finally, Phyllis rediscovered the entrance to the cave. It was not easy to recognize, just a dark spot near the bottom of a small dark cliff. When they climbed closer, Figures saw that the opening was big enough for a person to enter. They climbed over some rather large rocks that had fallen from the cliff to get to the actual opening. One boulder had a nearly flat top, so it became a table for their lunch. While they ate, Figures took a scrap of papyrus and a piece of charcoal from his lunch basket to sketch a rough map of their path and the location of the cave.

As he sketched, Phyllis talked. "A large hole in the side of the cliff does not happen by itself. Some ancient god, or maybe one of the Titans that came before the gods, must have made it for some purpose. Now animals may live in it. Perhaps we will find bears or wolves. But I certainly hope not. I don't see any tracks. If a Titan made it, perhaps it was to escape another Titan—the Titans were always killing each other in the days before the Gods. Or maybe it was to hide a treasure. That would be exciting, finding a Titan's treasure in the cave."

Figures finished his sketch. "I think it might have been an underground stream that dried up. It looks like something flowed through it. Let's finish lunch and see what's inside. First, I need to build a fire so that we can make torches to carry inside. Otherwise, we won't see anything."

He brought out the two rocks and wood shavings, then gathered some small sticks. He soon had a small fire burning outside the entrance to the cave.

Phyllis said, "Let's leave the fire burning while we go into the cave. We don't know what it is like inside. We may come out cold or wet and want a fire."

Figures agreed and added some larger branches to the fire. They each made a torch by wrapping dried palm leaves around a stick and lit these from the fire. Figures tucked the stones he used to start the fire into a fold in his chiton; if both torches went out he would be able to re-light them. Then they climbed over the rock pile and into the cave.

The ceiling of the cave was much higher than they realized from the opening--neither could reach it with an upheld torch. Figures looked at the walls and said, "Iblei must be a volcano. These black walls are just like the ones Hiero said he saw on Mount Etna."

They moved along the floor of the cave with caution, slowed by rubble on the cave floor. After about a hundred feet, they found a place where the rubble had been pushed aside.

Figures said, "We are not the first humans to find this cave. Someone before us built a fire here. And there are pieces of wood to feed the fire still stacked over here."

After another hundred feet or so, Figures and Phyllis

reached a place where the rubble was piled high. Scrambling up it, they discovered that the pile reached to the roof of the cave. That end of the tube was completely blocked.

The torches were beginning to burn down and there seemed to be nothing more to explore, so they crawled down the rubble pile and returned to the part of the cave where the fires had been. The cave was not as wonderful as either had hoped, but worth the long trip.

Figures said, "We should start back or it will be dark before we get home."

As they were about to pass into the cleared region, the ground began to shake beneath their feet, knocking both of them down.

"Keep your torch lit!" Figure exclaimed.

"What is happening?"

The ground shook again, harder this time. There was a great rumbling sound and the part of the cave they had just left was obliterated by the roof falling through, bringing with it enough rock and soil to fill that part of the cave completely. This time as they scrambled to escape the falling rocks, both torches were dropped and went out. They were in total blackness and the air was filled with dust.

Figures was terrified but strangely calm. He said, "We've got to get out of here. That was an earthquake. The whole cave may collapse at any second. Follow me. At least we know which is the right direction."

The two headed for the entrance. They stumbled over large stones that had dropped from the ceiling or rolled into the middle of the cave floor. But after picking their way for a few feet in total darkness, they saw a dim light in the distance. They also began to see the quake's devastating effects. Instead of a black wall, one side of the cave was now a pile of rubble.

The cave entrance looked different, too. It was much smaller and had a different shape. A large rock, fallen from the cliff above the entrance, nearly filled the cave entrance, leaving just a small space for daylight to pass through.

Phyllis said, "We've got to push it aside. Another earthquake can happen at any second and then we will be crushed. Why did Artemis lead us here to die?"

Figures shoved against the rock but it didn't move. "I can't budge it," he said. "Let's both try at once."

They pushed as hard as they could, but the rock did not move at all,

Phyllis said, "Perhaps there is enough room between the rock and the wall to squeeze through." She pushed her body into the curved opening, but although she was very thin, she could not fit through the narrow passage.

"Stop, Phyllis. You will get stuck partway, and then it would be even worse."

"How could it be any worse? We are trapped here and no one knows where we are. We are going to die here."

Figures thought she was probably right.

SCROLL 12

⬟ Figures and Phyllis tried several more times to push away the rock blocking the entrance to the cave, but it did not budge. They also tried stepping back and smashing into it as hard as they could, hurting their shoulders with the impact. The boulder trembled slightly when struck this way, giving the pair a flicker of hope. Perhaps they were not doomed after all. But they knew they could not rush the boulder any harder. Phyllis sat down and Figures thought she started to cry, but she had turned away so that he could not see her face.

After a moment, Figures said, "Even if we can't move the rock, we may still be rescued. No one knows where we are, but the smoke from the fire I kindled outside the cave entrance might help people find us." But when he peered through the gap, he saw that rubble falling from the cliff face during the earthquake had put out the fire. He decided not to tell Phyllis that this hope was gone.

"I am sure we can do something ourselves to move that rock," Phyllis said. "Artemis has been watching over us for years. She would not give us a difficulty we are too weak to overcome. I will pray, and help will come."

Figures still had fire on his mind. "I still have the stones that make sparks. Do you think we can find the torches and re-light them? We could go deeper into the cave and look for another way out. We didn't see another exit earlier, but the earthquake may have opened a new one."

⬟ They crawled deeper into the cave, searching between fallen rocks. The pair picked their way back over fallen rock and soon were enveloped in total darkness. Phyllis murmured prayers to Artemis as she moved deeper into the cave. Neither touched anything but the rocks that littered the cave floor. Figures said, "We have gone too far. The torches must be behind us."

Phyllis replied from several feet deeper in the cave, "You

go back. I can't get lost in here, so I will go farther. If there is a new opening, I will see its light."

"And if there is another earthquake, you are likely to be killed. We should both go back to the opening and find way to move that rock."

"I found something," Phyllis shouted from not very far away.

"A torch?"

"No, but it might do. Remember the old fire in the cleared space. Here it is. We can set partly burned wood afire to make a light."

"Keep talking. I'll be right over." Figures began to crawl toward the sound of her voice.

Phyllis said, "This feels like charred wood. I will have black marks all over when we get out. Wasn't there some unused wood nearby? Yes, here it is. This branch is too long for a torch. It is more like a pole than a log."

The word 'pole' gave Figures the start of a new plan. "Don't let go of that pole. We can use it as a lever. I have seen Tono move heavy stones using a long pole. You push down on the long end of the pole, and the short end can push a stone so heavy that you could not lift it."

At this point he bumped into Phyllis. After they determined how their bodies were positioned with relation to each other in the total darkness, she handed him the branch.

Figures felt along the length of the branch. "This might help, but I don't think it is strong enough. It is more likely to break than to move the rock. Search around. There may be a thicker branch that is just as long."

"It would be easier if we could see. Do you think that you can get one of these charred sticks to burn?"

"I'll try. Let's bring some wood back to the entrance where we can see." They each took a piece of partly burned wood from the ancient hearth. Figures also carried the pole. At first they tried to crawl along the rubble-strewn floor while holding pieces of wood in their hands, but it hurt their fingers and knuckles.

Phyllis said, "I can't crawl with this stuff in my hands."

"We have to stand up. I can wave the pole around to warn for rocks on the floor or to keep from running into the sides of the cave."

Phyllis said, "I don't have a long pole, but I can follow you." Both stood and she grabbed Figures by his hair. Figures led her on a zigzag course toward the entrance. When they could see the light coming around the edges of the boulder, she let go.

It was time to start another fire.

⬟ The original wood shavings had been burned, so Phyllis and Figures both began using sharp-edged rocks to shave thin strips from the partly burned wood they had brought. After several tries, Figures lit the pile of shavings, and soon they had a small fire. Using the light from the burning sticks they were able to locate the palm-leaf torches and re-light them.

The better they could see, the clearer it became that there was little hope of finding a way out through the back of the cave. Piles of rubble nearly filled the farther reached of the cave. Figures said, "We are not going to find a way out farther back in the cave. We can't go deeper into the cave. The only way to escape is by moving that boulder out of the entrance. Let's try a lever. Look for the strongest and longest pieces of wood. This pole is too weak." He broke it in half over his knee.

The two gathered several long branches from the small woodpile and brought them to the front of the cave. When they reached the blocked entrance, Figures chose the most promising branch, one longer and straighter than most. It was thick enough to be strong, but thin enough to fit into the opening. He inserted one end between the boulder and the cave wall, rested the pole against the wall, and shoved hard. The boulder moved but immediately hit the other side of the cave. He needed to push the rock forward, not to one side. He found a rock about the size of his head and rested the lever on it, then used the short end of the lever to push the big obstructing rock directly up and away from him. When he pushed down on the long end of the lever as hard as he could, the big rock moved a little, but not enough to roll away.

"I'm not strong enough. Help me," Figures said. Phyllis grabbed the lever and the two put their combined weights on it. The rock began to move away from the entrance.

Then the pole broke and Figures and Phyllis dropped to the floor of the cave.

"It almost worked," Figures said. "But that was our best lever, and it's gone. We need a lever that is longer and stronger if we are going to move the rock, and we already broke the best branch. None of the others are even as long."

The two sat on the floor, trying to think what to do next.

● Suddenly Phyllis said, "My dream! I was naked in the cave. If we use our clothes to make a better lever, we can move the rock. I am sure that is what Artemis meant to tell me." With that she began taking off her chiton.

Figures had no idea what she meant until she took two of the longest and strongest branches and began using the chiton to bind them together. She made knots in several places, combining the branches into a rigid lever. The result was half again as long as the lever that had broken, and thicker, too.

"Brilliant!" said Figures.

"No. Inspired," replied Phyllis as she moved the new lever into place on the small stone with one end under a projecting bump on the big rock. Figures grabbed the other end and pushed as hard as he could. The big rocked moved about half a foot before the long end of the lever touched the floor of the cave, but when Figures took his weight off the lever, the rock slipped back to where it had been.

"Phyllis, when I move it out again, take a rock from the floor and jam it into the gap to keep it from slipping back." She found a rock that seemed to be about the right size and

Figures again moved the rock. This time Phyllis blocked it from slipping. The open space was now wider, but still not wide enough to pass through. They tried the same idea again, moving the rock another half a foot away and keeping it there by moving the small rock forward. But then they found that the boulder was pressing against the top of the entrance. No amount of pushing on the lever would move the boulder any farther. Finally they broke the lever.

For a while, the two simply crouched on the floor. Figures thought that Phyllis must feel especially powerless since she was naked.

Phyllis studied the opening. "For once it is good that I am so thin. I think I can squeeze through. It will be easier to slip through because I don't have a layer of clothes to catch on the rock."

Figures did not like the idea of being left alone in the cave for even a moment, but her plan might work. "You try it. I don't think I can make it through that gap even if I take off my clothes. If you can get out, you might be able to move the rock from the outside with a lever placed on a different part of the opening."

Phyllis just managed to squeeze through the gap. As Figures watched her pass through the narrow opening, he noticed that her breasts had grown. He had not seen her naked for a long time, and he noticed that seeing her gave him an odd feeling he had not experienced. She was not so beautiful as the girl who had appeared to Pyrrhus that day by Arethusa's spring, but there was something very interesting about her skinny, athletic body with the new breasts. But he only saw this for a moment and then she was gone. He peered through the opening and saw that the rock had rubbed off a small patch of skin on her back, and she was bleeding.

Phyllis stuck her face in the opening and said, "Untie my clothes from the lever and hand them out. I scraped myself on the cave wall, but I can put leaves over the wound and my chiton will hold it in place. I see plenty of wood out here that

I can use for a longer lever. The earthquake shook down lots of dead branches."

Figures untied her clothes from the poles and passed them through the hole. He waited beside the big boulder for what seemed a very long time. Then he heard Phyllis' voice. "Watch out." Within seconds the rock rolled away and down the cliff. Figures stepped out of the cave to see Phyllis sitting on the ground with the other end of a large branch in her lap.

"It moved so fast, I fell down," she said. "That long lever made it easy, and I could push the rock from the other side."

"Yes," said Figures. "Someday I am going to find out more about levers."

● Phyllis said, "I must go to the temple and thank Artemis for rescuing us."

"I am happy to thank *you* for rescuing me. After all, it was your idea to use your clothes to make a longer lever."

"I should thank you, too. You were the one who thought to use a lever. But I needed the dream from Artemis to see how to escape."

Although Figures did not want to argue with her, he said, "If the gods got us out, then who caused the earthquake that almost killed us? And did not Artemis lead us to the cave where we almost died? It is not clear to me that she is on our side."

Phyllis was silent for a moment. Then she said, "It is not always obvious what the Gods do and what just happens. But suppose Artemis wanted you to experience the earthquake. Maybe there is something in the future, which we can only glimpse when the Gods let us, something that will be important to you that happened today. Most of the time mortals can only guess what the Gods have in store."

Figures said, "Perhaps Hades, the god of the underworld, caused the earthquake because he wanted us to join him, but we were both too clever to let that happen. Or maybe just too lucky. It all depends on chance, from being there when the earthquake happened to not being killed at first to knowing enough to be able to use levers. If we had been pigs or bears, we would have died from ignorance."

They argued all the way back. Phyllis remained convinced that Artemis watched over them. Figures argued that if gods protected people why did so many bad things, such as earthquakes and disease, occur? Phyllis told Figures that her father said earthquakes had destroyed several cities in Sicily, but Syracuse had always been spared because it was sacred to both Artemis and Athena. Figures said that this did not explain why temples to those goddesses had been lost in the earthquakes that struck other Sicilian cities.

He finally decided that there was no convincing Phyllis — if gods could do anything, then everything was possible. But the argument made the long trip back to their homes seem much quicker than the way to the cave had been.

SCROLL 13

● A few days after Phyllis and Figures escaped from the cave, Figures began to train for the Games. Jason was spending most of his time with boys who looked to have better chances of winning, mainly Narcissus and Faunus, hoping to learn training tips from them, so at first Figures practiced his long jump alone. To keep from being bored, he worked out the mathematics of the jump, counting steps, trying to establish which geometric curve his body followed while in the air, assigning a number to each impact, and so forth. Sometimes he focused so much on the mathematics that he forgot to jump.

After three days of decreasing practice, but increased understanding of the mathematics, he knew he had to do something different. He asked Phyllis and Herc to join him at practice. Since Phyllis was a girl and Herc was too young, they had not been training themselves. Phyllis was happy to play the aulos while Figures jumped and to remind him to practice when he forgot about jumping and immersed himself in a problem. Herc, however, competed with Figures. He had changed over the past year.

● Herc was always interested in food and money. Shortly after the army was exiled from the city, he had picked a bagful of apples and pears from his family's orchard. It was more than he wanted for himself, so he set out to sell the rest to the soldiers. They were happy to supplement their rations and paid well for his fruit. He came home with a small bag of coins tucked into a fold in his chiton.

Some older boys who noticed the coins overpowered him and took the money. Phyllis said he needed to build up his strength to resist bullies. She told him the story of Milo of Croton.

"Milo was an Olympic wrestler long ago. He won the Olympic wrestling championship five times in a row. His great strength started when his father gave him a baby bull.

Whenever the father asked Milo how the bull was doing, Milo would run out to the field, pick up the bull, and bring it for his father to see. Every day the father would ask about the bull, and every day Milo would carry it back and forth from the field. The bull grew faster than Milo, but because Milo picked up the bull every day, his muscles grew stronger as the bull grew larger. Even after the bull had reached his full size, Milo could lift it in his arms, carry it from the field to his house and carry it back. Milo became the strongest man of his time, often challenging others to match his strength by trying to remove a pomegranate from his hand or to push him off a greased disk or to bend one of his fingers. Milo invariably won these contests. You need to become strong like Milo."

Herc was inspired by the story. His family, richer than Figures' family, owned cattle as well as sheep and goats. Herc first went to where the cattle were kept, but realized that it was the wrong season for young calves and that he could not pick up even the smallest of the cattle that were there, so he went on to where the sheep and goats were kept. The sheep were also too heavy for him to lift and when he tried to lift a goat, it butted him first and knocked him down. Clearly, he could not begin with adult animals to imitate Milo, and he did not want to wait until spring for the young animals to be born.

Figures suggested, "You need to work with something inanimate, Herc. The point is not that Milo lifted an animal; it is that he lifted a weight that increased every day. Get a strong leather bag and fill it with rocks until it is so heavy that you can barely lift it. Better yet, get two bags, one for each arm. Lift those bags every day. Carry them around with you. Then every day add one more rock to each bag. That would do the same for you as lifting a calf, and probably more."

Herc tried Figures' idea. After he got the bags of rocks, he lifted them several different ways—up above his head, behind his back, just with his forearms, just with his shoulders, and even with his legs by squatting and then standing up. And he added a rock to each bag every day.

Soon the bags were too heavy for Figures or Phyllis to lift, but Herc was still able to lift them, although it was not easy for him to do.

His big, overweight arms had changed from floppy fat to massive muscles. So it was a different Herc who trained with Figures and Phyllis.

Herc encouraged Figures to do more than practice jumping. They worked through the five parts of the pentathlon. Figures easily won over Herc in racing and jumping. They were about equal with the discus and both had trouble with the complex javelin toss. That left wrestling. Herc's weight and strength gave him an advantage in wrestling. In their first test, he had Figures flat on his back within seconds.

"Try me, Herc." Phyllis said. "I have been able to outfight you all your life and I can still do it." Following standard procedure, they stood with their foreheads touching to start. Figures said, "Begin!" Phyllis soon proved herself. Herc was stronger, but she was faster. Phyllis ducked as Herc came at her and grabbed him behind the knee. He was already off balance and fell heavily to the ground.

Phyllis said, "That's one. Get back up. I need to throw you to the ground three times to win the match." Herc got up a little warily. He remembered that his sister had always beaten him in fights before, but he was stronger now.

Figures said, "Remember in Homer's story of the Trojan war how Odysseus felled the mighty Aias. He kicked him in the back of the knee. At least your sister only grabbed you there, so count yourself lucky."

In the second trial, Herc tried the same knee grab on Phyllis that she had used on him. But even before he had his hand behind her leg, Phyllis took advantage of Herc's lowered head to put both her hands behind his neck and once again throw him to the ground.

"That's two. One more and I win."

Herc was determined to make his sister fall, but he was also feeling battered from the first two trials. For the third time they stood with their heads together. Figures said "Begin!" and Herc succeeded in wrapping his arms around Phyllis. He used his weight and strength to push her down toward the ground. Phyllis went down on one knee.

"I have you now," Herc said.

"Knees down don't count," Phyllis said. She leaned suddenly backward. Herc was already pushing down, so he lost his balance and flew over her head. "I win!" shouted Phyllis.

Figures said, "I could learn to fight like that. If you know how to use your body as a lever, you don't have to be strong."

⬟ Phyllis said, "I have some important news that I have been saving for a good moment to tell you. Every year a young girl fourteen years old is chosen to be the main priestess for the temple of Artemis. Next year it will be me. I asked our father to help me be chosen. He donated some books, animals, and other items to the temple. He may even have given some gold. Whatever he did, it worked."

Figures was startled. Although he knew that Phyllis had long been devoted to the goddess Artemis, it had not occurred to him that she could be a priestess. He said, "That's amazing. Tell me about it."

"Although my father's gifts certainly helped, I was really chosen by the Goddess, of course. A stag was sacrificed and the women who attend the temple prayed for guidance. I was told to walk before the Goddess who lives in the temple. When I was directly in front of the Goddess, one of the women saw the Goddess nodding. Everyone agreed that this was the proper sign. Since I was the only one asked to walk before the Goddess, thanks to father, it was unlikely that She would choose someone else."

Phyllis seemed to Figures to recognize that the gods control not everything in life; humans could change outcomes. "And what will you do as priestess?" he asked. Since his family paid little attention to gods and goddesses, he was ignorant of much that was common knowledge to most citizens.

"I will be the one with the key to the temple. Every morning and evening, I go to the temple. In the morning, I open the temple doors. I will usually stay in the temple with the Goddess for a while, but I don't have to be there all day, every day. Usually there are handmaidens to the priestess around. We want to protect the Goddess and also any treasures She may be watching over. In the evening I return and lock the temple for the night.

"On the main festival days, I lead the procession to the altar. You surely have seen women and the animal that will be sacrificed going through the town, led by a young girl holding a key and followed by other girls with baskets on their heads. The baskets contain the tools used in the ceremony."

"Do you have to kill the sacrifice yourself?"

"I could kill the sacrifice—after all, I have butchered a stag--but I do not. I prepare the altar, and the women in the procession draw lots to see who will carry out the sacrifice. I help cut up the flesh and cook it for the feast. We all eat and also drink much wine. As the priestess, I will be expected to drink the most wine, and when I am out of myself from the wine, I can answer questions in the voice of the Goddess, who will come to inhabit me for a short time."

Figures, who had begun to think more and more of how he felt when he saw Phyllis naked at the cave, wondered how she would behave when she drank too much wine. But he could not mention that. Instead, he asked, "Could I come to the temple and take part? I'll be 14 next year, too."

"Even though you do not take Artemis seriously, She has always treated you as special, so She would be pleased if you joined Her worship. I might have to give you lessons on how to act. But wait until I am the priestess. Then you can join a procession. Although Artemis is special to women, men join in her worship on the feast days, perhaps so that they can get their share of the feast and the wine. On the main feast day, most of the town will get drunk, not just the priestess."

⬟ *That night Figures dreamed of an object floating in the water. It was shaped much like the breast of a woman, but rounded at the tip with no nipple. It was the shape formed if a parabola was rotated around its axis. The object floated like a boat in the water with the curved tip down. Then he saw that it was a boat after all, and he and a girl were passengers inside the curve. He was not sure whether the girl was Phyllis or the nymph Arethusa. The girl was trying to climb up the inside of the boat, which caused the shape to tip alarmingly over. Figures called to the girl to come down to the safety of the bottom of the boat, but she kept climbing higher and the boat tipped more and more. It also began to rock back and forth from her motion or perhaps from waves in the water. Figures began to calculate the angle at which the shape would tip, and they would drown. He knew that before it reached that angle, the shape would rock back and forth, but stay essentially upright. She was still climbing. The shape was beginning to tip. Water poured into the boat. Figures was surprised that it was warm, like a small pond, instead of cold like the sea. The water poured over him and he drifted into a dreamless sleep.*

⬟ One afternoon when Figures came home from training with Herc, he was surprised to find a stranger talking to his mother. He was reminded of the time he had run home so frightened by Malchus and met Hiero for the first time. But this was no frightening soldier still wearing his leather jacket; instead, it was a girl who appeared not much older than he was, a deeply tanned girl, dressed in clothes not much better than rags, and wearing the poorest sandals he had ever seen.

Andromeda said, "Archimedes, I want you to meet your father's cousin, Hypate. She has traveled a long way to visit us."

Figures recalled that "Hypate" was one of the names mentioned by his father the night they discussed the Pythagoreans. Could this be the daughter who with her mother had fled after her father had been killed? If so, what had become of her mother--Claudia?

Hypate spoke with an unfamiliar accent. "Hello, Archimedes. My father often spoke of our relative, Phidias the astronomer of Syracuse. So when I escaped from Eryx, I came to Syracuse to see if I could find an astronomer named Phidias. Happily, everyone in Syracuse knows Phidias, so here I am."

Figures could not decide which question to ask first. Where is your mother? Why were you in Eryx in the first place? How did you get from Eryx to Syracuse? What happened to your clothes?

Before he could ask any of these questions, his mother said, "Hypate has yet to meet your father, but I have asked her to stay with us for a while. There is room in the women's quarters. But Hypate is tired from her journey and should rest until Phidias gets home. So save your curiosity for later." And she took Hypate by the arm and led her away, leaving Figures standing in the courtyard.

⬟ In the days that followed, Hypate spent most of her time helping Andromeda run the household, but she spent her free time with Figures when she had the chance, so he soon was able to learn her story.

Hypate began with history. "It really started four years ago. The Epirote King General Pyrrhus came to Italy intending to defeat Rome on behalf of Tarentum. There were many fierce battles. Croton became involved. Pyrrhus left Italy for Sicily, but then he came back and started fighting again. Finally, Pyrrhus went back to Epirus. By then the whole south of Italy was devastated by war. Half the population of Croton had either left the city or been killed. My family was lucky to still be alive and safe, but times were very hard in Croton and gangs controlled different parts of the city."

Figures interrupted to tell her about *his* adventures with Pyrrhus. He hinted, not quite truthfully, that he was one of the general's advisors. Hypate appeared impressed.

When Hypate could resume, she said, "My father, Leon, was a teacher, like your father. My father taught music. When I was a child, we lived peacefully at home, and all was well. Then, my father began to work with a young man whose name was Pasion, who would become his favorite pupil. Soon Pasion was at our house every day. They were together constantly. Father told him the secret of our family life—that we belonged to the Society of Pythagoras, which had long been suppressed in Croton and elsewhere. He was hoping to induct Pasion into the Society. Soon he declared that as soon as I became 14, I was to marry Pasion. This was *not* a good idea. My mother was against it, but could not break father's attachment of Pasion. Moreover, Pasion's family was a part of a gang that ruled our neighborhood."

"Did you marry him?"

"Not at all. Pasion's family was also against the marriage and begged him to break off his relationship with my father, but Pasion defied them and stayed at our house. One day, Pasion's father and some of his gang captured Pasion and dragged him back to his father. Also we began to be persecuted in another way. Pasion must have told his father that we were Pythagoreans. A pentagram was painted on the side of our house."

Figures said, "That's the 'secret' sign of the Pythagoreans."

"It was known as such in Croton. The priest of Hera denounced us from the temple. One night, voices outside our home awakened us. Pasion's father and the priest of Hera had gathered a crowd to drive us out of town. The mob began to throw rocks at the house. We stayed inside. Then the attackers piled hay and branches up against the side of the house and set the pile on fire."

"What did you do?"

"We ran from the house. The mob threw rocks and we all were hit. My father was hit in the head by a large rock and fell to the ground. Mother and I rushed back to help him even as rocks continued to fall around us. Father was not conscious, so we each grabbed a leg and pulled him into the woods as deep as we could. Finally, we stopped running. Or we may have stopped because we reached a stream. We certainly stopped by the stream. There was a glow in the sky from our burning house."

Hypate had begun telling her story in a calm voice, but when she reached this part of it her voice shook. She appeared close to breaking down and crying. After a pause she returned to relating the awful events in something like the voice with which she had started.

"Mother soaked the edge of her dress in water from the stream and used it to wipe the blood from Father's head. We knew we had left a trail of blood through the forest. We were terrified that we could be followed. Mother said we could use the stream to hide our trail. We picked up Father by the shoulders. We could not lift him to a standing position, but we were able to drag him into the stream. His head rolled about in an alarming way. After a while, Mother said, 'It's no use. Leon is dead.' I could not believe it. She dragged him to the bank. She had to pry my fingers away. I was not ready to give up. After a while, I finally was convinced that Father was dead. His body grew cold and I did not want to touch him. We stayed by his body all night. We had no tools to dig a grave, so the next morning we covered him the best we could with leaves and branches, hoping to keep the wild beasts from devouring his body. Pythagoreans believe that a person's soul does not die, but is returned into another body—perhaps another human but perhaps an animal. Mother and I prayed someday to meet Leon in his new body, but of course we could not count on it."

Figures had no experience with human death and thought that he could not stand to spend a night next to a dead body, even if it was his father.

⬟ "After we covered Father's body, we began to plan what to do next. Mother said, 'We'll follow the stream. All streams run to the sea eventually. We will be safer on the coast. . If we can get to the sea, we might be able to find a boat that would take us to Rhegion. I have relatives in Rhegion, which is around the southern tip of Italy, far south of Croton. Rhegion is allied with Rome, so it should be safe.' We traveled downstream all that day and the next, moving to larger streams as one flowed into another. As Pythagoreans, we did not kill animals to get food. My mother showed me what we could safely eat—berries, fruit, certain mushrooms, leaves of some small plants, and roots of others. We also stole what grains we could from farmer's fields. The stream flowed into the Esario, the river that practically encircles Croton. There were ships at the river's mouth, but we had no way to pay for transportation.. When Mother found a ship going to Rhegion, she persuaded the captain that, her family in Rhegion would pay him handsomely if he let us travel with him. Mother was a very attractive woman. The captain may have been interested in more than the money. Whatever his motive, he took us aboard."

Figures wondered how Claudia looked and if he would ever meet her. Hypate would be very attractive, he thought, if she gained a little weight.

"Rhegion is across from Sicily. After several days at sea, we rounded the tip of Italy. Rhegion would be our next stop and we could leave ship if my mother's family could pay for our fares. We saw Sicily on one side of the ship and Italy on the other. The captain said we were sailing between Scylla and Charybdis, as Odysseus had done."

Figures said, "I cannot believe in a many-headed monster like Scylla, but a whirlpool like Charybdis is possible—it would just be bigger than an ordinary whirlpool."

"We saw neither. Suddenly, the ship's captain began to scream orders to his men to put down the sails and man the oars. 'Row for Italy!' he shouted. Another ship was fast approaching us. It drew up to our side and great hooks were thrown onto our decks. Our ship was tied by these hooks to the other ship.

"A giant man with black skin jumped onto our ship, brandishing a sword. Many other armed men followed him. Our own sailors were unarmed and clearly did not want to fight. Most of them fell to the deck and just lay there. Mother and I moved to be near the captain. Mother asked, 'Are these pirates?' The captain replied, 'Yes. It is better not to resist them. Let them take our goods and leave us with our lives. This ship is too slow for them to use, so they may sink it. I hope you can swim.'

"But the pirate leader, whose name was Atban, had different ideas."

Figures broke into her story. "Atban! I know him. He tried to kidnap me once, but I escaped."

"Atban was more successful with Mother and me. He succeeded in kidnapping us. Men from his crew bound us hand and foot and carried us to their ship along with any goods of value our ship had been carrying. When Atban and his pirates had everything they wanted, they sunk the ship. Everyone from our ship grabbed something that would float, then jumped overboard. In a few moments the ship sank beneath the surface of the sea. Its sailors were using flotsam to stay afloat and paddling toward the Italian shore. If they had been Greeks, they would have known how to swim.

"Atban took off the ropes that bound us and made us take off all our clothes. As we stood there naked, he walked around us a couple of times. He looked in our mouths and even into other parts of our bodies Finally he said, 'We can keep these. They are worth more alive than dead. Indeed, I know just the person who will buy them.'"

● Figures could not help himself from glancing at Hypate and, almost ashamed of the thought, picturing her naked.

"After we put our clothes back on, Atban locked us in a small room below the decks for the rest of the trip. When we were allowed on the deck, Atban made sure that our hands were tightly bound behind our backs and that one of the pirates constantly watched us. We were taken ashore in western Sicily, loaded into the back of a cart, and carried inland for a day before we were given food, drink, and a place to wash ourselves and generally clean up. We were in a town called Eryx."

Figures remembered Eryx. It was where Pyrrhus had used an elephant to mount the wall and end a siege.

"Mother said, 'We are to be sold into slavery. They want us to look our best so that we command a higher price.' But we did not go on the auction block at the slave market. Atban had a friend in Eryx, and we were sold directly to him. Atban is a spy. He stops at ports to collect reports from his agents. He knew the whole story of the attack on our family in Croton and even that we had escaped on a merchant ship heading for Rhegion. When he captured our ship, he expected to find us. Atban's friend is the agent of Carthage in Eryx. Carthage has controlled the whole west coast of Sicily since Pyrrhus withdrew, so Malchus is a very important person."

Figures said, "I should have guessed when you first named Atban. He and Malchus worked together. They were the ones who kidnapped me and nearly drowned me. Malchus is a terrible man—the enemy of our entire family."

"He certainly is my enemy, too. When we were brought before him, we expected to join his field slaves, although we hoped to be made household slaves. Malchus knew that our family were Pythagoreans. Malchus is very religious, a great believer in Baal. He considers Pythagoreans, who believe in no gods, to be the lowest form of human life. Owning us gave him a chance to injure Pythagoreans."

Figures remembered with a shudder how Malchus had believed sacrificing him to Baal could win a war. If Malchus had recognized that Phidias was a Pythagorean that would account for Malchus's hatred of his family.

Hypate said, "We were back in prison for only a few hours when men came and took Mother away, leaving me in the cell. She was gone only a few hours, but returned weeping and unable to talk to me. I never learned what

Malchus had done to her. I think he forced her into acts that shamed her greatly."

Figures was horrified. He had learned in the dormitory that soldiers often took women by force when they captured a city. This demonstrated their power over the losers because it insulted the woman's husband or father, but soldiers also liked forcing women, even though it often harmed them. He could not imagine doing such an injury to anyone. His hatred of Malchus mounted even higher.

⬟ Hypate continued, "The next morning we were taken to Malchus with our hands bound behind us again. Mother whispered to me that the person with Malchus was a priest of Baal. Malchus dismissed our guards. He told Mother and me that we must abandon our Pythagorean beliefs and worship Baal. Mother said that this would be impossible—for one thing, Baal demands human sacrifices. 'Exactly,' said Malchus. 'You are to make a sacrifice to Baal to start your worship of Him. If you accept our beliefs, then I will spare you the life of a field slave and keep you here in the household, for I find that I am greatly attracted to you.'

"The priest produced a sharp knife and said, 'Baal considers your young virgin daughter a suitable sacrifice. He would especially find it pleasing that you conducted her soul to him yourself. A fire has been laid on our hilltop altar to burn her body so that the smoke rises to please him.'

"I cannot describe the look of horror that I saw on Mother's face, but she did not argue with Malchus. She said, 'I am in your power and can only do what you order me to do.' I believe that she immediately began to seek a way for me to escape."

"Malchus took Mother by the arm and the priest grabbed my ropes. We were pushed through the town, outside the town walls, and up a small hill. People we passed did not seem to find it strange that we had our arms bound, for we appeared to be slaves. At the top of the hill, we were led to a much-used altar laid with branches. Human skulls ringed the altar.

"The priest and Malchus lifted me and placed me on the branches on the altar. But they laid me on my back, which let me work with pieces of wood to try to untie my hands. Malchus asked Mother if she was sure that she was strong enough to cut her daughter's throat. She appeared to think this over, finally replying 'I have no choice, but you assume too much about my relationship with my daughter. When you are ready, give me the knife.' I was sure Mother's words were meant to mislead; she had a plan of some kind. But I continued to pick at my bonds,--that was my plan.

"Malchus told the priest to begin the ceremony. The priest spoke for a long time in Punic, praying to Baal. Then Malchus spun Mother around so her back was to the priest, who used his knife to cut the ropes off Mother's hands. As soon her hands were free, she flung herself backwards, knocking the priest off his feet. She landed on top of him and called out 'Run, Hypate, run!' By then I had loosened the ropes enough to pull my hands free. I rolled off the altar and ran toward the woods.

"Malchus followed close behind me. I heard a cry of agony. Malchus and I both looked back. Mother had the priest's wrist and was using his wrist to pull the knife from the priest's stomach and stab him a second time, more deeply than the first. Malchus stopped chasing me and ran toward Mother This time the priest screamed again and let go of the knife, which Mother took.

"Mother rose to her feet as Malchus reached her. He was behind her and wrapped his arms around her, pinning her arms to her side. Mother saw me watching and cried out, 'Hypate! Run to the woods and escape!' I ran, glancing back over my shoulder once. Although Mother could not harm Malchus, she still had the knife in her hand, and she plunged it into her own body.

"I started back to help Mother. But Malchus had taken the knife and Mother lay on the ground. I did not know whether she would live or die, but she had chosen to let me escape rather than to try to save herself, so as my last act of obedience I determined to save myself. I ran into the woods. I believe that she preferred to die rather than be a slave to Malchus."

Figures said, "Your mother was amazing. But how did you get from Eryx to Syracuse?"

"I ran through the woods as fast as I could. I decided to aim for Syracuse because I knew that it was in Sicily and Greek and your father is a relative. I used the Sun to find east. It was good that I had traveled through the woods with Mother, for I knew which wild food I could safely eat and how to steal from farmers. I did a lot of stealing while journeying east. Sometimes I went a day or more without food, but I was always able to find water. One day I climbed a ridge and saw the sea spread out below. I was on the eastern shore of the island. I had no idea whether I was north or south of Syracuse. I had to ask for directions.

"It was easier than I thought to strike up a conversation with a young man who I took to be about my own age or perhaps as young as you."

Figures thought Hypate was not more than a year or two older than he, so he felt rather insulted.

She continued, "My new friend told me that I was on the south slope of the famous volcano Mount Etna. Syracuse was a long way south. Eventually the large city by the sea that I saw from the top of a cliff was Syracuse. I felt safe enough after I passed through the gates of Syracuse to ask anyone I met where the house of Phidias the astronomer might be. When I found it, your mother welcomed me in."

Figures knew the woods and streams well, from mapping them since boyhood, but he wondered if he could have lived in them the way Hypate had. After hearing her story, he treated her with respect.

SCROLL 14

● As the days went by, Hypate's body, emaciated when she arrived, began to fill out on Luce's good meals. Eventually she resumed her normal weight, somewhat more than most girls her age, although she was never fat the way Herc had been. After she learned that the Games would take place in a few months she watched Figures and his friends training when she had time. She had a way of finding where Figures was and would sit nearby, using a spindle to make yarn from wool to occupy herself while Figures trained or even when he studied.

Phyllis nearly always was part of the boy's practice sessions as well. Hypate and Phyllis tried to talk to each other when Phyllis was not playing the aulos, but it always seemed awkward.

One day Phyllis said, "Syracuse is very fortunate to be under the protection of Artemis. Have you been to Her temple?"

"My family were Pythagoreans. We did not believe gods live in the temples."

"But when you traveled through the forests on your way here, you might have seen or felt Artemis there. I sometimes see Her in the woods. It is Her hunting ground."

"No gods, just occasional animals. Can you hold the end of this yarn for me? This skein is ready to wind up."

"Don't you think that spinning wool into yarn is the most boring task in the world?"

"No. Don't you find playing the same tunes over and over on the aulos boring?"

"No."

They didn't say anything more while Hypate wound up the yarn. Phyllis picked up her aulos and began to play the melody Figures used to get his timing right for the long jump.

● He was beginning to make some very good long jumps. Phyllis said, "I think you are getting the rhythm from my playing much better now. If you pay even more attention to what I play, I am sure you will win the long jump." He thought that his understanding of the geometry of the jump had more to do with his improvement, but he decided not to tell her that.

By watching other boys jump, he observed that the path of the jumper through the air affected the distance achieved. There was a point inside the jumper's body that traveled on a well-known curve, the parabola. The flatter this curve, the longer the jump.

He also studied the weights, called halteres, that the jumper throws behind him at the end of the jump to gain greater distance. Both the heaviness of the haltere and the speed of throwing seemed to influence how much added push he could get. His arms could help his legs jump. His own weight affected how far he could push himself against the halteres, with less being better. To help gain distance he ate less than usual and became even thinner. The halteres used might move against the wind better, he thought, if the front and back were each rounded into half spheres with the two half spheres were connected by a cylinder.

One night Figures dreamed of the sphere and the cylinder, but it was a nightmare.

He was trapped in the cave again, but this time the cave had been transformed from rough rock to the inside of a perfectly round bronze cylinder. Instead of the fallen rock blocking his way out there was a huge bronze sphere. Hypate was trapped with him. Figures and Hypate were not alone in the tube. Both Malchus and Atban were behind them, running to catch them and make them slaves or worse.

There was no space between the cylinder and the sphere, so they could not get on the other side of the giant bronze ball. They were trapped! They rolled the sphere forward and ran behind it, but this slowed them. Malchus and Atban were fast approaching.

But when Malchus and Atban were about to catch them, the sphere dropped into a well. The well was another cylinder exactly the same diameter as the sphere, but just as deep as the height of the sphere. The well was filled with water, most of which splashed out on Figures when he and Hypate and the ball fell into the well. But both could step on the top of the sphere and across the well. Once they were on the other side of the well, they tried to reach down and pull the sphere up so that they could put it between them and their pursuers. But the sphere fit in the well, so they could not get their hands below it to lift it up. Malchus was stepping on the sphere and about to grab Hypate when Figures woke up, covered with sweat.

⬟ In addition to practicing the long jump, Figures experimented with the discus, and occasionally ran races against Phyllis, who won every time—but he was getting closer. The discus flew somewhat like the body of the jumper, but the curve could be even flatter if the discus were slightly tilted with the leading edge up. If he got the angle just right, he could throw farther. Other boys threw the discus in the accepted way—vertical instead of at an angle.

One day when Figures and Herc were training at Figures' house, Phidias came home from Ortygia and stopped to watch the two boys. Figures was working on strengthening his legs by squatting down and jumping straight up while holding the weights he would throw during the long jump and working on his arms at the same time by pushing the weights behind his body. Herc was lifting two leather bags repeatedly above his head.

Phidias said, "Heracleides, what are you doing with those bags of rocks?"

Herc put down the bags and replied, "I was going to lift a young bull like Milo of Croton so that I could become strong and be a winning wrestler at the Games, but I did not have a young bull. When I tried to lift a young goat, the goat got the better of me, so Figures suggested that I use bags of rocks and add a rock every day."

Phidias walked over to the bags and lifted them with

some difficulty. "It seems to be a good plan. Maybe in five years when you are eligible the Games you will be able to lift your opponent and throw him to the ground. I'm glad you learned about Milo. Milo was a Pythagorean in the days before their neighbors persecuted Pythagoreans. He was once in a meeting of Pythagoreans when the main column supporting the roof of their meetinghouse began to buckle. Milo was able to hold the column in place until all of the other Pythagoreans were able to escape. He escaped that time, but finally met a living creature that could defeat him. Do you know that part of his story?"

"No," said Herc.

"Milo became famous everywhere for his great strength, always winning every contest he entered. He believed that there was no test of strength he could fail. One day while walking through the forest, he saw where a woodman had been trying to fell a very large tree using a wedge. Driving a wedge into a tree lifts one side of the trunk. The weight of the tree should cause it to break and fall down; but this tree did not fall. Instead, the wedge became stuck in the tree. Milo thought that he could fell the tree himself with his great strength. He put his fingers into the cleft made by the wedge and opened a little further. The wedges fell out. But Milo was not able to open the cleft further. His fingers tired slightly, and the entire tree pressed down on Milo's fingers. He could no longer move the tree, and he remained stuck there. The forest did not have many visitors. By the time someone found him, Milo had died of lack of water and food. I have always wondered if the tree had not in an earlier life been one of the many wrestlers Milo had defeated, now finally having a chance for revenge."

Figures decided that it was time to ask his father more about the Pythagoreans. Figures by then had reached a number of conclusions on his own, but he wanted to make sure that he was correct and also to learn more than he was able to do by himself.

Before *Eureka!*

⬟ At fourteen, Figures home schooling came to an end. He had passed beyond his father in both mathematical ability and knowledge. Phidias, the professional teacher, still volunteered details of astronomy or anything he had forgot to mention previously. One day Phidias remarked that Pythagoras originally discovered the laws of harmony and that Hypate was named after the most beautiful chord on the lyre. Figures felt he it was the right time to ask a question that had been on his mind ever since he learned Hypate's story.

"Father, I know that Hypate's family was attacked for being followers of Pythagoras, and that Malchus counts himself an enemy of the Pythagoreans. Our family lives by the Pythagorean rule but never mentions that we are Pythagoreans. Is this kept a secret for fear that we will be killed by an angry mob?"

Phidias said, "The days when mobs attacked the Society have faded in most cities, despite what happened to Leon and his family. We could tell nearly anyone in Syracuse that we follow Pythagoras without fear of harm, but we might lose many friends and most of my students, which would be a great hardship. When my father and mother set up shop as goldsmiths in Syracuse—I was just a small boy when they bought this land—they decided they would have more clients if they did not tell their new neighbors, and even when I was a child, I was taught to keep it secret. Eventually they gave me the sacred scrolls of Pythagoras to study. I still have them."

"I think they are in a locked part of in your scroll trunk and that the brass whistle you wear is the key."

"I can hide nothing from you. I was probably about fifteen or sixteen when my father gave me the scrolls to read. He had forged the brass lock and the whistle key for the hidden compartment: Well, not very hidden, since you found it. Let's go to the trunk, and I will show you how to work the lock. From now on, you should be the one to wear the whistle and keep the scrolls safe." And he took the whistle off his neck and handed it to Figures.

Following direction from his father, Figures unlocked the compartment in the trunk. Phidias showed him how to remove one scroll--very carefully, saying, "These brittle with age." The papyrus was aged and frayed, but had been kept dry and free from mold, so it could still be read easily.

Phidias said, "This reports Pythagoras' words that were written down by followers as *Sayings of Pythagoras*. Other scrolls contain the life of Pythagoras and theories of the universe, music, or mathematics. Don't try to read these all at once, especially since some of them contradict what others say. Read each one slowly and try to determine the truths for yourself."

Phidias left Figures alone to unroll the *Sayings of Pythagoras*.

⬟ In the following months, at times when no one was likely to see or interrupt him, Figures read the ancient scrolls. He was surprised to learn that earlier Pythagoreans revered their teacher so much that they never used his name, but said "He" or "Him." The words of Pythagoras were more like poetry than mathematics--many sayings could be understood in several different ways. There were rules for the Society to follow, but his father and mother only followed the rules that made sense to them. Figures thought that he would do the same.

Some mathematical works were stored in the hidden compartment. For Pythagoreans, the biggest secret was that everything could not be reduced to numbers, as Pythagoras had taught. A Pythagorean named Hippassus of Metapontum had discovered that the lengths of some lines cannot be measured with the ratios of two numbers. One proof of this came directly from Pythagoras' theorem that the sum of the squares on two short sides of a right triangle equals the square on the long side. If the two shorts sides are equal, then the long side cannot be the ratio of two numbers because that would imply that the same number is both odd and even. Figures loved this way of making a proof—show that the assumption of the opposite leads to a contradiction.

Although he was disappointed to learn that numbers are not the basis of everything, he still believed that mathematics rules the universe, not the gods.

⬟ When Figures told Phyllis about the writings of Pythagoras, she said she, too, had been reading old writings that were new to her. It began when she became the priestess of Artemis. She noticed an ancient, weathered statue inside the temple--a short, attractive woman holding a book.

"At first, I could find no one who knew anything about the statue, but the historian of the temple said it was an image of a wonderful poet named Sappho."

Figures said, "I know about Sappho. She wrote beautiful short poems and songs."

"Sappho lived here. She was born and raised on the island of Lesbos, but a rebellion there caused her to move to Syracuse. She became popular here. The people of Syracuse erected a statue of her in the public square. The priestesses of Artemis rescued the statue when it was becoming worn from the weather and people passing by no longer knew whom it honored.

"It is unusual for a mortal woman to be honored by a statue. I asked my father about Sappho, and he started telling me about all the famous writers who had lived in Syracuse — Sappho, of course, Pindar, Aeschylus, Plato, and I can't remember them all. But he had no useful information about Sappho, only that she had been universally beloved.

"The temple historian took me to a room in the back of the temple filled with scrolls, saying that some of these were poems of Sappho, but she did not know which. It was easy to find them. And the poems are wonderful. They are about love. I had not thought much about love before, but now I know I must make it a part of my life."

"What does she say about love?"

"Much. Here is a short sample that I memorized from one of the scrolls:

'Some say horsemen, some say warriors,
Some say a fleet of ships is the loveliest
Vision in this dark world, but I say it's
What you love.'

That is truly beautiful. Someday I hope that I can write beautiful words. I don't expect that I will ever get close to what Sappho wrote so long ago."

⬟ Training for the Games occupied a large part of most days, but Figures found time to visit Hiero, camped with the army outside the walls. He would bring Hiero news of Andromeda and Phidias and also carry messages from Hiero back to them.

Hiero also began to assign small tasks to Figures. Hiero was trying to persuade the Assembly to allow the army to return to the city, so he asked Figures to carry messages back and forth to the various members of the Assembly. He also took notes from Hiero to Philistis, daughter of Leptines, when she was not visiting the camp herself. Figures began to suspect that the relationship between Hiero and Philistis might involve more than politics.

Hiero was determined to move the Syracusan Army back inside the city walls, despite the Assembly's explicit prohibition. He asked Figures to bring a message to Philistis and Leptines and said, "Archimedes, I am counting on them to help me, and I am counting on you to help them. Do whatever they ask of you."

Figures agreed, which led to his becoming part of a plot to open secretly one of the gates in the City wall. The conspirators planned to distract the guards at the darkest part of the night. Then the first part of the army could enter through the gate; after that, Hiero's men would take care of the guards and keep the gates open while part of the army passed through.

When the appointed time arrived, Figures started a small

Before *Eureka!*

fire inside the wall, near the gate, which drew the guards' attention. At that point, Leptines opened the gate, and Hiero and his best soldiers streamed through. Figures helped put the fire out—he had a large jar of water with him—and returned home.

His mother and father were at the door when he arrived.

"Where have you been?" Phidias asked.

"On a secret mission, but it is all right now to tell everything. Leptines, Philistis, and I let Hiero bring his army through a gate in the wall; Hiero's troops are now all over in the city. They are planning to appear invincible. Leptines is to argue in the Assembly that they have no choice but to accept the army back."

"I think that might work," said Phidias. "Leptines will certainly bring Hiero before the Assembly and ask him to speak. Hiero will promise that his soldiers will not disturb the peace in any way."

"It will be wonderful to have Hiero back in the city," said Andromeda, "He can come and live with us." However, Hiero said he preferred to live with his soldiers. Figures soon learned that Hiero had moved in with Leptines and Philistis.

⬟ In the autumn, when daylight and darkness became equal, the Games began. People streamed into the city from the countryside and cities across Sicily and even from nearby parts of Italy. Every building in town was filled, and many visitors camped outside the walls. Both harbors teemed with ships that provided not only transportation to Syracuse but also living quarters.

Before competition started, ceremonies dedicated the Games to the gods. The Syracuse Games had once honored the god of a river where Syracuse's navy triumphed over that of Athens, but that victory was over two hundred years past. Now the Games were offered to Artemis. But to take no chances with the gods, sacrifices in Syracuse were offered to Zeus as well as to Artemis. Meat from sacrifices was cooked and distributed to become a feast for the competitors, officials, and judges assigned to direct the Games.

Because the Games at Syracuse were dedicated to Artemis, Phyllis, as priestess of Artemis, led a procession to the temple, starting from sacred caves near Epipolae. Phyllis first decorated a cow with garlands of flowers and then led the cow near the head of the procession to the altar in the temple. Other girls and women in the procession carried on their heads baskets of tools for butchering. Figures followed the marchers and then watched the ceremonies outside the temple. He had seen animals butchered before. It always upset him that some soul must go through that pain before its next reincarnation.

Phyllis distributed the cow's meat among the worshipers, keeping the rank of each woman in mind. The meat was cooked and eaten by the women, the athletes, and the judges as part of the festival, accompanied by wine that was also shared. Being a vegetarian and skeptic, Figures did not take part in eating the meat, although he was happy to drink a jar of wine.

Hiero was honored to be named among the officials who supervised the Games. Since he would be an official, Hiero gave up his plan to participate in the race for soldiers wearing armor. Leptines was also an official, representing the Assembly. Jason's father, in honor of his famous victories, was chief of the judges.

Figures' official participation in the Games began with swearing before the judges that he had trained fairly for the Games. Then he rested and fasted so that he would be in his best shape when the pentathlon took place.

⬟ All of the adult events were held before the boys' Games began. Figures arrived late at the stadium and found his friend Jason just as the adult pentathlon race was beginning with the one-stadium race. While the runners began to line up on each balbis, Figures counted the number of lanes. He asked, "Is there a reason why there are 24 lanes marked? There might be more than 24 runners."

Jason said, "There is one lane for each letter of the alphabet."

"That makes sense; we have 24 letters in Syracuse. In Greece they use a shorter alphabet, so there are probably 22 lanes for the Olympics."

At this point the judge cried "foot to foot" so Figures stopped talking and watched the race.

When the race was complete, Figures said, "That was exciting. What is the winners name?"

"There is no winner yet. This year there are more than 24 competitors for the pentathlon. So today the race will be run in sections. Then the winners of each section will compete.

"The system is not fair. The runner who was second in one section might be faster than the winner of the other."

"That doesn't matter. No one cares who is second because the only runner who counts is the one that is the fastest, and that boy would be in the final race."

Figures said, "Sometimes one whole section might run faster than the other, so the second in a really fast section might be swifter than the winner of the slow section. "

"Winners are winners, and no one else counts. The winner of a section does not matter unless he also wins the final race. For the two-stadium race there are often several sections, since each runner uses two lanes, one for the first half of the race and an adjacent lane to return to the starting point."

Figures said, "So that race can only be run by twelve runners at a time. Will the winner of this race have to wrestle the runners of the other events?"

"Yes. If anyone wins all four of the first events, he is the winner of the pentathlon, but that almost never happens. Nearly always three or four different people win the first four events, and the wrestling competition determines the pentathlon winner.

"It is not really fair. Someone who wins two of the other events and a wrestling match should be the winner instead of someone who just won one other event but came in first in wrestling."

"Rules are rules. The first events are really just ways to get into the wrestling competition—unless you can win all four other parts. Wrestling most years is the only thing that really counts in the pentathlon. This is the same as it was for the original pentathlon of Jason of the Argonauts."

⬟ The competition for the long jump and the two tosses that followed amazed Figures with how far the adult athletes could jump or toss a discus or javelin. But he soon lost track of which athletes were leading in the events because he began to calculate the possible ways that a pentathlon could occur.
- The winner of the race might or might not also win the discus—so there would be *two* ways the pair of wins could happen—one with the same winner and one with different winners.
- Then if one person won the first two events he might also win the long jump—*one possible outcome*.
- Or the race winner could win the long jump but not the discus—which makes *two ways* the first three events might end.
- If someone lost the race, and then won the discus and long jump, that would be *a third possible combination*.
- Or the winner of the long jump could be someone who had not won either of the first two events— a *fourth combination*, and that could happen for me, Figures thought.
- Using the same reasoning, there would be *five* possible combinations that included the javelin toss.

The problem got a lot more complicated when including the wrestling because the wrestlers must have won at least one, but not all four, of the first events. Figures began to draw sketches in the sand to work out all the possibilities.

Jason interrupted Figures' thoughts. "Brascidas has won the pentathlon! He will go to Greece to compete in the Olympics. "

Figures said, "Was there wrestling?"

Jason looked at Figures' sketches in the sand. "I don't

think you watched anything. The wrestling was the best part."

⬟ That night Figures dreamed about the pentathlon events, but in his dream each event was a shape, like the shapes of the pieces of the Bellyache. *He tried to put the five shapes together to form a square. The square would reveal the winner of the pentathlon. He took a piece and found that only two sides could match the next piece he picked up — the other sides were either too long or too short. So there were two ways to combine these two shapes. A third piece could be put in any of four positions. He tried all eight ways that he could combine the first three pieces. Then he realized that he was not going to make a square. He saw that the five pieces could combine to make a pentagon. As he gazed at the pentagon, he remembered that the pentagon was the symbol of the Pythagoreans. Were the five events of the pentathlon connected to the Pythagoreans? He asked Hypate if the pentathlon was sacred to Pythagoras. She said, "We are Pythagoreans: You are One and I am Two, but you are also Three. Two and Three are Five." Figures solved Hypate's puzzle: Two and all even numbers are female, while three is the first male number. The least combination of male and female is the pentagon.* While gazing on the pentagon and thinking of Hypate and numbers, his dream ended and he fell into a sound sleep.

⬟ The next day, the Games for boys started. Figures brought his discus and his cylinder-and-sphere weights for jumping to the stadium, along with the javelin he had been using in practice and the leather thong used to throw it. He placed these around the edge of the stadium next to similar equipment from the other boys..

Figures asked Jason, "What happens now?"

"A tunnel leads into the stadium. We wait there. When we leave the tunnel, there is a brief ceremony. Following that, we go to an official who has a jar filled with small pieces of broken pots—shards--that are our markers. Each shard has a letter written on the side that bends in. After you get your marker, hold your hand out with the letter side down. The judge will wait until we all have our letters. When he says 'turn them over,' we can look to see our letters. Looking before then disqualifies you."

"What do the letters mean?"

"The letters determine which lane you will occupy for the race and the order of competition for the other events. You should keep your letter in a safe place during the race for you will need it later. Since we compete naked, you should give the shard to someone to hold for you. Most boys give the shards to their fathers."

Figures followed Jason into the tunnel, where he recognized Narcissus, Faunus, and several other boys among the younger ones already waiting. He counted the group; there would be only eighteen boys in the pentathlon. Every boy was silent, readying himself to compete.

The ceremonies when they left the tunnel consisted of Phyllis, in her role as the year's priestess, offering a prayer to Artemis for a fair competition. Then Phyllis and her handmaidens left the stadium.

The judges and an official carrying a large jar walked into the stadium. One at a time, each boy reached into the jar, and took out a single shard. When the judge let them turn over the shards, Figures had letter digamma, the sixth lane in the race—alpha, beta, gamma, delta, epsilon, digamma (digamma is a letter used in Syracuse but not in Greece). He knew this was not as auspicious for Pythagoreans as the tenth lane, or iota, would have been, since 10 is the sum of 1, 2, 3, and 4, but 6 had its own special meaning. Not only was it the sum of 1, 2, and 3, but also the product of 1, 2, and 3, what the Greeks called a 'perfect number.'

Figures looked for Phidias among the men in the amphitheater. Phidias was partway up the stadium. Some women sat in a section near the back of the stadium. The separate section was for the mothers or grandmothers of the

Before *Eureka!*

athletes, so Andromeda was there. Figures also saw Hiero, in the front row among the officials. He decided that it would be easier to give his shard to Hiero.

Hiero was surprised when Figures gave him the pottery piece. He said, "You should give this to your father, Archimedes."

"He is far up in the stadium and busy talking. In any case, I would be happy for you to hold this for me because I am only here today because you suggested it."

Hiero said, "Thank you. You had better go to your place—the other boys are already lining up at theirs." He glanced at the shard in his hand. "Digamma, the sixth position. Not the best start for the race."

⬟ Each lane for the race had its own balbis, the stone slab with grooves to mark positions of the runners' toes. Figures located the balbis for digamma. After placing his feet properly, with the left foot on the forward groove, he stretched out his arms and leaned forward. He tried to concentrate on the correct position but nearly fell forward. The other racers appeared relaxed and ready, but he did not feel that way at all. He stared at the wooden bar in front of his position. Other racers watched the official holding the rope; pulling the cord would cause all the wooden bars to fall at once, starting the race. He found Narcissus far to his right, three places from the other edge of the track.

It was a good day for the Games. The Sun shone brightly, and the air was not too warm or heavy. Sometimes, even in autumn, the athletes and even the watchers were coated in sweat, but not this day.

With the runners all lined up, the starter cried out "Foot to foot," the signal that the race was about to begin. Figures' muscles became even tenser. In the stadium, everyone stopped talking and concentrated on the field. When the starter pulled the cord, the bars all dropped, and the runners took off, stepping over the fallen bars.

Figures did not get a good start. Like the other runners,

he flailed his arms wildly while running, which Jason said provided extra speed. In Figures' case, however, his swinging arms hit fellow runners, who gave him hard looks while they ran past him. He wound up in last place a few seconds into the race, but, running as hard as he ever had, he caught up with the back of the pack and stayed in that group until the race was over. He was glad that he was not all alone in last place, but part of those all more or less in last place together.

The race was over quickly, in about the time that it takes the heart to beat 30 times. Figures did not see the finish because of the boys in front. When he crossed the finish, he saw Narcissus already standing beside the track. Figures went over to him, excited to think that Narcissus had won. But then he saw the disappointed look on Narcissus' face. The winner had been one of the older boys.

Later he talked to Narcissus, who by then had cheered up. Figures said, "I am sorry you did not win. I thought you would."

"So did I. Next time I will win. I was only a step behind the winner and he was much taller than I. I took more steps than he did, but he won because of his height. Four years from now, I will be taller and surely win. Also, I am entered in the other two races, so I still have chances. And of course losing the race does not mean that I will lose the pentathlon, for I am good at all the events."

Figures wished he had Narcissus' self-confidence. After his poor showing in the race, he was sorry that he had entered the Games at all.

⬟ Figures followed the other racers over to the stands, where they were retrieving their shards. Then, ashamed of being among the last in the race, he slowly walked to Hiero. As he handed back the marked shard, Hiero smiled and said, "You are too young to expect to win this year, but now you are on your way for the Games four years from now." Figures then took his discus from his equipment pile and found his place, sixth in line, for the toss. The first discus thrower had already stepped up to a spot just behind the balbis and raised his discus to its starting position. Seconds later the boy put his whole body in the service of pushing the discus into the air. When it landed, the boy ran and handed his shard to the judge, who used it to mark the spot. The boy picked up the discus, ran back across the balbis, and tossed again, throwing slightly farther the second time, so the judge moved his marker to the farther landing spot. But the third toss fell short of the second, so the marker did not move. The first boy's second toss was the one that counted.

The same routine continued with the next boy, although the second contestant excelled with his first toss. The next three saved their best toss for last. At this point the boy labeled gamma, the third in line, had the longest toss.

Then it was Figures' turn. His form was not the same as that of the others. They held the discus vertical, the way their elders threw. Figures held his discus nearly horizontal, but with the front edge raised, aiming to get extra lift from the wind. He threw the discus the way he did because his experiments showed him that a raised front edge and lifting motion produced greater distance. When he started, he held his right arm lower than the conventional form, raising it as he spun around. His nervousness affected his first toss, but it still landed a long distance away, but to the left of the others. He had not let go of the discus soon enough. It was more difficult to aim in a straight line when launching on the wind.

On his second attempt, the landing was so far to the left that it was hard to tell whether the second toss traveled farther than the first. The judge did not move Figures' marker. Figures heard the boys behind him laughing and someone saying, "Figures should stick to his numbers. He can't even throw like a man." He recognized Narcissus' voice.

Narcissus' insult enraged Figures, who turned that anger into energy for the third toss. This time everything worked the way he intended—the angle of attack was perfect, and he let go of the discus at the moment that it headed straight. The flight was low at first, but then the discus caught the wind and rose instead of falling to the ground. When it landed, the discus was farther by a foot than that of the previous leader, gamma.

Still shaking with rage, Figures walked over to stand by the wall of the stadium with the earlier competitors. As he did the boy who had been given gamma grabbed his arm and said, "Good throw." After hearing that Figures felt relieved and calmed down for the rest of the discus toss.

By the time the line had dwindled to Narcissus and two other boys, Figures' third toss had already been surpassed several times by older boys who threw in the accepted manner and also by Jason, whose toss was also in first place for a few turns before being bested. Figures knew that he had not won, but now his main interest was to hope his best toss was longer than that of Narcissus.

Both of the first two of Narcissus' throws fell short of where Figures' marker was still on the field. Figures thought for sure he had won his own private competition. Before the third toss, Narcissus stared at Figures, leaning against the wall, and his look made it clear that he, too, would consider it a win to surpass Figures. Narcissus took great care to lift and aim his discus, then twisted his body in a mighty throw. From the moment the discus left his hand, Figures knew that Narcissus had thrown too high. The discus seemed to rise above the stadium walls. When it finally came to ground, however, it was right beside the wedge marked with a digamma. Neither had won this round, but neither had lost.

The discus toss, like the one-stadium race, was finally won by one of the older boys. Jason had been the best of those entering the Games for the first time, but he had not thrown as far as three of the older boys.

● Figures became excited and nervous again, for the long jump was about to start, and that was the event that he hoped would redeem his earlier showings. He always jumped farther than Herc or Phyllis, who sometimes put down her aulos to jump against him. Also, Figures had developed several rules for the long jump. The weights should not press against the wind. When he threw the weights behind him, the farther they traveled, the farther he would be propelled forward. The arc of his jump must be flat; he did not want to see a high curve like the one that had prevented Narcissus from beating his discus throw. So, although nervous, Figures also felt confident that he would make his father and Hiero proud of his performance, although he did not really expect to win the event. His father, who had sometimes watched him practice, seemed to know that this would be the best event, for Figures could see that Phidias had left the Assembly members and moved down to a position just behind Hiero.

SCROLL 15

● The two judges for the long jump marked a starting line and then walked six steps ahead. Each used a pick to break up the ground where jumpers were to land, making the soil a rough meal that would leave an imprint.

An aulos player began the rhythmic melodies used to improve timing, not exactly the same as Phyllis played, but Figures believed he could adjust. The alpha jumper began his first trial. Figures watched, but there was nothing special about the first few jumps. The contestants all did everything about the same and all jumped similar distances.

His gaze drifted from the slow action on the field to Andromeda among the women. She had never been to the Games before and her excitement showed, especially now that Figures' turn was next.

Figures took his position for the first of his three trials and studied the roughened soil. The shard marking the longest earlier jump now seemed far away. He bent his right knee as he leaned back and put his left foot forward. He held the two weights in front of his body with his arms extended as far as he could manage. He listened to the aulos and began to sway slightly to its steady rhythm. When he felt completely ready, he ran rapidly forward, making sure that he left the ground just before reaching the starting line, shoving the weights toward the ground to provide extra lift. As soon as he was airborne, he pumped his legs, then tucked his feet and pulled the weights forward. At what he believed to be his highest point he swung his feet forward. As soon as his legs were completely extended, he swung both weights behind with all his strength. During this maneuver, his speed increased slightly. He bent his knees a little and landed feet down in the roughed up soil. He was delighted to see that he had cleared the marker for the previous longest jump. He thought: I may be a winner after all. He handed his shard to the judge to mark the distance, retrieved his weights, and hurried back.

Before *Eureka!*

Again he extended his arms to lift the weights, and swayed to the melody. Again he ran, jumped, released the weights, and landed. But he was disappointed. He had jumped half a foot shorter than his first try. As he picked up the weights and headed back toward the start, he replayed every portion of the jump in his mind. He had not made any big error, but each phase had been executed with less intensity than the first time. He had been too sure of another success.

He lined up for the third time and rocked to the melody for several seconds before starting to run. He was taking a chance that the judge would strike him for lingering, but he needed the time to concentrate. His arms stretched so far that they seemed to have grown longer. He made a last-second decision to keep the weights in front of his body as he left the ground instead of swinging them downward. He gained more speed and distance by pushing back on the weights at the end. In the air he pumped his legs as before, using the motion that makes a swing rise. Finally, he flung his weights backward with all the speed he could muster, releasing them as soon as his arms were extended completely behind him.

Figures was surprised not to see the marker as he landed, but then he saw it behind him. His third jump was at least a foot longer than the first. As the judge moved his shard to the new location, he had time to see his whole family, including Hiero. His father, mother, and Hiero were all standing in excitement, although that was improper for Hiero as an official. Figures waved to them, then took his weights over by the wall where the other boys were standing.

Figures' marker was not moved as the next few jumpers took their turns. Then one of the older boys, tall and skinny like Figures, but several inches taller and as thin as Phyllis, leaped past Figures' mark on his second jump, and past his own winning marker on the last jump. Eventually three other older boys also jumped farther than Figures, but none came close to surpassing the tall, skinny one. Figures thought that he had jumped farther than Narcissus at least, although not by much. He was beginning to think that he might win the long jump in the next Games.

⬟ The next Games were four years away, however. Today he had to compete in the javelin toss. The first of the boys had already wound the leather thong carefully around his javelin and was standing with his right hand on the shaft while the left held the tip of the thong to keep it from untwisting prematurely. He pushed the javelin through a long arc as he ran toward the starting line. As he released the shaft, he continued to hold the end of the leather thong, so that the javelin began to spiral, and its arc expanded. The javelin traveled most of the way across the stadium. A judge ran over and marked the landing spot. Each boy would be allowed five tosses.

Figures worried as he waited for his turn, sure this would be his least successful event; there were many different ways his toss could go wrong. Instead of watching the other boys, he rehearsed each step in his mind over and over, but when it became his turn, he made serious errors on each of the five tosses.

- For the first, the thong, not wound properly, became tangled as he tried to throw, causing the javelin nearly to pierce one of his feet.
- He took much more time with the second try, carefully winding the thong and earning a tap from the judge for delay, but he managed to lose his grip on the thong as he ran. The throw, with no help from the thong, was very short.
- For his third try, he overcompensated and held the thong so tightly that he released too late and the distance was even less than the second.
- Then for the fourth throw he threw the javelin too early and it soared high in the air. He heard Narcissus call from the sidelines "You need distance, not height."
- Figures had one last chance to redeem himself, but he was totally rattled. Although he wound the thong correctly and held on until the proper moment for releasing, he became

so concentrated on what his hands and arms were doing that his feet tangled with each other as he released the javelin. He fell on his face and did not see the missile fly past his previous mark.

He was sure that he was the only athlete who had ever fallen while throwing. His place in Syracuse history would be assured, Figures the Faller.

Figures slowly got up and returned to the line of boys. This was worse than being kidnapped. He was not surprised when the other boys began to taunt him. "Figures, you throw like a girl—when you can keep standing!" "Figures, guess the javelin is smarter than you are." "Figures, are you still wrapped in your thong?" "Hey, Figures. Show me how you did that. I want to throw my javelin into the ground, too." Not all the boys called out to him—the older ones did not know him, and Jason was clearly embarrassed for his friend.

Narcissus just said, "If I was that bad, I would go home and kill myself." This idea struck Figures more as good advice than the insult it was meant to be. He pretended not to care what the boys were shouting, but of course he heard everything.

Jason proved to be the leader among the younger boys at the javelin toss—he had done well in the discus, too, so his incessant practicing had paid off. But as in the other events, the winner was one of the older boys.

⬟ None of the boys near Figures' age had won an event, so none wrestled, which took place on the following day. Since a different boy had won each of the first four events, the wrestling took place in two phases. The four winners put their shards in a jar and a judge reached in to determine which boys would pair up. After these two matches, a final match determined the pentathlon winner. The boy who had won the foot race was given the crown of laurel leaves. Figures was surprised when Phyllis emerged from the tunnel to present the crown to the winner. He hoped that she had not seen his terrible performance with the javelin toss.

Normally a young girl would not have been allowed to see the competitions, but Artemis' priestess had her special role in the Games. He was glad that Hypate at least had not been there to witness his disgrace. It was bad enough that his father, mother, and Hiero had seen him falter and fall.

⬟ After the pentathlon completed, the crowd in the stadium swelled considerably. The pentathlon proceeded too slowly to interest the larger audience. The one-stadium and two-stadium races provided more excitement—and more betting. Many timed their arrival at the boys' Games so that they could watch the wrestling and the ceremony for the pentathlon winner and then the two races.

Figures walked over to Jason and Narcissus, who were discussing the upcoming races. Narcissus said, "I am entered in these. Do you know how the races will be set up?"

Jason said, "Yes. I am entered also. This year, 37 boys are in the one-stadium race. The first section will be 18 boys, while the second will be 19. We all will have to draw new shards to see where we compete."

Narcissus said, "Well, I expect to be in the third group as well as one of the first two." Figures knew that he meant that he expected to compete in the two-person match between the winners of the first two.

Jason said, "That is not likely—the older boys always win. You might get into the finals in the two-stadium race, however. Since all 37 boys also entered the two-stadium race, it will be run in 3 sections of 9 boys each plus a final section of 10 boys, so there will be the four winners competing. "

Figures said, "You have twice as many chances to win, Narcissus."

Narcissus said, "Even I can figure that one out. But in any case, I am really good at racing and should be able to beat anyone in Syracuse."

⬟ Figures and the other boys who were not racing left the field and joined the audience, where most found their fathers. He was so unhappy about his terrible javelin tosses that his success in the long jump had receded from his mind, so he was surprised when Phidias said, "Congratulations, son. I did not realize you had gotten so good."

"But Father, I fell down when I was throwing the javelin."

"That's not so bad. Some of the best athletes put so much effort in their throws, both for the discus and the javelin, that they fall. But you really have to learn how to wind and unwind the thong a lot better." As they talked, they followed the crowd as it moved toward the finish line for the one-stadium race.

Figures suddenly decided that he would enter the next Games. He might win the long jump. He could improve the way he tossed the javelin. He thought: I had better practice my wrestling more; I might win the long jump next time.

Now the crowd fell silent. The first section of the one-stadium race was about to begin. The starter cried out "Foot to foot" and then "Go." By the time Figures started paying attention, the race was underway. He looked for Narcissus and Jason. Jason was running but Narcissus was on the sidelines. Faunus, however, was in the first section with Jason. Figures held his breath in during the whole race, then exhaled at the finish when an older boy that he did not know won the heat. The second section now moved into place. Narcissus had drawn a position near the middle of the 19 runners. Figures counted from the first place and decided that Narcissus must be kappa, the tenth letter. Ten is a lucky position according to Pythagorean beliefs, but not a good place for a race—the first position, alpha, had the greatest advantage.

When the race started, Figures tried to keep his eye on Narcissus, but it was difficult to locate one Greek boy in the middle of nineteen naked runners. He thought the racers would be easier to follow if each boy wore a colored ribbon. Bright colors would be easy to tell apart; red, orange, green, blue, purple. But there were not enough bright colors. Duller colors would have to be used to make enough, such as black, white, brown, and gray. If there were two shades each of red, green, and blue, it totaled 12 colors. Or each runner could wear two colors—striped ribbons, or a ribbon around the neck and a different color around the waist. If the two colors had to be different, each of the 12 colors could match with any one of the other 11, so there would be 123 different combinations, plenty for any contest.

By the time he had thought this through the race was over. He looked to see if Narcissus was the winner, but once again it was an older boy.

Then the most exciting part of the one-stadium race took place. The two winners from each section lined up in the alpha and beta positions. With just two runners, it would be much easier to watch. It seemed to Figures that the runners were ready, but the officials were taking a lot of time to set up the wooden bars. He said to his father, "Those judges are very slow."

"They want to be sure there is enough time for everyone to place their bets. More money changes hands on the final one-stadium race than on any other event."

The bettors were right about this race. It really was very exciting, even when you knew nothing about the runners.

After the race ended, Phyllis brought the crown to the winner. Everyone applauded as she placed it on his head. As soon as the winner had the crown, she returned to her tunnel. Figures guessed that she must be able to see the Games so that she would know when to come out with the crown. He hoped she wasn't looking during his struggles with the javelin.

⬟ Now the first section of runners for the two-stadium race was lining up along the finish line of the previous race. In the two-stadium race, the runners used the same track as for the one-stadium race, but turned at the end of the track and came back to their starting lines. Unlike the runners in the one-stadium race who bumped into each other for better position, the runners in this race were required to stay in their lanes. This start was also the finish.

An older boy won the first section of nine runners. Jason had been one of the racers in that section, so now he was through for the day. Since his father was busy as a judge, and boys were forbidden to join their mothers in the women's section, he joined Figures and Phidias in the stands.

Narcissus was in the second section. When the race started most of the runners tried to pace themselves so that they did not run out of energy halfway through the contest, but Narcissus took a different approach, running flat out from the start. As a result, he was the first to reach the end of his lane and turn around. Despite the many quarrels he and Narcissus had, Figures began to cheer for him to win. He noticed that unlike the other runners, Narcissus did not flail his arms as he ran, but instead carried them down at his side, elbows bent and fingers curled into a fist.

In the second half of the race, the older and taller boys began to run much faster, and soon were gaining on Narcissus. But he was able to maintain his fast pace throughout the race and won the heat by a step in front of the closest competitor. Figures by then was jumping up and down and shouting.

For Figures at least, the third and fourth sections were much less exciting. He was already looking toward the final match when the four winners of the heats would compete. Phidias commented. "I don't think the bettors will lay much money on that young boy who won the second heat. He did everything wrong and was lucky to win once. I suspect that none of the really good runners were in the second group with him."

Figures began calculating the chance that none of the best runners would be in one of the four heats, but it was hard to do without a place to draw diagrams. "I'll work it out later," he thought, for now the winners of the heats were ready to race. The judge called "foot to foot" and the four competitors raised their arms. At "go" they took off. All four runners started off at a much faster pace than usual. By the turn, Narcissus was in fourth place by one step going in and behind by two steps after the turn.

On the run back, as Figures jumped and cheered him on, Narcissus steadily gained on the three other runners. Toward the finish line, one of the older boys began to slow down from fatigue and breathlessness, and Narcissus passed him. Encouraged, he also passed another boy, but that was not enough. The race was over and an older boy won.

Phidias said, "That's it for this year. But I think that you have a chance to win the long jump four years from now. But remember, as much fun as the Games are, you cannot let them be more important than your studies. Let's find your mother and go home."

They hurried out and did not wait for Phyllis to crown the winner.

⬟ At home, everyone gathered in the courtyard. Phidias and Andromeda told Hypate and Claudia about the Games, although they omitted describing Figures' embarrassing failures in the javelin toss. Phidias also told of the young boy who had run so well, and Figures supplied his name since Hypate knew Narcissus. Jason also was praised for his showing in the javelin toss and discus throw. Andromeda, who had never been to the Games before, had many questions about how the events were organized and what the rules were. Hypate knew some of the answers because she had watched the boys practice so often.

Andromeda said, "Your friend Phyllis certainly looked poised and mature."

Hypate said, "What was Phyllis doing there? I thought only the boys' mothers could see the Games."

Phidias said, "In Syracuse, the priestess of Artemis is always at the Games. She crowns all the winners."

Hypate looked a little unhappy at learning this, so Figures tried to soothe her feelings, saying, "But Hypate, I don't think she actually saw the Games. She had to wait in the tunnel until a contest was over. Then she would come out and give the winner a crown of olive leaves."

Hypate said, "So she had to walk out in front of everybody in the stands. I don't think I would like doing that."

Figures, however, thought that Hypate would have liked to be the center of attention.

⬟ In the next several days, as talk of the Games continued—the slaves all knew more about the actual winners than Figures did—Figures felt that he should spend more time with Hypate, who clearly felt left out. Before this, Hypate always seemed to be wherever he was. Now she seemed to be avoiding him. He could not think of activities the two might share. After her long trip across the entire island of Sicily, she showed little interest in walking in the woods.

Instead of cheering up Hypate, Figures began to spend more time on mathematics. He felt that he did not have to practice his sports for the next couple of years. He re-read the works of Hippocrates of Chios, who had found a way to construct a square equal to a particular curved figure, and of Hippias of Eliis, who had found a curve that could separate an angle into three equal parts. But he was especially interested in some mathematical papers he found among the Pythagorean scrolls that Phidias kept hidden in his scroll cabinet. These included a work by Archytas of Tarentum on how to make a cube exactly twice the volume of a given cube.

The problem had a long history. Many years earlier a serious plague affected Athens. Apollo is the god of good health, so the Athenians went to Apollo's temple on Delos, the birthplace of the god, to ask how to halt the disease. The priest reported that Apollo wanted to have the size of his altar, a perfect cube, doubled; then he would rid Athens of the plague. The Athenians dutifully made a new altar with every side twice the size of the old one. The plague only became worse. The priest asked, "Why did you not do as

Apollo asked? He required you to double the size of the altar, and you have made it eight times as large. This has offended all the other gods and goddesses, who have agreed that the plague should continue." The Athenians now consulted mathematicians. The mathematicians who agreed that the new altar had eight times the volume of the old, but they found that they were unable to find a way to construct a cube with twice the volume of one that had been given. The plague continued. Finally, Archytas became the one who as a young man found the way to double the cube properly, although by then the gods had tired of the plague and it had already ended.

Figures studied the way Archytas doubled the cube and wondered about doubling other figures. It was easy for Figures to find a way to double a square—making a new square on the diagonal of the given square did the trick, a version of the Pythagorean theorem. Thinking of squares reminded Figures of the Bellyache game. If he had two sets of Bellyache tiles, could he use the pieces to make a square double the area of the square made from one set of tiles?

He decided to find out. He had his own set and of course Phyllis had a set. He had Herc lend him hers. It took only a few seconds to see that the larger square could not be constructed. He needed to have the side of the larger square equal to the diagonal of the original square, which was not available from any combination of tiles. Since he could not make the large square, he began to move the tiles around to see if he could make some sort of interesting shape from the two sets taken together.

⬟ Hypate stopped by his doorway and said, "I am glad to see someone is here. I don't know where your father and mother have gone, but apparently they took the household slaves with them."

"They are visiting Hiero and Philistis. I think Dromio and Luce were going to fix a special dinner, or something like that. I thought you went with them."

"I thought I would stay here with you." She stepped through the doorway and asked, "Is that what you are studying? It looks like a game."

"It is a game, called the Bellyache because some people get sick trying to play with it. I am trying to see what can be done with two Bellyache sets combined. Each set has 14 pieces of different shapes. With one set you can make as simple a shape as a square or as complicated a one as an elephant. Come, let me show you."

Within a few seconds he had moved the tiles from his own set into a square. "I think there are hundreds of different ways to make these squares." And he took the tiles from Phyllis' set and moved them almost as fast into a different pattern that still had the overall square shape. "See, here are two that are totally different."

Hypate said, "Let me have one of the Bellyaches. I think I can make a flying bird." And, after a few false starts, she succeeded. "This is fun. What else can we make?"

Just at that moment they heard heavy footsteps outside the doorway.

⬟ "There they are!" a man shouted, and four persons poured through the doorway into Figures' small room. Although it had been years since he had seen them, Figures immediately recognized Malchus and the pirate Atban. Atban had a large knife in his hand. The two strangers, carrying bundles, looked mean as well, especially one with a prominent scar across his face. The other looked inhuman because his hair was braided in long ropes that appeared coated in mud.

Hypate recognized Malchus and Aneabal, too, exclaiming "Malchus! What has happened to my mother?" as she recoiled toward the far wall of the room, then began to slide toward the doorway.

Malchus said, "I traced you here. Baal does not take it lightly when his sacrifices fail. Bad fortune has plagued Carthage since Archimedes escaped and it has gotten much worse since you got away. Take them, men." The men behind Malchus and Atban stepped forward with nets and hoods.

Hypate stuck both her arms up high to make it more difficult for anyone to put a net over her and kicked Scarface, who was trying to capture her. But Malchus stepped behind her and pulled her arms down, while Scarface lurched to one side to avoid another kick and then pulled the net over her head and shoved her to the floor.

Atban's knife was at Figures' throat. He considered trying to kick Atban, but immediately decided he had a better chance of living if captured. He simply asked, "What do you want now?"

Atban did not answer, but Mudlocks slipped the net over Figures head as Atban withdrew the knife and pinioned Figures' arms. Within seconds, the men had pulled hoods over Hypate and Figures' heads. Figures could not see through the cloth.

Malchus said, "You are not going to escape so easily this time, Archimedes. You both will be taken off this island before anyone knows you are gone. Then I can sacrifice you properly."

Atban growled, "Don't waste time with threats. Both these children escaped before, so let's get them safely aboard ship. We can be out of the harbor and on our way to Carthage in an hour."

Figures tried to struggle with the net as he had the first time these two had trapped him, but clearly this net was much stronger than that first simple fishing net. He was unable to move his arms or legs as he felt himself being lifted up by four strong hands and carried out of the house.

⬟ Figures was carried along a rough path. The bag over his head interfered with his breathing and added to his terror. It felt like drowning again. He tried to calculate their chance of escaping death but did not know where to start. Phyllis would have said that Artemis had rescued him from Malchus and Atban when they had him before, and he would be saved again, but he did not believe that gods had anything to do with it. He had been *lucky* not to have been drowned. Everyone's luck sooner or later runs out.

The men occasionally broke the sound of heavy footsteps and occasional grunts with short comments.

"This way," someone said.

"Give me a hand with the girl. She's heavier than that skinny boy."

"It was easier to carry her by myself."

"Not far now."

"Good. My arms are numb."

The distinctive smell of the sea began to penetrate his hood. Then someone said, "Toss them in the boat."

Figures fell onto a hard surface. His shoulder and elbow radiated pain throughout his body. There was a loud thump next to him, and he heard Hypate cry out. He asked, "Are you all right?"

"Quiet!" one of the heavy voices commanded. A boot crashed into Figures side.

Through the pain, he could feel and hear the boat scraping along the sand, and soon he heard the sounds of oars and waves splashing.

Malchus said, "I thank Baal that not only will I bring Him the runaway girl but I can also bring the wretched Archimedes to the altar. They will not escape Baal this time."

For a long while all Figures heard was oars rowing and the boat moving though the waves. Then he felt and heard a sharp bump. Someone said, "Get the hook. Haul these two on board." He felt a sharp point poke his back, then the net pulled tight around his arms and snapped his head back. He felt rough hands gave him a shove. First he was flying and then he was falling. His head hit something hard. A loud clang filled his skull. Then there was nothing, and then he was among the stars.

SCROLL 16

⬟ Figures began to feel something. He was being pushed and shoved. When he tried to push back, he kicked something.

Hypate's voice. "Keep still. I thought you were dead, but you don't have to kick me to prove you are alive. Sit up so that I can get the net off. Hold your hands at your sides so your fingers don't get caught."

Figures' feet and legs were free of the net. He struggled to sit up. When he succeeded, he felt the net slide up his body and off his head, causing a sharp pain as it passed over the back of his head. The bag around his head was lifted. His head ached fiercely.

"Are you all right?" said Hypate.

"My head is really sore. What happened?"

"We were lifted onto the ship with a hook, then dropped. I was lucky to land on my behind, but I think you hit your head."

"How did you get out of the net?"

"When we were lifted out of the boat, the hook tore part of the net. I found the hole and could reach to the string that tied the net shut."

Figures said, "I had a strange dream. I saw stars."

"People who bump their heads hard often see stars."

"These were real stars, but instead of being points of light, each star was a ball floating in space. They were not fixed to the inside of a sphere; they floated in space. I was floating among them. I was trapped among the stars. I had to move them aside to escape. I had a very long lever, like when I was trapped in the cave with Phyllis.

""I could use one star to rest the lever on and then use the lever to move another star. I needed a place to stand, so I stepped onto one of the larger spheres. At first I wasn't able to move the other star. Then I was able to make the lever longer and actually moved a star. But there was still no way

Before *Eureka!*

for me to escape. I had to move more stars. Then I woke up, and you were taking me out of the net."

"Do you think your dream is a clue that might help us escape? We are trapped."

"I doubt it. Where are we?"

"On board a ship at sea, but tossed down a hole. I think it's open at the top, although the night is so dark it is hard to be sure. Maybe there is a stair or ladder up. Let's see what we can find out. You move around the walls starting left and I'll go around the other way." For a few seconds they didn't try to talk as they reached up and down and worked their way around the wall until they bumped into each other.

Figures said, "No sign of a stair or a door on my side."

"Nor mine. And the walls are slick. There is no way we could crawl up to the opening."

"Maybe if you stood on my shoulders, you would be able to reach the top and lift yourself out."

"You weigh less than I do. I am strong enough to hold you if you can climb up."

Figures said, "I am stronger than you think. I'll crouch down and you get on my shoulders."

They tried this according to Figures' plan.

Hypate asked, "Are you standing straight now?"

Figures replied, "Yes. Can you reach the top?"

"No, it is still about a foot away.

After this for a long while the two sat on the floor in silence as they tried to think of some way to escape. Figures rejected one idea after another. Finally he said, "I have an idea. We can tie the nets and masks into a sort of a rope and throw the top over the edge in hope it will catch something."

But when they did the best they could without a knife to make long strips, the nets were not long enough to reach the edge. Figures remembered how Phyllis had used her clothing in the cave to tie sticks together for a longer lever. Figures said, "We can take off our clothes and tie them on the bottom. Then the nets should reach."

Quickly they disrobed and tied the two chitons to one

end of their nets. But as soon as they began to throw the makeshift "rope" at the top, a sailor appeared and looked down at them. He caught the nets that had reached the top.

"Hey!" he said in Punic. "You stay down there until Malchus is ready for you." He pulled the cloth up and took a knife from his belt, then cut the nets off from the chitons. He tossed the still-tied-together chitons down and added, "Get dressed. We don't want anything to go on. Baal prefers virgins, although I suspect that, like the rest of us, He takes what he can get." With that the sailor disappeared.

Figures said, "They are guarding us. I don't have another plan, do you?"

Hypate had gone beyond tears now. "No, but we will find one. " A long time passed with no new ideas and Figures found himself nearly falling asleep.

⬟ A woman spoke to them from the top of their container. "Hypate? Are you there? Talk to me."

Hypate jumped up. "Who is that? I know that voice." She cried, "Is that you, Mother?"

The woman whispered, "Quiet. No one knows that I can walk around the ship. I watched until your guard fell asleep, but he will awaken if he hears us talking."

Hypate said to Figures, "That voice sounds like my mother. But it can't be. She is dead."

The woman continued, "Even if you could get out of the cistern, you would still be on the ship. I can't steal any weapons, but I can give you this. Reach up and take it so it does not make any noise."

Figures stretched his hands up in the general direction of the voice until his fingers touched something cold and hard. He grabbed a thin edge and pulled it down. As it scraped against the sides of their prison it rang softly but like a piece of metal."

"What's this?" he asked.

"Think of a way to use it. Now I have to get back. Your guard is stirring." With that, she was gone.

Hypate said, "What did she give us?"

"I don't know exactly: A piece of metal, I think, but too thin to use as a weapon. We really need a ladder, but this isn't it. Maybe we could use it as a shield. Do you think that was your mother?"

"It sounded like her voice, but the last time I saw Mother, she had stabbed herself to distract Malchus so I could escape. I thought she died. If she lived, Malchus could still be keeping her with him. Do you think we could rescue her?"

"We can't even rescue ourselves. I believe we are going to be carried to an altar on some mountain and sacrificed to Baal. Even if my family has discovered that we are gone, they won't know where we are, not even that we are on a ship. They might guess we were taken from Syracuse by sea. But they can't find us in the middle of the sea. We are doomed," Figures said.

⬟ Dawn arrived. A thin sheet of metal leaning against the wall gleamed gold in the early morning light.

Hypate asked, "What can we do with this piece of metal?"

"This copper sheet? It bends easily into any shape, but I can't think of a shape that would save us."

Hypate looked out the top of their prison. "The sun is very bright on the sail. We soon should be able to see the sun down here. Then it will get hot."

Figures repeated the phrase "get hot" and closed his eyes for a few seconds. Opening them, he said, "I know something we can do with a copper sheet, but I don't see how it will save us. It might cause us to die even earlier. But that would be better than being sacrificed to Baal. One way they sacrifice to the god is to put a person into a metal image that has many sharp blades projecting from its inner wall. Then the Carthaginians close it, putting all the blades into the sacrifice at once. They place the metal image over a fire to complete the job."

"I am willing to take any chance to avoid Baal and his

wicked priests. What can you do with the sheet?"

"I can set the sail on fire."

"That doesn't seem like a good idea. Why would you do that?"

"I am not sure what would happen. I can't think of any way to escape from here, but we might have a chance under different conditions. The pirates would certainly try to put a fire out. We might find a way to escape in the confusion. Maybe when everyone is fighting the fire, your mother, or whoever that woman was, can get free and help us get out of here. But the ship might burn and us with it. I don't know what will happen, but somehow we will be better off in a burning ship than if we do nothing."

"How can you set the ship on fire? Copper is not hard enough make a spark, and our walls and floor are wood. You need stones and tinder to start a fire."

"I know another way. We'll bend the copper sheet so that it concentrates light. When the sun appears, we'll direct concentrated sunlight toward the sail. Sunlight aimed at a tiny spot becomes very hot. The spot will burst into flame. I have done it with curved bright metal and wood shavings."

Hypate said, "I wish we had a better plan. Your idea might distract the sailors when they see the sail burning, but we still would be down in this hole. If I thought they had human feelings, they might pull us out before we burn. But they might just think that this is another way to sacrifice us."

"Better to burn honestly than to be sacrificed to a false god. Let's do it."

Figures described the shape he wanted and she helped him work with the copper. When they finished, it looked like the top of a mushroom. Soon after, the sun appeared over the edge of their prison.

⬟ When the sun became completely visible Figures moved the copper mushroom so that it reflected the sun's rays onto the sail.

Figures said, "Look! There is the white spot from the sun

on the sail." Figures moved the mushroom around, and the spot of bright light expanded and contracted. "We need the place where the sun's image is smallest." He soon found it and held the copper so that it stayed with the spot.

Hypate said, "I can see a hole in the sail." The small hole replaced the bright spot and began to grow larger. "Is it a fire? I don't see any flame."

"The sun is so bright that the flames can't compete. But it is burning." The hole, now ringed with black, continued to grow. Soon they could see smoke.

Figures moved the copper mushroom so that he could start another fire on a different part of the sail. When that was flaming, he aimed at a third spot. Very quickly the whole sail was aflame, sending up a column of smoke. Soon the ship itself would be on fire.

⬟ Figures and Hypate heard sailors rushing to put out the fire. They could see water splashed onto the lower parts of the sail, but the fire was moving upward and out of reach. The sail dropped to the deck as sailors cut the ropes holding it in place. Now the pirates could pour water on the whole sail, but the upper portion of the mast was already on fire. Figures did not think that the pirates could easily put out the blazing mast.

"Look!" Hypate said. She pointed where a rope from the fallen sail dropped into their cistern. Figures grabbed it and pulled hard. The rope did not give—it was still connected to something on the deck.

"Can you climb?" Figures asked. At Hypate's nod "yes," he grabbed the rope with both hands and, pushing his feet against the wall, was able to reach the top of the cistern. Hypate was right behind him.

"Keep low and look around before we stand," Figures said, "We need to find a place to hide."

⬟ All the sailors, including Malchus and Atban, were busy fighting the fire. Most were splashing water on parts of the sail to keep it from igniting the deck. Two pirates with axes were chopping the base of the burning mast, while others pulled at a rope attached high up on the mast.

Hypate said, "This is the same ship where Mother and I were held prisoner. I'll bet that Malchus is holding Mother in the same room where we were kept Follow me." Hypate, keeping her head low, quickly entered the nearest opening to below decks, with Figures close behind. They descended a ladder to the deck below. She looked around for a second and then started down a passage into the ship's interior. She stopped at a door and said, "This was the prison room."

Just at that moment, there was a loud boom and the ship lurched as the falling mast struck the side and then fell into the water.

Figures pulled at the door, although he expected it to be locked. To his surprise, after it caught for a second, it opened. A woman about the same age as his mother was inside, sitting on a bench that was the only furniture in the room. She immediately rose up and said, "Hypate?"

Hypate rushed to the woman and threw her arms around her. "Mother. I thought you were dead."

Figures closed the door behind them, pulling the worn wooden lock beyond the jamb. "That lock is too short to work." He looked again as Hypate's mother, Claudia. She was beautiful like the girl who had appeared before Pyrrhus near Arethusa's fountain, but she seemed worn and the Phoenician-style dress she was wearing seemed far too large for her thin body. But, as thin as she was, he could not help but notice her breasts, larger than those of Greek women and still firm and pointed. Her complexion was darker than most Greeks, her eyes were large and widely spaced, and her lips were full and red.

Figures took his eyes off her body and said, "Thank you, Claudia, for the copper sheet. With it we escaped from the cistern, but I have no idea how we can escape from here. Even if we could kill Malchus, Atban, and their whole crew, we would be left on a ship somewhere in the sea, we don't know where. The ship has no mast or sail in any case. Our best hope is to be killed here instead of being sacrificed to Baal."

Claudia said, "I had a dream about seeing Hypate in the cistern. I dream about Hypate almost every night. Last night seemed like just another. I don't know anything about a copper sheet, although in the dream there was some bright, shiny thing. I can't imagine where any copper came from. If it wasn't a dream, I must have been walking in my sleep. If I were awake and really saw Hypate, I would never leave her. But in my dream, I just walked away. Maybe I was enchanted. I often dream I am Persephone, the Queen of the Underworld. Hades kidnapped Persephone just as I have been kidnapped, and Hades treated her both as a wife and a prisoner, as Malchus treats me. Persephone was rescued by her mother, but I seem to have been rescued by my daughter."

Hypate said, "We will rescue you from Malchus's Underworld. This is my friend Archimedes; he and his family saved me after I wandered all across Sicily. We all must escape from Malchus. Then you no longer will be Persephone, but will stay as my mother forever."

⬟ Suddenly, there was a huge bump. All three of them were thrown off their feet. The shouting and general commotion became much louder. Figures guessed that with everyone fighting fires, the sailors might not have paid attention to where the ship was heading, and it struck a reef. They might be sinking. Instead of dying in the fire, they might drown. After his experience in the cage, Figures was more frightened of drowning than of fire. Being inside the ship was not that different from being in the cage if the ship sank.

"We had better go on deck," he said. "The ship hit something. It may be sinking. We have no chance to survive down here if it sinks. Better to see if there is a chance to swim to safety."

Hypate said, "But we can't go on deck. Malchus and

Atban will see us. They would kill us rather than let us escape again."

Figures said, "We should look for some weapons. We could be stuck on a rock. If we can get off the ship, we might reach land. The pirates have been fighting fires or maybe trying to escape a sinking ship. They probably don't have their swords with them."

Claudia said, "I can show you where Atban lives. He must have a sword or knife. Follow me."

They re-entered the passage. A lamp swung from the ceiling, the only light below decks. Although it was dimly lit, Hypate noticed something in the passage.

Hypate said, "It's a weapon. Do you know how to use that thing?" She pointed to a big crossbow mounted on wheels and armed with a metal spear.

Figures said, "It's a catapult. I know how to use it. I used to make catapults myself. It's supposed to shoot that spear into a wall to make a hole, but we need something for hand-to-hand fighting. Even the spear is too heavy to use."

Claudia said, "There might be something more useful in Atban's room. Follow me." They reached a closed door. "This is Atban's room."

Before they could enter Atban's quarters, however, Atban himself rushed out, carrying a sword in his right hand and a dagger in his left. He ran past, saying. "I'll deal with you later." He swiftly mounted the ladder to the deck.

⬟ Hypate said, "Listen! Hear the fighting up on deck. What's going on?"

Figures said, "Stay here. I'll climb up and see what's happening." As soon as he could see the deck, he said, "It is a fight. Another ship rammed us. Men from that ship are fighting with the pirates. I think they are Greek soldiers. We are better off down here than up there. If they are soldiers, they are probably better fighters than pirates."

Hypate said, "Are you sure they are soldiers? Maybe they are just pirates themselves."

Claudia said, "I hope they are Greek. I cannot live much longer with Carthaginians."

The three listened quietly. They heard screams among the sounds of fighting. Suddenly they were startled as a figure started down the ladder from the deck. Figures looked for anything he could use as a weapon. He grabbed the lamp, pulled it off its hook, and raised it to strike the intruder.

With the lamp raised, he saw that the intruder was Phyllis, who said, "Figures! I was sure we would find you here. Stay here until Hiero and his men take the ship. The pirates are losing, but they don't stop fighting."

Figures said, "Hiero is here, too? How did you find us?"

Phyllis replied, "We found the Bellyaches you left. Your clues showed you were on a ship. I knew as soon as I saw the two designs."

"Clues? I don't even remember what we were doing with the Bellyaches when we were captured. How did you find any clues?"

Phyllis explained, "Everyone was at a special dinner to celebrate Hiero's engagement to Philistis. Herc and I were left at home so we walked over to your house to see what we might do for fun. But your house was empty. I went into your room and saw the two Bellyaches. I knew right away it was an important message. The arrow pointed to a ship. For some reason you had gone to a ship."

Hypate interrupted, "I don't remember making an arrow or a ship. I made a bird. Then Figures was going to show me some other shapes."

Figures said, "I could have made an arrow. That's one of the easy shapes to make. I don't even know how to make a ship."

Phyllis said, "Well, someone did. I saw the arrow pointing at something that looked like a ship to me. I was sure it was a message. I told Herc that you had gone to harbor. But I wasn't sure which harbor you meant. The small harbor was closer, so we went there.

"When we got to the harbor, we saw a big boat being

rowed out to a ship, not a fishing boat. I said, 'Herc, they are on that boat.' We could see the two men rowing and another two men standing up in the boat. The boat moved close to the ship and people on the ship used a big hook to lift bundles us and swing them over the ship's deck. A man on the ship pushed the bundles off the hook and they fell out of sight. I told Herc 'Those bundles were Figures and Hypate. They've been kidnapped.' I don't know how I knew that, but I was sure of it."

Hypate said, "You guessed right. They dropped us into a cistern. Figures landed on his head and was knocked out. I was afraid that they had killed him."

"They still want to kill me — and Hypate, too."

Phyllis continued, "Herc and I ran to Hiero's house and told everyone that you and Hypate had been taken onto a boat that was sailing out of the small harbor. Hiero ran to one of the warships in the harbor and ordered it to look for you. Your father and I followed him and got aboard the ship, too. We headed out to sea immediately, even though it was night. But Hiero was not sure where to look for you. Your father told Hiero that most likely the ship was headed for Carthage. But the sea is very large and at dawn, we saw nothing but water. Then our lookout saw smoke on the horizon. We headed toward it. Soon we saw this ship with its sails and mast on fire.

"When we were close enough, your father spotted Malchus, so we knew that this burning ship was the right one. We rammed the ship and used grappling hooks to stay fast so we could board. Hiero and his men have been fighting the pirates, but pirates are no match for soldiers. Your father stayed aboard Hiero's ship, but when no one was watching, I slipped down here to look for you. And I found you, too."

Hypate asked, "Do you think it is safe to go up and see what has happened?"

Figures said, "It sounds like the battle has quieted down. Let's go."

Hypate said, "If you want to go up to see what is

happening, you ought to have some sort of weapon. Are you sure that the catapult would be of no use?"

Figures thought it over. He said, "It would take two of us to carry it up. I don't think we could do much with it. If we had it cocked, I suppose the spear could be shot at someone or something, but the spear would travel far beyond the ship. And we would have to make sure that we aimed it so that it did not punch a hole in our ship or, even worse, in Hiero's ship. Remember that the main use of this kind of catapult is punching holes in city walls."

Phyllis said, "I remember when you built a catapult. Let's take this one up on deck with us. Even if it is impractical, it should frighten anyone who tries to attack us. I am sure that the two of us can carry it."

⬟ Figures and Phyllis had to maneuver the catapult up the ladder to get it on deck. At first Figures thought that he should be on the bottom because now he was larger and stronger than Phyllis. But then he realized that if he were on the bottom, Phyllis would be in danger as she emerged on deck, so he decided that he should pull the catapult up the ladder while Phyllis pushed from below. Phyllis, however, argued that Figures was the one whose life was in danger, so she should go first. Hypate agreed with Phyllis, but Figures ended the argument by grabbing the catapult and heading up the ladder. Phyllis had no choice but to push from behind.

Figures reached the deck, followed almost immediately by the other three. Fallen remnants of the burning sail and mast had cast cinders all over the deck. Smoke still rose from several places. Some Greek soldiers were using their swords to chop out pieces of burning wood, then tossing the charred and smoking pieces into the sea. Other Greeks were guarding or tying up pirate prisoners, while one or two battles between the Greeks and the pirates were ongoing.

Figures suddenly recognized that Hiero was one of the Greeks still fighting.

"Look, Phyllis," he cried. "Hiero!"

The pirate attacking Hiero was Atban, who still had his sword. But Atban's dagger was lodged in Hiero's right shoulder, so Hiero was trying to fight Atban with his sword in his left hand. Hiero was not faring well.

As Figures began to search the deck for something he could use to help Hiero, Phyllis cried out, "And there is Malchus!"

She pointed into the sea, where Figures could see a man in a rowboat rapidly leaving the ship. Phyllis continued, "We have to stop him before he escapes."

Figures said, "But first we need to help Hiero. He has just been wounded again. If Atban triumphs, the pirates may win after all." The soldiers and the pirates had stopped fighting to watch Hiero and Atban. Figures remembered how Pyrrhus had changed the course of a battle by winning in single combat.

SCROLL 17

● Phyllis noticed that one of the fallen pirates had a bow and arrow, a weapon she knew how to use well. With the speed of a practiced hunter who sees a stag burst out of the forest, she picked up the bow, tightened the bowstring, and threaded an arrow from the dead pirate's quiver onto the string. Even though it was not her familiar hunting bow, and really too large for a young girl, she drew the bow with a strength born of fear for Hiero and launched her arrow at Atban.

The arrow struck him in the heart and pierced his body, lodging in a rail behind him, for he was fighting without armor. With a fierce cry Atban dropped his sword and plunged to the deck.

Hiero turned to see who had rescued him. Despite pain from the dagger still stuck in his arm and his surprise at seeing Phyllis with the bow in her hands, after a slight pause he cried out, "Thank you."

The pirates saw their leader die. The noise of clashing swords died down, and the pirates began to give up their weapons to Hiero's soldiers.

Figures said, "Can you shoot Malchus before he escapes? Then we will be safe." To Hiero he said, "The man in the boat is Malchus who has twice tried to kill me."

Phyllis picked out a new arrow and threaded it as she ran to the side of the ship. By now Malchus' rowboat was distant and moving rapidly away. Phyllis pulled the bowstring as far back as she could and fired the arrow. But it fell into the sea short of Malchus' boat. Malchus looked back at the splash and began to row faster.

"I think that is the best I can do. My arm already hurts from trying to shoot as far as I can. You may be stronger than I. Do you want to try?"

Figures said, "I have never used a bow."

Hiero said, "I might be able to shoot him at this distance, but I can't even pull the bowstring with my arm wounded.

Pelias is my best archer. Where is he?"

One of the soldiers replied, "Pelias is wounded. I saw him being carried back to our ship. Let me try."

Phyllis handed him the bow and an arrow. He was quick to shoot, but his arrow, while it traveled what appeared to be the whole distance and perhaps even a few feet farther, was to the left of Malchus' boat, which seemed to pick up even more speed as the arrow fell. Phyllis quickly passed the soldier the last arrow from that quiver.

As the soldier drew back the bow, Hypate called out, "Try the catapult." Perhaps the sound distracted the soldier, for this shot not only did not reach the vicinity of the rowboat, but also was off to the right.

Hiero asked, "Do we have a catapult?"

Figures said, "Yes, a small one. I know how to operate it."

⬟ Figures ran to the catapult and said, "Someone give me a spear — no, two spears would work better." Several were immediately thrust at Figure. He took two and placed their points on the deck of the ship while their shafts pressed against the handles used to pull the bowstring of the catapult back. Hanging onto the upper parts of the spears, he leapt onto the back of the catapult and leaned back as far as he could, using the spears as two levers to pull the setting mechanism into place. Hiero, who had also fired catapults before, reached with his left hand between Figures' legs and set the catapult for firing.

Figures jumped down and said, "We have only one missile, so our aim has to be perfect. This is not like breaking down a city wall."

Phyllis said, "Let me aim it. The catapult is just a big bow and I have learned how to shoot a lark out of the sky with a single arrow." She moved behind the catapult and began turning it on its wheels while raising the spear slightly higher by pushing the back of the machine down. " We have to take the roll of the ship into account. I'll say 'foot by foot' when we are almost at the right point and then 'go' when you should release the spear."

Figures grabbed the handle that would loose the spear and waited for Phyllis' command. She let the ship roll twice before saying "foot by foot, go," On "go" Figures let the bronze spear fly.

By this time, Malchus and his rowboat were far from the pirate ship. Everyone's eyes were on the spear as it curved over the sea. One sailor cried out, "It will overshoot."

But he was wrong by inches. Although the spear sailed past Malchus, it hit the front of the rowboat and pierced through the boat's prow. The rowboat quickly began to fill with water.

⬟ Hiero said to one of his soldiers, "Arion, gather a boat crew to capture the pirate. That wooden boat will not sink. He will use it as a raft and cling to it, hoping to drift ashore the way wily Odysseus did after the gods wrecked his ship. I want Malchus safely in our power. Everyone else put these pirates below and guard them. Throw the bodies of the dead overboard before they start to stink. I'll talk to the children and this woman, who seems to be a captive. I want to find out what's going on."

Hiero turned to Figures and asked, "These are the same villains who tried to drown you several years ago. Why did they come back now?"

"They're also the ones who captured Hypate and her mother and tried to kill Hypate. This is Hypate's mother, Claudia, who Malchus kept as a slave."

Hypate said, "Maybe Malchus learned that I survived and was living with his old enemy, Phidias."

Hiero said, "Whatever the reason, they are gone now, and I am delighted to meet Claudia again. You could have been killed long ago, but you survived everything and are still as beautiful as when I met you in Croton." Figures thought that Hiero was saying the last to flatter Claudia, for she looked tired and confused, although Figures also could see that a little rest and perhaps a few meals would restore her to extraordinary beauty.

Phyllis said, "Can a man continue to live in the open sea clinging to a piece of wood? Even if the wood continues to float, Malchus would die of exhaustion and thirst before reaching the shore."

Figures said, "Hiero was right about Odysseus. After his crew angered Zeus, the god caused a great storm to wreck Odysseus' ship and all the crew except Odysseus perished. But Odysseus clung to a piece of wood from the ship. After floating for ten days in the sea, he was cast up alive on the island of Calypso. We don't want to take a chance of that happening to Malchus."

Hiero said, "If he is alive, my men will find him."

⬟ When Hiero's ship returned, Arion reported that Malchus had not been found. "No one clung to the rowboat. My crew turned the rowboat over with one of our oars to make sure. The oars were missing and the prow was shattered, but there was no sign of any person."

Hypate said, "The bronze spear appeared to pass just over Malchus, but it may have grazed his head. That might have knocked him senseless. If he was still breathing, his lungs would have filled with water and he would have sunk out of sight."

Figures said, "Drowning in the sea was the fate he had in mind for me when I was tossed overboard in a weighted cage, so it would be fitting if it happened to him instead."

Hiero said, "We all come close to death many times before the gods take us. It was not your turn or mine, thanks to Phyllis, today. Now let's put up the sails, set a tow line to the pirate boat, and return to normal life in Syracuse."

⬟ Life in Syracuse was not exactly as it had been before the kidnapping, however. First of all, Phidias' household now included Claudia. With a better diet and no more abuse, she soon returned to good health. Her mind did not return to normal as quickly as her body, however. She often was heard screaming from nightmares, wakening and frightening her daughter, who slept in the same room.

Claudia relied on Andromeda for friendship and direction. Phidias at first seemed attracted to Claudia, but appeared to have difficulty conversing with her. After a few days he treated her as he did Hypate and nearly all other women, with a kind of awkwardness and polite reserve—Andromeda appeared to be the only woman with whom Phidias felt totally comfortable.

Figures continued to study the mathematics books that his father had collected, but he also began to create new theorems of his own. His childhood custom of drawing geometric figures on any available surface was ingrained by now.

Figures interrupted his mathematical work each day, however, for a practice session with Jason and Herc for the Games. Even then, however, he tried to find ways to use ideas from mathematics to improve his performance on the five tasks of the pentathlon. Earlier either Phyllis or Hypate would have joined the boys for this daily workout, but now Phyllis spent nearly all her time at the Temple of Artemis while Hypate devoted herself to activities that would engage her mother, hoping to rid her mother of her dark memories and to restore the sunny woman she remembered from before all their troubles began.

⬟ One day Andromeda said to Phidias, "Archimedes is old enough to have an occupation--pentathlon practice and reading mathematics books take all his time. Figures was in the room as Andromeda spoke and resented that she talked about him instead of to him, as if he were three or four instead of fifteen.

Phidias said, "I agree with you. But what can we do?"

Andromeda said, "I spoke to Hiero. Remember how Archimedes was a messenger for Pyrrhus. I asked Hiero to employ Archimedes in the same way now that he is in charge of Syracuse's armies. He said he would be happy to have Archimedes by his side."

Figures said, "I certainly would rather work for Hiero than for Pyrrhus. But I am just beginning to do a lot of mathematics on my own. And Jason and Hero count on me for practice."

Phidias said, "I am sure that Hiero would allow time for study. Being with the army would keep you more fit than the amount of practice you manage these days. Running errands for Hiero would be healthy exercise, and you can do math while you wait for the next errand."

Andromeda said, "Hiero did not plan to have Archimedes run errands. He said Archimedes could devise war machinery. Most soldiers think that whatever worked in the past will work forever. People say the army always plans to fight the last war, not the next one."

"I certainly like being with Hiero, and it would be fun to design war machinery. I would need help building machinery."

Andromeda said, "Good. Then you will do it. It will be better than hanging around here with the women and slaves."

Phidias added, "Consider it part of your education. I sometimes think my life would have been better if I had served as a soldier. I spent my entire life studying and teaching. I missed out on a part of real life, I fear, and now I am too old and settled."

Andromeda said, "And too married — don't forget that."

⬟ Soon after that, Figures was sent to live with Hiero and Philistis in Tyche, the fashionable section of Syracuse. Hiero had married Philistis. Philistis' father Leptines lived with them, but it was a large house and there was plenty of room, even after Philistis gave birth to a boy. Hiero named his son Gelo, after an earlier king of Syracuse. Although Hiero claimed to be a direct descendant of Gelo, Andromeda said she had never heard such a thing about their family.

Figures spent most of every day with Hiero at army

headquarters, eating his meals with the soldiers. Hiero insisted, however, that Figures continue to meet Jason and Herc for training sessions. He now trained for all five pentathlon events. He did not want to be humiliated as he was the year before when he failed so badly in the javelin and racing. And he might really win the long jump, which would put him among the wrestlers.

⬟ Hiero asked Figures for ideas to improve the machines used by the army, such as the siege engines. Siege engines were called "tortoises" by the army. Their armor was like a tortoise's shell that protected the soldiers inside, and these armored towers on wheels moved very slowly--like real tortoises--as the engines were pushed close to the wall of a town under attack. Tortoises contained a few soldiers at the top of the tower. These soldiers could reach the top of a town wall without danger from missiles or boiling oil and leap out from the tortoise onto the wall. The soldiers then held back the town's defenders while the rest of the army rushed forward and used the siege engine as a ladder to reach the top of the wall and swarm into the town.

When Figures observed soldiers practicing with the tortoises, he noticed that the tall, awkward towers on wheels leaned far over if they traveled over the slightest incline. Once he saw the tortoise tip over completely, injuring some of the soldiers; he was told that this happened often in actual battles. He had the carpenters make model tortoises. He glued rocks near the top to represent the weight of the soldiers. By testing the model tortoises on slopes he found that one central point determined whether the model stood or fell. If this point was above the interior of the rectangle formed by the engine's wheels, as determined with a plumb line, the tortoise remained upright, even when tilted. Once that magic point was above a location outside the rectangle, the tortoise toppled.

He decided to enlarge the rectangle formed by the wheels by moving the wheels to the edges of a large platform that extended beyond the tower in all directions. Figures first tested this design with a model. The toppling point was above this platform even on steep slopes, so the model remained upright.

Hiero was delighted when Figures demonstrated that the traditional tower fell over on the side of a hill, nearly crushing the men pushing it. But the one on a platform stayed upright whether pushed uphill or sideways or rolled down a hill. When the front of the platform reached a city wall, the tower was detached from the platform and pushed forward against the wall.

⬟ Shortly after the demonstration of the new kind of tortoise, Hiero summoned Figures just as Figures was returning from his regular practice session with Jason and Herc.

"Figures," Hiero said, "Go home to Andromeda and Phidias. We are going to war."

SCROLL 18

⬟ Hiero continued, "It is necessary for Syracuse to defend itself from the Mamertines, and the best defense will be to surprise the enemy and attack them first. However, you must reassure Andromeda and your father about your safety in this war—and mine as well." Hiero then told Figures how he wanted the experience to be explained to Andromeda and Phidias.

Following Hiero's instructions, Figures started home to say farewell to his parents, Hypate, and Claudia before going into battle. When he reached Epipolae, however, he stopped to tell Phyllis and Herc that he would be traveling with Hiero's army to fight the Mamertines.

Phyllis asked, "Why is Hiero going to attack the Mamertines now? My father told me that the Mamertines killed most of the men in Messana, then took the wives of the dead as their own. But that was about the time I was born. Syracuse has had fifteen years when it could have fought the Mamertines. Now that Hiero and Philistis have a young son, it is a bad time for Hiero to go to war."

Figures said, "Hiero's spies tell him the Mamertines are planning to attack Syracuse as soon as they finish plundering Enna."

Phyllis said, "I will pray to Artemis to shield you and Hiero from harm. She may find a way to keep Syracuse's army safe, since she is our main protector."

Herc said, "I wish I could go with you, Figures, but I am sure that our father would not permit it."

Phyllis changed the subject. "I also have news. Although I am not going into war, it is something similar. Father says I am to be married."

Figures was taken by surprise. Nearly everyone eventually married, but it had not occurred to him that this would apply either to Phyllis or to him. He said, "Married! Who are you going to marry?"

"I don't know, and I don't think Father knows either. He said that I am fifteen and should be married. He will offer me to his friends and see if any will accept me. I told him not to try the father of Narcissus, but Father said Narcissus was already taken."

Figures wondered if he should offer himself as a groom.

After a pause, Phyllis went on, saying, "Don't think about it too much, Archimedes. I don't think Father will find many takers. He will start with the wealthiest and work his way down. That puts your father near the bottom of the list. We may know more when you get back from the war. But you had better go now. You only have one night to be with your parents before you leave."

Figures kissed both Phyllis and Herc and said goodbye, then continued home to tell his parents that he was going to war with Hiero.

⬟ Andromeda said she would stop it. "I will tell Hiero that you cannot go. You are only fifteen. He will listen to me." She raised both her hands in front of her as she spoke, as if trying to stop a cart.

"Hiero told me you would try to prevent my going. He said there is no danger. He will not let me fight. Instead, I will help him with maps and locations for camps. He promised that when fighting starts, I will be kept safely far from the action."

This information did not convince Andromeda, but Phidias took Hiero's side, saying, "Hiero will keep our son safe. And Archimedes will have a chance to travel with the army. He will see the world beyond Syracuse. I think this is an opportunity, not a danger."

Figures could see that his mother was not happy, but she reluctantly abandoned the argument. He suspected that after he was in bed, he would hear more protests if he managed to eavesdrop on his parents. But when he went to bed, he fell asleep without hearing voices from the other bedroom.

● The next day Figures and Hiero started with the army on the journey north to Messana. The natives of Syracuse and the nearby countryside formed the cavalry, long a famous fighting force in Sicily. Hiero rode at the head of the cavalry. Figures marched with the archers and spear bearers; he did not know how to ride. Figures' family had never owned a horse.

His fellow marchers were mercenaries, mostly Celts or tribes of Italians along with a few natives of Sicily, the Sikels. Figures felt an affinity for the Sikels because of Tono, who had saved his life from Malchus. Still it was awkward because Figures could not speak the mercenaries' languages, even Sikel, and few of the mercenaries knew much Greek. Despite this, Figures recognized that the mercenaries were unhappy. He heard Hiero's name mentioned often, and the tone of voice used was far from respectful.

When he found an Egyptian mercenary who spoke Greek, Figures was careful not to identify himself as Hiero's cousin. He said to the Egyptian that he had noticed that the mercenaries seemed unhappy.

The Egyptian said, "We were hired by a great warrior, Pyrrhus. He left us behind and we have had only a small salary instead of rich plunder. Pyrrhus was always fighting, but under Hiero there have been no battles. At last we are going to war but the rumor is that Hiero plans to fight the Mamertines as they travel between towns. When the army takes a town, we reward ourselves with treasure and women. When you fight in the field, there is little plunder, even if you win. The Mamertines are famous warriors who destroy those who oppose them. The risk is great and chance of reward slim. So we are unhappy. Some say we would do better to side with the Mamertines than fight them. After all, they were originally mercenaries, too. We have more in common with them than we do with the horsemen of Syracuse."

● After a few days march north, Hiero encountered Figures with the mercenaries and asked him to start exploring the countryside on horseback and improve the maps they had available.

Figures said, "I don't know how to ride, and in any case I have no horse."

"You should not be marching with Pyrrhus' mercenaries, Archimedes. I will find a horse and someone to teach you to ride. An army moves only as fast as its marchers, so a man on horseback can explore the land and still keep up. You can compare our maps of these territories with the terrain and improve the maps as necessary."

"That would be wonderful. I am not happy being with the mercenaries. They don't like you or the people of Syracuse. I worry that some rabble rouser will lead them to leave you for the Mamertines."

Hiero laughed and replied, "Mercenaries are always unhappy. I should know—I was one myself. Don't worry about rebellion. I have spies among the troops to make sure nothing serious occurs."

⬟ Next day Figures left the mercenaries and began his riding lessons. A young cavalryman named Celphalos taught him. Hiero introduced Celphalos as a relative. When Figures asked Celphalos about the relationship, Celphalos said only that his family claimed descent from Gelo, one of the early rulers of Syracuse. Hiero also claimed descent from Gelo, although the exact line was unclear.

Celphalos was able to locate a docile mount for Figures. Figures was delighted that the horse was named Plato, after the famous philosopher who had once been important to the history of Syracuse and who famously loved geometry. Plato the horse had been named for his placid, philosophical style; he seldom moved fast, stepping methodically through the countryside.

Not only did Celphalos teach Figures to ride, but he also was able to tell him about the region they were mapping, since he had grown up locally. Every natural feature came with a story of the minor god or goddess who had created it by some magical means. They were in a region Odysseus passed through on his way home from the Trojan War. It was once the home of giant cannibals, among them one-eyed Cyclops Polyphemus, who devoured several of Odysseus' crew. The rocky islets in the sea were stones Polyphemus flung at Odysseus and his remaining crew as they escaped.

Figures knew the story from Homer's Odyssey. Polyphemus captured Odysseus and twelve of his crew and kept them in his cave, killing and eating two crewmembers for each meal. But Odysseus used his wiles to make Polyphemus drunk and with the remaining members of his crew put out the Cyclops' single eye. With Polyphemus blinded, the crew were safe but still trapped in the cave that the Cyclops had closed with a giant boulder too heavy for humans to move.

As Figures recalled the familiar story, he had a vivid recollection of how he and Phyllis had been trapped in a cave closed by a boulder. Although there was no Cyclops in the cave intending to eat them, it had been a terrifying experience.

Odysseus and the remaining crewmembers escaped from the cave when the Cyclops let his giant sheep out to graze. Blind Polyphemus felt the top of each sheep as it left the cave to makes sure it had no rider. But each Greek clung to the bottom of a sheep and rode to freedom. After the Greeks escaped from the cave, Odysseus could not refrain from taunting Polyphemus, who blindly threw the giant boulders that became islands in the sea.

⬟   Hiero supplied Figures with his maps of Sicily. Figures rode Plato around the countryside, comparing streams, hills, and villages with positions shown on the maps. He used an astrolabe to measure the height of the Sun or stars, which revealed how far north or south he was. It was more difficult to determine distances east and west so he rode back and forth and guessed at distances.

When he thought he had done the best he could, he went

to Hiero and said, "I have been studying the maps you gave me. They are good near the sea, but not very reliable for inland locations."

Hiero said, " We are to join forces with the Carthaginians, who failed to protect Enna. Their leader, Hanno is prepared to suppress past differences so that both armies can work together to defend Sicily from the Mamertines. We should do this near where the Mamertines will be traveling from Enna to Syracuse. I have been also hiring local scouts who think that the Mamertine army is heading east toward Centuripa. So see if you can locate the best way from here to Centuripa."

Figures already had a map in his hands. "We should aim toward the river Cyamosorus. There is a ridge along the river, and you will have the high ground if you camp there. If the Mamertines attack, you would have the advantage."

Hiero said, "I need to send a messenger to the Carthaginian forces. If we can meet near the Cyamosorus, then we might surround the Mamertine army. Figures, you and Celphalos ride ahead to Cyamosorus with a scout to select a location for the army to set up camp. The scout can then return here to lead the army to the campsite. Remember that the Mamertines also have scouts riding around the countryside, looking for places to plunder, so watch out for strangers on horseback.

"Make a good map that shows where we will camp. Celphalos can carry the map to the Carthaginians. Celphalos should tell the Carthaginians to camp on the other side of the Cyamosorus; we can attack from both sides at once."

● Figures and Celphalos and one of the scouts located a level area near a tributary of the Cyamosorus that would provide water. Figures made two copies of a map showing its location. He gave one to the scout to take to Hiero and the other to Celphalos to take to the Carthaginian army. Because he could not ride fast enough to keep up, he stayed at the campground. As the two rode off with the maps, he found himself alone in what might be enemy territory.

But he was not alone for long. The next morning he heard the sound of horses and splashing coming from the Cyamosorus river, just over the bluff from where he had spent the night. Leaving his horse tethered by the stream, he carefully crept through the trees and bushes to the edge of the ridge. In the distance he could see a large army crossing the river and headed toward him. The army could be the Carthaginians, but they had been told to camp on the other side of the river. These were the Mamertines on their way to attack Syracuse. If they found him, Figures thought, he would most likely be killed.

He decided to hide until Hiero's army appeared. This army, like Hiero's, was surely surrounded by scouts looking for food to plunder and any information available from local people.

He tethered his horse Plato on the ridge where it was screened by a thick stand of bushes. Then he climbed onto a large lower limb of a sycamore, where he thought he would be safe from any scout's eyes. The limb, as large as a tree itself, was a nearly horizontal branch that poked out over the ridge, so he could see the enemy camp from his hiding place. He lay flat on the limb and watched the Mamertines below make camp beside the river.

⬟   As the day grew warmer, Figures wriggled into a fairly comfortable position on the great limb of the sycamore and fell into a shallow sleep. Late in the afternoon, Figures awoke completely at the sound of a creature moving beneath his tree limb. Peering cautiously around the edge of the limb, he saw a man who appeared to be watching, keeping himself hidden as he studied the army camped below the ridge down by the river. He thought it was one of the scouts from Hiero's army, but he was not completely sure. If he was wrong and let himself be discovered by a Mamertine, it would be the end.

Another soldier appeared. The first pointed to the camp by the river and said, "That is the Mamertine army."

The second scout replied, "We should wait at the campground and make sure that our army keeps hidden until we are ready to attack." With that the two scouts melted into the woods and vanished.

Figures did not want to startle armed soldiers, so he waited for a few moments before climbing down, retrieving his horse, and riding into camp, where he found the two scouts and also the first few horsemen from the Syracuse cavalry, who were being briefed by the scouts. As soon as he appeared, the whole party drew their swords and began riding menacingly toward him, but as they drew near, one of the cavalrymen called out, "Hey! It's Archimedes, the mapmaker." Swords were sheathed as several called out his name.

The first of the scouts Figures had seen from the tree said, "This is a fine campground you found for us, Archimedes, but do you know that it just over the ridge is the whole Mamertine army?"

At that point more of the cavalry arrived, including Hiero. The scouts and Figures each described exactly what they had seen. Hiero finally said, "I am still counting on the Carthaginians. I don't think from what you tell me about the size of the Mamertine army that we have good enough mercenaries nor enough Syracusan cavalry to win. We have to draw up a battle plan based on the troops we have. "

⬟ Just after nightfall Celphalos arrived with the Carthaginian Hanno, the general in charge of the Carthaginian troops. Soon after that an aide appeared to summon Figures to Hiero's tent with his whole map collection. When he arrived, he learned that after Hiero asked when the Carthaginians could be in place for the battle, Hanno produced a map showing where he thought his forces were. Because Hanno's map did not resemble Hiero's, Hiero told Hanno that they needed to consult his chief mapmaker.

Hanno asked, "Who is this boy? And why do you think he knows more about where my army is than I do?

Hiero said, "He is Archimedes. Although he is young, he has spent his life making maps and studying the stars and mathematics. I can assure you that his views can be trusted completely."

Hanno argued about the maps for a while and then offered his plan. The Carthaginians would cross the Cyamosorus during the night and move into a position to join the attack from the northwest. The basic idea was clear to all—the Carthaginian troops would mass in the northwest, the Syracuse cavalry would move to a position along the river southeast of the Mamertine camp. The battle would begin when Syracuse's mercenaries stormed over the ridge from the south. These mercenaries, who were on foot and had not yet reached the Syracuse campsite, would have to march through the night to be ready for an attack at dawn.

⬟ Dawn arrived, and with it the Syracuse mercenaries. Although the mercenaries had marched all night, Hiero said that they had to attack now while all the allied forces were in place. When the mercenaries attacked, the Carthaginian force would sweep along the riverbank from the northwest. Meanwhile, the Syracuse cavalry would gallop up from the southeast. No one would escape. The river would prevent any Mamertine retreat.

As the message was translated from Greek into the various languages of the mercenaries, Figures could hear an increasing babble of the different languages as small groups talked over the plan. Figures did not know what they were saying, but it sounded agitated and unhappy. Some of the Syracusan cavalrymen drew their swords, as if expecting resistance to the plan. Nevertheless, the mercenaries were grouped into battle formation with their pikes held parallel to the ground before them.

Hiero saw Figures watching the mercenaries and rode over to him. "Archimedes, get on your horse and move to a safe spot a long way from the battleground. I promised your mother to keep you safe."

Figures shouted, "I'm on my way," but when Hiero returned to commanding the armies, Figures ignored his orders and began to seek a place on high ground where he could watch the battle unfold but not be easily seen. The sycamore branch was not satisfactory, as the mercenaries would be moving directly under it. A large boulder to its east looked suitable. He hitched Plato to a tree branch behind the boulder and scrambled on top. He could see the Mamertines' camp on the plain near the river. In the distance to the northwest, he could see a few glints that probably came from the weapons of the Carthaginians. And far to the east, a small amount of dust rising above the treetops showed where the cavalry was assembling. The mercenaries formed ranks on the ridge.

⬟ There was a shout from the ridge, and the mercenary forces began to advance down the hill. It was a thrilling sight as they marched with their spearlike pikes held high and their shields at their breasts.

A Mamertine lookout saw them, too, and raced down the hill toward the camp. The nearest mercenaries threw pikes at him but they fell short. Figures could hear the lookout shouting something in Italian. Mamertine soldiers began to race around, arming themselves, collecting and mounting horses, and forming into military order. In what seemed only a few seconds, Mamertine archers began firing at the mercenaries.

The mercenaries were only armed with pikes and swords for hand-to-hand combat, so they needed to close in on the Mamertines to fight. They dashed toward the archers. Arrows felled some the mercenaries as they ran, although most parried the arrows with their shields. Meanwhile, the Mamertine cavalry moved up the hill and pivoted toward the mercenaries. As the horsemen reached the mercenaries, the Mamertine riders used long swords to slash the mercenaries on the head or calves, parts unprotected by leather armor. Some horsemen stopped to behead mercenaries felled by arrows.

A mercenary could sometimes dismount a rider with his pike. Figures saw a Mamertine who had a pike through his side still fighting the mercenary who had impaled him. They fought sword to sword and he could hear the metals clash until the mercenary managed to strike the Mamertine below his helmet, putting him down. The mercenary was pulling his pike from the body, when a Mamertine cavalryman swept by and cut off his arm.

Some of the mercenaries turned and ran up the hill toward the ridge. They left their swords and pikes behind to run faster. But they could not run as fast as horses, and the Mamertine cavalry followed those up the hill and killed all those trying to retreat.

Where were the Carthaginian forces and the Syracuse cavalry that should have relieved the mercenaries? Figures looked to the north. The Sun was higher now and he could see the Carthaginian army. It was not advancing toward the battle. Instead, the horses and marching men began moving away from the fight.

On the battlefield the Mamertines were destroying the mercenaries. Some mercenaries threw down their weapons and kneeled before their foes, but the Mamertine soldiers attacked them with swords anyway. Figures could smell fresh blood and hear the cries of the wounded.

Figures expected that the Syracuse cavalry to appear and change the odds. Although he could see quite far up the river valley, however, there was no sign of a relief force. Had his own cavalry chosen to abandon the battle the way the Carthaginians had done? He could not imagine Hiero making that choice. Although he had disliked the mercenaries when he marched with them, their destruction left him shaking at the horrors he was witnessing.

He also shook with terror for his own life. Some retreating mercenaries who had escaped the Mamertine cavalry were heading directly for his rock and his tethered horse. If one saw his horse, he would surely leap on it and ride away as quickly as they could. He would be stranded on top of the rock and possibly visible to a Mamertine on horseback. He thought he should climb down and ride away from the battle.

As the fighting neared his hiding place, Figures tried to estimate the chance of escaping death. The rock he lay on was too small to conceal him from the passing Mamertine horsemen. Although he was sure that his chance of safety was vanishingly close to nonexistent, for once he could not concentrate on numbers.

SCROLL 19

⬟ Figures heard the thunder of galloping hooves as a horse came directly toward his hiding place. He pressed flat on the boulder and held his breath.

As the galloping horse reached his rock, he lifted his head, half expecting a Mamertine sword to sever his neck, but the horse had no rider. The horse must have belonged to a Mamertine whose rider had been killed. Figures raised his head higher. Dead men--mostly mercenaries from the Syracusan army--and dead horses littered the field. Mamertine warriors on horseback chased mercenaries fleeing on foot.

He wanted to flee on Plato, but his riding skills and docile steed were no matched for trained cavalry. He was sure to be seen and killed; the Mamertines were not taking prisoners.

He remembered Odysseus and the Cyclops. Odysseus and his men escaped by hiding under giant sheep, hanging on the wool coats. He could use Plato instead of a sheep. He could not hold onto Plato's belly, but he could hide behind the horse. If he hung low on the far side of the horse, the Mamertines might not see him. His small size and large horse would make that possible.

Plato's saddle was a pad held in place with leather straps across the horse's breast and belly. Figures could hold on to the pad and dangle on one side. He slipped from the boulder and ran to Plato. As he released the rope tying the horse in place, he reached across the horse's back and grabbed the far edge of the pad and swung his feet under the horse's belly. The horse tried to shake him off. He held on tight and said, "Get going." Plato responded by trotting off.

Plato, smelling the dead animals on the field, turned away from the battlefield, and galloped toward where the army had camped the night before. This was not safe since Figures could easily be seen from the rear. He let go of the pad with one hand and grabbed the bridle with the other to try to turn the horse and hide from the battlefield. But he nearly fell from the horse in the effort, so he quickly let go of the bridle and clung to the pad.

Plato turned, anyway. Figures thought he heard a woman's soft voice soothing his horse as Plato slowed to a trot. Plato moved as if being led at exactly the angle needed to keep his rider hidden, while the horse trotted through the wood. Soon Figures no longer heard the sounds of battle, although he thought he heard a person running along before the horse.

As Plato and Figures entered a small clearing in the forest, the horse stopped and began to graze. Figures was surprised to hear a man speaking Greek.

"Was that a woman slipping into the forest?"

"Probably one of the local wives trying to hide from the battle. But that looks like Archimedes' horse. He was supposed to be a long way from here by now."

"There is a boy clinging to the side of the horse. I think it is Archimedes."

Figures was no longer afraid. In the excitement of meeting, he did not worry over who the woman might have been. Phyllis might have a theory—perhaps she might be right about protection of the goddess after all. Instead of concerning himself with Artemis, however, he wanted to talk to Hiero to tell him of the slaughter of the mercenaries and to find out why the cavalry had not come to their rescue.

⬟ The soldiers were the two scouts he had met earlier. Figures asked, "Did you see the battle? What happened to the troops led by Carthage? Where was Hiero?"

"Carthage betrayed us. I was there when Hanno ordered them to retreat. But I don't know what happened to Hiero and the cavalry."

The other scout said, "I'll go to Hiero and lead him to a place safer than our last campground, which the Mamertines have already found." He pulled out one of Figures' maps from under his saddle and pointed to the location of a distant hill. "We will go there. Take Archimedes with you and circle around so that the Mamertine army does not find you." With that, he galloped off.

Figures mounted Plato and followed the other scout in the opposite direction. It took almost all day for Figures and the scout to reach the hill where Hiero was camped with the cavalry. Hiero saw them entering the camp and immediately went to Figures.

"I knew you were safe, but it is good to see you with my own eyes. Tell me what you saw."

Figures said, "The Carthaginian army just moved away, letting the Mamertine cavalry destroy our mercenaries."

Hiero said, "I had scouts on all sides of the battlefield, so I learned almost immediately that Hanno had betrayed us. I considered the sizes of our forces and theirs. Our mercenaries would lose badly. Without allies, sending my cavalry into battle would result in more deaths without affecting the outcome. So we did not join the battle. I think I can justify my decision to the people of Syracuse."

Figures heard a very different view when he met Celphalos the next day. Celphalos said, "Hiero should have aided the mercenaries. Most of the cavalry are unhappy that they traveled so far and did not fight. Hiero is going to be very unpopular when we get back to Syracuse."

⬟ Because Hiero controlled the army that occupied Syracuse, he had the powers of a tyrant although he tried to govern through the Assembly as much as possible, fearing that the people would rise against him. Because of the loss to the Mamertines, his popularity was dwindling fast.

After the Mamertine fiasco, Hiero's wife Philistis became pregnant again. Soon after the baby was born, a girl this time, Hiero told Figures to continue to return to living his parents' home instead of staying with Hiero and his family.

"It's not that we don't want to see you," said Hiero, "But you need to be getting ready for the Games, and I need to devote time to my family, to Syracuse, and to rebuilding my army. But please make time to help with Gelo."

After his experience at the Games when he was 14, Figures knew that to be a serious competitor he must be strong as well as clever, so each morning he started his day by running for several stadia, working on mathematics problems while he ran. Some mornings he became so distracted by trying to prove a complex result in geometry or by creating a puzzle that he forgot where he was going and ran into trees or fell into streams. He also planned new ways to improve his performance in the five events of the pentathlon.

In addition to trying to improve his strength and speed, he redesigned all the tools used in the pentathlon: the halteres of the long jump, the discus, and the javelin.

- He tried various shaped for the halteres, finally settling on a half-sphere for the front and a cone for the back.
- He invented a discus with a curved top and bottom instead of being flat on both the top and bottom. The curved discus seemed to rise and float.
- Perhaps his most important change was to the javelin.

The memory of his disgrace in the javelin toss at the previous Games returned often, and he was determined to excel in this event to erase that pain. A key element was how effectively the athlete wound the strap around the shaft.

Jason told him, "You should be able to improve through practice."

"That helps, but my problem is getting a good spin that keeps the javelin flying straight. If I use a thin strap, it would fit into a spiral around the shaft. Not only will this help me wrap the strap, but when I release the javelin it will always have the same amount of turning."

"I don't think anyone has tried that, but I can't see why it would be against the rules."

Figures studied different varieties of spirals, which vary mostly in the distances between turns. He needed a spiral that maintained the same distance between any two points on the spiral along a line drawn from the center of the spiral. He drew a flat version of how that would work to show Tono.

The spiral Tono carved into the shaft was a three-dimensional version of this. Figures thought that it would be interesting to study spirals further. How would a ball move if

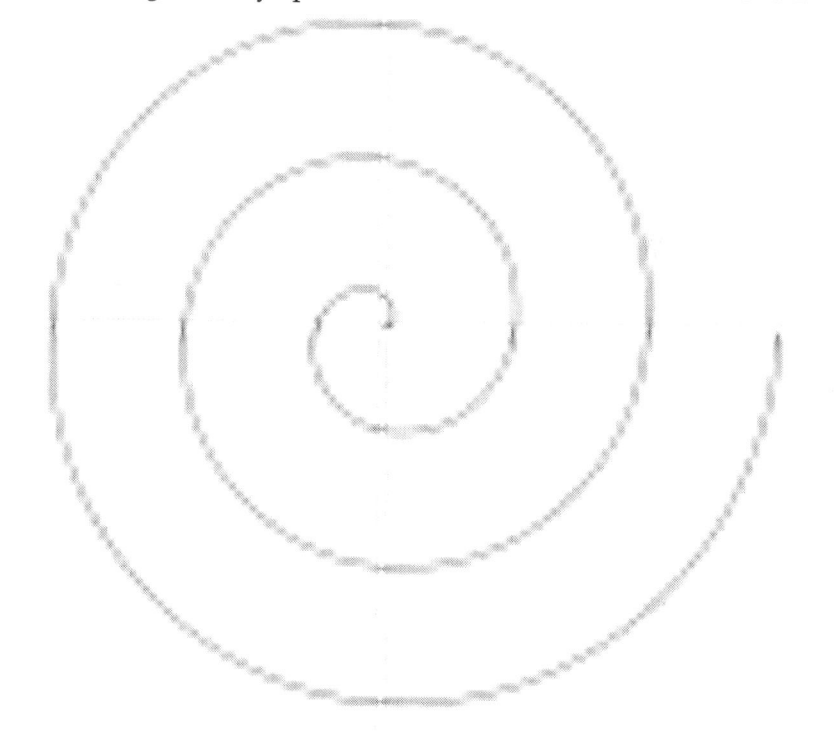

it were inside a tube formed into a three-dimensional spiral?

The experiments with the equipment and constant practice went on for months. He also practiced wrestling with Phyllis, Herc, and Jason whenever he could persuade them to give it a try.

⬟ Although was no longer living at Hiero's house, he continued to help take care of Hiero's young son Gelo, teaching him skills such as putting correct geometric shapes into holes in a board.

Hiero no longer was popular with the citizens of Syracuse. Citizens accused him of planning the slaughter of the mercenaries by the Mamertines. Meanwhile, the Mamertine armies pillaged towns closer and closer to Syracuse and appeared to be gathering strength to attack Syracuse itself. Hiero was blamed for every advance the Mamertines made.

Hiero told him, "Archimedes, the Mamertines are threatening Syracuse. I have a new mercenary corps that I can trust. My cavalry is still intact, and very well trained. We are now strong enough to defeat the Mamertines without any help from Carthage."

Soon after, Hiero left Leptines in charge of the household as he again went to war.

Several days later, Phidias returned home early from the agora and announced, "Hiero has met the Mamertine army and defeated it. Any Mamertines who managed to escape are fleeing back to Messana. At least this time his mercenaries were loyal. And the plan didn't require treacherous Carthage. When Carthage is your ally, you don't need an enemy."

Figures asked, "How did the Assembly take the news? Are they satisfied now that Hiero does not send his men to be slaughtered? Or are they still against us?"

Phidias said, "I heard much cheering. I suspect that Hiero will always have some enemies, but for now they will be silent."

● When Hiero returned to Syracuse with his army nearly intact, the fickle population of Syracuse had turned completely in his favor. The Assembly sponsored a huge celebration of the triumph.

Phyllis' father had been unable to make a suitable match for Phyllis. Some families said she was too independent. Instead of trying less suitable families, Phyllis' father bribed the temple of Artemis to allow another year as priestess. Although this was not common, it was not unprecedented, and Phyllis was very happy to accept the idea.

Consequently, she was the priestess who conducted the rites that were performed at the triumph. She sacrificed several bulls donated by the Assembly for the occasion. A ritual of prophecy followed this. After pouring some wine over the altar in front of the statue of Artemis, Phyllis took the remainder into one of the secret places of the temple.

Phidias, attending the celebration with his family, said, "She will drink all the wine in the jar, which is not mixed with water as we usually do. Then she will emerge with a message supposed to be from the goddess."

Andromeda said, "I have heard that a powerful herb is added to the wine to make the priestess believe that she has become the goddess."

Phidias said, "They had better be careful. Remember how Socrates was killed by the herb hemlock."

Figures said, "But the Athenians meant to poison Socrates. The keepers of the temple don't want to poison their priestess."

Phidias said, "I just hope that they are careful."

Time passed. The crowd enjoyed feasting and drinking. Finally Phyllis returned to the temple steps, helped by two of the temple keepers. The help was needed as Phyllis was staggering and her eyes held a strange shine.

The crowd all turned to listen as she began to speak in a low voice that was like her own, but different.

"I am Artemis, Goddess of maidens and protector of childbirth."

"My arrows pierce the bodies and horses of enemies of Syracuse.

"I travel with the wind over all of Sicily, Greece, and beyond.

"When Hiero conquered the Mamertines, I was with him."

Phyllis paused for a long time. As she slumped a little, the two attendants pulled her body straight. She opened her eyes again and continued.

"Great is Syracuse, but greater powers contest for the Earth.

"Syracuse sides with one power but wins with the other.

"If your king chooses rightly, Syracuse prospers as before.

"Once you defeated the power of Athena, but she will return."

Once again, Phyllis seemed to stagger a little, but the attendants holding her arms kept her from falling. Now her voice rose in both pitch and volume.

"I will protect Syracuse until I am celebrated beyond reason."

She began to shake violently and the attendants had difficulty holding her in place. Finally she gave a great shout:

"I will change my name and spend time on the Moon."

Phyllis threw her arms in the air, causing the attendants to lose their hold. Her eyes, unblinking during the recitation, rolled up and back, showing just the whites. She pitched forward in front of the altar and lay still on the rock floor.

The crowd gasped and then all was silent. Figures started to rush toward Phyllis, but his father held him back. Figures was certain that the potion in the wine had killed her.

SCROLL 20

⬟ Phyllis lay on the floor at the top of the temple steps. Her eyes remained open but her collapse was as complete as if she were a toga tossed on the floor. Only his father's grip on Figures' shoulder kept him from going to her.

Phidias said, "A lot of nonsense as usual. She says, 'When Hiero conquered the Mamertines, I was with him.' but I remember seeing Phyllis in Syracuse that day. She says 'your king" but we don't have a king, and neither does Rome or Carthage."

Figures said, "It was the goddess, not Phyllis. She was speaking as Artemis." He was trembling with fear for Phyllis, now being lifted by her attendants.

"Pretending to be the goddess. Don't worry about Phyllis—she is already on her feet. It's nonsense, but people here will repeat her statements over and over, trying to make sense where there is none."

With two attendants helping, Phyllis slowly walked back into the inner recesses of the temple.

Claudia said, "We don't believe in the gods, but a lot she said seemed meaningful. It must have been about Rome and Carthage, but which is supposed to be the winner?"

Hypate added, "And where is the king she said would decide?"

Figures answered, "According to Phyllis' father, Syracuse once had a king. The most famous king was named Hiero."

"My cousin Hiero was named after that king," said Andromeda.

"My recollection is that the first Hiero was a tyrant, not a king" Phidias said. "Although the younger Dionysius was sometimes called a king, for it was during his reign that the famous incident with Damocles took place. "

Hypate, who was not worried about Phyllis, asked, "What happened to Damocles?"

"He was a rich man in Syracuse who should have envied no one. But he envied the king and said that to be king must make Dionysius the happiest person on Earth. Dionysius told Damocles that he would allow Damocles to spend a day as king, sitting on the throne, provided that he remain on the throne all day. When the day arrived when Damocles would be king, he eagerly climbed on the throne. No sooner was he seated that everyone present gazed above his head. He looked up. A heavy sword, point down, was suspended by a single strand of horsehair. 'What is this?' asked Damocles, pointing to the sword. Dionysius replied, 'Every king must live with a sword pointed at him every moment of the day.' With that, Damocles jumped from the throne and no longer envied the king."

Andromeda said, "I think that is just a fable and not really a true story. The point, of course, is not to be envious of others, for you get their burdens along with their blessings."

"The historian Timaeus told it to me himself as if it were true, but perhaps Andromeda is right. There are several morals to that tale."

Figures thought that, like a king, a priestess lived in danger. Mathematicians are safe from most hazards, although one mathematician might envy another or steal a proof. But he was unlikely to face a physical hazard.

Everyone went home, but Figures, who remained outside, hoping to see Phyllis. Eventually one of the temple attendants emerged and said, "The Priestess is fine, but resting. Go home." And he did.

⬟ With the Mamertines defeated, Figures' time was split between training for the games and young Gelo. It was not easy to help Gelo learn, since he was just beginning to talk. Gelo played with wooden blocks in various geometric shapes, but often Figures would conceive an idea about geometry from seeing the blocks. Then he took the blocks away from Gelo and arranged them himself. But he succeeded in teaching Gelo to count almost as soon as Gelo began to talk.

Hiero and Philistis became concerned that Archimedes did not have enough time to train for the Games, now fast approaching. They decided to hire someone to help Philistis with Gelo and Gelo's newborn sister, Damarata, so that Archimedes could practice more.

Hiero said. "Could I hire Hypate to take care of the babies and relieve both Philistis and you? You need more training time, but Philistis, while she loves the children, needs time for herself."

"I could also use more time for mathematics. What about Claudia? She is experienced as a mother."

" I suggested that to Philistis, but she thought it would not be wise to have Claudia here. She said that people might find fault with me having two grown women around, one a widow. It is very important to us and to Leptines what people think of me."

"I will ask Hypate. But even though you have a good position as head of the army, can you afford to keep hiring servants? Maybe it would be better to have a slave watch the children."

"The Assembly is working on a plan to greatly increase my fortune, so do not worry about me. Worry about getting ready for the Games, Archimedes. And mathematics can wait until after the Games."

Figures arranged for Hypate to visit Philistis to talk about taking care of the babies.

Andromeda said, "That's a good idea, Archimedes. It would be good for Hypate to learn more about how to care for infants. One day Hypate will marry and have children of her own. Claudia and I can handle everything here."

Soon it was settled that Hypate would be with Gelo and baby Damarata during the afternoon, while Figures taught Gelo in the morning. Philistis played with the baby in the morning and had afternoons free.

⬟ Phidias reported that citizens were to gather the next

day on a matter of importance. The Assembly numbered all adult male citizens of Syracuse as voters; normally, however, only a few leaders met regularly to establish laws. From time to time, all citizens met for major decisions.

Next morning the theater was as filled as if the Games had started. Figures spent the morning with Gelo as usual, while all the women in Figures' extended family stayed home and performed their regular household tasks. When Phidias returned from the Assembly everyone but Hypate, who was with Philistis, gathered in the courtyard, eager to learn what had occurred.

Andromeda asked, "What is it, Phidias? Are we at war again? Or have we made peace with Carthage?"

"Hiero is to become King of Syracuse." Phidias paused for Andromeda to comment, but she appeared to be shocked speechless. "A spokesman for the Assembly announced that those who met had voted him king. In response, the entire group of citizens shouted in his favor."

Andromeda regained her voice, but could only say "Hiero a king?"

"I am generally opposed to kings, although democracy often fails, too. But I think Hiero will rule Syracuse as fairly as our current Assembly—in truth, he has been doing it already. And he will keep an evil tyrant, such as Hiketas, from arising. Hiero will be granted great privileges and a large income, which may be helpful to us as well. The city will also rebuild the palace at the tip of Ortygia for him."

Andromeda said, "King Hiero! Hiero is a wonderful man, but I am not sure he should be a king."

Figures said, "I thought kings were chosen by the gods, not elected. At least, most kings claim to have been born, not made." The idea of Hiero as a king did not seem logical, despite his great respect for his cousin.

"The Assembly claimed that Hiero should be king because they say that he is a direct descendent of Gelo, the tyrant who made Syracuse into a great city. That Gelo's brother, Hiero, also a king, will now be known as Hiero I, while Andromeda's cousin is Hiero II. "

Claudia said, "I think that Phyllis started this. She prophesied that 'If your king chooses rightly, Syracuse prospers.' Listeners thought Syracuse needed a king."

"Whether or not Phyllis started the idea, she will crown him — although my memory is that the patron of Gelo and the first King Hiero was Demeter, not Artemis, but none of this is entirely proper."

Andromeda said, "I have never heard that any of our family was descended from Gelo. But I don't think I will remind Hiero of that."

⬟ Some days Phyllis left the Temple of Artemis for a few hours and visited Figures. Then he performed long-jump practice to the accompaniment of her aulos.

The first time Phyllis visited, he asked, "What did you mean by all that odd prophesy?"

"I have no idea what Artemis meant. The temple attendants had to tell me what She said, since I cannot remember anything after I drank the potion. That drink helps the priestess leave her body so that the Goddess can inhabit it. It seems that I left my body more completely than earlier priestesses have. They were concerned that I might not return to the body of Phyllis."

"I think you are so thin that there is less of you compared to the amount of potion than for earlier priestesses. That is why you collapsed as if dead."

"They say the prophecy took only a moment, but it was a long time before I felt like myself. I am sure that what Artemis said will become clear in time. Remember what your father told you about Pandora — people are not allowed to know the future."

"One part is already clear. Now we have a king."

⬟ Phyllis had put a wreath of gold olive leaves on Hiero's head at a ceremony watched by almost the entire population of Syracuse — or at least as many as could get near enough to see.

Later Phyllis told Figures, "Now I will make another prediction—as Phyllis this time, not as Artemis. When the Games are over, Hiero will have more for Archimedes to do than teach Gelo. You are the one he counts on for important tasks."

"He already has a project for me, but I must do well in the Games to learn what it will be."

"You will do well, especially in the long jump, even if I cannot play the aulos for you that day. But I worry that if you win the long jump, you will quickly be eliminated in the wrestling. Although you are much stronger now than four years ago, you are far from being the strongest boy your age."

"You may be right. But I remember how you beat Herc at wrestling when he first tried it. You were not as strong as Herc, but you were faster and cleverer. That is what I will have to be if I am to make any showing in the wrestling. Provided that I win an event and am allowed to wrestle."

● Figures began to spend more time thinking about wrestling. He practiced with Jason, who was not only stronger than he was, but also very fast.

He also closely watched other boys wrestling to learn their special holds. He then made model wrestlers from clay that could be put into each position a boy might assume during a wrestling match.

He suspended the models with hairs attached at differing locations and also balanced models on sharp points. The goal was to develop ways boys could be overbalanced so they would topple with pressure. Gradually, he developed techniques to try. Testing these on Jason often failed in practice, but some methods worked, surprising Jason and putting him on the ground.

For example, when Jason first approached with his arms reaching out for him, Figures surprised by reaching behind him with one hand and grasping Jason's right arm by the part between the shoulder and neck with the other. From that position, he put his right foot just beyond Jason's right foot and half squatted, bending the left knee while keeping the right straight. A quick twist to the left unbalanced Jason and threw him on the floor.

Most of the best ways to down an opponent or to keep upright were already known to Jason, since he had been wrestling with his father all his life. Figures studied these common methods and had Jason try — usually with great success — to toss him to the ground. He tried to find unexpected methods of gaining advantage from the opponent's hold. One effective method not common among other wrestlers was to jerk an opponent by the ankle instead of inside the knee. If he achieved a real wrestling match, he would save that for last, since it could only be a surprise once.

Hypate noticed Figures testing his models in various wrestling positions. She said, "When you are finished playing with those dolls, let me have them so that I can give them to Damarata."

"They are not dolls! I am conducting research with them and not playing," but when he thought he could learn no more from the models, he did let Hypate take them. Hypate made tiny togas and chitons for the models and Damarata played with them for weeks.

⬟ Politics dominated the talk in Phidias' household, but now Figures, because he saw Hiero so frequently, often knew more than his father. The main news as the Games approached concerned the two big powers that both were trying to expand their influence — Rome and Carthage.

After Hiero decisively defeated the Mamertines, the Mamertine army held a shaky control over its stronghold, Messana. Hiero might be able to take Messana from them. Carthage also threatened the Mamertines. So the Mamertines turned to Rome for help.

Rome now dominated Italy, but had never occupied Sicily. Messana was conveniently just across a narrow strait from Italy. The Roman Senate launched an army to Sicily to defend Messana against Syracuse and to counter Rome's main rival, Carthage, which still controlled most of Sicily.

Hiero learned of these developments and called a council of war, bringing together the leaders of the Assembly, including Phidias, and his principal generals, and Archimedes.

Hiero addressed the council, "Rome has sent a large army to Messana. The Roman legions have been defeated in some past engagements. Pyrrhus won major battles against them, but his forces never quite recovered from the effort. But no matter how often Roman legions have lost a battle, they never have lost a war. Instead of dealing with Carthage's influence in Sicily, as we have long managed, we may find ourselves in danger from a major war between Rome and Carthage on Sicily's soil. What do you recommend?"

Several advisors spoke, but each speech in slightly different words carried the same message: King Hiero should declare war on Rome, march to Messana, and send the Roman legions back across the strait to Italy.

Hiero said, "I consider this important advice. Now that you have all done your duty to your King, I dismiss this council." But he beckoned Leptines, Phidias, and Archimedes to stay. He told them, "You heard what the Assembly wants. Is this good advice?"

Leptines said, "King Hiero, they are right to urge you to war. If you don't turn back the Romans now, they will continue to pour troops across the strait. There will be war between Rome and Carthage, and Syracuse will be a victim no matter which side wins."

Phidias said, "If we had time, it would be better to strengthen the walls around Syracuse and improve the fortress Euryalus, which Dionysius showed was beyond taking by anyone's army. War is never a good solution, but we do need to be protected."

"But we don't have time," Archimedes said. "I have spent many hours at Euryalus. It is not close to being ready to protect Syracuse. Roman catapults can easily break through those worn-out walls. It would take a year or more to create the defenses Syracuse needs."

Hiero said, "I have to agree. The Romans will attack us if we do not attack them, and we will surely lose here. Carthage may help, since their future is at stake, too. I will send an envoy to Hanno. If Carthage is with us, we may have a slight chance—at least the battleground will be elsewhere, so that the Romans won't destroy Syracuse and kill its citizens, which they surely will do if the battle is waged in the city. So there is no choice but to assemble the army and head north once again. Archimedes: while we are gone survey Euryalus, and see what can make it impregnable again. We are going to need it someday, especially if Leptines is right about Rome and Carthage."

Hiero's army traveled up the coast toward Messana for the third time in a few short years. Hanno brought his Carthaginian forces into alliance with Hiero's army. Despite the combined armies, Hiero and Hanno failed to defeat the Roman legion. Hiero's troops lost the first battle with the Legions. The next day Hanno's troops were routed and scattered back to villages across Sicily. Hiero recognized that his weakened forces would also lose, so he retreated to Syracuse.

Seeing Carthage routed and Syracuse in retreat, Rome sent additional troops to Sicily. One contingent occupied Messana and prepared to march with the Mamertines across Sicily. But two legions moved south and surrounded Syracuse. The city did not have strong enough walls or a working fortress. Syracuse seemed fated to fall to Rome. If it fell, no one would be safe from pillaging Legionnaires.

SCROLL 21

◆ While King Hiero was fighting losing battles against Roman legions, Archimedes surveyed the city walls and Euryalus fort. He did not like what he found. Meanwhile, Roman Legions besieged Syracuse, trapping Hiero and his army in the city.

Archimedes reported to the king as soon as Hiero returned to Syracuse.

Hiero said, "I should have known better than to try to ally with Carthage. Hanno's army fled as soon as they confronted the Romans. Hanno had told me that Carthage would prevail because he had excellent intelligence from his agent, Malchus, who knew Sicily well, but intelligence cannot prevent cowardice."

Figures heart seemed to stop when he heard the name. "Malchus! We killed Malchus at sea."

"I said the same to Hanno. But it was certainly another Carthaginian with the same name. We know your Malchus drowned. But enough of that. What have you learned about our defenses? The Romans are at our gates. "

Figures, still shaken by hearing the name Malchus, had bad news about his project. He said, "The walls, which have protected the city since the time of Dionysius, are no match for modern catapults. There are places where two men with a battering ram could push a wall down."

"What about the fort?"

"Euryalus is in ruins. It could be repaired, but it would be better to redesign it. I have been making sketches. We could use the existing stones and tunnels to create a truly impregnable fort. But it will take years and many men to build it."

Hiero was silent for a long time before speaking, as much to himself as to Archimedes. "The Romans attack will soon enter the city. Our best force is the cavalry, not very useful for street fighting. There will be hand-to-hand fighting in the streets. There is no chance of rescue from Carthage. Syracuse is doomed."

There was another long pause. Finally, Figures said, "We could surrender."

Hiero glared at Figures for a moment and then broke into a smile. "There is an old army saying that the meaning of 'surrender' is 'joining the winning side.' Maybe Rome *would* agree to leave us alone if we promised tribute. In a street fight the Roman commander would lose a lot of his men, too. And if we bought off the Legions, he could divide some of the ransom among his men so that they would not mourn the lost chance of plunder. The Assembly would not like it, but they elected me king."

Figures, who had merely been considering all possible actions when he mentioned surrender, asked, "Do you really think that would work?"

Hiero said, "Better to try surrender and fail than to be overrun by Roman Legionnaires." He gazed up at the sky for a moment while Figures wondered what Hiero was thinking. After a moment, he said, "I will send an message to the Roman general, Appius Claudius Caudex, proposing that Syracuse surrender under terms to be negotiated."

⬟ The next day Hiero summoned Archimedes to the palace, where he told him, "When I met Appius Claudius to work out terms, I proposed a bribe of 100 talents of silver, expecting this to be turned down for being too small, but he said that amount would be acceptable if I allied Syracuse to Rome eternally and added the same value in foodstuffs. I had to promise that, as a faithful ally, Syracuse would feed the Roman Legions in Sicily. I agreed, provided Syracuse would continue to be independent. Appius Claudius added another condition. We had to allow the Roman Navy, such as it is, to use our harbor. So, although Syracuse would be 'independent' instead of being absorbed into Rome the way their conquests usually are, we would be 'independent' only on terms that require us to cling closely to Rome. Since we were certain to lose everything if Rome attacked, I was surprised at how sensible the terms were, so I accepted them before Appius Claudius could change his mind. I know how to rule Syracuse so that we are loyal to Rome but not its slave."

● Hiero asked for all citizens of Syracuse to meet in the theater in Neapolis. When the crowd had gathered, he appeared on the stage dressed in a purple toga and wearing the gold laurel-leaf wreath that Phyllis had placed on his head. Figures was in the crowd with Phidias.

Hiero addressed the Assembly: "Citizens of Syracuse, I am happy to report that I can continue to serve Syracuse as king and general. We are not going to suffer invasion by the Roman legions that now besiege us."

The crowd cheered.

"Consider Rome and Carthage. Carthage has long been an enemy of Syracuse, besieging us as recently as a decade past. Although Carthage has captured and ruled much of Sicily, Syracuse and its allies have always prevailed against Carthage."

Another cheer.

"Now think of Rome. Rome is far distant from us. The affairs of Rome have not mattered to Syracuse. Recently, however, Rome sent its Legions to Sicily to help expel Carthage from Messana, which it accomplished. Now the Roman Senate has concluded that Carthage should be driven from Sicily. We can help Rome achieve this goal. We do not have to send our armies out. We only need supply the Roman army with food, since they cannot bring enough from Italy. Therefore, as your king, I hereby impose a tax of one tenth of all the wheat raised in the region controlled by Syracuse, that tax to be entirely used to feed the Roman army."

Hiero paused. There was no cheer this time.

"Rome is our ally against Carthage. But I do not want to risk the lives of our young men in battle. We can help Rome in other ways. I am withdrawing 100 talents of silver from the treasury to help the Roman Legions in their efforts to rid Sicily of Carthage. Their armies will immediately leave the vicinity of Syracuse and begin the campaign. Life here will continue as before. We are not a part of this war except insofar as our enduring friendship with Rome. Syracuse will continue to be the greatest city on Sicily and will once again be the greatest on the Mediterranean Sea." Hiero paused for a shout in his favor, but none was forthcoming.

Phidias said, "Hiero is wiser than I thought. A hundred talents of silver and a tenth of our wheat crop is a small price to pay for keeping his kingship. Especially since the citizens are paying the price."

Figures said, "I gave him the idea."

Phidias said, "I'm not surprised."

Hiero continued, "Now that our city is safe, I declare that all is ready for the Games, which I had feared we would have to postpone. I shall consult the priests and priestesses of Zeus, Artemis, Apollo, and Athena to determine the most propitious day for the Games to begin. Also, in honor of Zeus for our escape from the Roman Legions, I will build the largest altar ever constructed. We then will sacrifice many bulls, which I shall supply to the God."

Phidias said, "Hiero is an even better politician than he was a general. Give the people sacrifices, festivals, and games, and they will forget that he has bribed the Romans for our release."

It appeared that Phidias was right, for once again the crowd was cheering.

⬟ The Games were scheduled about a month later than usual. People said that the priestess of Artemis, who had the final say on setting the date, still had the power to interpret the signs correctly, for during the period when nights and days were equal — the usual time for the Games — the heat was intense. If the Games had taken place then, many competitors would have collapsed, and, it was said, the ones who fought the hardest to win would have died. Days had cooled by the time the Games were launched, beginning with sacrifices to Zeus on his new altar and general feasting.

After the adult Games concluded, the boys' Games began. Figures and his friends, now 18, were old-timers who knew how everything should be done. Herc was among the oldest newcomers and took the lead in explaining rules and procedures to the others.

This year only twenty boys were competing in the pentathlon—many others were saving themselves for the races that followed the pentathlon. Narcissus was one of the few who entered all three events. Figures, who doubted that he could win a race, stuck with the pentathlon.

Figures drew the tile labeled "Iota," a good omen for a Pythagorean, since iota is the symbol for ten. Tenth, however, is not a great position for the race with twenty runners. He was next to Faunus, who drew iota. Narcissus was happy to get Beta, next to the inside lane, while Herc drew Theta and Jason Sigma, meaning that Herc would go eighth in most events, while Jason was at the eighteenth position.

Both Figures and Narcissus appeared to have made the correct decision about entering the race events outside the pentathlon, for Narcissus easily won the one-stadium race that was the first event in the pentathlon, but Figures was well back in the middle of the pack. "At least I did better than last time," he told Jason, who had been close behind Narcissus.

Jason said, "I knew the race was not the best event for either of us. But it is too bad that Herc finished last. He will be too old for the boys' Games four years from now, and it is unlikely he can make up this disgrace in the adult games."

Figures looked over to where Herc was standing. "Herc is no longer fat, but his legs have not grown any longer, and these days he carries too much muscle to run very fast. He will do better where strength is more important than quickness."

"Maybe, but he still has a lot of weight to lift for a long jump. And the javelin toss requires skill and speed, not just

Before *Eureka!*

strength. But he does have a chance to do well in the discus, I think. And that is next."

Figures, who did not like to recall his earlier javelin failure, said, "Herc doesn't have a chance to win the discus — I have seen you at practice. You are almost as good as your father."

Although Figures did not tell Jason, he thought that he might also have a chance for success in the discus. His discus soared on the wind when thrown right. It was not flat like ones other boys used, but had a rounded top and was partly carved out on the other side.

⬟ Herc did do very well in the discus, easily beating all of the other newcomers and several of the older boys, although Herc's best was short of the most distant mark set to that point, set by Narcissus, the event's second competitor.

When Figures' turn came, the judge said, "Archimedes. That does not look like a discus to me. Let me look at it."

He meekly handed his discus to the judge, who turned it over from side to side several times.

"Let me compare this with another." He looked at the next contestant. The judge said, "'Kappa: give me your discus."

The judge took the discus and compared it with the one Figures had developed. The two were about the same diameter and weight, although Kappa's discus was flat while Figures' curved into a flattened dome. He said, "Wait here, Archimedes," then took both discuses to the officials and held a brief discussion. Then he left Figures' discus behind and returned with the one belonging to Faunus. Figures was sure that he was disqualified.

"Here, Archimedes," the judge said, handing Kappa's discus to Figures, "Compete with this one. I was going to disqualify you, but I was reminded that you are a good friend to the king, so the officials will let you compete. But you cannot use your trick discus. I am sure Kappa won't mind you borrowing his for a few moments."

The other discus felt odd to his hands, accustomed to his own device, but all three of his tosses were respectable, although were well short of the most distant mark, set by Narcissus.

Figures was disappointed but glad that he had not been taken out of the competition. If he did not compete in all events, he would be eliminated from the pentathlon.

At the end, however, the event went to Jason, who easily surpassed everyone else, throwing not only with strength and speed, but also with a grace in motion that the other competitors lacked. Figures heard one of the older watchers in the crowd murmur, "He is just like his father, maybe even more nearly perfect." Another said, "He will go to the Olympics for sure."

● The long jump was Figures' best event in practice and the only one that he thought he could win once his special discus had been outlawed. He studied the shapes of the hand weights, called halteres, the first nine competitors used, fearing that if his halteres were judged out of order he might be disqualified. He had redesigned his halteres several times to get them to move faster through the wind. Now they were like teardrops, spherical in front and a cone behind.

Narcissus made competent leaps that set the distance others needed to surpass. Jason had been right about Herc. Not only was his weight an apparent handicap, but also his jumps were awkward. It was clear that the contestants who were tall and thin, like Figures, tended to do the best in this event.

By then the time it was Figures' turn, he was relaxed, because he observed that each competitor carried halteres that were shaped and sized differently from the others. His would not pose a problem for the judge.

As he began to rock back and forth for his first jump, he was surprised to notice that the aulos was playing the tune Phyllis played for his practice sessions. The tone and melody were so familiar that he looked back to see if Phyllis had somehow replaced the young man who accompanied the earlier contestants. But it was the same player as before.

With the familiar sound and rhythm backing him up, Figures began with an immense leap that easily passed Narcissus' lead. But he was not satisfied—he thought he had released the halteres too soon, and he knew that he had jumped too high, losing additional distance.

The second jump was better than the first. He traveled in a low curve that was more forward motion than height gain. He pushed hard on the halteres when his feet approached the landing, which produced a slight lift and acceleration. After he landed, he looked at his heel prints in the soft ground the judges had tilled for the landing area. He was almost at the far edge. It would be difficult to surpass this jump, not only for Figures but also for the ten competitors who would follow him.

Now for the third jump. He mentally checked off everything he had done right for the second jump. He did not think he could push off harder, keep his angle of ascent smaller, time his use of the halteres better, or improve in any way. He thought: The only way I could do better would be if Phyllis' goddess Artemis gave me a push when I lifted off the ground or if she carried me through the air.

Perhaps it was because of his odd thought about Artemis, but he did feel as if he had an extra push just when his feet were leaving the ground. And he did sail farther before the moment came to push back on the halteres. He pushed the heavy weights so hard that muscles in his arms were sore for days afterward. Then he landed with a much harder thump than before, a hard landing that threw him off balance so that he fell face down.

As he embarrassedly struggled to stand up, he realized that the crowd was shouting. He thought that he would be shamed the way he was at the javelin toss four years earlier. But when he looked at the crowd and at the judge the shouting was *for* him, not against him at all.

The judge said, "Archimedes, you have just done

something that very few boy athletes achieve. That jump was greater than the winning distance of the adult long jump. I did not expect such a prodigy, so I failed to soften the ground far enough for your landing."

Figures was too astonished to reply. He simply walked over to the group of other boys who had jumped already. As they congratulated him, he turned to watch the other competitors. No one exceeded even Figures' second jump, although Jason came close, so he knew that he would compete in the next day's wrestling finals. Now there were three wrestlers set — Narcissus, Jason, and Figures.

⬟ The javelin toss was much less exciting. Figures' spiral channel for the leather thong insured that all of his tosses had a proper rotation and attitude, but his sore arm muscles led to a poor distance for each of the three tosses — instead of traveling farther with each toss, they successively did worse. Herc had tossed the javelin much farther than Figures' best and so had Narcissus, who was the leader when Figures took his turn. Jason however, outdistanced all of the previous tosses with each of his three throws.

So there would be three wrestlers next day to complete the pentathlon--Narcissus, Jason, and Figures. Since Jason had won two of the four events, Figures and Narcissus, who won just one each, would be pitted against each other first. Then the winner of that match would face Jason to determine the pentathlon winner, the person in first place, the only place that counts.

⬟ That evening Figures visited the temple of Artemis in hopes of talking to Phyllis. He approached a tall woman standing at the temple's entrance.

"May I speak to the priestess?"

"She is not available to men or boys for petitions, and in any case it is the wrong time of the day. "

"This is a personal matter among friends. The priestess lives near me, and I have news of her family." Of course, he did not have any news, but he thought that the idea that he was a messenger might break through the temple rules.

The tall woman leaned into the entrance to the temple and said something he could not hear. Then another woman stepped out, and the tall one entered the temple. The new guard glared at him. But after a moment, Phyllis emerged."

"Figures, tell me everything is all right at home."

"Everything is fine. I just wanted to talk to you, but your guards…"

"Handmaidens."

"Handmaidens…your handmaidens did not seem to want you to talk to a boy, so I lied about my message."

"They are just following the rules. Iphigenia will have to watch while we talk. But I am glad you lied to the other handmaiden, since being a priestess can sometimes be tiresome. Although I am very fond of the women of the temple, I miss seeing you. Congratulations on the long jump. I prayed that Artemis should help you win that event. You were unlikely to win any of the others."

"Thank you. Perhaps Artemis did help me win. How did you manage to get the aulos player to play your melody and to sound so much like you?"

Phyllis laughed. "I taught him. When his wife came to pray for his success. I told her he would play perfectly if he learned one tune from me and played it when I commanded. I thought you would do better with a familiar tune, even though I could not play for you myself."

"I think it helped my timing—and right timing is the most important part of the long jump. "

Phyllis said, "Winning is wonderful. But I have not been doing much winning recently. My second year as a priestess is coming to an end soon, and my father has failed to find a husband for me. In addition to rejecting me for being too independent or too boyish, the other families—at least the ones who have not already married off their sons—fear me because of that notorious day when Artemis occupied my body. They think I am haunted."

"That what I wanted to talk to you about. If you can predict the future, what can you tell me about tomorrow's wrestling matches? I have to wrestle Narcissus. Remember the day that Pyrrhus arrived and Narcissus easily beat me. Can he do it again?"

"I know nothing about that. Sometimes Artemis comes in a dream, and I believe she has inhabited my body, but on my own I know nothing. You will wrestle Narcissus, because that is the rules. One of you will win."

"Actually I am glad to know you lack magical powers. I like you as a human."

"Then you may like this. Now that my father has exhausted every possible rich husband for me, he is thinking of asking Phidias for you to marry me. But with no magical powers, I can't predict whether it will happen."

"Marry me? Me marry you? I thought that was out of the question. I had put the idea out of my mind. No rich father would choose a poor boy that everyone laughs at to be his daughter's husband. No one else is offering Phidias a daughter either. I have tried to forget about marriage completely. Not all men get married."

"But most do. My father may have changed his mind about you because you are the cousin of the king, and therefore more desirable, although still poor and of course still in love with mathematics, which will likely keep you poor."

Figures said, "But you cannot predict whether it will come true, whether we will marry or not?"

"Nor can I tell whether we would like it if we married. I don't want to run a household like your mother. And I like my life with the women of the temple. I have made close friends, here. But we have no real choice. If our families choose to have us married, that will happen."

"Of course, I cannot predict the future either. We will have to make the best of what we are given." Impulsively, he gave Phyllis a tight hug and kissed her with considerable abandon.

The handmaiden Iphigenia pulled Figures away. "You are not allowed to touch the priestess. Phyllis, you need to return to your duties."

Phyllis said, "All right. Figures, good luck with the wrestling. If it is your fate to win, I know you will. But you are already a winner with the long jump, so all your practice paid off. And you can beat me in wrestling, and I am very good."

Iphigenia said, "Say goodbye."

Figures and Phyllis said goodbye together as Phyllis was steered through the temple door. Figures thought about luck and fate. He believed in luck, but he was not sure about fate. He tried to guess whether this new turn of events was luck or fate, and he was not sure. He was sure that it was not the work of Artemis.

⬟ That night Figures lay awake for a long time, uncertain whether to worry about wrestling or marriage. Finally he fell asleep.

He dreamed that he and Phyllis were to be married. After ritual baths in the women's quarters at Phyllis' home, attended only by women, she is transported at night to his house. Following the marriage custom, Phyllis cuts her hair and gives the hair to Artemis for a wedding offering. But since Phyllis habitually wears her hair at a boy's length, when she cuts her hair, she removes all of it and comes to the wedding bald. Figures tries to grasp the hand of Phyllis' father to symbolize the transfer from her father's household to the new one. But he cannot connect with her father's hand.

Figures is back at Phyllis' house where she is being bathed by several women — Hypate, Claudia, Andromeda. But as Phyllis emerges from the bath, she turns into the beautiful woman he had last seen persuading Pyrrhus to abandon the war. People thought that she was the nymph Arethusa, turned back from a spring into a nymph. Then Arethusa steps back into the bath, and changes back into water, keeping her shape as a woman for a moment, then flowing back into the bath.

Figures looks for Phyllis. One of the women holds locks of hair, but she is not Phyllis. She is Hypate — or perhaps her mother, Claudia--coming to Figures as if they were to be married.

Figures searches for Phyllis. She is no longer bald. He says, "I could not find your father's hand." Phyllis holds out both her hands toward Figures, but takes his right wrist with her left hand in the pose wrestlers use to start a match. She says, "You must practice wrestling," and grabs his body and throws him to the ground. He pulls her down with him. He is wrestling with Phyllis, then Arethusa, then Hypate, then Claudia, then Phyllis.

Then he woke up. He remembered everything but understood none of it.

SCROLL 22

● Figures arrived at the stadium early for the wrestling, but Narcissus and Jason were there already.

Narcissus was saying, "I don't expect my match with Figures will take much energy or time, so you and I will be at it soon, Jason."

"You may be surprised. I have been practicing with Figures. He is better than he looks."

Figures wished Jason would keep quiet. It would be better for his strategy if Narcissus assumed that he would be easy to beat. He hoped to win through leverage and changing centers of balance rather than counting on strength or speed, and surprise was essential. But Narcissus would not believe him if he bragged, so he said, "I have been practicing. I am not the same boy you took down so quickly on the day Pyrrhus arrived." He thought that reminding Narcissus of how easily he had once been beaten might counteract the remarks by Jason.

By now the audience was entering the stadium. A judge told the boys to enter the tunnel until religious ceremonies were complete.

When Artemis had blessed the contest, the judges summoned the boys from the tunnel. The crowd roared, for all three already were winners.

Narcissus and Figures each won only one event, so they were to wrestle first. The winner would wrestle Jason for the prize, a crown of olive leaves placed on the champion's head by Phyllis. Her handmaidens also would present the winner with a ceremonial tripod—a metal bowl with three long legs that must be carried to the temple of Artemis and left for an offering.

Figures and Narcissus had left their clothing in the tunnel, so there was nothing more to do than fight.

● Narcissus appeared eager to start the match, which

Figures thought would be helpful. He lingered outside the dug-up place at the center of the stadium, hoping to make Narcissus even more eager to attack. His planned first move depended on Narcissus attacking vigorously.

Narcissus said, "Come on Figures. I am eager to get to Jason."

Figures stepped forward. With their foreheads touching, each encircled the other's right wrist with his own left hand. The judge stood ready with a flexible rod, ready to strike either boy if he moved before the match started.

The judge said in a voice loud enough to be heard outside the stadium "Begin!"

As Figures had anticipated, Narcissus released his hold on Figures' right wrist while pulling his own arm away. The classic opening would be for Narcissus to lunge forward with his hands rising to take Figures by the shoulders. This common plan takedown began by pulling your opponent close. Then the aggressor drops his right hand to the opponent's waist. With one arm on the right shoulder and the other behind his waist, the aggressor lifts his opponent and throws him to the ground, winning the point.

But Figures had practiced this with Jason many times. At first Jason always succeeded. Figures observed that the lunge toward the shoulders left his opponent leaning slightly forward. With his models, he tried several different holds that might use that posture

The next time he and Jason practiced, he tested his new plan and for the first time succeeded in gaining the point. But it had only worked a few times, for soon Jason learned not to lunge forward at the start of a match.

So when Narcissus reached for his shoulders, Figures took a step backward, as if afraid to fight. Narcissus reached for the shoulders, but Figures raised his hands faster and put them both behind Narcissus neck. As Figures stepped back again, he clasped his hands together and pulled hard. Narcissus began to fall forward and Figures stepped back a third time. Narcissus stumbled and both knees touched the ground. First throw to Figures, with two more needed to win.

Narcissus said, "You can run from me and make me stumble, but you will have to fight me to win this match."

Sometimes the winner of a point paraded around and waved his arms to the crowd. But Figures decided that it was better to appear frightened of Narcissus, so he simply stood with his arms and head down. In fact, he was frightened. When he pulled Narcissus down, he realized how hard Narcissus' body felt and how strong he seemed.

⬟ He knew that he could not surprise Narcissus the same way again, so he had planned a different strategy, although it depended on how Narcissus attacked. In all cases, his idea was to use the weight, strength, and position against the opponent.

The judge summoned them back into position. While they put their foreheads together and took hold of the wrists, Narcissus murmured, "Your tricks won't work this time." Figures worried that he might be right.

The judge called out "Begin!" and both fighters loosed their grips on the wrist and for a second just pressed their heads against each other. Figures felt his head moving backward, but could not press hard enough to hold it in place.

Narcissus put an arm around Figures' waist and, partly spinning Figures around and partly stepping around him, he moved behind him. Narcissus now put both hands around Figures' middle, but Figures knew what was coming and what he needed to do.

The plan was to place one foot between Narcissus feet and bend whichever way he was leaning to get him unbalanced. They might both fall to the ground together, but in that case, neither wrestler would receive a point. It was not as good as gaining a point, but certainly better than losing one.

But Narcissus was too fast this time. He lifted Figures' feet from the ground before there was a chance to place his foot anywhere. This point would be lost unless Figures could pry Narcissus' fingers away and escape the hold. But Narcissus' fingers refused to be pried. Figures struggled with the fingers, while Narcissus turned his body around in midair, then flung him to the ground hard.

As Figures slowly got up, he realized that not only had he lost the point, but also his left shoulder hurt from where it hit the ground. But he could not show how much he hurt, so as soon as he was on his feet, he moved swiftly toward the center of the dug-up area.

"You won that point, Narcissus," he said, "so we are even. But we are not even, since I know how to win and you do not. Let's get on with this match."

⬟ Figures knew that the racer Narcissus' legs were his strong point; there were advantages to attacking your opponent's strength. A successful attack tended to make the opponent fear you more. Also, if you forced the muscles to move the body in the proper direction, their strength would help propel the fall.

Once again their heads were together and wrists clamped. Figures tried to forget about his sore shoulder. The judge shouted, "Begin!" Moving as fast as he could, he bent down and with both hands grabbed the back of Narcissus' right heel. Pushing his good right shoulder as hard as he could into Narcissus' stomach, he pulled as hard as he could on Narcissus' heel.

Narcissus was unbalanced, and when he tried to keep himself from falling by thrusting his left foot strongly down, he pushed himself farther off balance. At the same time, he tried to hang on to Figures so that if he fell he would take his opponent with him. But Figures, with his shoulder pushing into Narcissus' stomach was not easily reached.

Narcissus fell backward but managed to grasp Figures by one arm, but Figures, with his feet planted firmly in the ground and knees bent, was in a stable position and able to stand up straight. Narcissus sprawled on his back.

Now Figures had two of the three points needed to win. But he could see that Narcissus arose with a new purpose and a wild look of anger on his face.

⬟ This time the two opponents did not speak as they moved into position. Figures knew that when he was angry, he found a strength that he did not normally have—and that was probably true of Narcissus also. On the other hand, strong anger could lead to rash moves, which could be an advantage.

This might be one of those times when it would be helpful if Artemis intervened, the way Phyllis often thought She did. But since he did not believe that Artemis existed, he did not think he could count on Her help.

When the judge shouted "Begin!" Figures saw Narcissus start to bend down and take his legs, like Figures had done to him. But Figures knew the defense against this move, which Jason had often tried—usually successfully—against him. He took Narcissus by the shoulders, turned, and knelt on one knee, which the judge would not call a takedown. Because Narcissus was already leaning forward, it was possible to pull him farther. With Narcissus on his shoulder, he raised up, lifting Narcissus' strong legs off the ground. Meanwhile, Narcissus had reacted to this change in position by reaching to take him around the waist again, hoping to repeat his successful throw from the second encounter.

As Figures used all his strength to push Narcissus over his shoulder, he realized that he was being held tightly. Narcissus would not be dislodged and thrown to the ground. Narcissus was upside down, but his arms were firmly locked on Figures' body. He tried to pull Narcissus' arms away, but the opponent was too strong for him

At least they both could go down, scoring no point for either wrestler. Figures stepped forward and deliberately fell so that Narcissus would have little time to improve his position.

But when Narcissus landed on his back, something

unexpected happened. Later Figures decided that Narcissus had made the mental error of assuming that both were down and no point would be awarded to either one. For this reason, or perhaps just because of the impact--made more powerful because Figures' weight was added to his--Narcissus relaxed his grip on Figures body just enough that he could escape.

His luck continued. Now he pushed hard on Narcissus chest and was able with this move to put his own feet on the ground. If he pushed hard enough, he thought, he might have enough momentum to stand upright. In fact, he had more momentum than needed, for he felt himself falling backward. He was barely able to keep his footing by extending one leg behind him.

He was standing and Narcissus was on the ground. It was the third takedown, so Figures had won. The crowd cheered. Later Phidias told him that no one had really believed he could win against Narcissus and that none had ever seen a move like that last point.

He thought, I did this without any help from a goddess, but I was very lucky to win at all.

● Figures still had to wrestle Jason. A few minutes passed between the matches so that the audience would have time to make final bets on the outcome. During this time, Figures realized how sore his shoulder was. During his struggles with Narcissus, the injured muscles had been forgotten.

The match with Jason was much less dramatic than the one with Narcissus. Because they had practiced wrestling together, Jason had learned the ways he could keep an opponent off balance and how to avoid them. From the beginning, Jason held on to his wrist and if Figures released Jason's wrist, Jason took his other hand. Jason was strong enough that once he had both of his hands, there was little Figures could do with his arms.

The second line of attack for Figures involved using his legs to unbalance Jason or to push one of Jason's legs out from under him. Jason had thought about this also, so he simply stepped hard on both of Figures feet as soon as the judge said, "Begin!"

With Figures disarmed (and dislegged, for that matter), Jason simply used his superior strength to push him sideways to the ground the way an arm wrestler pushes down an opponent's arm. It worked for the first point, and Jason saw no need to abandon it. On the second point, Figures pulled his feet back quickly to escape Jason's stepping on them, but this had the effect of leaving him unbalanced himself, so once again Jason easily pushed him to the ground — somewhat faster this time, so he once again landed on that sore left side.

As they positioned themselves for the third point, Figures' left arm hurt even as he moved to grasp Jason's wrist. He hoped that Jason had not seen him wince. Jason surprised him this time by using one of the leverage-based moves that Figures thought he had invented — but of course Jason knew this takedown from their practice sessions together. Jason stepped forward, turned, and lifted the sore left arm over his shoulder. Then, bending over, Jason threw him to the ground, winning the point, the match, and the pentathlon.

Figures, now aching all over, stumbled up. He gave Jason a hug and limped to the side of the stadium where Narcissus stood.

Narcissus said, "I could have beat him. He never could have done that to me."

"I practiced with him. I should have known that I might face him in wrestling, but I did not give it a thought. But I am glad. Jason wanted to win more than anyone."

"Not more than anyone. But wait until we race. I will trample over him on my way to winning."

They stopped talking when Phyllis and her handmaidens came forth to present Jason with the crown of olive leaves and the ceremonial tripod.

Later that day, Narcissus proved himself a better racer and predictor than he had been a wrestler. He won both the one-stadium and two-stadium races easily.

⬟   Shortly after the completion of the Syracuse Games, Hiero summoned Archimedes to the palace. When Archimedes arrived, he was introduced to Duilius, who was in charge of the Roman Navy.

Hiero said, "As part of the peace with Rome, we agreed to help fight against Carthage, although we are not at war with Carthage ourselves. The Roman Navy has a problem."

Duilius said, "The land war is going well, but we are being beat badly at sea."

"I told Duilius that I have a wonderful inventor working for me. He improved our siege engines so they no longer tip over. I said that this magician, Archimedes, would consider the problem of fighting ships and enable the Romans to succeed."

Archimedes said, "I know very little about ships, but I am always at your service, King."

Duilius said, "We look forward to your aid, Archimedes. We can begin by watching a mock battle in the harbor so that you can see how naval wars are fought. Hiero, if you could arrange for the merchant ships and fishers to keep out of the harbor for a day, I will have our Navy ships perform the battle. While we watch from the harbor wall, the people of Syracuse can be the audience. Mock sea battles are very popular in Rome."

Hiero said, "I will ask the priests and priestesses to declare a feast day. We will celebrate the winners of the Games, sacrifice to the Gods, and the mock battle will be the highlight of the day, to be followed by a distribution of food and wine. The people of Syracuse are due for a festival."

When Duilius left to return to the Roman camp, Hiero asked Archimedes to stay behind.

"I have faith that you will have an idea that will work for the Romans, but I am more interested in using your talents for the people of Syracuse. We have several times discussed improvements at the Euryalus Fort. Make that your next project. I will assign as many men and as much money as you need to redesign the Fort so that it is once again the impregnable defense of our city."

"I have already mapped the old Fort and I have ideas for improving it. I will begin immediately." Archimedes knew he had to help Hiero, even though he preferred to use his time studying mathematics.

⬟   The Euryalus Fort was not far from Archimedes' home in Epipolae, so each night he slept in his old room. In the morning, he would walk to the Fort and make sure that the workers were following his plans.

Many of the stones in the original Fort were huge, hard to lift, and tough to set into their new places. Workers handling the stones could barely fit their hands under one to lift it. Archimedes invented a device to help them clear away the rubble of the old Fort and move the stones.

He remembered how a lever had moved the huge boulder when he and Phyllis were trapped in the cave. The secret of the lever is trading distance for strength. The short end of a lever lifts a heavy stone a short distance while the other end moves farther. Ropes with pulleys can be arranged to that pulling one end of a rope a long distance could move the other end a much shorter distance, as effective as a lever but more versatile. Working in the open instead of inside a building, however, there was no place to attach the pulley arrangement.

Archimedes developed a combination device that used a long beam attached to a weight. The weight rode on a wheeled platform, while the beam was attached to a structure on the platform about ten feet above the ground so that the beam functioned as a lever, with the long part and weight on the platform and the short part projecting beyond the platform base. A pulley was attached to the short end of the beam. A large claw was suspended by the pulley from the projecting beam.

To lift a stone, the operator used a rope to open the claw.

Then the claw was positioned over the stone and lowered to the top of the stone. Releasing that rope let the claw close. The operator raised the stone by reeling in the main rope of the pulley.

⬟ The day of the mock battle arrived.

Figures came to the festival with his family, Hypate, and Claudia, but he left them to report briefly to Hiero on the work at Euryalus. When he started back to his group, he saw Phidias engaged in what appeared to be a very serious conversation with Phyllis's father. Meanwhile the three women had made their way from the seats in the amphitheater down toward the stage. He thought they were heading toward the location where Phyllis and her handmaidens were working with the priests of Zeus and Apollo to prepare the meat for the feast that was to take place after the mock sea battle.

Figures stood still and tried to analyze what his family was doing. He was sure that it had to do with him. Most likely Phyllis' father was bargaining with Phidias over the wedding arrangements, while the women were visiting Phyllis, perhaps to remind her of what a bride's duties and responses should be. Phyllis was not likely to know much about marriage ceremonies.

Figures did not want to be part of either of those conversations. First of all, it would not be appropriate. Also, he realized that he was not sure about the idea of marriage at all. He was hoping that after he finished rebuilding the fort and found a way to help the Roman navy, if he could, he would be able to spend his time on mathematics. Hiero might reward him sufficiently that he would not need to teach the way his father had always done. Instead of building devices, he could build theories and solve problems. That needed time to think. He was not sure that marriage to Phyllis would allow that.

⬟ Archimedes moved to a location where he could

watch the mock battle, conducted with ships whose prows were covered with bags of hay to prevent too much damage from ramming. The Roman triremes all carried a large flag with the image of an eagle, while the flag of the Syracuse navy bore an odd symbol featuring three equally spaced legs that radiated from a central face of a woman with snakes for hair—the woman, known as Medusa. The three legs represented Sicily, which is shaped somewhat like a triangle. Medusa, whose face was so terrifying that looking directly upon it turned the viewer to stone, is associated with protection, so her central location on the flag shows that Syracuse protects Sicily.

The warships were maneuvering into place and Syracuse appeared to be winning easily. Some of the Syracuse vessels swung around and rammed Roman ships in the side. Other Syracuse triremes moved beside Roman ships and tried to grab them with grappling hooks so that the marines from both sides could engage. From where Archimedes watched, every movement of the ships seemed to be happening in slow motion. Whenever a Syracuse ship rammed a Roman one or managed to grapple itself to one, the crowd roared.

It was very difficult to grapple another ship. Even though the Syracuse navy moved faster and with more accuracy than the Romans, a grappling attempt was usually foiled because the Roman ship could turn so that the ships did not become side by side. Often the more aggressive ship that was trying to connect with grappling hooks was rammed for its attempt.

On the rare occasions when a ship of either navy succeeded in grappling and boarding another vessel, the Roman marines showed their superiority by simply overpowering the marines from Syracuse. The commanders of Syracuse's navy switched their tactics to rely entirely on ramming, where they were more successful.

Archimedes thought: If I could think of a way for the Roman marines to board ships from Carthage, the Romans would have the advantage. Grappling is too difficult, however. There must be a simpler way to connect two ships that would work when one does not want to be connected.

As he struggled to find an idea, one of the Syracuse triremes was more effective at ramming a Roman ship than expected. Despite the hay, it stove a large hole in the side of the Roman vessel, which began to sink. The Roman marines did not know how to swim, so the "battle" halted while the Syracuse sailors tried to save the Romans from drowning.

At that point, with his attention distracted from trying to find a solution to his problem, Archimedes had an idea. There was too much confusion and noise for him to work out the details, so he left the festival and headed for Euryalus. There he would be alone and also would have some tools that might help him see how the idea would work. He left without telling his family where he was going. They were used to his disappearances and also he was not ready to talk to his father about marrying Phyllis.

⬟ After he left the region around the Great Harbor, he was out of the crowd. Nearly everyone in Syracuse had gathered to see the mock battle. There were a few people around, however, so Archimedes was not surprised when he heard footsteps behind him. He turned to see if perhaps Phidias had seen him leave and was following him, but saw no one there at all.

As soon as he reached the fort, he went through a tunnel to a small platform where the apparatus with the giant claw designed for moving stones stood unattended near the top of the cliff that marked one of the least approachable sides to Euryalus. His idea was that he could mount such a machine on the front of a Roman trireme. The claw could be dropped on the opposing ship and pull it beside the Roman ship.

Archimedes slid into the operator's position and raised the claw. But he realized then that his idea would not work. A claw landing on a deck would have nothing to grasp. A much larger device might capture the whole prow of a ship, but a machine that big would be so heavy it would sink the ship that carried it. He needed something lighter, something that would hold the ship in place.

Now he did hear someone approaching. Maybe Phidias had followed him after all. But the person who walked out of one of the tunnel entrances was someone else, someone carrying a short sword in his right hand.

With feeling of intense shock and fear, he recognized Malchus.

The man with the sword shouted, "I see you know me, Archimedes. Now I will be the last person you ever see."

"Malchus? But you are dead. You drowned when my catapult sank your boat."

"Your sailors are idiots. First I hid behind the boat. When they approached, I pulled the oars a few feet behind the boat. Then I held myself below the sea, dangling below the oars, putting my mouth up for air just for a second until your crew was gone. Like Odysseus using the wreckage of his ship, I floated and swam with the aid of the oars until I reached land. I was nearly dead, but not as much as you believed. Now you are the one to die."

Figures said, "You still want to sacrifice me to Baal? Did you bring your priest?"

As Malchus advanced toward Figures, he said, "I can sacrifice you myself. First I think I will cut off your hands, then your feet. By the time I remove your head, you will be praying to die."

SCROLL 23

◆Archimedes looked around the fort, but there appeared to be no way to escape. The cliff behind the terrace dropped many feet to piles of rocky debris, and Malchus was between Archimedes and the tunnel entrance, the only exit. He thought of a plan that might work, which was better than no plan at all.

Malchus began to advance toward Archimedes, who crouched behind the machine, his hands on the controls. He wanted Malchus to see him cowering as if hiding would protect him. Malchus raised his sword high as he approached. Timing his move carefully, Archimedes swung the claw over his enemy and dropped it on him.

The jaws closed around Malchus. Archimedes ratcheted the claw into the air, lifting Malchus's feet off the ground.

Malchus shouted, "This won't save you." His sword hand, raised high, stayed free. He began cutting the ropes that held the jaws in place.

Once Malchus escaped from the machine, Archimedes would have no other weapon. Something had to be done quickly--Malchus's sword was halfway through the rope.

They were near the edge of the cliff. Archimedes summoned all his strength and pushed the machine toward the cliff so that Malchus was suspended over the edge. A large rock in front of the machine's wheel stopped it before Archimedes could push it over. At this moment, however, Malchus cut far enough through the rope that its remaining strands broke, and the jaws swung open.

Malchus shouted, "Baal save me!" as he fell onto the rocks at the base of the cliff.

Figures was shaking with fear. He crouched low, ready to run as soon as he heard Malchus scrambling up the base of the cliff. But he heard only the wind and birds.

After a few moments, he felt calm enough to crawl to the edge and peer down. At the base of the cliff, Malchus lay

Before *Eureka!*

unmoving, draped over the stony rubble with his sword flung aside. One arm met the body at an angle never seen in life, and there was a small pool of blood near what appeared to be a new joint between the knee and ankle.

Figures stayed by the cliff edge for a few moments. Then he rolled one of the smaller boulders to the edge. If Malchus moved, he could drop the rock on him. But Malchus did not move.

Archimedes stayed by the edge of the cliff. As the sun grew low in the autumn sky, he heard a movement behind him. First, he glanced down to make sure Malchus's body was still there; then he faced the tunnel entrance, sorry that he did not have Malchus's sword.

⬟ Phidias emerged from the tunnel, saying, "I thought I might find you here, Archimedes. You disappeared from the feast. Your mother was frantic. After asking many and discovering no one who had seen you leave, I went home, but you were not there. Then I thought you might have come to work on the fort and been hurt. You seem well, but why are you still here? It will be dark soon."

Archimedes said, "Oh, Father. I almost was killed. Malchus is—was—still alive. He followed me here. I believe I killed him."

"Thank the gods! But where is he?"

Archimedes took Phidias to the cliff and pointed, then told his father all that had happened. When Archimedes described Malchus cutting through most of the rope and then falling, Phidias said, "Then you did not kill him. He killed himself trying to escape. Do not feel bad. He was the most evil person I have ever known. He deserved to die."

Archimedes said, "We must make sure he is dead. "

The two left the terrace and worked their way around the outside of the Fort to where Malchus lay. Phidias felt the body and listened for a heartbeat or breathing. He said, "We can have Hiero send soldiers to remove the body."

Then they started home.

⬟ While they walked Phidias asked, "Why did you leave the mock battle for Euryalus?"

"Hiero commanded me to help the Roman navy beat Carthaginian ships. I had an idea for something like my claw for lifting boulders, but when I studied the claw, it seemed too complicated and too heavy. Something simpler could work. The Roman marines are great fighters, so all they need is a bridge to cross from one ship to another. If one end of the bridge has a sharp spike, then a Roman ship could move close to an enemy trireme, then drop the spiked end of the bridge onto the other ship. The spike would penetrate the deck and hold the ships close while the marines stream over the bridge."

The two walked on in silence. Archimedes thought his father should tell about what Phyllis' father had proposed, so after a while, he said, "I saw you speaking with Phyllis' father before the mock battle started."

"Yes. He has been concerned about what Phyllis will do after she gets over this obsession with Artemis."

Archimedes said, "I hear that he hopes to find her a husband."

"He mentioned that. He is ready to let her go for a very small bride price. But Archimedes, although she is your friend, she is not a suitable wife. She has never shown any interest in managing a household. She plays the aulos and now has developed an interest in poetry. Clearly she expects to be a courtesan."

Archimedes knew otherwise, but if Phyllis had been offered, Phidias had clearly turned her down. Even though he had not thought much about marriage until recently, Archimedes felt a strange, hollow sadness overtake him. What would happen now to Phyllis or to him?

⬤ Hiero's workers built the device Archimedes had designed on the front deck of a Roman warship -- a raised bridge made of wood topped with a weighted iron point—

where it jutted up at a slight angle. Then Duilius, Hiero, and Archimedes stood on the wall overlooking the Little Harbor to observe its first test. While the triremes rowed into position, Duilius said, "Archimedes' new invention looks like a giant crow perched on the deck of our ship."

The ships began to maneuver, with the "Carthaginian" trireme trying to swing so that it could ram the Roman trireme armed with the "crow," a name that stuck. One marine aboard the Roman ship stood near the base of the crow, his hand on the lever that put it into action. Behind him, a troop of marines filled the deck.

As the prow of the "Carthaginian" ship almost touched the hull of the other trireme, the marine released the crow. The heavy iron beak plunged down and broke through the deck of the "Carthaginian" attacker with a crash loud enough for the watchers on the wall to hear. The ships were joined together. Now the marines rapidly ran across the bridge that connected the two ships.

Duilius exclaimed, "It works! Hiero, have Archimedes put a crow on every Roman warship."

⬟ The next few days were spent directing Roman shipbuilders outfitting the fleet with crows. When that was complete Figures went to the temple of Artemis to find Phyllis. After the usual struggle to get past the handmaidens, he was able to meet her on the temple steps. The same handmaiden as before posted herself in the door.

He said, "Is it necessary for your handmaiden to listen to everything you say?"

"Don't mind Iphigenia. She is very protective of me, but we have no secrets. I hear you have invented a device that will enable the Romans to defeat Carthage."

"I am not sure if it will do that, but the Roman navy may win some battles. My main work these days is rebuilding Euryalus, but that is nearing completion. What I want most is to be able to quit designing machines or forts and devote everything to mathematics."

"The gods should grant you that. I know that you are not interested in inventions and tutoring Gelo. But surely Hiero will reward you for all your help."

"I have been given a very good salary for working on the fort, although I have nothing to spend it on, so I give it to my family. They are supporting not only themselves and their slaves, but also Hypate and Claudia. But if I were married, I would have enough to start my own home, and I believe Hiero would support me well even if I only continued my tutoring."

"That's what my father thought also, which is why he offered me in marriage to you."

Figures was more angry than surprised. "My father would not tell me anything. He just rambled on about what wives are supposed to do."

"My father brought the matter up with Phidias at the festival with the mock sea battle. Your father thanked him for considering his family. Phidias spoke—I am told—about how talented I am. But he regretted that he could not accept, for Archimedes was already betrothed, which would be announced at a suitable time. I thought you must know all about that."

"No one has said anything to me. I cannot believe that my father would lie."

Phyllis said, "It looks like no family wants me to join them. It may all be for the best. This way we can still be friends."

"Are you going to become a courtesan and devote yourself to pleasing men for money?"

"I am not suited for the life of a housewife nor that of a courtesan. Although I play the aulos a little and I know the poetry of Sappho, I am not interested in entertaining or managing a household. Artemis will have to protect me and guide me through life. Don't worry."

At that point the handmaiden Iphigenia stepped toward them and said, "Archimedes, Phyllis has spent enough time in this interview with you. We need her in the temple."

Figures said, "What can you do? Will you become one of the handmaidens to the goddess yourself?"

Phyllis said, "I don't know for sure, but I am in good hands. And Iphigenia is right. We have talked long enough for today."

Figures left the temple in a state of total confusion. What plans did his family have? What would happen with the rest of his life?

⬟ Hiero summoned Archimedes to meet Duilius, who reported, "The Roman navy, once equipped with a crow on each trireme, sought and fought the Carthaginian fleet. The Carthaginians must have wondered what strange creatures were attacking. Some tried to ram our ships, while others aimed to attach grappling hooks. It did not matter. As soon as they were close, the crows bit and the ships joined. Our marines were ready to board the enemy and without fail took control of the enemy ship--a complete success."

Hiero said, "That is what I expected from one of Archimedes' inventions."

Archimedes was dressed in a toga for this meeting instead of his boyish chiton. He plucked at the still unfamiliar folds. "I am glad the crow worked this time. But you should keep in mind that you had the advantage of surprise. The Carthaginians are great sailors, and they may devise a way to prevent the crow from biting them."

Duilius said, "Even if they succeed, this battle has lost so many of their warships to us that I am sure we have the advantage whether or not the crow is still effective."

"I must reward Archimedes." Hiero took Archimedes' hand in his. "What would you most like? A house and some land? You are surely old enough to be married soon, and if you have a nice house it will help attract a suitable mate. I can provide a good bride price for you also."

Archimedes had been expecting a reward and had prepared an answer. "I want to devote myself to philosophy—to creating new mathematics and to using mathematics to explain the universe. But I can learn nothing more here—Phidias is the best teacher in Syracuse, and I learned all I could from him long ago. If you will grant me a request, then send me to Alexandria to study mathematics with the scholars at the Museum."

"I will do that on one condition. After you have spent a year or two there, you must return to Syracuse. I need you by my side. We need to go beyond rebuilding Euryalus and find ways to make Syracuse safe from attack by land or sea. You can do that and I cannot. Since I owe you a reward, I will grant you a year—at most two—in Alexandria, with money to support you while you study. And I will take care of your family while you are gone."

Archimedes thanked Hiero and as quickly as possible left to tell his family that he would be going.

⬟ While Archimedes walked home from Ortygia, he determined to ask directly about his parents' plans for him. They would be surprised that he was going to Alexandria, which might unhorse those plans.

When he entered his house, he found his father in the courtyard taking advantage of the sunlight to examine an ancient scroll. The house slave, Luce, was also there, watering some plants.

"Hello, Father. Luce, could you find mother, Hypate, and Claudia and ask them to join us? I have some news." Luce hurried off to the women's side of the house.

After Andromeda, Hypate, and Claudia appeared Archimedes said, "There are three new events. First, my invention worked well, and the Romans have had a great victory over Carthage's navy."

Andromeda gave her son a hug. "I was sure you would succeed."

"Second, Hiero has asked me what I would like as a reward. I asked for the chance to study mathematics."

Phidias said, "But you do that all the time now."

"I need to know more. I want to study with the scholars at the Museum, where the greatest thinkers of the world are. Hiero has agreed to pay my way to travel to and live in Alexandria for up to two years. I plan to go."

Hypate started crying, startling Archimedes, who would have not been surprised if it had been Andromeda.

Andromeda said, "We have other plans. Phidias, you must tell him."

"Claudia has agreed that you should marry Hypate. We are happy because she is also a Pythagorean, which is important. When you are married to Hypate, you will be able to maintain the same simple life you have now."

Andromeda added, "And she will be a wonderful wife. She has learned from her mother and me how to run a house. She has all the skills that are needed. And I am sure that you will come to depend on her, and she upon you."

"But I am going to Alexandria."

Hypate had stopped crying. She punched Archimedes hard in the arm. Her mother began to stroke her daughter's hair.

Claudia said, "That is all right. I am not sure Hypate is ready for marriage yet, and in any case I am happy to have her beside me for another two years. You can marry when you return. But you must promise to return."

"I have already promised Hiero that I will return."

Phidias said, "Then it is set. I have already arranged a suitable bride price for Hypate, which we can pay on your return."

"I would prefer to marry now, Archimedes," Hypate said. "If we must wait, then we must. And after we marry, I will be happy to let you think about mathematics all you like. You need a woman like me, who will keep you fed and bathed properly, to have the time to think and write."

Then she surprised Archimedes but throwing her arms around him and kissing him with more enthusiasm than Phyllis had ever shown. Archimedes thought that perhaps this new idea would turn out well.

⬟ And so it was arranged. Archimedes was to sail to Alexandria on the next ship that carried passengers.

During the few days that Archimedes waited for passage, everyone was surprised by the sudden death of Phyllis' father. He was found at his writing desk, with his massive history of Syracuse still unfinished.

Herc was overcome with grief at first. Soon after the funeral, however, he realized that he must deal with new duties.

He consulted Archimedes. He told Archimedes that his mother had explained his new situation. A wife keeps possessions she brought to the marriage, but the husband's wealth passes to the adult sons. She said she had little of her own to keep, and Herc owned everything else. Now he needed to decide what to do about his mother, his sister, and his own life.

"Archimedes, I am in charge of everything at a very young age. I have considerable property and some money, but less wealth than people think, for Father earned almost nothing for years and spent lavishly on books. I have a wonderful library, but hardly any money. I also need to care for my remaining family. What am I to do?"

"You need to find a trade. You should do what suits you. I don't think you could make your living as a cook, nor do I think you would enjoy that line of work. What else do you enjoy doing?"

"I enjoy bargaining and I believe I would enjoy travel. What would you think if I came with you to Alexandria and became a trader?"

"You need to have something to sell."

"Alexandria has the greatest library in the world, and I have the greatest library in Syracuse. I can sell my father's books, which do not interest me very much since they are nearly all ancient documents. With what I make from the books, I can buy goods in Alexandria that are not available in

Syracuse. When I return, I can sell those items here. I am good a bargaining and I think I could make a living that way."

"Clearly you have already thought this through. Why are you asking my advice?"

"Although I would listen to any objections, I really don't need advice about my career or even how to take care of mother, who can take care of herself and our property if I make sure she has money. The problem is Phyllis. I ought to marry her off, but father has shopped her all over Syracuse without finding a husband. You were my favorite possibility, but your family has given you to Hypate."

Archimedes said, "Hypate is a good choice for me. She and I have quickly become much closer now that we know we are to wed when I return. I don't think either you or I are qualified to decide about Phyllis. Her term at Artemis' temple lasts only a few more weeks. My impression is that she will be miserable when it ends."

Herc said, "I believe she has become very close to the handmaiden Iphigenia. She would regret losing that relationship even more than no longer being priestess. But I don't have enough money yet to set the two of them up in their own house."

Archimedes said, "Let's consult Hiero. He has the power to change almost anything in Syracuse."

⬟ Archimedes and Herc found Hiero in the palace, playing dice with Gelo. Gelo was winning, but Hiero was cheating to give Gelo the advantage.

Archimedes spoke first. "King Hiero, my friend Heracleides has a puzzle we hope you can solve."

Herc said, "Archimedes and I want to find a place in life for my sister Cleoboule, known by her nickname of Phyllis, who is nearing the end of a second term as the priestess of Artemis. She seems not to be suitable to be someone's wife, and I would not be happy to see her become a courtesan. I barely have enough inheritance to support my mother properly. Furthermore, I plan to travel to Alexandria with

Archimedes, so we need a solution for her in place before we leave."

Hiero said, "Gelo, go to your mother. I need to think about this."

While Gelo picked up the dice equipment and wandered off, Hiero appeared to be deep in thought. Finally he said, "Who is the next priestess of Artemis?"

Archimedes said, "She has not been chosen yet."

Hiero said, "I know that the tradition is that the priestess is always a young girl. But Cleoboule has shown that she has a special relationship with the Goddess. When the Goddess occupied her body, she predicted my kingship and, I believe, our alliance with Rome. What if we changed the tradition and kept Cleoboule the permanent princess?"

Herc said, "Can you do that?"

Hiero said, "I can talk to the Assembly. Since they declared me king, they have let me make the decisions. This might startle them, but I believe they would accept my advice."

And that is what happened.

Archimedes was allowed to tell Phyllis, who had not been consulted about her own fate. After the usual wait while a handmaiden summoned her, Phyllis and Iphigenia emerged and met Archimedes on the steps.

Archimedes said, "I have just come from the Assembly. Hiero has proposed and the Assembly has accepted a new rule: You are to remain Artemis' priestess for the remainder of your life."

The two girls screamed happily and both rushed to Archimedes and got in each other's way, hugging him tight. Archimedes was taken aback, but decided that the plan for Phyllis was probably the right thing.

⬟ A few days later, Archimedes and Herc arrived at the boat that was to take them to Alexandria. They had to wait for a merchant ship that had room for Herc's many boxes of scrolls that he planned to sell to the Library. Archimedes also

Before Eureka!

was bringing scrolls—precious mathematical works that his father gave to him to help him in his studies.

Both families came to the ship to see them off. Phyllis kissed her brother goodbye, but then pulled Archimedes apart from the others. She said, "Artemis was with us when we were trapped in the cave and she guided my hand when I shot Atban. So I am sure that she will watch over you in your travels. I would love to go to Alexandria with you and see the temples there and along the way, but now I am tethered here by my duties as priestess and also by Iphigenia."

Hypate walked closer and said, "Do not stay away too long, Archimedes. I look forward to your return and our marriage. Hiero has told me that his wedding present to us will be our own house and some land in Epipolae. I am eager to set up housekeeping, although of course Claudia will come to live with us."

Andromeda said, "I am not sure that I can part with Claudia. It is difficult enough to lose Hypate and Archimedes. But Archimedes, Hypate is right to ask you not to stay too long in Alexandria. You can learn everything you need to know in a year or less. I suspect you will teach the mathematicians of the Museum as much as they teach you. "

Phidias said, "These women would have you lose the opportunity of a lifetime. It has been years since I was in Alexandria, but it was already the most exciting place in the universe. Take advantage of this opportunity while you are young. You can live a long, happy life in Syracuse with Hypate, and missing a few years should not hurt."

Claudia said, "Pay no attention to your father, Archimedes. Hypate needs you more than Alexandria does."

Herc said, "The ship's captain is signaling us. We have to sail now while the tide is right."

Everyone hugged and kissed each other one more time. Then Archimedes and Herc stood on the deck of the ship while it sailed out of the Great Harbor.

Bryan Bunch

Before *Eureka!*

POSTLOG: THE TOMB

A small harbor filled with fishing boats slowly came into view. High above, a strong wall followed the bay and a strip of land that projected into the sea--an island, but so close to shore that it seemed a part of Sicily. My Sicilian adventure is about to begin, thought the lean, almost cadaverous, young man, his eyes intent upon the scene. Cicero had been watching the shore since dawn, waiting for this sight-- Syracuse at last. It was good to breathe the air of land again.

He thought about the esteemed visitors who preceded him to this great city — the philosophers Plato and Pythagoras, the playwright Aeschylus, the poet Sappho. The mathematician and inventor Archimedes had lived nearly all his life in Syracuse. His thoughts drifted from those men and women of fame to himself: In the future when historians tell the story of Syracuse, he mused, they will surely add the name "Cicero" to the list.

"We are arrived, Quaestor," the captain of the trireme announced, using Cicero's new title. Quaestor was an important title, bestowed by the Roman Senate, but only the first step up for an ambitious Roman politician. Cicero belittled the honor to his friends but in his heart was thrilled with the appointment to Sicily. As a Quaestor he now was eligible for a place in the Senate. Senators had real power.

Cicero turned to his personal slave and constant companion Tiro and said, "I recognize the battered harbor walls of Syracuse, once protected by Archimedes from both Rome and Carthage. Times change. Carthage is no more, gone these seventy years. Syracuse is no longer a kingdom. I expect that while I am Quaestor, it will be my own province of the Roman Republic. Make a note of what I just said, Tiro." Cicero exaggerated here, for he had not come to rule Sicily, but to purchase its wheat and to ship the grain to famished Rome.

If he succeeded in relieving the Roman shortage of food, he expected to enter the Senate with glory. Everyone would hail him as "the man who stopped the famine." In the past he had endured his share of derisive nicknames, beginning with "Chickpea," which is what *cicer* means in Latin, and then "the Greek," from his knowledge of the language of Plato and Aristotle. He liked "the man who saved Rome" as a new nickname. But soon, he thought, his name would be *Senator* Marcus Tullius Cicero. And after that, perhaps, just maybe, Consul, the highest post in the Roman Republic.

Cicero's reverie was halted by the bump of the trireme striking the dock. Tiro would take care of his baggage, so he jumped off the ship and headed toward the gate in the harbor wall. A pudgy man dressed in a formal toga was calling his name.

Cicero stepped forward. "I am Quaestor Cicero."

The pudgy man announced himself as representative of Sextus Peducaeus, the governor of Sicily, sent to guide Cicero to the governor's palace.

As they passed through crowded streets, the governor's man lectured to Cicero in a loud yet sweet voice. Cicero thought that his greeter had come by his role because of this exaggerated manner. More than a greeter, he spoke like a walking guidebook.

"Syracuse is as old as Rome, founded by Greeks from Corinth at about the same time as Romulus and Remus founded Rome. The Corinthian Greeks discovered our great harbor, the best port in the Mediterranean. The Corinthians were astonished to find a large fountain of fresh water flowing right beside the salty sea, surely a sign from the gods. The spring was once the beautiful nymph Arethusa, turned into a fountain by the goddess Artemis, whom you Romans call Diana. The site of the fountain of pure fresh water is the island of Ortygia, just across this bridge. Ortygia contains the oldest temple of the city, originally for Artemis, but now also dedicated to her brother Apollo."

Soon they reached a large stone building in the Doric style, standing behind an impressive statue of the Tyrant Dionysius. Their guide nodded to it, "Dionysius, the famous tyrant, who rule Syracuse when our city was more powerful than Rome. The governor's office is here." Cicero and Tiro followed the guide into the governor's office, off an inner courtyard.

The governor of Sicily, Sextus Peducaeus, was a powerful balding man with a pink skin and a snub nose that rather gave him the look of a pig in a toga.

"Welcome, Quaestor Cicero," Peducaeus began. "I am sure you will profit by your year in Sicily as I have profited greatly from being its governor. I am sorry to see that you are unable to bring your young wife on this kind of duty, but you will no doubt learn to adjust to that as other politicians do when they move up the ranks. Sicilian women are very attractive when young, but they do not age well."

Cicero was pleased to be addressed by his new title. "Thank you, Governor Peducaeus. I think my wife and I will manage quite well with a year apart. Her fortune is her best feature." A Roman politician was required to be wealthy, a problem Cicero had resolved with marriage.

Peducaeus said, "Getting the Sicilians to release their grain may be difficult. In the past farmers found many ways to delay shipments or to hide grain. Furthermore, the price they ask is far too high now, and they hope to sell for even more coin when Rome becomes desperate. The political situation is another impediment, Quaestor. Farmers lead the Assembly. I have had much trouble with the Assembly and indeed with every attempt to govern this unruly island."

"They still have an Assembly?" Cicero was surprised to learn that Syracuse continued some vestiges of self-government. He had assumed that the governor had complete authority.

"Although ruled by Rome for the past 140 years, the Syracusans continue their own Assembly, dating from their early days as a democracy. Even when tyrants such as Dionysius or kings such as Hiero ruled, the Assembly persisted. It continues to linger under Roman rule, although without real power to govern. This Assembly is the most disputatious and faction-ridden organization ever known. It opposes me on all fronts, and its members continually complain that Roman rule is too harsh. The warring groups within the Assembly have come together on only one issue -- Sicily's harvest must stay in Sicily. If the Assembly could be persuaded to cooperate with Rome, I think that the principal farmers would stop their illegal tricks, and the famine-relief shipments could begin, for Sicily has grain to spare."

Cicero bragged, "I am here to solve these problems for you and to get the grain on ships to Rome. I have had great success arguing cases before the Senate in Rome. Let me present Rome's case before the Assembly of Syracuse, since they appear to be the key."

Peducaeus loaned Cicero rooms just off the central square, or agora, in Ortygia. Slaves carried his goods from the ship to his new lodging where Cicero and Tiro arranged an office. Tiro had been a gift from Cicero's father four years earlier, when Cicero was 27 and Tiro 24. Tiro was well educated and often helped Cicero escape from scrapes. They had become more like friends than master and slave.

As soon as they were settled, Cicero told Tiro that he planned to appeal to the pride of Syracuse, since he suspected that the city had no honor. He would remind the Assembly of the importance of Syracuse in the world, whether true or not. He would then tell them that such a great city would bring even more grandeur to itself by saving its mother, Rome.

Cicero counted on his skill as an orator, but Tiro suggested that other measures might help more than speech. Tiro had learned from the sailors aboard the trireme that Syracuse, like much of Sicily, was only partly ruled by the governor and Assembly. A shadowy organization of criminals determined which services were available to businesses or citizens and controlled many judges and members of the Assembly. Tiro proposed bribing the leaders of the crime organization. He said, "I will tell them that Cicero will pay from his own pocket for the names of farmers with secret supplies of grain."

Cicero said, "Forget about 'from his own pocket.' They won't believe you. Tell them that I have a large budget from the Roman Senate."

Cicero thought it was an excellent plan and made a mental note to take credit for the idea if the plan succeeded. Thus it would be an effort on two fronts--Cicero moving the apparent leaders with rhetoric, and Tiro paying hard cash to the bandits who controlled the city.

The Assembly met in the agora outside Cicero's office. When Cicero entered the agora for his oration and gazed on the faces of the Syracusans in the Assembly, he suspected that Tiro would be contacting some of these same men with bribes later that day, for several, in his opinion, appeared to be criminals.

Cicero spoke in a low voice so that the Assembly members had to gather close to hear him. "O great men of Syracuse. I am the new Quaestor from Rome, Marcus Tullius Cicero. I come to this, the principal city of the immense isle of Sicily, on behalf of the Senate and Consuls of Rome. They have directed me to gather the excess grain of Sicily for the provision of Rome and the countryside of Italy. In Italy crops failed this year from lack of water, Meanwhile Sicily has been blessed with abundant rain and warmth."

Tiro recorded every word in shorthand. Cicero habitually had Tiro take notes for him before arguing law cases but also commanded Tiro to copy every word of his arguments in court as well as other speeches he might give. In response to this burden—a burden since Cicero argued many cases and was apt to give a speech on any occasion—Tiro had begun to develop an easy way to record whole words with just a few strokes. The method, called "shorthand," enabled him to capture Cicero's exact words no matter how quickly his master spoke.

Cicero glanced at him and was glad that he would have these words available when he wrote his account of the mission or perhaps when he compiled all his great speeches.

The men of the Assembly were startled to be addressed by this stranger. One of them, Aegestes, a stocky, powerful-looking man with a squarish head and a complexion even more olive than most Sicilians, spoke loudly. "Who is this ass that the Romans have sent? He brays like a scholar, not a farmer. A farmer would understand that even after a good harvest we need grain for our families and slaves and seed for next year. There is no surplus. Even if there were, we don't need some dandy from Rome to help us sell grain. The price of grain is rising all the time. The longer we hold it, the more it will be worth."

Cicero replied, somewhat louder than before, "I am no Roman dandy at all, but a humble man from Arpino, a town that has no history worth repeating. But you citizens of Syracuse live in the tradition of a great culture that shines forth over the whole Mediterranean."

Aegestes jumped onto the platform next to Cicero and shouted, "He is wrong. Syracuse has not been important since the tyrant Dionysius lived. He both ruled the seas and hosted great poets. There has not been his like in hundreds of years. Today Sicily is just a breadbasket for Rome. Syracuse is just a provincial capital. We are continually abused by Governor Peducaeus. Peducaeus has been stealing our wealth from us as fast as he can, shipping our treasures to his villa outside Rome. This man," pointing to Cicero, "has come to help Peducaeus. Let us resist."

Cicero groped for a response and remembered Archimedes. "Dionysius was a great tyrant. But Syracuse has had a much greater citizen than Dionysius, and much more recently. I speak, of course, of Archimedes. His name will keep that of Syracuse alive in the minds of men for all eternity."

Cicero paused for effect.

Aegestes shouted, "Archimedes? When did he rule Syracuse?"

"Archimedes," said Cicero. "Archimedes saved Syracuse

when it was attacked by land and sea." Cicero decided to minimize that Romans were the attackers. He started again.

"Archimedes was the greatest mathematician of all time, and a great inventor also. When I first came to Rome I saw the planetarium he built. It is the most intricate working model of the heavens ever made, although already well over a hundred years old. But he was no mere philosopher. Archimedes alone held the Roman navy and army at bay before Rome came to take Syracuse under its wing and save it from the Carthaginians and other barbarians. Syracuse will always be remembered because Archimedes lived and died here. Surely anyone who has even the slightest connection with civilization would rather be associated with the mathematician Archimedes than with the tyrant Dionysius, who, in addition to his other foul traits, was perhaps the worst poet ever in the Greek language." Cicero felt on safe ground here for his own poetry had won praise in Rome.

Aegestes shouted, "Dionysius was our greatest king! We had no 'King Archimedes.'"

Cicero ignored him. "Archimedes fixed his brain on scientific research and discovery, the most spiritual nourishment known. But Dionysius dwelt on murder and oppression, and fear was his companion day and nights. Surely there are monuments to Archimedes all over the city. So take me to one now that I may make a sacrifice to the gods in his honor."

Someone in the crowd shouted, "Never heard of him."

Cicero recognized an advantage over the Assembly and pursued it. "Even if you do not know of a monument to Archimedes, I do. It is his tombstone. The stone is famously inscribed with a sphere and a cylinder and the formula for the volume of the sphere, for Archimedes was the first to determine how to measure curved figures. The tombstone would have been erected about 135 years ago, not so long ago that inscriptions have been worn away by time. Let us go find this grave. Lead me to the cemetery."

Aegestes said, "The old cemetery is outside the

Agrigentine Gate, abandoned today. But there is no monument to this 'Archimedes' you have described."

Cicero walked past the statue of Dionysius and pushed through the crowd in the agora, while Tiro directed the bewildered Sicilians to follow him. Cicero asked the nearest Sicilian the way to the Agrigentine Gate. He did not know if Archimedes' tomb could be found or even if it really existed, but he thought it better to lead the members of the Assembly away from their natural place of business. He needed to establish as much control as possible. If the grave could not be found, he would blame them for destroying it.

The group walked through the Agrigentine gate. Greek cemeteries, like Roman ones, lined roadways outside the city wall. As Cicero expected, monuments to Syracusan noblemen and kings loomed on either side. Cicero paused at several monuments to read inscriptions that were still legible. While many of these tombs were old and in disrepair, the grass around most was cut short, and some showed evidence of recent sacrifices. None of the dead showed signs of being forgotten, which, if the Assembly members were typical, would be the case for Archimedes' tomb.

With that in mind, Cicero moved toward a weed-covered group of older tombs. The crowd behind him had grown larger now, for curious passersby were following the Assembly to see what might be afoot. Almost to his surprise, Cicero noticed a column topped by sphere and cylinder poking above the weeds. It could only be Archimedes' tomb. Now he could impress the crowd by knowing more about Syracuse and its history than the Syracusans knew themselves.

Cicero stopped. "I need help with these weeds. Summon the gardener and his helpers. We must clear away this thicket." Aegestes, immediately behind Cicero, called in a loud voice for slaves to help. Cicero sat on a convenient grave marker and considered his options as the gardeners worked. Within a few moments they exposed a small marble column topped with a sphere and cylinder.

Before *Eureka!*

Cicero strode to the grave marker. Peering at the column, he read from the partly eroded text "The volume of a cylinder is three halves that of a sphere whose diameter matches the cylinder's diameter and height--Archimedes of Syracuse." Cicero continued, "Since this poor tombstone appears to be the only monument to Syracuse's greatest citizen, I command that henceforward it be kept in perfect condition so that the citizens may visit it frequently and remind themselves of their greatest philosopher. Tiro, please arrange with the local priestess of Artemis (who, I understand, is the principal goddess overseeing Syracuse) for me to perform the appropriate sacrifice or rite here so that I may seek the gods' intervention on behalf of my mission."

Cicero stepped on top of the monument he earlier sat on and addressed the Assembly and the crowd. Still speaking without the trumpet sound of many orators, he continued loud enough that most people in the cemetery could hear.

"Men and women of Syracuse. I am Marcus Tullius Cicero, recently appointed Quaestor of Sicily with one mission, but grateful that I have been able to carry out another. I was sent to buy your grain and relieve the famine that has struck your mother Rome, but I am also proud to clear this monument, the tomb of the great Archimedes, whose achievements made Syracuse famous throughout the civilized world. Archimedes single-handedly saved your city when it was besieged by a powerful navy and even more powerful army. His practical inventions showed farmers how to water their fields and kept giant ships afloat. He built the most complex device ever assembled, one that faithfully keeps track of all the planets as they move through the sky. His studies of buoyancy showed why some solids float and how solids lose weight in liquids. The sphere and cylinder you see atop his tomb represent some of his deepest works of mathematics, which encompass ideas so subtle that only the greatest geometers understand them. He discovered and proved the law of the lever and how to count the ways to combine shapes. He set problems no one but he could solve.

Although he lived 150 years ago, he is still recognized as history's greatest mathematician and engineer."

Someone in the crowd shouted. "I know about Archimedes. He was a magician of long ago. But what Cicero says is true. With his magic he defeated great navies and armies, sinking ships at sea and unerringly hurling myriads of arrows at a time."

Cicero was about to go on to speak of the death of Archimedes, but he remembered that Archimedes' death was at the hands of a Roman soldier during the Roman sack of the city. It might not wise to introduce this tragic event into what he perceived had been a very successful speech.

"I will speak more of Archimedes later, when I come to make a proper sacrifice. First I must return to the agora. I will offer fair prices for all the grain that Sicilian farmers can spare. As I speak a fleet of ships travels to Syracuse to fetch that grain for a starving Rome. I know that I can count on the Assembly of Syracuse to aid me in this mission, helping me establish prices and finding ways to make sure my message reaches all the farmers of Sicily."

With that, Cicero returned to the Assembly and soon began the bargaining. That night, Tiro bribed several citizens to inform on grain hoarders and hired thugs to terrorize farmers who waited for higher prices. Within a few days Cicero collected enough wheat to fill the Roman ships.

Cicero's mission lasted a year, his term as Quaestor, plus one month. Much of his time was spent away from Syracuse. When he was in Syracuse, however, he visited Archimedes' tomb to commemorate the speech that he believed had turned the city to his favor.

He instructed Tiro to search the archives of the city and the homes of the oldest citizens for documents written by or about the great scientist, so that he could add them to his personal collection. Tiro located a trove of Archimedean documents kept by the priestesses of Artemis. Some scrolls were copies of Archimedes' mathematical works. There was a complete copy of the well-known life of Archimedes written by his lifelong friend Heracleides. The priestesses let Cicero purchase some of these scrolls and copy others for his collection.

The most surprising discovery from the temple was a set of scrolls in an unknown hand. These, when arranged in the proper order, contained a story that purported to tell the adventures of Archimedes as a boy. At first Cicero and Tiro thought that Archimedes himself might have written them. After comparing these scrolls to other writings kept by the Artemis priestesses, Cicero concluded that the narrative most likely was a fiction written by one of the priestesses — although many of the events were matched in the Heracleides *Life*. Women sometimes created such long stories, although men never paid much attention. Nevertheless, Cicero had Tiro copy the scrolls. He took copies of all the documents found in the temple back to Rome after his mission was over.

Cicero hoped his mission to Sicily would lead to great advances in his political career. On his return to Italy, however, Cicero discovered how much his mission really meant. After disembarking at Puteoli on the Bay of Naples, he encountered one of Rome's most eminent citizens and asked how his accomplishments across the sea were being received in Rome. The citizen asked, "Have you been away? Where did you go?" Almost no one in Rome knew more about his exploits in Sicily than that citizen did. Adventures outside Rome were appreciated only if they were military victories, and even victorious generals might not receive a hero's welcome.

Cicero devoted the rest of his life to politics and the law in Rome itself. Staying in Rome, Cicero was able to manipulate opinion and eventually achieved the high offices he so desired.

Bryan Bunch

APPENDIX

Before *Eureka!*

LIFE AND WORKS OF ARCHIMEDES

By Heracleides

Heracleides of Syracuse to Eratosthenes greetings:

I write to tell you of the death of Archimedes. Although you are now blind from age, surely someone at your Library of Alexandria will read this to you. You will recall that I once delivered messages from Archimedes to you on my regular travels between Syracuse and Alexandria carrying the finest in olive oil and other products, but as I am about ten years your elder, I no longer travel the trade routes.

Instead of simply sharing the news of the death of our mutual friend, I will report what I know concerning his life and also the personal circumstances that led to his great mathematical proofs. To understand his life, I also need to tell you of his cousin, King Hiero II, and the wars that affected Archimedes. It is a tale worth telling, and the truth has been hidden by wild rumors. Keep this history safe in the Library, for I want scholars down through the ages to know this wonderful man.

The greatest warrior of all time was Archimedes of Syracuse, even though he never lifted a sword or threw a spear. He won ferocious battles on land and sea almost single handedly. He succeeded by inventing deadly war engines. But he also created objects of immense utility and beauty. None of these meant much to Archimedes, however, for all he cared about was mathematics.

I knew Archimedes well, but I am deficient in mathematical knowledge and the understanding of the operations of the universe, especially when compared to Archimedes. I can only tell you what he told me about his discoveries. My only role regarding mathematics has been carrying copies of his work to his colleagues in the Museum in Alexandria. But I am sure you know his proofs, which are opaque to me, but have been recognized as both convincing and significant by the greatest philosophers throughout the civilized world.

Archimedes was born in Syracuse in Sicily shortly after the tyrant Hiketas overthrew the fourth democracy. It was one year before Herodorus of Megara won his second wreath in the Olympic Games for playing the trumpet more loudly than anyone had ever heard, causing some listeners to faint from the sound, and the year after Cimon won both races in the Syracuse Games. The mathematician's father was the astronomer Phidias and his mother was a cousin of the man who later became King Hiero II of Syracuse.

Sicily at the time of Archimedes' birth and for most of Archimedes' life was a contested prize. Lying between Italy and Africa, it was often the target of one or the other. Shortly before the birth of Archimedes, the tyrant Agathocles, who fought constantly to expand the region he could dominate, ruled Syracuse. A score or so of years before Archimedes was born, Agathocles attacked and nearly defeated Carthage, the Punic city on the coast of Africa more or less directly south across the sea from Sicily. Carthage later returned the favor and occupied most of Sicily save Syracuse itself.

During his wars against Carthage, Agathocles hired powerful soldiers from southern Italy. These soldiers were followers of Mamers, the God of War (known as Mars by the Romans). This army, known as the Mamertines, found itself unemployed when Agathocles died, so they ravaged the countryside of Sicily, living off their plunder. The Mamertines eventually settled at the northern Sicilian city of Messana, directly across from Italy. The continuing Mamertine ravages in and around Messana ultimately led to several events that I will recount later, including the rise of Hiero from soldier to king and the great war between Carthage and Rome. This war began when Archimedes was 23 and lasted until he was 46; then after an illusory peace, the war resumed when Archimedes was 69, continued until his death, and of course continues today.

Archimedes was a year older than I. Even as a boy he was recognized for his ability to solve problems and to build devices that no one else had thought of, but he was also known for his impiety and thoughtlessness. He had few friends as a boy. Because of his habit of drawing geometric figures on everything available, including food, as well as his ability to make complex calculations without aids, his friends called him by the nickname "Figures".

The young Archimedes was not strong or swift. Despite this, he participated in the Games at Syracuse and sometimes won events by using clever tricks. He was content to study, to explore the land around Syracuse, and to construct inventions. Although impious, the gods protected him and he survived various dangerous adventures.

His main teacher as a boy was his father, an astronomer. Phidias introduced him to the stars and planets, which he studied all his life. Archimedes built models of the universe as a boy, and in later years constructed the great sphere of the universe and the planetarium that are so famous today, although now carried off to Rome.

Phidias kept secret for nearly all his life that he was a follower of Pythagoras, since the Pythagorean society was often persecuted for their beliefs. I am the first to report this publicly, although his fellow philosophers knew his secret. Archimedes, thus, learned irreverence for the gods from his father, since the Pythagoreans believed that the foundation of the universe was number and that gods have little or nothing to do with the affairs of men. They also believed that the soul is immortal and will be reborn in another form--a man who is unlucky might be reborn as a beetle, while a beetle can aspire to be reborn as a dog or as a man. One joke that amused Phidias was that his son had the soul of an inchworm, which accounted for his habit of measuring and his close study of everything about him; or perhaps his son had the soul of a honeybee, since bees construct such geometrical combs. I have always thought that the reason Archimedes was so thin as a boy was the vegetarian diet his family maintained, which they did because it would be impious to eat the flesh of an animal that might have the soul of an ancestor.

When Archimedes was born, Hiketas had been tyrant of Syracuse for two years. Hiketas was a unpopular, despotic ruler. The Assembly obtained the help of King Pyrrhus of Epirus to drive Hiketas from the city. Pyrrhus, however, proved to be worse in many ways than Hiketas, turning against those who had invited him to the city and conscripting Syracuse's citizens for his army and navy so that he might, he planned, attack Carthage. Archimedes' cousin Hiero, a professional soldier, was lifted to the command of part of the Pyrrhic army.

Pyrrhus' plans to attack Carthage soon were in disarray. The Carthaginian navy set sail to attack Syracuse. The Mamertines also thought it was a good time to attack the city. With Carthage advancing from the south and the Mamertines from the north, and the uncertain allegiance of the Syracusans still in his army and navy Pyrrhus feared defeat. He announced that he had been summoned to Italy to help an uprising against Rome. Pyrrhus took his trusted lieutenants and the men of Epirus and his elephants, and all moved to Italy, leaving Syracuse and much of Sicily in disarray. The Carthaginian navy and Mamertines attacked Pyrrhus instead of Syracuse.

The Syracusan Assembly, fearful of the mercenary soldiers left behind when Pyrrhus departed, passed an edict driving all armies from the city, even the soldiers of Syracuse. These soldiers, who were forced to live off the country as best they could, elected their own co-commanders--Archimedes' cousin Hiero and a soldier named Artemidorus.

Hiero kept in touch with his cousin, Archimedes' mother, and with her husband Phidias. Phidias detested Carthage because Carthaginians, like their Phoenician ancestors, worship the god Baal, to whom they sacrifice children. Phidias complained often to his family and close friends, such as my own father, about the possibility that Syracuse might fall to Carthage. He said that it had been a mistake to rid Syracuse of its army.

Hiero conspired with his cousin, young Archimedes, on a plan to return to Syracuse. His first step was to position the loyal Syracusan contingent of his army directly outside the wall of the city. He moved that part of the army there under cover of darkness, while the mercenaries maintained camp and built their usual large fires. Any watchers from the wall would think that the fires were warming all of the outlawed army.

When the plan was set in action, Archimedes opened a city gate and let Hiero and his chosen forces pass into the city. When daylight arrived, with his armored men holding weapons at all the key points in the city, Hiero and his soldiers were in control of the city and the Assembly.

Hiero commanded the city but feared that the fickle Assembly would take action against him if he led the army into battle out of the city. The most popular and influential politician in the Assembly at that time was Leptines. Leptines had a daughter, Philistis. Hiero now courted and married her, giving him a much more secure place as commander of the city and its army.

Archimedes was often welcomed in the home of Hiero and Philistis, along with his mother and father. The couple treated Archimedes almost as their older son. He often played with their true son, Gelo, born soon after their marriage. To some degree, Archimedes was Gelo's tutor, much as Aristotle had been the tutor of the young Alexander in Macedonia. Hiero had recognized early on that Archimedes had an unusual ability to solve problems, especially mechanical problems, and so Hiero often turned to Archimedes for assistance. Because of these several factors, Archimedes, Hiero, and Gelo maintained a close relationship for all of their lives.

Although Archimedes had successfully designed equipment for the army and navy and advised Hiero on other matters for several years, he desired to study mathematics and philosophy at the Museum of Alexandria, the center of learning, instead of staying in Syracuse. King Hiero reluctantly let him leave for Alexandria on the condition that he would return to Syracuse as soon as he finished his education. With Hiero's backing, Archimedes was able to employ the best tutor available, Conon of Samos, the astronomer for Ptolemy, ruler of Egypt.

Conon is known today not for his many mathematical discoveries and studies of the times of eclipses of the Sun but for his explanation of how Queen Berenice's hair, which had been sacrificed for a favor from the gods and left in the temple, had disappeared. The disappearance of the hair was a great scandal in Alexandria, and Ptolemy threatened the full power of the state against the perpetrators when they were discovered. Hundreds of people were being arrested and tortured for information, when Conon came forth with the solution. Taking Ptolemy out of his home at night, Conon pointed to a spot in the sky between Virgo, Leo, and Boötes where he said the gods had placed the hair of the queen. The creation of the new constellation was accepted by the king and all of Alexandria, so any prisoners who had survived the torture were released from their bonds and freed. But this all happened before Archimedes came to Alexandria.

Conon and Archimedes studied a mathematical curve called spiral and found many wonderful properties. It was Archimedes' way, although he always was ashamed of this tendency, to seek practical applications of any idea. Archimedes believed that the philosopher must keep his thoughts above the material plane, but he could not keep his hands from making inventions. While in Alexandria, Archimedes began to wonder if he could find some uses for the spiral. At that time Archimedes saw how difficult it was for the common Egyptian farmer to raise the waters of the

Nile high enough to empty that necessary element into the canals that carried it to nourish the fields. That is when he thought of the spiral. When the spiral is rotated, it appears to carry the points of the plane within it to the outer rim of the plane. If a version of the spiral were made in space that had the same property, it might carry whatever was between its branches from one location to another. Archimedes took a small log and with some difficulty managed to cut a spiral into its surface. He called this version of a spiral the screw. When he turned this screw in his hands it appeared to carry space from one end of the screw to the other just as a spiral seems to carry parts of the plane outward. To make the screw carry water instead of space, however, the screw needed to be enclosed. Archimedes put his carved screw into a cylinder just tight enough to allow it to turn. With this device, he could put one end into water and by turning the device lift the water through the tube to the other end. There seemed to be no restriction on length, so the device was easily be extended to lift water from the Nile to a canal.

I do not know for sure, but perhaps Archimedes also showed his spiral device to a smith. In any case, around that time some smiths developed pointed metal screws that could be used to fasten sheets of metal or pieces of wood together. These work much better than nails or clips, but are very expensive and for that reason saved for special applications. Another application of the screw has become common since that time, an improved press for producing oil from olives, but I have no reason to think that Archimedes himself was involved in that invention.

I am also told that when Archimedes returned to Syracuse from Alexandria, the ship in which he was traveling began to leak very badly and appeared about to sink. Archimedes had brought with him the screw, which he was going to show his cousin, Hiero. The captain had heard stories that suggested Archimedes was a kind of magician and asked Archimedes if he could use his magic to save the ship and all their lives. Archimedes, as was increasingly the case, had been deep in thought and had not even been aware that the ship was sinking. When he heard of the difficulty, he immediately brought out his screw and showed the captain how to use it to remove the water that was seeping into the vessel. Members of the crew turned the screw and used it to keep the ship afloat until it could reach land for repair.

Archimedes was never proud of his inventions. Some of them were both practical and geometric, such as the screw, He also showed how to use a spiral to trisect an angle or square a circle, feats that no one knows how to do with the simple tools to which Plato limited geometry, the compass and straightedge.

But I have skipped ahead of my story. Return now to Archimedes' life in Alexandria.

Archimedes had from his youth loved astronomy and also always wanted to understand how even the simplest tool worked. He was a good friend to numbers, able to calculate results in his mind almost instantly, solving problems that others might need to work out in detail on a counting board. Although his father was a member of the Pythagorean sect, who believed in number as the basis of everything, Archimedes did not fall completely in love with mathematics until he went to Alexandria, where he learned the works of such early geometers as Hippocrates of Chios, who nearly squared the circle; Eudoxus, who discovered mathematics beyond ratios and whole numbers; Menaechmus, who first recognized the sections of a cone; and Aristaeus the Elder who wrote five books on the conic sections. Archimedes already knew geometry as it was taught by the famous Euclid, who had resided there just a few years before and written his *Elements* at Alexandria. I know that these were the main influences on Archimedes because he gave me the list himself when I inquired from whom he learned mathematics. He credited Conon of Samos as a principal influence.

Archimedes also traveled about Africa when he could, visiting the famous pyramids and Sphinx that were up the Nile from Alexandria. As he traveled between Alexandria and Syracuse he also stopped at Cyrene, which is about halfway between the two, although not on the seacoast. He visited Cyrene long enough to meet and study for a time with several of the famous philosophers who taught there, learning about the paradoxes of Zeno from Ariston of Chios, who was among the teachers.

While visiting Cyrene, he met and became friendly with the youth Eratosthenes, who was also studying philosophy and was considered by all to be the prize pupil. Archimedes recognized a kindred spirit in Eratosthenes and, although the two were not destined to meet each other face to face again, they later engaged in a correspondence on mathematical topics. Archimedes was in Alexandria for two years. Years after Archimedes had returned to Syracuse, Eratosthenes became the librarian of the famous Library at Alexandria, where he kept all of the letters and proofs that Archimedes had sent and continued to send to Alexandrian philosophers over the years. Fortunately all of these letters are still in the Library where they can continue to be studied by scholars forever. Some, of course, have been copied and recopied and are already known to philosophers in Rome and in the cities of Greece.

Archimedes had become interested in using geometry to establish and prove exactly how balances used in weighing, levers used in lifting, and similar devices work. He developed reasoning to explain the laws that govern these devices. Following the example of Euclid and others, Archimedes began with a few simple facts that all persons recognize. The main assumption was that equal weights placed equally distant from each other balance. With only a handful of similar assumptions, he was able to travel from this concept of a balance to the general rule for levers, which is as follows:

When unequal weights balance a lever, the ratio of the weights is proportional to the reverse of the ratio of the distances from the balance point.

He also demonstrated that by combining two or more pulleys, the same kind of proportion between two weights can be established. He told me that he also had observed that the same rules apply to the lever and the wheel, although he did not write this out because he was unsatisfied with his proof. But he demonstrated for me a device he had invented that used a movable lever to turn a wheel on its axle. I had never seen anything like it before. He claimed it to be exceedingly useful, and he incorporated it in some of his later inventions such as catapults and other war devices.

He wrote proofs of these principles in a letter on balances and levers that I delivered to one Polykrates in Alexandria, who had been a fellow student when Archimedes was there. It was more of a success with Polykrates than Archimedes had expected, for Polykrates copied the results and the proofs and issued them to other scholars in Alexandria as his own. Eventually a copy of the results, ascribed to Polykrates, reached Syracuse, infuriating Archimedes. Although Archimedes knew that he had originated these proofs, the results were being passed around to every philosopher under another's name. In time, Archimedes retaliated. He created some very clever results that appeared to be both remarkable and true, but in fact were remarkable because upon closer examination they were false. He also provided some misleading hints as to how the (false) proofs had been obtained. Then he sent the results and hints in a second letter to Polykrates in Alexandria. Of course he did not mention that he knew that his earlier work had been stolen.

In due time, he learned that Polykrates had once again stolen his work and was passing it around with apparent proofs. At this point, Archimedes let the truth be known among the philosophers he knew in Alexandria and also in Cyrene. He revealed the errors in the proofs and demonstrated that the results, although plausible, were false. The reputation of Polykrates was justly ruined, and he abandoned geometry to return to work for his father Kleon, an administrator of public works in Memphis.

Thereafter, Archimedes often issued his results without proof and often with a false proposition included among the true ones. At a later date, when any plagiarism would have already been broadcast, he would issue the same results, or at least those that were actually true, along with the proofs. Few dared to try to steal from Archimedes as this practice came to be known. In later years he continued to sometimes include false results in letters to mathematicians that he did not fully trust. He also sent correct results without proofs in one document and the proofs of the theorems later, often years later.

After Alexandria and for the remainder of his life, Archimedes worked continually on problems in geometry, sometimes even when I or others were speaking to him, including even the kings of Syracuse. He became famous for his concentration. His wife often had to summon him twice to meals or to remind him to go to bed, so intense was his concentration. He drew diagrams on any available surface, such as the oil on his skin that he had applied after bathing.

His memory for diagrams was acute and he could wake up in the morning and immediately redraw figures that he had sketched in dust the night before. Since he could keep a long chain of reasoning and the diagrams that went with it in his head for long periods of time, he did not commit his results to papyrus until he was sure that he had taken care of every detail. One result, the mathematicians to whom I delivered his letters would complain, was that while the results were clear and true beyond a doubt, the means by which he thought of making a particular diagram or line of reasoning was often obscure.

After the problems with the stolen results concerning balances and levers, Archimedes returned to the same subject and greatly extended the correct results and proofs as they applied to balancing, or putting into equilibrium, various plane figures, including triangles, parallelograms, and trapezoids. (*Translator: In modern terms he was finding centers of gravity for these figures, although he called the center of gravity the balance point. When there is a modern mathematical term different from that used by Archimedes, from now on I will give the modern equivalent in italics within brackets.*) Many of these balance points had been found previously, although he supplied new proofs in some cases.

Archimedes was exceedingly proud of these discoveries and sent two long letters to Conon of Samos in Alexandria. This became his regular practice--after he had worked out the proofs in detail of his mathematical discoveries, he put the results into lengthy letters addressed to other mathematicians, such as Conon or Eratosthenes; his lesser mathematical works were addressed to those who had asked him about specific topics, such as Hiero or his son Gelo. He also sent mathematicians in Alexandria and elsewhere propositions to be proved or problems to be solved. As I traveled frequently between Syracuse and Alexandria, I was privileged to be the bearer of the letters to mathematicians, most of whom were located in Alexandria at the Museum and Library. Archimedes chose not to describe most of his practical devices, such as the screw, crow, and odometer, in writing, however, although if the invention concerned philosophical knowledge he would write for the benefit of astronomers or other philosophers how it could be made.

His most astonishing achievement in these communications concerning balance points related to the figure one obtains by passing a plane through any part of a right circular, or isosceles, cone parallel to the axis of the cone [*the parabola*]. The section of an isosceles cone is a curve, just as the figure obtained by passing a plane through the cone parallel to the base is a curve, the familiar circle. Archimedes remained interested in the section of an isosceles cone for the remainder of his life. In his work on plane equilibriums, he computed the balance point for a section of an isosceles cone bounded by a line that is the base of the section.

Archimedes tried, with only partial success, to explain to me what he had learned and proved about balances, levers, and balance points. In the course of this explanation, he said to me "Give me a place to stand, and I can move the Earth." Archimedes did not mean this boast to be taken literally, but I relayed it to King Hiero in response to the question of what Archimedes was up to now. Hiero was always interested in any new device Archimedes had developed. Archimedes was summoned to the King. When Archimedes tried to explain what he had been investigating, Hiero quickly grew impatient. Finally Hiero interrupted an elegant explanation of how proof by contradiction works to ask if what he had been told was true--could Archimedes actually move Earth if he had a place to stand?

Archimedes explained to Hiero that he simply meant that with levers and pulleys he could in principle lift any imaginable weight with his own strength. Hiero would have none of this "in principle" talk. He wanted to know if Archimedes could use his pulleys to lift by himself any heavy object that was proposed. After some thought, Archimedes said that it was true, although even the strongest lever might bend and the strongest rope break and pulleys themselves, being made of material substances instead of being geometric circles, could also collapse when faced with a weight too heavy. Hiero began to search around for a heavy weight to propose as a test.

Gazing out on the harbor, Hiero observed the newly built freighter, the *Syracuse,* being loaded. Recalling how many men it had taken to slide the *Syracuse* off the dry dock into the water, he thought that the ship was as heavy as one might ask. Hiero summoned his ship builder and told him to bring Archimedes a sample of the strongest anchor rope and also a sample of the simple pulleys used in raising and lowering sails. After the ship builder presented Archimedes with these materials, Hiero asked if he could use them to lift the ship by his own power.

He told Hiero that he could draw the freighter *Syracuse* up onto the bank using only his own muscles and move it into dry dock that way. Furthermore, the ship could be fully loaded and the crew could remain aboard. The ropes were affixed to the *Syracuse* and Archimedes seated himself in a chair firmly attached to the stones of the city wall, where he could hold the grip on the pulley arrangement. The rope formed a giant web as it traveled around pulley after pulley. One pulley was fixed to the wall but the others were arranged so that they could move as the rope ran through them.

Archimedes astonished onlookers by pulling the heavily laden ship and its crew onto the dry land without much apparent effort, tossing excess rope behind him as he lifted the ship

A few years later, the war between Rome and Carthage was going back and forth, both on land and at sea. The Carthaginian Hamilcar Barca had landed on the other end of Sicily and was winning battles, expanding Carthaginian influence in an ever-widening arc. Hiero was greatly concerned that Hamilcar would attack Syracuse, either from land or with the aid of the Carthaginian navy from sea. He asked Archimedes to design impenetrable defenses for Syracuse. Hiero suggested that Archimedes might improve the catapult, which had been invented in Syracuse.

The catapult was one of those rare inventions that had completely changed warfare. It was a relatively recent invention from shortly before the time of Archimedes' father, when Dionysius ruled Syracuse. These first catapults used heavy bronze arrows, each as long as a tall man in the earliest catapults, with more recent ones using arrows twice that length. The basic mechanism of the early catapult was a giant bow to shoot such a heavy arrow. Archimedes developed a ratchet mechanism to hold the string as it was gradually pulled with back. A claw grabbed the string at its lowest position. Pulling on a rod raised the claw, which lifted the string off the ratchet and sent the arrow flying with such a force that it penetrated city walls. Over the next hundred years, one result of this invention was that most cities built new walls about themselves. These new defenses had to be more than twice as thick as the length of one of the catapult arrows. One reason that these thick walls were needed is that the catapult was also modified to propel heavy stones into the walls, which could produce more widespread damage than the bronze arrows did.

Hiero asked Archimedes to develop a catapult that could be transported by sea to defend Syracuse against an enemy navy. The device Archimedes had built was too heavy for an ordinary warship, but Syracuse had at that time the large freighter named after the city that could easily carry the mechanism. This was the *Syracuse*, which Archimedes had once pulled onto dry land. When the catapult was fired, a stone the weight of a man could be launched from the deck of the *Syracuse* and sent the length of a stadium, effectively sinking any vessel it hit. I do not think that this catapult ever saw action, but news of its existence helped deter attacks on Syracuse's navy.

The catapult was a powerful weapon but not very effective against an advancing army, other than by terrifying the soldiers. Only a few soldiers at a time could be hit by any single shot. Here the use of boulders as missiles was an improvement over arrows also. However, the time needed to cock the giant bow for a second shot was often so long that the army had advanced below the region where the missile could strike.

Hiero challenged Archimedes to solve these problems, also. He experimented with various devices that could change the angle of the catapult between firings, which changed the range. He also created combinations of levers and wheels that enabled quicker reloading. But his biggest innovation was developing a catapult that could launch a hundred arrows at once with each arrow following a slightly different path. This device rained down arrows over a wide swath of an approaching army. It could be quickly reloaded and aimed at a different group of the advancing soldiers. Hiero told Archimedes that if the Carthaginian army attacked, these varied showers of bronze arrows would quickly demoralize not only the foot soldiers but also the elephants and cavalry.

Seeing the great catapult on the deck of the *Syracuse* reminded Hiero of how easily Archimedes pulled this ship out of the water. It occurred to him that if Archimedes could lift that heavy freighter, he could unaided lift a warship, which, even with marines aboard, would be much lighter. When Hiero proposed this to Archimedes, he returned to the idea of a lever. He told Hiero that a lever might not be long enough or strong enough actually to lift a ship into the air, but it could be designed to pull the ship up enough to cause water to rush into the ship and sink it. Archimedes explained to me that the weight of a ship in the water is less than its weight on dry land. Thus, while a ship might be too heavy to lift with a lever, a ship in water would initially weigh less. Then, as it was lifted from the water, its weight would increase. So his idea was to use a long lever to lift one side of the ship a few feet only, putting the other edge into the sea, which would rush in and sink the ship.

There were many technical difficulties in creating such a lever, but eventually the device was made and stored at the top of the harbor wall. Pulleys lifted a long beam so that it could be swung over the edge of the wall. Archimedes used weights, large wheels, and pulleys to provide great forces—needed since the lever action was backward, with the force applied to the short end, causing the tip of the long end with a claw to move rapidly through space. The claw grappled a ship before it rowed out of range. Lifting one side of the ship a short distance allowed the sea to rush in, so that it sank when released.

Thus it came to pass that Syracuse had defenses for any possible Carthaginian attack, ranging from the mobile catapults aboard the *Syracuse* and mounted at various places on the walls of the city to the giant claw that could sink ships while they were still in the harbor.

For many years, however, these weapons were not needed. From time to time, however, a select crew from the army would be allowed to bring them out for practice, just in case they should be needed at some time in the future. This crew was enjoined to strict secrecy about the defenses, although some rumors did escape. Indeed, those who heard anything about the weapons usually heard an exaggerated account of how powerful they were, leading to many false beliefs among the armies and navies of Rome, the chief place that such rumors circulated.

Rumors of another invention of Archimedes also circulated among soldiers and sailors. They said Syracuse could set ships aflame in the harbor by concentrating the Sun's rays on the wood or on the cloth sails. Such an invention, as a weapon of war at least, did not exist. Archimedes had, however, once used a mirror this way to set a fire aboard a ship to escape from pirates. Perhaps the story that he could burn ships up from a distance began with people who knew about the pirate experience.

Even while working on these instruments of war, Archimedes continued to create new propositions in geometry. After sending the second of his letters on plane equilibriums to Conon, he had written a letter on the subject of the area of the section of an isosceles cone [*the parabola*]. While working on this problem, however, Archimedes learned that Conon had died. Thus, when he completed the proofs, he asked me to take them to a young man in Alexandria named Dositheos. Archimedes had learned that Dositheos, whom he had never met, had become Conon's favorite pupil after Archimedes returned to Syracuse. Thus it happened that the letter on the quadrature [*finding the area*] of the section of an isosceles cone was redirected to this Dositheos.

In the letter Archimedes showed by two independent methods that he had determined the relationship of the curve created by the section of a cone to a figure bounded by straight lines; that is, he had "squared" the conic section. In fact, he did not "square" it in the literal sense, but determined its exact relationship to a triangle, which, since any triangle can easily be converted to a square of the same size [*area*].

As always, he tried to explain both methods to me before giving me the letter to carry away. I gather that one method, which he called "mechanical," gave the correct result, which is that the section of the cone is 4/3 as big as an inscribed triangle. But he was not satisfied, since the mechanical method was equivalent to balancing the section and the triangle with a lever, then determining the ratio by measuring the arms of the lever. Instead he preferred the second method, which he called "exhaustion." I can report that his explanation exhausted me.

Apparently he could remove more triangles than one could count from part of the diagram and then add the areas of all these triangles to determine the region covered. I failed to understand why it was better to deal with untold numbers of triangles than simply to accept something he already knew to be true from the mechanical method. But he was much prouder of the proof by exhaustion than the mechanical one, although he sent both to Dositheos.

Dositheos in his reply listed a number of theorems of Archimedes that he had discovered in the Library, theorems sent without proof to Conon much earlier. He praised Archimedes for his calculations concerning the content of the section of a cone. Shortly after this, I received a second letter to carry to Dositheos, which Archimedes told me was regarding important discoveries he had made concerning the sphere and the cylinder. As I will recount later, Archimedes valued these discoveries so highly that he arranged for them to be placed on his tomb.

Archimedes was the first to determine the extent of the surface area of a sphere and also its volume, both of which he related to a cylinder that is inscribed in the sphere. Furthermore, he observed that, since he had supplied proofs for every step, any mathematician could read what he had written and see that it is correct. In this letter, also, he determined the extent of the surface of sections of spheres. There were so many ideas concerning these objects that I carried two separate letters to Dositheos concerning them. The reply to these and to the previous letter I had carried to Dositheos convinced Archimedes that Dositheos was indeed a proper follower of Conon and that he should receive the fruits of the mathematical labors of Archimedes. As a result, the letters on the sphere and cylinder were followed in fairly close order by letters on spirals, conoids, and spheroids. I cannot comment much about the mathematics, which is mostly more complex than I can follow.

Dositheos told me that the spirals were figures that either Conon or Archimedes had discovered, since no Greek before them had described such figures. Also Dositheos reported that in the work on spirals, Archimedes used a formula for the sum of the square numbers taken in order that appeared very Pythagorean, so I believe Archimedes may have learned this from his father. Archimedes also discovered the conoids [*paraboloids of revolution and hyperboloids of revolution*] as well as the elongated or flattened spheres he called spheroids [*ellipsoids*]. He was to prove many propositions concerning these figures, although he said that some of the propositions were much more difficult of proof than he had originally believed.

One of Archimedes successes during this period concerned the ratio of the distance around a circle to the distance across it. Here is how he explained it to me. He began by drawing several squares of different sizes in the sand. He asked if I could see that all squares have exactly the same shape. I agreed that they did. Then he asked me if the ratio of the perimeter of a square to the length of a side is always the same. Even I knew that this ratio was always the number 4, so I told him so. How about the ratio of the perimeter to the distance across the middle of a square, parallel to one of the sides? I said that this was also 4. Then he drew some circles in the sand and asked if, like squares, all circles have the same shape no matter their size.. I told him that they do. He said that therefore circles must have the same ratio of the distance around, or circumference, to the distance across, or diameter.

Archimedes drew a circle inside a square with the circle touching the four sides of the square. He asked if the diameter of the circle was the same as the one side of the square. And is the circumference of the circle greater or less than the perimeter of the square? I understood that the circumference is less since the circle is completely in the square. So, Archimedes asked me, is the ratio of the circumference to the diameter equal to 4, greater than 4, or less than 4? I said that it must be less than 4.

Then he had a harder question for me. He drew a square inside a circle with the vertices of the square touching the circle. What part of the square is the same as the diameter of the circle? It is the diagonal, I told him. After this part of the explanation he lost me for a while as he used the theorem of Pythagoras to compute the perimeter of the square, which he said, if we take the diameter of the circle as 1, is a number near to 2-4/5. Then, since the perimeter of the square inside the circle was clearly less than the circumference of the circle, the ratio of the circumference to the diameter must be greater than 2-4/5 as well as less than 4.

He proceeded to draw several more figures, first showing a hexagon inside a circle and then a similar hexagon surrounding a circle. Then he bisected the sides of the hexagons and connected those points to make figures with twelve sides, both inside and surrounding the circle. He told me that he had computed the length of diagrams within and without circles up to those with 96 sides each. His calculations showed that the 96-sided figure surrounding the circle has a perimeter of 3-1/7 times the diameter of the circle. Similarly, the 96-sided figure surrounded by the same circle has a perimeter of 3-10/71 times the circle's diameter. Thus, the ratio of the circumference to the diameter is between 3-10/71 and 3-1/7, which he said is good enough for any practical calculation.

Soon after he explained this to me and also wrote out the full mathematics for me to take to Alexandria, a problem arose that set him off on a different series of investigations completely. It began as a tribute to a goddess.

Carthage had capitulated to Rome without invading Syracuse. As part of the agreement that ended that war, Carthage agreed to remove all troops from Sicily, which it accomplished in short order. Rome decided that Syracuse, already an ally, should control the entire island, so Hiero became the ruler of all Sicily. His rule of the whole island continued for about 15 years or so.

When Hiero was given control of the entire island of Sicily, he went to the temple of Artemis and asked the priestess Cleoboule what he should do to give thanks for this great honor. Cleoboule told Hiero that a crown of olive leaves should be made and placed on the head of the goddess Artemis, the principal protector of Syracuse. This would insure peace throughout Sicily during his reign.

Hiero thought that this was a small thing to offer, since even winners of athletic contests were crowned in olive leaves. Surely a goddess deserved better. So he took a quantity of gold from his stores, consecrated it to Artemis, and gave the gold to the man reputed to be the best goldsmith in Syracuse. Hiero asked the goldsmith to create a golden wreath of olive leaves in the best detail he could manage. When complete, the crown was seen as an object of great perfection. Everyone was delighted when Cleoboule ceremoniously placed it on the head of Artemis during a great festival that was given in her honor.

Almost immediately, however, Hiero found that he had to put down rebellions in various parts of the island. Soon his forces were stretched thin and the Romans began to query him as to why he could not manage any part of the island beyond Syracuse. Hiero did not understand what the problem could be, so he returned to Cleoboule to ask her again what should be done to propitiate the goddess, for he accepted that the rebellions were a divine wrath unleashed upon Syracuse. Cleoboule assured him that he was correct in this interpretation. She suggested that perhaps something was wrong with his gift to the goddess. Hiero thought that perhaps he had overreached in making the crown of gold. He offered one of simple olive leaves taken from the trees in his garden, but the political situation grew worse after using it to replace the gold one. Cleoboule returned the metal wreath to the head of goddess but said that the goddess had told her that the problem was in the material of the crown. Artemis said specifically that the rebellions occurred because the crown was not appropriate. Problems continued to occur throughout the island.

Cleoboule's report baffled Hiero, who as he often did, sought the advice of Archimedes. Archimedes was puzzled, also, but with his typical intense concentration made the problem occupy his mind completely. Seeing that he was again neglecting himself, his wife ordered the slaves to feed him and then to take him to the baths. They followed these instructions. At the warm bath they filled a basin and put the naked Archimedes into it. He appeared to still be lost in thought, but suddenly leaped from the bath and, escaping his slaves, ran into the street and toward Hiero's palace, shouting "I have it, I have it" all the way, astonishing those in the street who saw him. Upon arriving at the palace, he was given a robe and escorted to Hiero.

Archimedes told Hiero that he had reached a conclusion on the problem of the golden crown. Cleoboule must mean that the crown did not consist of gold at all but had been adulterated with some other metal. Furthermore, he knew the way to determine if this was indeed correct. He explained that as he was being lowered into the bath, his weight decreased. This is why some objects float and others sink. All objects lose weight when they are immersed in a liquid. The amount an object loses depends on the weight of the liquid and the volume of the object. It will always be the same ratio for a particular material. He asked Hiero to supply him with some of the same gold that he had given to the goldsmith, which Hiero did, trusting Archimedes in all matters.

Archimedes took the gold sample to his workshop. There he weighed the sample carefully and then he put his scale next to a jar of water big enough to contain the gold. Suspending the gold from one pan of the balance, he dipped the gold sample into the water. In the liquid, the weight of the gold was diminished. Carefully Archimedes adjusted the weights so that the gold suspended in the water now was once again in balance. Then he divided the number of the original weight by the sum of the weights of those he removed from the pan to achieve balance, obtaining the number 19. Still somewhat like his Pythagorean father in his reverence for numbers, he now knew that the mystical number for the gold sample was 19. That should also be the number for the gold in Artemis' crown if it were made from the same material as Hiero had taken from his stores. Then he performed the same exercise with the wreath. This time he discovered that the number for the crown was 15, not 19. Archimedes knew that this meant that the goldsmith had substituted some lighter metal for the consecrated gold.

Hiero had the goldsmith brought to him and forced him to tell the truth about the crown. The goldsmith, who was treated very badly, admitted that he had kept the consecrated gold and substituted instead a golden-colored mixture of gold and silver. This, he claimed, was a better metal for manufacture of the crown, being stronger and better able to retain the fine markings he had incised on the leaves. Hiero did not believe this account. The king concluded that the goldsmith had kept the original gold for himself because it is much more valuable than silver. In any case, there was no longer any chance of recovering the original gold, as it appeared to have been mixed into other materials or used as a thin covering for objects of bronze.

Hiero started the process all over again with a different goldsmith, who was guarded night and day as he fabricated the new wreath from pure gold. By the time this was placed on the head of Artemis, all the rebellions had been put down so harshly that it was some time before any cities in Sicily thought of trying to throw off Hiero's rule. Thus, Hiero was satisfied that he now had the goddess on his side again and offered many ritual sacrifices to her.

Archimedes, however, was more interested in what he had learned about how weight changes in liquids. He began a series of investigations that took years out of his life because the problems were so difficult. When he finished, he described his results in two long letters concerning floating bodies that I eventually delivered to mathematicians at the Museum. In these he described how bodies of various shapes float upright or tip over depending on what parts are immersed in a fluid. He was able to use much of his previous work on equilibriums and his proofs concerning the content of shapes formed when the section of a cone is rotated. One might say that this was a lifelong project, extending to studies he made long before his sudden thought in the bath that day.

Exhausted by the intensity of his work on floating bodies, Archimedes instead of simply resting, relaxed by turning to abstract problems concerning numbers, almost abandoning geometry for a while. He found a new correspondent in Alexandria, Zeuxippus, who was especially interested in numbers as well as some geometry and philosophy.

In his correspondence with Zeuxippus, Archimedes first considered a puzzle that he had played with as a child, known as the Bellyache. This consists of a wooden square cut into 14 pieces, mostly triangles and also one each of irregular polygons with four or five sides. As a child, Archimedes learned to arrange the shapes to make elephants, flying or sitting birds, boats, dancing humans, and various geometric shapes. He learned very early that he could re-create the original square using many different arrangements, and he began to count these different ways of making a square from the fourteen pieces. He also became interested in how many movements of pieces were needed to go from one shape to another. Another game he played with the toy involved creating a shape that in outline was a familiar geometric figure, such as a larger square or a large triangle, with the opening inside forming whatever strange irregular shape that resulted. Archimedes had long become familiar with the areas of each of the pieces and it was easy to compute the total area enclosed by the outline of the larger shape; then by subtraction he could easily find the area of the inner shape. I do not believe that he did this because he could not compute the size of the inner region by some other method, but he told me that the idea behind this had been useful to him when dealing with curved figures. In any case, he finally wrote a brief discussion of the kinds of problems he was solving and of his general interest in the Bellyache to Zeuxippus.

He followed up this short book with another that he said had emerged from his work with the Bellyache. As he had counted the various possible configurations of the toy, he soon reached some numbers that were too large to express easily. These numbers were not the quantity of possible different squares he could make, which was only a few hundred, but they included some of the numbers concerned with quantity of ways of getting from one figure to another and even the total numbers of some of the possible configurations other than squares. As a result, Archimedes found that he needed some method of indicating numbers much larger than a myriad [*ten thousand*]. With characteristic ingenuity he invented his own system and sent Zeuxippus a description of the principles for this method. Much later in life, Gelo, who had come to occupy the throne along with Hiero by then, asked his old teacher for an account of large numbers. Gelo had heard that Archimedes had somehow counted to infinity, which was not true, but Archimedes obliged Gelo with a discussion of how to use his system for writing numbers to indicate the number of grains of sand in the universe. Because Gelo was not a mathematician, Archimedes wrote in the simplest possible way and for once even I could understand most of what he was saying.

Archimedes did not abandon geometry while he was advancing the methods of counting and of writing numbers. Like other geometers he was greatly impressed that there are only five regular solids--figures formed with a particular regular polygon, such as an equilateral triangle, square, or regular pentagon for each face. The five are the tetrahedron or four-faced solid; cube or six-faced solid; octahedron or eight-faced solid; dodecahedron or twelve-faced solid; and icosahedron, or twenty-faced solid. Archimedes told me that it was well known that no other such figures could exist provided that any line from one face to another must lie completely within the solid. But he wondered if it would be possible to construct solids that used two or more different polygons as faces, but that were otherwise like the five regular solids. Soon he discovered a way to do it. He first created such a figure by taking a cube and cutting off equal-sized triangles at each of the vertices. The resulting solid has six faces that are regular octagons, which are all that is left of the former faces of the cube. Its other eight faces are equilateral triangles, each of which replaced a former vertex of the cube. Since each octagon was exactly like all the other octagons and all the triangles were also congruent, the solid was half regular.

A similar approach, he showed me, produces a different half-regular solid (that is, with two kinds of equal faces) from each of the other four regular solids. In addition to those five, however, Archimedes discovered eight more figures of the same general type, some with three different regular polygons as faces. One solid has 92 faces in all, consisting of 80 equilateral triangles and 12 regular pentagons. Archimedes satisfied himself that these 13 solids are all that are possible under the given conditions. He had Hiero's workmen build a large and a small model of each solid, and I carried the small models to Alexandria to show to the mathematicians in the Museum. The large models were displayed at court, for Hiero and Gelo wished all to know of their relative's great discoveries. Unlike his more difficult mathematical discoveries, these were easy for even the poorest slave to recognize.

Archimedes was over 40 years old by this time, and one would think that his best ideas were all behind him, for it is common knowledge that mathematicians generally do their most original work while they are young. As I shall describe, however, he continued to devise new mathematical ideas for the remainder of his life. He also continued to make inventions that amazed all who beheld them. I believe that he made many discoveries that were never written down, for he increasingly was preoccupied with his thoughts, and his wife and slaves needed much more often to remind him to eat or to bathe.

You, Eratosthenes, are in possession of all of his writings from this period. Some of these writings concern some specific problems in geometry that he had solved. But the most important one explains in detail the method by which he made some of his greatest discoveries. He told me when he entrusted the manuscript of this to me to bring to you that the method itself was more significant than any theorem he had discovered using it. With this method it is possible to determine the area of almost any figure no matter how curved its boundaries are. Archimedes believed that the same general method could be used to solve many other kinds of problem as well. The secret, he said, was to make an approximation of the shape using rectangles, which are easy to measure. Then allow the rectangles to become smaller and their number to increase until finally they cover the entire figure exactly.

Although this method was a great achievement in geometry, he also continued to study other matters. For example, he had me bring you a puzzle he had written concerning the Cattle of the Sun. Recall that regarding this puzzle he said that it would be well if you read one of his books concerning very large numbers before you try to solve the problem. As far as I know, however, you have not succeeded in solving it.

Beginning in his youth, Archimedes made many different machines that imitated the movements of the Sun, Moon, and planets. Each one was based on his understanding of these movements at that time in his life. He also mapped the universe in several different ways. One occupation of his later years was building what are now recognized as the most spectacular examples of such machines and maps anyone has ever seen.

His great map of the universe is a solid sphere of glass

with every star and constellation engraved upon it at the appropriate location. It is so clear that one can look through the sphere to see what Archimedes had concluded were the stars visible only from the continent at the far side of Earth. He based this part of the sphere on what travelers had told him and on the writings of those who had sailed the farthest south, even to the tip of Africa.

The machine that displays the movements of the planets is even more impressive. Because it shows the positions of the planets for any night, it is sometimes called the planetarium. This machine is largely made from bronze and moves according to how a gear is turned. The gear mechanism can be operated slowly by a water clock. When powered in this way, and set for the ratio of one year to one day or less, the planetarium will show in a few hours how the sky looks all during the year. Alternatively, the planets can be set by hand to any night of the year, showing how the sky appears on that night. Archimedes had to do many calculations to determine the positions of all the stars and planets. His written description of how to make such a device is the only time that he felt that it was worthwhile to describe his mechanical techniques on papyrus. But he said that other astronomers of the future should know how to make these devices, which not only are useful in explaining to others how the universe works, but also give insights into new discoveries in astronomy. For example, if a similar machine were built showing the universe with the Sun at its center instead of the Earth, as my namesake and also Aristarchus of Samos had supposed, then by comparing how these two machines move over time it might be possible to tell the true center of the universe. Archimedes has told me that no mechanism that he knows can determine the difference between a steadily moving Earth and one that is the stationary center of the universe. Thus, although there are good philosophical reasons to think that the universe operates as Eudoxus and Hipparchus have supposed, it may in fact be as suggested by Aristarchus and Heracleides Pontica.

The fate of the sphere of the universe and of the planetarium is part of the story of Archimedes' death, which I must now sadly relate.

For nearly a quarter of a century the peace between Rome and Carthage held. Syracuse prospered under the kings Hiero and his son Gelo, who had become co-ruler of the state soon after the first war between Rome and Carthage ended. When Archimedes was nearing 70, however, war between the two great powers broke out in Spain. With that, the whole situation changed drastically. For Syracuse, it was further complicated by the deaths of both kings--Gelo about two years after the war started again and his father, who died as much from grief as old age, a year later. Hiero had remained a strong ally of Rome, sending soldiers and grain to aid the Roman legions in their battles against the Carthaginian general Hannibal, who had crossed the Alps into Italy.

When Hiero died, Syracuse was plunged into political turmoil. Many who had long awaited a chance to take over the state began to act. Hiero's former allies fought back by looking to Hiero's family for a new king. The majority of Hiero's children and grandchildren were women or girls, but Gelo had produced one son, Hieronymus. Hieronymus, although only 15 at the time, was made king. But the real power was in the hands of the "advisors" who had put him on the throne. Some of these favored Rome, others Carthage, and all wanted to control Syracuse themselves. Swayed one way or another as different groups in the Assembly were ascendant, Hieronymus negotiated both with Hannibal of Carthage and with Rome. His goal was complete control of Sicily. Rome at that time ruled western Sicily with a governor while Syracuse reigned over the eastern half of the island. Rome showed no sign of giving up half of Sicily, but favored Hieronymus with much flattery that disposed him toward the Roman side. But the advisors supporting Carthage plotted against Hieronymus and arranged his assassination. They also killed the other members of the royal family, including not only the daughters of Hiero and Gelo, but also their husbands and granddaughters.

In the turmoil that followed, the Assembly elected as consuls two brothers, Hippokrates and Epikydes, Syracusans who had close ties with Carthage. These two had been behind the negotiations between Hieronymus and Hannibal. Now they raised an army that consisted of mercenaries and even legionnaires who had turned against Rome. With that army behind them, the brothers declared Syracuse independent of Rome and left Syracuse to start attacks on towns in the western half of the island, aiming to take the island by force and then to ally it with Carthage.

A large part of the Roman army and navy had just arrived in northern Sicily under the commander of the consul Marcellus. He quickly defeated an army of Roman dissidents and moved toward Syracuse itself. Now for the first time in decades, Rome had become the enemy and Carthage, in theory, the friend. At that time, however, Carthage had no troops in Sicily or navies in its waters.

It was at this point that Archimedes became involuntarily involved in the war. The devices he had built to defend Syracuse against Carthage were still in place on the walls of the city. Although long a supporter of Rome, Archimedes, on threat of death, was asked to aid in the city's defense against the Romans by employing these weapons.

Knowing that rumors of Archimedes powers had circulated in the Roman legions for years, they brought the old man, now in his mid-70s, to the top of the wall when they learned that Marcellus and his army and navy were about to attack. They thought this would contribute to the fear that they hoped Archimedes' weapons would inspire. And they were entirely right.

As the Roman troops approached Syracuse by land, great clouds of bronze arrows rained down on the Romans. The Legionnaires observed the old man standing on the wall and believed that Archimedes himself was killing them by magic, and they turned back in terror. Then the Roman navy tried to employ two massive siege engines, so large that each had to be carried on two boats lashed together up to the walls along the coast. These engines were covered ladders that could be raised to the top of the wall, permitting the marines aboard the ships to fight their way into the city.

Using levers and winches Archimedes had arranged for long beams to extend from walls. These carried heavy weights of rocks and lead that were dropped on the siege engines, breaking them to pieces. Then grappling hooks were lowered from the ends of the beams. These grasped the sides of the ships, and then the beams were lifted higher, which turned the ships on their sides. Sailors and marines were thrown across the decks into the sea, and water rushed into the ships, sinking them. Catapults also launched great stones that smashed into the ships as they sank.

Marcellus soon realized that his troops would not continue their attack and turned back. Marcellus left two thirds of his army and navy at Syracuse to blockade and starve the city into submission, and with the remainder left to capture the towns in the countryside around Syracuse.

Occasional attempts at direct attacks on Syracuse, however, all resulted in Archimedes' weaponry appearing and the sight of a long pole and claw emerging from the wall or a few bronze arrows flying at the troops was enough to provoke panic and retreat.

As the Romans and Syracusans met from time to time under a white flag to exchange prisoners, commanders from Marcellus' army and their staffs were able to visit the tower where these negotiations took place. During these visits, one of the Romans was assigned to count the number of stones along the outer side of the tower below a window that was always open. He determined the number and simple arithmetic told Marcellus the height of the window. He had a ladder built on one of his largest ships that would just reach the window and waited for an opportunity to sneak a group of his soldiers into the city, where they might then overwhelm the guardians of the main gates and also the operators of Archimedes' machines.

It was the time for the annual festival honoring the patron goddess of the city, Artemis. At this point Epikydes was in charge of Syracuse while Hippokrates controlled that part of the Syracusan army operating outside the city. For the festival, Epikydes declared that since bread was in short supply, he would sustain the citizens' courage by providing free wine in a large quantity. For three days, anyone in Syracuse could have as much wine as he or she could consume, all in honor of the goddess. Marcellus, who had spies in the city, saw his opportunity and on the third day, when most of the citizens were drunk, he moved his ladder to the tower and sent his troops in. A city gate was soon opened and the army moved in to take charge of a large part of the city. But Syracuse is a huge city, and Epikydes was able to move his armies to Ortygia, an island that is part of the city, where they could continue to defend themselves and also to defend the harbor.

The region still held by Syracusans included soldiers, mostly mercenaries and deserters from the Roman forces, who wanted to hold out against Marcellus and the Romans to the end, since they calculated that they would be tortured and executed by the regular Roman legions. But the citizens of Syracuse and some nonmilitary foreigners who had been trapped when Marcellus occupied the main city all were eager to surrender. Moericus, a Spanish officer hoping to gain favor by his actions, was able to reach the Roman occupiers and offer them a deal. He slipped a contingent of Roman soldiers from a ship into Ortygia, where they quickly took charge. After that it was relatively easy for Rome to occupy the city completely.

Marcellus saw that resistance had vanished and hoped to save the city intact, for a rebuilt and rearmed Syracuse with the right leaders would once again be an ally of Rome or even incorporated into the Republic. He determined that the highest part of the treasure he himself would bring back to Rome would be the globe and planetarium of Archimedes, which for his triumph would symbolize his victory over the one man whose inventions had kept the Roman legions and navy at bay for so long. Thus he particularly ordered the Roman soldiers not to harm Archimedes, for Marcellus wanted the great mathematician as well as his globe and planetarium.

But when the Roman troops recognized that there was no resistance, they began to riot and plunder the treasures of this rich Greek city. The soldiers broke ranks and ran through the town, taking what they could carry, raping the women, and killing anyone who tried to stop them.

One of these rampaging soldiers came to the home of Archimedes. He encountered the philosopher at his work, studying figures that he had drawn in the dust and deep in thought. The soldier ordered Archimedes to get out of his way, for he planned to enter the house and steal as much as he could carry. Archimedes, concentrating as only he could, ignored the order and the soldier advanced on him, sword drawn. As the soldier stepped closer, his foot invaded the drawings and Archimedes, roused from thought, told the soldier to step back and not disturb the drawings. The solider took this as insolence, and killed Archimedes with a single thrust of his sword.

Stepping over the old man's body, he entered the house and found the place of honor occupied by the globe and the planetarium. Even a simple soldier could see that these must be valuable--although he took the glass globe for a crystal and the brass of the planetarium for gold. He grabbed the two and ran out the door, where he immediately ran into the officers Marcellus had sent to take charge of Archimedes and the globe and planetarium. The officers commanded him at sword point to relinquish his plunder and tell what had happened. When they realized that he had killed Archimedes, the officers retaliated by likewise killing the soldier.

Marcellus took possession of the globe and planetarium and, I understand, brought them back to Rome as he had planned. They are to remain in the Roman Senate chambers as a special display honoring the capture of Syracuse.

Archimedes body was buried with honors. I was consulted on the burial and I told the Roman officials that Archimedes considered his greatest discovery to have been the unraveling of the secrets of the sphere and the cylinder and that he had once told me that he thought their relationship should be displayed on his tomb. This request was granted although when I saw the tomb, near the Agrigentine Gate to Syracuse, I realized that the Roman officials had failed to grasp that Archimedes discovered that the volume of the cylinder is 3/2 the volume of the sphere placed exactly within the cylinder. While they inscribed upon the column that Archimedes had discovered this relationship, following wording I had supplied, they topped the column with a sphere next to a cylinder instead of trying to show the sphere within the cylinder as Archimedes intended. Nonetheless, although small, the tombstone is a fitting monument to the greatest warrior of all time, a man whose inventions changed the course of civilization and whose knowledge of astronomy exceeded all that of the ancients, but who cared only for numbers and geometry.

ABOUT THE AUTHOR

Bryan Bunch is the author of *The History of Science and Technology* (Houghton Mifflin Harcourt, 2003) as well as author or coauthor of many other trade nonfiction books about mathematics and science; reference books and articles on medicine and science, notably *The Penguin Short Encyclopedia of Science and Mathematics* (with Jenny Tesar); and science textbooks. His specialty in addition to the history of science is mathematics, which he taught at Pace University—his popular mathematics books deal with paradoxes (*Mathematical Fallacies and Paradoxes*), symmetry (*Reality's Mirror*), and number (*The Kingdom of Infinite Number: A Field Guide*). This is his first work of fiction.

Made in the USA
Charleston, SC
10 December 2014